I0771751

The Hobo Code

THE HOBO CODE

Kristoffer Ryan

This novel is just a work of fiction relax. Any resemblances would not only be coincidental but pretty scary.

Copyright 2024 Kristoffer Ryan

All rights reserved.

First Edition eBook and paperback

Cover art by Norbert Yates

ISBN: 979-8-9909594-1-5

TABLE OF CONTENTS

The longer he spent living in his parents' dank smoky home, the more claustrophobic and dungeonlike it felt. He had outgrown the place a couple of years ago by his own estimation—he was freshly eighteen, but he knew he could have cared for himself just fine at sixteen. Hell, he'd had plenty of practice by that point of not only caring for himself but the mongoloid as well. In his mind he would have been gone a long time ago had it not been for what they were calling Black Friday in the newspapers. A normal day for him but one when all the bankers and stock traders in the cities had messed up in a big way. Some of the muckety-mucks had even leaped from open windows rather than face the repercussions of pouring one's life savings into questionable assets then seeing them fail. Had the Depression waited a month or two, Vincent would have already been long gone. Not sitting in his corner of the loft dreaming about freedom like a prisoner who had been locked away and forgotten about.

As it was, the Depression the big city businessmen had caused was affecting all corners of almost everyone's lives that he knew, which to be honest was limited. It had especially affected his family's. Dad hadn't worked since he smashed his leg to bits with a misguided ax and a knotted piece of hardwood (the ax was likely misguided from booze) and the healing went all to hell with him getting an infection all the way through to the bone. Vincent felt slightly lightheaded just thinking about the bandages and rot during the summer he helped his father recover.

Mom on the other hand hadn't been much help since Jamie Lynn, the mongoloid, was born. Seeing her daughter born with the affliction killed a piece of her, and it seemed like a sadness engulfed her. The only way Mom had seemed to find to feel better was to eat. So, she did. She ate until it was hard for her to get up and out of the chair by the fireplace, so she didn't. The repulsion he felt for his dad melted into anger for his mom. It was wrong to feel like that about your own parents—he knew that—but he was having a harder and harder time lying to himself, telling himself that everything was fine.

As if to accentuate his point, there was a louder than usual shout that came from the argument downstairs that he had been casually listening to. The usual arguing shifted tones and volumes so many times, it became background music to which he was now so accustomed. The familiarity of his parent's strained lullaby helped him fall asleep on more than a few nights. Tonight was different. The chords being struck were all wrong and he could feel a tension that was usually absent as the arguing was mostly for entertainment purposes, not to hurt each other. Tonight's argument was more than just surface-level. They were so heated down there; he was sure the boys would wake up at any second from the noise they were making. The shitty part of him got a little excited at the prospect of a heated argument. He wasn't tired, and a good argument would keep him entertained if he could listen hard enough to hear what they were saying. He strained trying to pick vowels out to string together words. The kids' heavy breathing from their beds opposite him and Jamie Lynn snoring in the corner weren't helping.

"VINCENT, COME DOWN HERE!" his father yelled from downstairs, breaking the silence and scaring the life out of him.

It took a minute for him to swallow the scream. Too long for dad.

"Vincent are you awake?" his father said a little more softly.

"Yeah...yes, sir, I'm coming." Vincent slid his pants on, put his undershirt back on, and hurried downstairs.

The living room stank of Mom, booze, cigarettes and whatever she had thrown in her cauldron (which she would try to call soup) that was perpetually bubbling on the fire. It was the one thing mom did was toil over her soup relentlessly. Continuously burning the firewood that had taken Dad's leg regardless of the temperature inside their house or out. Ironically, chopping firewood was just about the only thing left Dad was capable of or wanted to do. Chop more wood, take more laudanum with a shot of whiskey, and whine about his life. That pretty much was the summation of his father's days. Mom, on the other hand, ate from sunup to sundown if she could; if not, she spent the rest of her day complaining about Dad or Vincent for being lazy or not helping enough. Most of this was done with Jamie Lynn perched on her lap like some demented gargoyle, soaking it all in ready to repeat it as soon as she left her lap to try and egg Vincent on.

"Vin, your dad has something to tell you and you better pay attention." She nodded towards his father, who looked confused and hurt. "Go ahead," she urged.

"Why don't you tell hi...."

"Get it over with or you can go, too!" she hollered, cutting him off. Something on the edges of her grin let Vincent know this was not going to go in his favor. She was enjoying making Dad tell him, so it was bound to be bad news. She knew it would hurt more coming from his father.

"Vin, your mom decided that...."

"WE!" she shouted over him again.

"Yes. WE decided it would be best for the family if you could pack up some things and...."

"Not *our* things, though," she added.

This time, Dad gave her a look that told her to be quiet. She didn't listen often, but this time she would. There was after all a happy ending for her.

"Either way, pack some things and head to Kingston to look for work to support yourself. You are eighteen now and with the problems you had with Jamie Lynn last week, your mom... and I...." He looked at her with more than a little anger, but he was a beaten man, the fight was long over. "Well, we think it's best for you to be on your own now. So, in the morning, I'll give you a hand packing, but you need to be gone by sundown, she says." At this, it was Mom's turn to flash an angry look back at his father.

Vincent's head was congested with anger, and no rational thoughts or arguments would form in his mind. He wanted to say something to defend himself but like his father, he realized the fight was over. During Dad's little presentation when he'd referred to his problem with Jamie Lynn, Vincent knew he was beaten.

Last week after being perched on Mom's lap, Jamie Lynn had jumped down with a smile on her face and ordered Vincent to make her a bath on Mom's orders. This was nothing new for Vincent—he had been feeding her, changing her diapers, making sure she was dressed and keeping her out of Mom's hair for almost her entire life. He had even tried to teach her things, but with the mongolism it was too much of a struggle and keeping her just behaving like a child was a chore. So, like usual, Vincent had taken the water from the wood stove and prepared a bath in the tub. When he came back with the last load of hot water, she was already in the shallow steaming bath. Her naked, white, fleshy body was packed into the small tin tub. Vincent could see the folds of her flesh and that she was beginning to look more and more like Mom. With a smile on her face, her beady little eyes locked onto his and she began screaming.

"Mom, he did it just like you said he would, he looked at me in the tub!" she shouted, still smiling, almost giggling. "MOMMMM!" she continued.

There was a tremendous crash from the living room.

"Jesus, Vin, what are you doing?" With a speed that had shocked and scared him, his mother had gotten out of her chair and into the entry of the bathroom to see him standing there shocked with Jamie Lynn screaming bloody murder, pretending to cover what little of her body the rolls weren't already hiding.

After the initial shame and trying to explain to his mother what happened, Vincent got the impression that she wouldn't believe him because she had orchestrated it. So, he had spent the last week casually trying to convince his dad he wasn't a pervert, trying his hardest to not seem guilty. He obviously hadn't been peeping on his sister, but it sure didn't look good, and he couldn't tell whether his dad believed him or not. On top of that, he felt guilty for something he didn't do, so he was probably coming off insincere or desperate, likely both. There was a sense that if he kept his head low and didn't mention it, this situation would blow over eventually. That was what he had hoped for, anyway.

At the time he felt set-up but couldn't put his finger on a motive for his mom in doing so. However, it was all clear to him now and the grin on Mom's face let him know he was right. She had coached Jamie Lynn into giving her all the ammunition she would need to get rid of Vincent for good. There was no underlying issue between them that Vincent could put a finger on. Just a tension that existed between the two of them since he had taken over the parent role for her years ago. Vincent figured, now that the hard part of raising Jamie Lynn was over, and his brothers were not mongoloids, the job was done. In mother's eyes Vincent had reached peak usefulness and only remained as a reminder of her own failures. Plus, Vincent was the only one who ever balked at her for bossing everyone around like a queen on her throne. With him gone, she could rule with impunity.

Dad looked like he was just glad that he wasn't the one being asked to leave. It was Mom's family money keeping them afloat, even if just barely, but it was enough for desperate people to feel grateful for. He was hopelessly addicted to his laudanum and whisky—the latter of which was now illegal, and buying illegal hooch was another asset Mom provided. Dad was no asset to anyone. Someone who was looking for a laborer would be out of luck, and his brains weren't so great either after years of pickling it with poppy and rye. He had expressed to Vincent on more than one occasion during his frequent drunken babbling sessions that he was one limping step away from being homeless and one bullet away from relief. Vincent didn't believe his father had enough fortitude for either. His father's choice to support his mother rather than himself made sense. Even if it was cowardly. Also, if his dad genuinely thought he was a pervert, it was all the reason he needed to justify his own cowardice. Mom had planned this very well.

Now it was Vincent's turn to speak. His parents both looked at him for a response. There was nothing except anger. Just minutes ago, he was dreaming about being on his own out of this house, away from Mother's whims and Father's drunken ramblings. But that would have been on his terms, leaving the way he wanted to leave. Now that he was being forced out, it hurt. Badly. He looked pleadingly at his parents, from one to the other, hoping to see a crack but he could tell they were resigned to him leaving. Mom had won.

"By the time dinner is over tomorrow, I want you to be packed up and on the road. Got it?" It was just like her to keep time by meals, Vincent thought.

Finally, not lost for words, Vincent managed one.

"Fine" and turned his back on her.

He went back up to his corner of his room, tears threatening him the whole way, but he fought them off. Giving her the satisfaction of hearing him cry was unacceptable. Now, he let his anger take over; it was easier that way, with less feeling.

Why wait? He thought. He grabbed his bag from under his bed and started stuffing everything he owned into the too small bag. Football and helmet, baseball glove with his ball, his tinker toys, tin cars, modelmaking kit, blanket, both of his jeans and all his shirts even his church clothes that hadn't been worn in years, a knife, and his small but loved collection of science fiction books. It barely fit with just enough room for him to jam his pillow on top of the hoard.

His packing took all of three minutes, and this made him even sadder and threatened to derail the anger. He wished he had some money and or some food to take with him, but he would figure it out. He had been to Kingston once with Dad. They had taken the horse to go buy another horse, so he needed him to ride it back. It was the most exciting thing he had ever done. The city seemed huge compared to the dusty road they called town with the general merchant and a gas station. His dad had given him some pocket money. It wasn't much but it was enough to burn a hole in his sixteen-year-old pockets. He couldn't wait to get there and when he did, the options on which he could spend it seemed endless. After too much time looking, Dad was getting pissed, Vincent settled on some exotic candies he could share with his brothers and Jamie Lynn when they got home.

Now with the fond memory of Kingston fresh in his mind, he felt some excitement mixing with the anger. There were bound to be plenty of opportunities in a place like that. The biggest hurdle would be getting there. On horse, it had taken just a day back and forth, so he figured if he got started early, he could make it before lunch the next day. They hadn't been riding the horses hard, so him walking a brisk pace would be about the same. Now giddy and angry, he wanted to leave tonight even more. Although he didn't want to go back through the living room and face the humiliation of losing to Mom as she gloated by the fire. He had snuck out once before to get drunk with his friends. The one and only time he had ever been drunk. He could sneak out again.

Thinking back on sneaking out made him sad thinking of leaving his dad. Even though he knew he was a coward, he also knew he had fought with Mother on his behalf, which meant he still cared at some level despite the fact he had been emotionally blunted from inebriation all the time. The night he snuck out to drink with his friends, he was too drunk to sneak back in the same way through the window. So, he had resorted to trying to sneakily get in through the front door. He was successful in his attempt to be quiet. So successful that his mom sleeping in the corner and his father weeping in the other corner didn't notice him. His dad was a broken man physically and mentally by this point in his life, but he was still his dad. Seeing him crying in a corner alone at night was a sobering and shameful experience. As a result, Vincent had avoided ever drinking again, and if he were to ever hurt himself, he would try to just feel better and never take the laudanum—it seemed like father fell off a cliff once he started taking poppy extracts for pain. Mother had her own vices, but Vincent had always been too picky of an eater to worry about falling into that hole, and the smell of cigarettes disgusted him.

Now Vincent was teary-eyed from thinking about leaving his father to cry in the corner alone again tonight. He looked from the windowsill to his sleeping brothers. They were going to miss him too. They looked up to him and followed him around their small farm plot, constantly bugging him to entertain them or find something fun to do. He would miss them, too. All the invented games and stupid names they called each other, and even the constant nagging would be missed. He wiped a tear from his cheek and held back a sniffle, not wanting to let Mom hear a sound. Then he looked at Jamie Lynn. Even with her eyes closed, they looked beady. Her face was twisted into a snarl like a bulldog's. Her gut was exposed from the too-small pajamas riding up. He felt a tinge of guilt like he would be caught from the corner of her not-so-sleeping eye looking at her naked gut, and Mom would come thundering up the stairs for one final confrontation on her terms. Vincent's anger returned, he slung the heavy bag over his shoulder, and slipped out the window. Now dangling from the sill to reduce the drop, he let go and landed softly on the ground outside his house. He was free from the dungeon, he told himself to try to cheer himself up.

He made his way around the house and down the walk to the dirt road leading to Kingston.

"Not gonna say goodbye, huh?" his dad said quietly from behind the woodshed.

A startled Vincent spun around, both instantly glad to see him and regretful as he saw fresh tears in his father's eyes as well.

"No, I was uh…."

"It's fine. I would have wanted to leave, too. I know how she is, but she's all I've got. I hope you understand that." He sniffled a bit and a fresh tear rolled off his red nose. "You're a good kid. You always have been, and you'll be good out there on your own. You're smarter than I ever was, and you are a hard worker, too." He looked up and locked wet eyes with Vincent. "Here." He held out his silver Dunhill lighter. "I know you don't smoke, but you might could sell it for a meal or two down the road if you need to."

This broke Vincent's resolve and he let the tears fall. He took the lighter, knowing how much Dad had loved it. It was probably Dad's favorite possession and now it would be his. He would never sell it. It would be in his pocket to remind him of Dad until he made his way back home to return it. And in that future as a successful businessman, he would take his brothers and his dad out of this farm and leave it to Mom and Jamie Lynn. He would get his brothers all the best toys, and he would get Dad some help for the pain in his leg so he could stop taking the laudanum. They could move to Kingston together and start fresh.

They hugged until their tears dried. Then before they could start up again, Vincent started down the driveway.

"Love you, dad."

"I love you, too. Be good, be strong, and don't forget to visit someday."

Vincent couldn't turn around just yet or he would start to cry. He made it to the end of the driveway, hoping to turn around and see his dad waving and smiling. But it was just his back and him limping into the house. He never looked back.

Vincent was on his own. He took the first steps as an independent man. It was dark and he was scared. He gave his new lighter a squeeze in his pocket and felt a little better, even if it brought the lump in his throat with it.

The ground around the farm was cracked and dry and useless for growing anything. As his tears spilled, they disappeared into puffs on the silty topsoil. That amount of moisture wasn't going to stop the next black roller. This part of the country was so desperate for rain, the soil was blowing away to try to find it on its own. Maybe the whole farm would just blow away at some point, and then he wouldn't have anything to miss.

The farther Vincent got from his driveway, the darker it felt. The moon was a waning sliver of silver in the sky. Tomorrow would be the new moon and it would be black. Still, it was too dark to make much progress tonight. There was another source of light he could only imagine was his neighbor's yard light or shed. Either was fine with him as it would be a bastion from the darkness. Part of him wanted to get off the road because of the stories about the dramatic increase in child abductions in the last two years. He knew he was a man, but in the eyes of a large part of the world, he could still play the part of a boy well enough. Whatever they were doing to all the missing children, they were probably fine doing to him as well.

That train of thought motivated him, and as the hairs stood up on his neck, his pace quickened. The tiny point of light grew until he was so out of breath that walking was the only option. But it was fine now, as he was close enough for the light to comfort him, and he was still relatively close to home—regardless of the fact it didn't offer safety any longer. He could make out the light was coming from their neighbor's shed and not the front porch. Lucky break. A couple of hours ago, the thought of sleeping on a shed floor would have seemed crazy to him, but now, he was grateful for the walls and the light.

Not much sleep made itself available during the night. Thoughts of home and mother pissed him off. The thought of the farm and his brother and father made him cry. Dreaming of the future made him giddy. Sleeping on the ground hurt. But not as much as his feelings from being kicked out. He wanted to leave anyway, he tried to tell himself over and over, so it felt more and more like his own idea…but it was hard to buy his own bullshit.

He couldn't tell if he had been asleep when he noticed the sun was coming up. The last thing he wanted was for the neighbors to come out thinking he was stealing from them. They were notoriously hot-headed, from what Dad had said and, in his mind, they were not above shooting on sight. He put his now-filthy blanket and pillow back into the bag the best he could. They still poked out the top in a ridiculous fashion, but he would sort it out later; he had to get moving.

As he walked and did his best guessing about how long it would take to walk to Kingston, he had a stark realization. He was overly ambitious when it came to packing, and if he was going to make any serious progress, he needed to lighten his load. He started thinking of his possessions and what he could sacrifice and what he couldn't. His hand reached protectively into his pocket and rubbed the Dunhill. Not this. He knew a couple of kids' houses he would be walking past to get to the main part of "town" where the road to Kingston started. Maybe he could peddle some of his stuff to them and make some money for the road. It made him sad thinking of getting rid of anything, but there wasn't much choice in the issue; keeping going like this wasn't practical. He could already feel the straps from his bag forming blisters on his shoulders.

The first stop he made was an older kid who had a bunch of brothers. They weren't rich but were definitely better off than his family. They actually owned a vehicle. He wished he knew them well enough to beg a ride to Kingston from them or just beg to live with them. He didn't, though, and in fact, he didn't know a whole lot of anyone outside of his family. School was never an option after Dad was hurt, so after second grade he did his learning at home along with the chores Dad had to relinquish.

Luckily, the older boy was interested in Vincent's sports gear. For Vincent, that was fine, as he doubted he would be playing football or baseball anytime soon. The gear had been birthday and Christmas gifts, so that hurt, but he needed the money more than the memories. He got a dollar fifty for all the sports gear. It wasn't a great deal for Vincent, but he was lucky to get anything as not many people had anything to spare.

His second stop was less fruitful. He tried to sell his toys and models, but the kid had no interest in them. His father, however, walked by and saw the pile of goods he was trying to sell his son. The man stopped to grab the science fiction novels.

After turning the H. G. Wells over a couple of times, he grabbed the entire stack. "I'll give you fifty cents for the lot." This hurt but beggars can't be choosers, so he made his best compromise offer.

"Only if you buy the other stuff, too...a dollar total," Vincent said, trying his hardest to sound like a man making a deal and not a boy begging for help.

Maybe sensing his desperation, the boy's father softened and gave him a smile. "Ok, that'll work. Here." He handed him a nice, crisp, new-feeling dollar bill.

"Thank you," Vincent said, both sad at losing his novels and happy he made a better deal while also lightening his load considerably.

The last thing he got was a handshake and a good luck as he left their house and headed for the end of town. He had wasted much more time than he wanted to trying to make a deal and getting rid of stuff. It was noon now and according to his math he would barely make it to Kingston if he hurried.

Just then, a train let out a loud whistle signaling it was making its stop at the yard. Vincent had a brilliant plan. He knew the train was going from here to Kingston; if he could sneak onto the back of a car, he would get there in no time. Probably early enough to find a meal, as his stomach reminded him how hungry he was.

He hurried across town to the other side of the street. The train had come to a stop and people were unloading mail bags or bags of goods for the store—he wasn't sure which. Actually, it was probably both. He realized the train was multipurpose, so it only made sense. There were also a couple of passengers who looked to be unloading suitcases. There was no one waiting to get on from here, though, besides himself but he doubted they would count a stowaway. He saw a break in the action and there was no one standing guard, so like a flash he bolted to the open cargo door and vaulted inside with ease. The car was empty, so he did his best to be hidden and tucked himself into a corner.

That was easier than he thought it would be and Vincent felt a little proud of himself. His body relaxed and while he waited for the train to get going, somehow, he nodded off. He had been busy thinking of what he would do for work in Kingston and closed his eyes briefly…only to have them betray him and stay closed.

They didn't stay closed for long. Suddenly, a flash of white and blinding pain jolted him from sleeping in the corner to standing up and defending himself by shielding his face with his arms as blows rained down.

"You little shit" *smack* "what the fuck are you doing on my train" *smack* "I've had it with you damn bums shitting in my cargo cars and stealing fucking rides" *smack*.

This time, the smack was followed up with aggressive manhandling. The man serving him a beating was rummaging through his pockets and ripping his shirt at the same time. The man pulled out the two dollars and fifty cents, spilling the change and crumpling the crisp, new bill in his giant fist.

"There, that'll cover the ride, you little shit." And with that, he tossed Vincent from the train.

Ungracefully, Vincent tumbled the three feet onto the ground, landing mostly on his face.

Without thinking much about anything except getting beaten again, he grabbed his bag and ran for the tree line. Once he felt safely out of danger, he stopped and ducked behind a tree. He was more than out of breath with the running and hitching at the same time. He stopped breathing and crying just long enough to throw up a thick, green bile. He had never been in trouble with anyone outside of Mom and Dad. His adrenaline was higher than it had ever been, and he was shaking and crying and puking and bleeding. Still, the one thing that stuck out and hurt most of all was being called a bum. But what else was he if not a bum? The realization struck a chord and he puked again.

He spent the better part of an hour crying and feeling more alone than he thought possible. It was getting close to lunchtime and he was starving, but with all of his money gone and his prized possessions already hocked, the only prospect he had for a meal was getting to Kingston and trying to appeal to someone's humanity. He gathered his limp bag and his pride and dusted himself off. His shirt was ruined but it was good enough for walking. He made his way around town, giving the buildings and the tracks a wide berth. Then, a half a mile outside town, he got on the road to Kingston. He wasn't sure how far it was exactly. More than fifteen miles, he thought he remembered. But with his barely-there bag and his young body, he would make it just fine, he thought with confidence.

Just a little over what he thought was an hour into the walk, he realized he had made a miscalculation. His math would have been right had he figured in the fact he hadn't eaten since lunch yesterday. His body was reacting as it should and was sluggish. He tried to keep his pace up but found himself constantly fighting the sluggishness. He spent more time reminding himself to pick up the pace than he actually did picking up the pace. As a result, he was starting to regret his decision to cry in the woods and wasting time selling his stuff. He was never going to make it before dark. But he tried. He only stopped for breaks when he felt like he was going to faint. More than anything, he wished he had brought something to drink. The skin on his lips was starting to peel and his tongue wasn't much better, feeling flaky itself. First priority was a bottle for water when he got to Kingston. He was sure if he dug through the local bottle dump, he would find an old whisky bottle or something that would suffice.

Every so often, a car would pass. Part of him wanted to flag them to try to get a ride or a drink, but his pride stood in his way. Another part of him heard the cars coming and got scared thinking of the child abductions. This part wanted to dive off the road and hide like a kid when there were signs a car was coming. As a compromise, he decided he would walk staring straight ahead, not making eye contact with the passersby, and crossing his fingers he wouldn't hear them slow down and fling their doors open. Aside from choking on the dust from them passing so quickly, it was uneventful. No one wanted to stop and help any more than he wanted them to. Everyone was barely hanging on, so he understood and appreciated the solitude a bit at first. Then the sun started to set and the infrequent traffic became a memory as the world around him prepared for bed.

At first, he thought he could manage just fine walking on the road in the dark. That was until the sun really went down, revealing the predicted new moon. Why hadn't he considered this with his late start? He knew last night it was just a sliver and tonight it would be gone.

"Shit," he cursed himself in the dark.

He managed to keep the road under his feet by feeling the gravel crunching, and the stars were giving just enough light to illuminate the dry dirt road just slightly compared to the dark scrub brush on either side. His pace quickened and his anxiety grew. The dark was thick, his breathing was heavy, but there was an underlying sound that seemed in tandem with his footsteps. He slowed and the sound he thought he heard slowed. Now he was scared but curious. Without any indication, he stopped walking and strained his ears.

Crunch...crunch.......

The sound was unmistakably dried grass being walked on, which in itself wasn't scary, but the fact that something took two steps and stopped like it was trying to blend itself with his footsteps—that was terrifying. What was following him? Or who? Kidnappers out this late? he wondered. His hand reached into his pocket looking for hope, and found his knife and his Dunhill. His hand clutched the lighter and he found enough strength in it to keep walking. Now on high alert, he was listening to the pace of his stalker match his own. When he tried to jog, the footsteps beside him in the ditch matched his pace. When he stopped to listen again, they stopped as well. Only this time, he heard the sound of a predator sniffing the air. Was it smelling his blood or his fear? He wasn't sure but rather than stand around wondering, he sprinted.

The lights from town were glowing on the horizon up ahead of him. Had to be less than a mile, his worn but sharp mind told him. The straps from his pack were digging into the grooves the heavier pack had left, and the blisters were screaming at him. There was nothing left he couldn't live without, so he decided to ditch it. There was an outcropping of large white rocks coming up quickly on his left. On the fly, he ditched the bag, throwing it beside the outcropping, noting it in the back of his mind so maybe if he made it through tonight, he could come back and get it in the safety of the daylight.

As soon as he tossed his bag, he could hear the footsteps beside him stop. Maybe he scared it away. Maybe it was just a deer following out of curiosity. He had seen bucks do some pretty bold things during mating season. This eased his mind a bit, but his body was still in flight mode. His heartbeat was pounding in his ears, and the whooshing sound of his own breathing was starting to block out all other sounds. He was dehydrated and exhausted, but he could also start to see individual pricks of light through the trees. Kingston was so close now, he thought he could smell food cooking.

Within a couple of minutes, he was passing the first houses on the outskirts of town. They didn't have porch lights on; they were either conserving money or in bed, he thought as he slowed his pace, feeling confident he was no longer being followed. Luckily, one of the dark houses had a spigot in the front yard. It was a manual pump and he didn't have a bottle or cup, so he put his face under the tap and pumped the handle with his free hand. The cold water tasted so good; it temporarily replaced all other thoughts. He drank until he was full as he didn't expect a meal, and that would help his belly be tricked for a while. He also took the chance to change his shirt. He used the torn one as a rag and gave himself a quick rag bath sans soap. He put his overshirt back on without the undershirt, and it felt odd like he was still naked from the chest up. He would go back for his bag in the morning and get another shirt. If locals saw him like this, they would never give him a job.

Feeling a little better, he looked around for a safe place to sleep for the night. There was obviously nothing in the pitch black, so he chose to take a risk and sleep on the porch of this house. If he was lucky, he would still be there to get yelled at in the morning. If, he was really lucky he might beat them awake and make it out of there in one piece without catching a beating. Either way, he wasn't taking his chances in the dark again with the stalker. It was warm, so he didn't miss his blanket, but he would miss his pillow, so he used his shirt/rag and balled it up into a damp, stinky pillow. He lay down on the porch, way off to the side where he might go unnoticed. Somehow, despite the day he had just had (or maybe as a result of it), he fell asleep quickly and stayed that way until the morning, damp dirty pillow and all.

Had he stayed awake for five more minutes, he might not have gotten any sleep at all as the silence was broken by something loudly sniffing the air around him.

To his benefit, Vincent was a light sleeper and the early sun along with a couple of neighborhood roosters got him up and off the mystery porch before he had a chance to be chased off or beaten again. He rubbed his head, feeling the knots still angry and swollen from the beating on the train. Regretfully, he put the still slightly-damp undershirt back on, as it was the lesser of two evils when compared to the naked feeling of just the overshirt. First priority was water. He was still starving and could stand another belly full of water. Second was to go get his bag and get out of this ridiculous outfit into something only slightly less ridiculous, he hoped, thinking of the too-small Sunday shirt.

He went and pumped the spigot and got his fill, then let it run long enough to rinse his hair out and wash his face. The water was delicious, not like the muddy-tasting water from home. If he found a bottle, he should remember this house to come back to and fill up. He looked around and saw a neighbor giving him a funny look. Reflexively, his arm shot up and offered a wave, which was reciprocated with a shaking of his head and shambling back inside his own house. It was time to move on.

The road was much more welcoming in the daylight. The sun was poking through the trees and the birds were singing. If he hadn't been so hungry and feeling faint, he really would have enjoyed the morning walk. His feet felt heavy in his boots and his head was cloudy from exhaustion and no food. He still had to grab his stuff and head back to town and look for a way to earn a meal or two, maybe a bed if he was really lucky. It seemed impossible to fathom completing all of that feeling like this. All he could do was keep going and do one thing at a time. If he got too far ahead of himself, he saw disappointment was going to be a trend.

The rock outcropping was coming into view now, at least. It wasn't nearly as far as his sprint for his life the night before had felt, thankfully. Only now, the fear of the stalker returned. What if they were waiting for his return, hiding amongst the rocks waiting to jump out and snatch him up, to subject him to whatever whims they used abducted kids for. It probably wasn't pleasant, whatever it was. Then, the sound of a car's motor came from just around the corner up ahead. The same hiding spots he was scared of a second ago now became a place to seek safety. He didn't know why, but he just didn't feel like waving or talking to anyone or even seeing anyone. Maybe they were kidnappers, and that was why he was hiding, he tried to tell himself. It wasn't true; he just felt unwanted and anxious about someone judging him now that he was a bum. Shame was the word he was looking for and when he found it, he felt it. He stayed hiding for longer than he needed to, then dried his eyes and went looking for his bag.

"What the hell?" he said out loud when he rounded the side of the boulders.

There was his bag alright, but everything was dumped out and looked to be stepped on or rummaged through...maybe both. There was a series of footprints circling and trapesing over the clothes and his pillow and blanket. They were smooth-soled shoes with no tread. The only shoes he'd ever seen with smooth soles were the shoes of bankers and businessmen with shiny leather tops and smooth leather bottoms. He wondered what the hell a fancy guy like that would be doing looking through his bag. Looking for more clues was futile, as there was nothing but now dirty clothes and those strange footprints all over. There was a sense of violation, but there was nothing to be done about it. So, he dusted and shook out everything the best he could. Then, he grabbed the nicest undershirt he had and switched it out. It felt so much better against his skin than the woolen-feeling overshirt had. His nipples were raw and he noticed blood on the inside of the shirt. That was going to hurt for a while, he thought, regretting having to wear any shirt at all now. He packed up the rest of his possessions, which didn't take long. Also, he made sure to put the knife in the bag so his pockets didn't look chock full of stuff like a little kid when he went looking for work later.

The Sunday shirt fit terribly. It rubbed on his nipples even worse as he walked, guaranteeing there would be bloody spots on his undershirt that he would have to try to hide. It was three years past the point of fitting even uncomfortably, but his other options were farm work shirts, and he doubted there was going to be much if any of that kind of work in a big town like this. It was the best option he had if not his only, but it still made him feel even more shame. He had never really experienced feeling self-conscious, being at least as well off as the neighbors that he did know. And around his family, he was smarter and stronger than all of them, so no discomfort about himself there. But out here in the real world, a kid, a bum, with the whole world so worried about themselves that no one would give anyone a second look, he felt small and unimportant and silly. What were his parents thinking kicking him out? They might as well have killed him themselves. He was vastly underequipped to deal with this. His hands reflexively went up and held the fabric away from his sore chest to give it a break.

The longer he stayed on this train of self-pity, the worse he was going to feel. He knew that much of himself, so he course-corrected and tried to get excited for what kind of job he might find. He thought back to his trip here with dad. The streets were lined with all kinds of stores selling anything you could think of, and more that you couldn't. He was walking past the house he stayed at last night and now considered stopping for another drink, but when he got closer, he could see the neighbor who gave him the stink eye that morning talking to the owner of the house on the porch. Neither of them had seen him yet, so he scooted around the property on the side road. No more delicious water, he thought.

Main Street was just up ahead if he remembered correctly. Already, though, the town felt sleepier and less vibrant than it had. It was late spring and in his mind, the town should be busy or at a minimum, alive. As it was, there were groups of men here and there sipping coffee on porches, gossiping about some far too-important secrets. There were women too, but they were out in front of the church he passed, and more than a few in gardens. The oddity was that they were working-age men and women. These coffee crowds were usually reserved for the elderly. As he passed by the bored-looking, working-aged people they all stared at him. They were probably wondering who the newcomer was. In his mind, they were all passing judgment on his ill-fitting shirt and messy hair. This took his self-consciousness to another level and he convinced himself subconsciously to cross streets to avoid their criticisms.

As he made his way to Main Street, it all started to make more sense. Most of the businesses he passed were shuttered or had signs in the windows telling people not to apply or were closed permanently. More than a few were just boarded up with no answers at all; they probably didn't have any to offer, Vincent thought. Those businessmen must have really screwed up badly. The reaches of the Depression hadn't yet changed much of his rural life. They had always been rural and poor. Even if they were the least poor people he knew personally, they were still poor. This shook him in a way he hadn't expected. The main street had seemed so alive when he was with Dad, that he never imagined something could kill it. But it was dead. There was not going to be any work for him here. They couldn't help him. It looked like maybe they needed help more than he did. His stomach growled, reminding him that he had better figure out something.

Swallowing some pride, he ducked into the first open business he came across. Already feeling like a burden and a bum, he nervously asked if they had any work. The older guy behind the counter chuckled like he was kidding, then looked up and saw the scrawny dirty kid standing there.

"Uh, sorry, kid, we are barely keeping the doors open and we aren't paying any staff. Got the whole family working here already and no one takes a paycheck." He shrugged then added, "Feed store might have some work if they get a delivery. Not sure when that is, though. You'd have to check yourself...good luck." He pointed to where Vincent figured the feed store was located.

"Thank you. Have a good day...good luck to you as well." It could have been worse, Vincent thought, grateful just to not catch a beating.

He went back outside to look for the feed store. It was easy to spot with the largest sign on the street. There was a row of shops between where he was and the store, and not one was open that he could tell. When he got to the feedstore, his hopes of finding work were gone. There was already a group of six guys unloading pallets from a flatbed truck. They saw him coming and with their body language told him to beat it as they stiffened and stared. He could take a hint but not another beating, so he moved on. The rest of town was the same, nothing. Well, nothing for him, anyway. There was an older guy at the edge of town sitting on a bench feeding stale bread to birds. Vincent's stomach growled and he briefly considered asking him for some, but before he could get very far into that fantasy, he was cut short.

"Nice shirt, kid. Did you steal it from your little sister or what?" And with that, the older guy let out a great belly laugh at how hilarious his joke was.

Vincent's face turned red. He knew he looked ridiculous but hated that he pointed it out. His shame turned to anger in a flash, and he ripped the stupid small shirt off and tossed it into the street. He swung his bag back onto his shoulder and ran for the edge of town. This only made the old guy laugh even harder as he yelled some unintelligible insult while Vincent ran away. It didn't matter what the insult was; he had already cut as deep as any stranger could have. For the second time today, he was crying. He felt stupid for it. He wasn't prone to being emotional, but over the last two days, he felt like he had done nothing but cry. He was done looking for work today. Maybe he could find some early strawberries or raspberries if he looked around the edge of town. Something, anything to eat really.

He spent all of ten minutes looking until his body told him he couldn't go any longer. It was warm and the sun felt good. He was still thirsty but there was a river he could hear, so he walked down to its banks. The water was crystal clear and cold. He drank his fill and sat on a nice big warm flat rock that was in full sun. His eyes dried out and he lay down to stretch out for a minute, using his bag as a pillow. As he lay down, his undershirt pulled away from his chest, taking the scabs from his nipples with it. The spots on the front of his shirt were dark brown from the dried blood. He thought about washing it in the river but as he thought about it, he drifted off.

It must have been a great nap, because he didn't wake up until much later in the day. The smell of food roused him. He thought he was dreaming it, but now that he was awake, it was still there and still delicious. With no thought of how he looked, he gathered his stuff, and his stomach guided him back to town. Just out of curiosity. He saw a line forming and recognized some of the women from the church earlier in the day were guiding people into a large building handing out plates and silverware. He saw the banner that read, "Kingston soup kitchen." Vincent had heard of these. It was a ploy to get goodwill from communities by the organized crime families that were in trouble with the law. The mafia mobsters figured if they filled bellies, the communities would look the other way when they sold their illegal hooch. It worked. For one, they were glad to be fed. But also, most of them liked to drink. Vincent didn't care either way;

they could do whatever they wanted if he could get something to eat.

Now excited at the prospect of a meal, he hurried to get a place in line. He got sideways glances from everyone in line, but he didn't care—he was starving. As he neared his spot at the back, a kid a little younger than him grabbed his arm. Vincent started to say something, but the kid was already pointing. He followed his directing finger and saw a placard that wasn't visible from his angle across the street.

"Locals only, thanks for understanding."

No, he didn't understand. But the faces of the "locals" told him he had better figure it out. Then his shame dug the hole a bit deeper for him and opened his mouth.

"No…" Vincent faked a laugh. "I wasn't gonna get in line. I'm not even hungry…I'm on my way home." He regretted the lie instantly. Their faces told him they knew he was lying. They knew the truth. He was a bum, and he was starving. All he could do now was put his head down and look for cover.

He considered the rock at the river again; after all, he'd gotten a good amount of sleep there earlier without interruption. Then he remembered the footsteps and the blackness from the night before. Tonight wasn't going to be a whole hell of a lot brighter, he thought miserably. The sun was racing toward the horizon now and he knew he'd better figure something out. The community really seemed on edge, so squatting in a shed or on a porch seemed daunting and dangerous. He continued walking through town, zigzagging, and killing time while looking for a good spot to tuck in and hide for one more night. Tomorrow, he would figure out his next move. One step at a time, he reminded himself.

Most of the lights had gone out now. In the past, they likely would have stayed on through the night, lighting up the corners of the town. But with the Depression, they were pinching pennies and burning electricity on lights not being used was foolish. However, one remained blazing and it was highlighting a great spot for the night. It was a giant oak tree behind a shop. At its base was a bramble of some kind, maybe blackberry. At the side he was looking at, it appeared there was a tunnel leading to the base of the giant tree through the tangle. The closer he got, the better it looked. Now down low, almost prone, Vincent crawled through the opening, pushing his bag in front of him. To his surprise, it opened up to a nice-sized space, perfect for a discreet safe place to sleep for the night. Relief washed over him as he had considered just roaming the streets zigzagging all night.

The shop's outside lamp was providing just enough light to let him get an idea of his surroundings. The "floor" was covered in dry grass that had obviously been harvested and brought in, probably for the same reason he was here, as a bed. He looked at the base of the tree and saw a patch of bark had been scraped away, leaving a white canvas on which someone had scratched a drawing of a crude bed, confirming his suspicions of his current whereabouts' use. There was another drawing, but it made no sense; it was a plus sign with what he thought was a cat. He wondered what it meant, but it didn't matter very much as he was already settled on this spot for the night. Now cozy feeling, he started to get his bedding out and ready for the night. Only then did he notice something dark interrupting the matrix of beige dried grass. He tried to get a better look, but the sun was long gone and the shop's light wasn't quite bright enough to make it out. Oh. The Dunhill, Vincent remembered. He grabbed the silver lighter from his pocket and gave it a flick. He wished he hadn't. It revealed the stain on the grass was what could only be blood. Dark blood, like the kind from an animal with a wound it would die from. It was concerning but he could get rid of it. Out of sight, out of mind.

As he gathered up the stained area of grass to toss it out, he discovered a bottle. It had a lid, too—perfect, now he could carry some water with him. He shook it in the dark and felt the liquid inside slosh around. Curious, he unscrewed the cap and gave it a sniff. Whisky. He knew that smell anywhere. Dad was suddenly in the tangle of blackberries with him. It gave him a boost of confidence and helped him gather the rest of the bloody grass and toss it aside. Now, as he sat in the dark fingering the bottle and thinking of Dad, another thought crossed his mind. Who in their right mind that felt it necessary to sleep under a tree would also leave booze behind...the same guy who left the blood behind, he told himself sarcastically but correctly. Suddenly, he didn't feel so cozy. He put the cap back on the booze and darted his eyes around the dark.

He stayed like that for a couple of hours, like an owl craning his neck every which way, but only seeing what the light from the shop would let him. Then more bad luck. The shop owner who Vincent thought had left hours ago came out the back door with a bag of trash then went back inside. Thirty seconds later, the light clicked off and the door opened again with the owner locking it behind him.

"Shit," Vincent muttered under his breath. Only not loudly enough to alert anyone to him, of course.

He was finished with people for the day, maybe for his whole life, he thought bitterly. Now that the light was gone, tonight was going to be one long guard shift. He was glad for the nap he had taken, but was still exhausted to his core, and starving.

After a couple more hours of fear, boredom and tossing on his makeshift pallet, his mind wandered to the bottle of booze again. Just the smell had given him some comfort earlier, and his dad had always told him he drank at night to help him sleep (not as if he hadn't been drinking all day anyway). Thinking of the advice and home made him also think of Mom and her contempt for his dad's drinking. Spite took it from there. He grabbed the bottle and tried to get an estimate of how much was in it. Not much, he decided after shaking it. He spun the cap off, careful not to lose it as the bottle would serve as a canteen after this. Without another thought, he upended the bottle and tried to drink it in one masculine chug. It didn't work. The bottle was fuller than he had given it credit for. It took two manly chugs. Good, he thought, hoping it would bring sleep. Instead, it brought fire. He had drunk sips of whisky from Dad before and with his friends that one night, but it had always been that, sips, chased with plenty of water. There was no relief from water in his near future, so he just sat there with whisky now hitting his empty stomach, making it clench and turn. For a while, he felt like he would puke again, but it passed.

He could feel the warmth spread from his belly into his blood. It was coursing all through his body, working its way to his brain. It unwound his tension, and all the humiliation from the past couple of days was comical. He laughed to himself, thinking about his ridiculous outfit with the bloody stains on his shirt, and how he must have looked running away from the old man teasing him. He lay back on his pillow and thought of home and what his brothers had thought when they woke up and he was gone. He hoped they gave Mom a mountain of shit about it. Jamie Lynn probably celebrated with Mother but that was fine. He thought in time he may come to miss her, too...maybe, or maybe that was the booze talking.

Crunch...crunch...sniff

Something was walking around the back side of the tree. Vincent held his breath, listening for more. His head was swimming.

Crunch...crunch...sniff...sniff....SNIFFFFF

It sounded like a dog trying to locate a treat and finally getting close, taking in the last huge whiff of its scent before it eats it. The hairs on his arms bristled and his mouth hung open in the dark. Feeling drunk and unable to handle this situation, he froze. Why did he drink the whisky, he asked himself regretfully. That was two times now that he drank, and both times were awful. Despite his growing fear, he noted that if he made it through tonight, he would never drink again.

The crunching and sniffing intensified on the other side of the tree. It had to be the same animal that had chased him last night. His hands searched the ground around him for a rock or a stick, anything really to defend himself with, but they came up empty.

Whatever it was, was coming around the side of the tree now to the tunnel through the bramble that Vincent had crawled through. He was trapped. The bramble's tangle was far too thick to try and climb through. The only way out was to go through whatever was standing out there now. His hands were desperate and shoved themselves into his pocket looking for help. They found the Dunhill. For an instant, he just held it hoping for the best, wishing for Dad. Then his brain turned back on, and he had a flash of genius. He grabbed a fistful of dry grass and flicked the lighter to it. It went up in flames shockingly fast, almost burning his face. He held the makeshift torch in front of him now, shoving it toward the hole, thinking he would see the eyes of a wolf or a mountain lion, or maybe a bear—he wasn't sure if they lived around here, though he had heard stories from his dad (which he had mostly assumed were more drunken slurred babble), but had also read about them in books.

Instead, the flames illuminated shoes. Fancy, shiny, leather shoes. The kind with flat leather soles. Expensive shoes whose owner should have no business being here and now.

Vincent was screaming now. The owner of the shoes began laughing and tearing at the tangle of branches above him, forcing his way down and through the new opening he was creating inching towards Vincent. Vincent flattened himself to the ground and tossed the torch in the direction of the hole. It landed on the dry grass bed and instantly, flames were all around him. The kindling dry brush pile exploded into flames around him. The brambles were burning, the bed was burning, his bag was burning, and in a minute, he would be burning too.

Then he heard what sounded at the time like angels.

"Fire, fire! Grab buckets, wake up, FIRE!"

The laughing from the smooth soled man stopped as well as Vincent's own screaming. The shiny shoes disappeared from the firelight and Vincent was left alone inside the burning bramble, looking for an exit but seeing nothing but growing flames.

The heat from the flames felt like it was about to ignite his clothing. The air was being sucked from his lungs and what little he managed to pull back in was full of smoke. Screaming wasn't an option; he could barely breathe. His survival instinct kicked in and he scrambled toward the area the smooth-soled shoes were at a few seconds ago. He would have to face the threat eventually, he figured, but doing it on fire would be much worse.

Just then, Vincent was hit by an unexpected icy blast. Followed by two hands reaching through the flames and pulling him hard. They pulled him through the flames and into the smoke-filled night air. He was still holding the empty whisky bottle, so he let it swing in giant clumsy arcs. Two huge arms wrapped themselves around him and stopped his flailing.

"Calm down, kid! What the hell are you doing, how drunk are you?" the very normal-sounding man said.

"More water, more buckets, we're gonna lose the store if we don't hurry up," another voice in the night yelled.

The same man holding him now grabbed his bottle and tossed it, shattering it on the hardpacked gravel. He shoved Vincent to the ground.

"What the fuck were you thinking, kid?" he asked, getting more pissed off as he watched the fire consume the brambles and start on the tree itself, which was more than likely bone dry like the rest of the county. "Who are you and where did you come from?" he pressed further.

Vincent just stared up at him, still in shock from the attack and the fire, but he was now coming to grips with the fact that an angry mob was forming around the fire and him. The current most pressing threat was coming from the mob itself. He looked for words to explain what had happened, but the booze was still sloshing around in his head.

"I'm Vincent," was all that came as he held his hands out in front of him and tried to get to a kneeling position. He felt vulnerable.

The man kicked some gravel at him and scoffed at his defensive posture. The murmurs in the crowd were growing angrier. But finally, the others with buckets and water seemed to be winning the fight with the fire, although the bottom third of the tree was destroyed, and that would likely kill it in the near future. Vincent felt guilty but was still terrified as he scanned the crowd for shiny leather smooth-soled shoes. Maybe if he could point out his attacker and form a cohesive sentence, he could manage to make it out of this mess unscathed.

Instead, his guts retched, and he puked. It tasted like bile, smoke, and whisky. He was glad to be rid of it. However, the impression it left on the hulking man and the angry mob was less than flattering.

"Well, listen up, Vincent." It felt strange to hear this angry man use his name. "You have worn out your welcome and I suggest you get out of town before the owner of the store whose tree you just destroyed shows up." He paused and added, "The last thing we need is another town drunk costing us resources we don't have and causing trouble we don't need." He added another pelting of gravel with his foot for emphasis.

Vincent tried to stand up but between the booze and starvation, he lost his vision and ended up on his face. He lay there for a second catching his breath, listening to the laughter from the softening crowd, who no longer sensed danger just another pathetic drunk. His body gave him no option to walk away so he just had sit back up and listen to the insults a bit longer. He stayed there sweating and shivering for another thirty minutes, watching the remnants of the fire die down and the jeering from the crowd as well. As he noticed the sun was starting to creep over the horizon, giving a faint grey look to the East. That gave him a little comfort. At least the night was over. He had better heed the huge guy's advice and get out of here as soon as possible, before the tree's owner arrived.

The river was an obvious first stop. He went to his huge rock and attempted to lie back and collect himself a bit, but without his bag for padding it was worthless. He sat on its edge and almost let himself start crying again. Crying wasn't helping, he told himself drying the tears with flutters of his eyelashes before they could fall. He had been crying since he left home, and nothing was getting any better as a result of the tears. Just one step at a time. Last night was over. Today was a new day. The next town over was a mystery, and as such was full of opportunity. He repeated all of these positive thoughts in his head and filled his belly one last time at the river.

Feeling exhausted but more positive than he probably should be, he made his way cautiously through town. Hoping with every step that he wouldn't have to pass anyone or hear anyone yelling from a coffee-crowded porch. He just wanted to be gone as much as they wanted him gone. The sooner, the better, he thought and tried to quicken his step, quickly realizing he didn't have the energy for that much effort and slowing to a shuffle again.

On his way out of town, one last thing caught his eye. It started catching his eye because on a block full of lawns manicured to perfection by freshly unemployed and bored men, there was one yard that was a tangle of weeds and had grass as tall as the dilapidated fence that was surrounding the yard. As he got closer, he could hear a cooing voice talking sweetly to something. He peered through the tunnel-like archway formed by low unmanaged branches toward the front porch. A lady was holding what looked like a dozen kittens, maybe singing or just talking in a high sing-songy voice to them and petting them with the tips of her fingers. She saw Vincent looking at her and smiled a pleasant smile and gave him a wave.

Vincent's intuition told him that if he didn't feel as if he were being chased out of town by an angry mob, he could strike up a conversation and offer to clean her yard in trade for something to eat. It would likely end up with a bed and a roof, and maybe even some clean clothes, her smile told him. As it was, he wished he had seen her eight hours ago. Instead, he only gave her a smile and a wave back. The last thing that caught his eye about her yard was the last crooked corner post of her fence. It had been etched with the same bed and cat combination he had seen carved into the now destroyed tree which he tried to sleep under. This set of carvings had another drawing though; it was a bottle but instead of the usual three X's, this one had two. He wasn't sure what the X's meant and was even more unsure of why there would only be two and not the usual three.

He turned the mystery around in his head the first couple of miles of his walk to the next town, not coming up with much in the way of answers. The walk started out not so terribly. He was a few miles in before the sun started to get hot. The smoky smell from the fire was mixing with his body odor and the smell reminded him of Mom's soup. His stomach flipped and threatened to empty itself of the river water which he couldn't afford to lose. He was so hungry, it was passing hunger and entering into a new territory he was unfamiliar with, but even thinking of food was nauseating. His feet felt heavy and even Dad's silver Dunhill lighter in his pocket banging on his thigh with every step felt like it was made of lead.

A few cars had broken up the monotony of the walk and added some excitement as he hid from them in the ditches. It was becoming a game to avoid attention and judgmental looks. One, however, snuck up on him. He realized that if he were to jump in the ditch now, he'd look like a fool. So, reluctantly he put his head down and kept walking, trying avoid even looking at the passing car. Just as he thought it was safe to look up, he realized it had slowed down and was now stopped in the road. He cursed his luck, now wondering what they wanted. Was it the store owner? Was it the man with the fancy shoes? Was it a kidnapper?

Vincent looked into the back window of the car, trying to get an indication of what he was dealing with. Whoever it was had a big white and red hat that resembled a peppermint pinwheel with a red bow and reddish curly hair.

Probably safe. Vincent cautiously made his way up to the side of the car, only hurrying when he saw the lady wave him up with a lace gloved hand.

"Hey sweety, you need a ride?" she said before she could have even gotten a good look at him. Vincent hurried a few more steps and stooped a bit to be able to look in the car. The woman behind the wheel was beautiful. She was wearing a dress with a red and white pattern similar to the hat. Her skin was flawless. Her long neck led down to cleavage that she looked like she was unsuccessfully trying to hide with a blouse underneath.

Suddenly, Vincent was humiliated. She was welcoming and beautiful, but he was filthy and smelled like Mom's smoky soup. He had stains on his shirt from where his nipples had bled and patches of his pants were burnt from the fire. He was too self-conscious to even respond like a gentleman.

"No," he almost snapped. But not at her; he was snapping at his situation and instantly felt bad when he saw her recoil at his rudeness. "No, thank you, ma'am." He paused. "I'm in no shape to get in your nice car. I'd dirty it all up and I don't mind the walk," he lied.

"Are you sure? It's a pretty long ways to anywhere from here," she said in a manner that offered the ride again.

"No, really, I know where I'm going. Thank you, though." He felt a little better knowing he saved himself from looking like he was being rude. At the same time, he was regretting passing on the ride. Any other normal day, he would have done just about anything to ride in a car like this with a woman like her. He had no idea how far it was or what the town was even called that he was walking to. All the positive things he had told himself by the river suddenly seemed foolish.

"Ok, well, good luck, then." And with that she put the car in gear and gave him a smile before getting back on the road.

Vincent waved at her mirrors as he watched her disappear around the corner. He got back onto the hardpack and kept walking. This time making sure to listen harder for any car signs. He didn't think his ego could take another hit. It had been a long few days, and there was no end in sight. One step at a time, he reminded himself.

About a million heavy torturous steps later, he could see a town coming into view. He was going to make it before nightfall. Thank Christ, he thought, not believing he could make it another night in the dark alone. Even if town felt unwelcoming, it sure as hell wouldn't feel as dangerous as the sniffing man in the smooth-soled shoes. The thought of the stalker made him whip his head around to the tree line on either side of him. Nothing.

Up ahead, the town's sign came into view, welcoming him. He wondered if the sign meant it or if it would have the same unwelcoming feeling as the last. Main Street seemed livelier than the last one had, which made Vincent feel slightly more hopeful for finding a quick way to earn enough to buy something to eat. People were in and out of stores and there were fewer porches lined with working-aged men. Vincent wondered what was sheltering them from the scourge of the Depression. But he didn't care very much, if it meant people had more to spare. Maybe they would be more willing to let him earn a meal or a place to stay. The only thing was that there was an overwhelming fishy smell all throughout the downtown. He followed his nose, and it led him to another soup kitchen. This one was proudly sponsored by a man Vincent recognized from the papers. He was a big-time gangster who ran illegal booze in the area after they started the Prohibition. Suddenly, the hardiness of the town was a little clearer. Maybe this was the gangster's hometown, and the locals turned a blind eye to the underhanded dealings for the shelter it provided them from the worst of the Depression. Vincent wondered if they were at all generous.

Part of him wanted to get a head start on the hunger and look for a job. His body refused to comply. He was wasted physically. The best he could manage was to wait around the side of the soup kitchen until dinnertime and hope they were more hospitable than in the last town. He leaned his back on the building and rested his head between his legs. A passerby would probably not even notice him from the pile of refuse he sat beside. His shirt was the same color as the dirt street. His pants were burnt and filthy, looking like detritus rather than clothing. He was just a heap of trash waiting for burn day. Oddly, Vincent noticed a charcoal drawing of a plate with a knife and fork etched into the bricks beside him much in the same fashion as the cat and the bed on the fence post and tree from the last town. He noted these symbols for reference later. Right now, however, he was spent.

For the better part of the day, he was in and out of consciousness. His grey periods were interrupted by the musings of passersby on the smell of the fish. "Oh, the smell of fish is hanging so thick down on this end of town." "Jesus, that fish is strong." "Smells like an oriental fish market." "All you can smell is the smell of fish in the air" and so on, all day. It seemed everyone he could hear was talking about the smell of fish. Vincent had never felt so worthless in his whole life. Here he was starving to death right under their noses and all they could report on was the smell of fish. Vincent was jealous of the smell. He wished he were in the air and people were even slightly concerned for him, or hell, even *about* him, he would take any attention at this point. But there was nothing all day—not one person even seemed to notice him as the smell continued to get all the attention.

The last thing he remembered thinking was wondering when they would be serving dinner. Then his head rocked back, smacking the brick wall and his body tipped to the side. He lay there unnoticed for hours. Dinner was served. The line was long, stretching right past him, and no one cared. They were here to eat, not wake up hungover bums.

After the kitchen was closed and the lights were off, Vincent still lay there in the dark. Two hands grabbed him and shook him. Shook him so hard, it startled him into a scream.

"AAAAHHHH!"

"Jeezum crow!" a scratchy high-pitched voice yelled back in response to his scream. "I thought you were dead kid. I'm sorry...you scared me half to death."

Looking at the man's shoes, Vincent realized this couldn't be the stalker. He could see part of a knobby toenail poking through a hole at the front of what used to be a shoe. And the man had an air of harmlessness about him that would be hard to hide for someone with ulterior motives.

"I'm sorry, mister. I was just tired and fell asleep earlier. What time is it? Are they gonna serve dinner soon?"

Vincent could tell by the look on the older man's face that he had missed his chance to eat today.

"Nope, they served that up hours ago." The man looked as if he could sense his disappointment. "If it were fish you were after, I can help with that." He held a bag out in front of him.

Confused, Vincent took the bag and looked inside. It was chock full of strips of white, hard, dried fish. He looked at the filthy man questioningly.

"Go ahead, eat it all if you want. That's my specialty, always more where that came from."

Disregarding the unsanitary conditions in which the fish was prepared and even where the fish came from, Vincent ate. Surprisingly it was delicious. The man had sprinkled it with salt and pepper, which woke up every corner of his mouth. The salt was for curing and the pepper for tasting, the man would later explain in depth. For now, Vincent gorged himself. Little blisters formed on the roof of his mouth and an ulcer opened on his tongue. The salt stung and irritated these, but his stomach wanted more. He gave it to it, as much as it would take.

As he stuffed his face, the man held his hand out in front of him. "Elmer," he said with a smile.

It was the second bit of kindness Vincent had experienced since leaving home if you included the pretty woman who had offered him a ride. Eagerly, he reached out and offered his own.

"Vincent."

"Ok, Vin, if you...."

"Not Vin, Vincent," he said more hatefully than he intended. Where did that even come from? Why did he aim his anger at the one guy being nice to him? "I'm sorry, mister. I just hate that name I guess...you can call me whatever you want though." Feeling sheepish, still chewing this man's food, he regretted everything he had just said. "Sorry," he added again under his breath, the chewing now slowing.

"Don't be sorry. I'll just call you Vinny," he said, winking and still smiling. "What I was saying is that there is a deputy in this town that ain't super friendly to outsiders." Vincent wondered if this was going to be the guy's nice way of telling him to get out of town. "But if you want a safe place to sleep tonight, I can show you one. It ain't much but it's a roof and it's out of the way of the law. In fact, it's just a barn where you won't be bothered if I'm being honest, nothing special but it's safe."

Again, Vincent blurted out the first thing that came to his mind.

"Is it dark?" He regretted saying it, but it was an honest question. There was no way he was going to sleep anywhere he couldn't see what was coming from the dark.

"Well, it's nighttime but I think the streetlight is close enough to give it some shine," Elmer replied, measuring the boy's fear. "I'll be there, too, and I've slept there before. I'm sure it's safe."

Elmer had said all the right things and with a now full belly, Vincent could feel the exhaustion catching up to him. Even though he had slept most of the day, it wasn't a restful sleep.

"Ok, sure thanks." Part of him thought back to the kidnappers he had been so scared of only a couple of days ago, but since his encounter with the smooth-soled shoes the worries he'd had as a kid seemed much less important.

Another part of him prayed this guy didn't want to have a non-consensual dalliance in this supposed barn. Vincent's intuition told him he was fine. He looked at the old guy, who was smiling and chatting about his kids being busy somewhere with their own lives and jobs. Vincent wasn't paying very close attention, which he felt bad for, but he couldn't help but feel paranoid and was looking over his shoulder every few seconds not knowing what to expect but expecting something. After sizing up the situation and the old man Vincent decided that, if the old guy tried anything, he could lick him in a fight. He was larger than the older guy and a lifetime younger, by the looks of it.

As they walked on, Vincent's mouth was on fire and his feet were still made of lead from the miles behind him. Luckily, it wasn't very far to the barn. There was fresh hay on the ground and the light from the street was flooding in just as promised. He sat across from Elmer, dying from thirst now and sweating bullets in the too-warm stale air.

"I don't suppose you know where I can get a drink, do you?"

For the first time since meeting, he sensed anger or something dark from Elmer.

"NO," he said firmly. "Not a drop in this damn town. You see this?" He pointed to a drawing on the wall. It was an exact replica of the bottle with two X's Vincent had seen in the last town. "You see them two X's on that bottle. It's like those talkies with the cartoons at the start that get the X's in their eyes when they die. A bottle with two X's means you don't drink no hooch in that area unless you want to die."

Vincent was confused.

"I was talking about a drink of water, though, mister. I don't drink hooch," he lied even though it was only the two times. Vincent had sworn off liquor altogether, so maybe it was a white lie.

"Oh, well that's a different story, Vinny. I thought you meant the other." He reached into the bindle he was carrying. "Have at ya," he said and tossed him a bottle full of what must have been water. "Sorry to get a bit testy there but I've told more than a few fellas now who wouldn't listen and ended up in a shallow plot because they couldn't control their urges."

"What do you mean?" Vincent said, then chugged the water greedily. He was genuinely interested now, feeling like he was on the brink of solving the mystery of the drawings.

"Well, I'm not too sure to be honest, but wherever the code tells you to avoid certain things, you better listen. It's all I'm saying. This time of day ain't the time of day to discuss it anyhow." Elmer seemed to remember the fear on Vincent's face when he asked about the darkness.

"Oh, ok." Vincent tossed the bottle back. He was disappointed in the answer he was getting. But he didn't know Elmer well enough to press him for more. "What's the code, though?" he prodded a little further, not able to help himself.

"Well, if you stick around me a bit, maybe I can teach you a thing or two about that and a thing or two about this life." Elmer hadn't pried but with the country in the state it was in, he didn't have to.

Homeless men traveling looking for work was the rule, not the exception. Vincent was glad for his understanding and apparent offer to take him under his wing without wanting his life story. He didn't feel like sharing that with him anyway, he barely understood it himself. He thought of Jamie Lynn yelling in the tub and blushed even now in the dark.

"Yeah, maybe I will, thanks." Vincent started fluffing some hay for a pillow.

Elmer tossed him a clean shirt from his bindle. "Use that so it don't make your face itchy."

That night, Vincent dreamed of salt. He could taste it on the tip of his tongue, then it was in his entire mouth. Slowly, the ball of dream salt dropped into his guts and started to boil. He woke up retching and sweating, and he barely made it outside in time to empty his stomach. Luckily, it seemed like less fish came out than had gone in, so hopefully, he was digesting some of it. Thoughts of the dream of salt came back and he retched again. The thought of the fish was turning his stomach as well. He wiped his face clean and returned to the barn. Elmer was sleeping in a sitting position up against a support post for the stable he was in.

The sun was starting to poke some gold into the grey that had preceded it through the trees. At least it wasn't dark. He lay back down, wanting to let his stomach settle a little bit before he figured out what Elmer had in store for them. The older man seemed eager to help and friendly enough, and he seemed to know how to survive this lifestyle. Looking at him, he must have lived this life for a while. He had his bindle clung tight full of

God knew what. Canvas pants with more patches than original fabric paired with a flannel shirt with more grime than stitches. This ran against the grain of how he presented himself however. He seemed like a learned man and was charismatic enough. There was a friendly smile on his face most of last night, from what Vincent could see in the half-dark of the poorly lit town anyway. And there was the bag of fish. It may have made him puke from his over eager attempt to eat it all, but it didn't diminish its value. Thinking it over in the now almost daylight, Vincent thought it might be nice to have someone who knew how to survive. He could always just leave whenever he wanted if it got burdensome or weird.

There was freedom in that thought. Vincent had always felt under his mom's thumb or the burden of the chores and responsibilities that Dad couldn't handle or wouldn't because he was too drunk. The fact that he could just pick a direction and walk was liberating. Scary but safe in the knowledge that if he didn't like what was going on, he could just leave. If he could learn to feed himself and learn the tricks of life on the road from a guy who lived it, he would take the opportunity. There was also the not-so-small fact that Vincent had some burning questions about this code that Elmer seemed to understand better than he was letting on last night. His mind was made up; he would stick around this Elmer guy until he exhausted his teachings, then he would be unshackled from everyone. When he could survive on his own everyone could abandon him, and he wouldn't care. If he could feed himself and find safe places to sleep, he could live whatever kind of life he wanted to. That was if Elmer hadn't changed his mind about helping him during the night.

Almost like he could sense him thinking about him, Elmer interrupted his thoughts.

"Breakfast?" He tossed the bag of fish at Vincent, who still felt green.

"Oh uhh…." He gagged and his eyes watered. "I think I got sick from it last night. I was sleeping and dreaming of salt. It woke me up and I was sick to my stomach."

"Right right right." Elmer paused and then offered an alternative. "I doubt it was my fish. Not that I'm against criticism cos I ain't no cook, but I think you were dehydrated. How long did you walk with no water yesterday?"

"All day, I guess. I had a drink at the river before I left the last town." He blushed thinking of the fire and the mob thinking of him as the town drunk. "But, uhh, I was in a hurry to leave town, so I didn't take any with me."

"See, I had that salt dream a couple of times myself, but it was always on days I couldn't find any fresh water, or I was just being a jackass and not drinking any," Elmer said, not in a know-it-all fashion, but didn't leave any room for arguments either.

"Oh." Vincent thought he was probably right, but there was no way he would eat that fish again unless he had to.

"Well, let's make sure that don't happen again, and make sure you stop drinking all my water in the process," Elmer said. Vincent was a little shocked but after seeing the smile on his face, realized it was only a joke. "Let's get you a bottle of your own. Hell, we might as well put you together a kit if we can manage it."

Vincent was suspicious of the man's desire to help him. "Are you sure, mister? I mean you don't gotta help me. I can manage."

"No, you can't. I found you yesterday and I thought I was rolling over a corpse. But it's fine. I want to help. It'll give a frugal tourist like myself something to do…and stop calling me mister; it's just Elmer," Elmer said, trying to play it cool. The look he gave Vincent told him he was dying to keep Vincent around.

Vincent was in no position to refuse help even if he wasn't sure of this older man. "Ok, but what's a frugal tourist?"

"I'm glad you asked. I dropped that as bait, you see. I wanted you to ask me that. Frugal tourist is what I am. Not a bum or a hobo or a vagrant. You see, I have a home; I had a family, but they are gone, and my house got too big, so I left. I didn't have much money at the time." Elmer paused and handed his bindle to Vincent as he got to his feet. "You carry that, and I'll carry the conversation." Elmer laughed at himself and the two of them started walking. "Not having much money, I had to adapt if I wanted to see all the corners of this great country of ours. So, I adapted. I became the frugal tourist, on a mission to see as much as I can as cheaply as possible."

Elmer proceeded to enlighten Vincent with a didactic rendition of his life since leaving the home, a home Vincent wondered if he really ever owned. It seemed impossible someone would just leave a whole life behind on purpose. Perhaps it was all crazy talk from a crazy old man. Regardless, the information he was getting already seemed valuable and practical. So, he paid attention, not wanting to miss an important bit amongst the ramblings.

Once again, Elmer seemed to be rummaging around in Vincent's thoughts, saying something oddly pertinent to his train of thought.

"Maybe I'll go home someday if I can remember where it is at that point." He paused and laughed. "I sure hope the next thing I remember is the last thing I forgot. Otherwise, I fear something will be lost forever."

For some reason, this stuck in Vincent's head. His subconscious was already repeating it so he wouldn't lose it like so many other random thoughts that were, just like Elmer said, lost forever. This one Vincent wanted to keep. And for the first time maybe in months, Vincent laughed, which made Elmer laugh. By the time they got close to downtown, they were still laughing. Elmer had to remind them people were going to assume the worst if the two of them, looking like they did, came stumbling into town laughing their asses off this early in the day. So, they both corrected themselves and Elmer continued his lesson.

"First thing we gotta do is get you a bindle for yourself, but its trickier than you might think." Elmer said.

They were rounding the corner to the alley behind the storefronts. Elmer seemed to know where he was going. As they came up to the trash cans behind one of the stores, he stopped and tipped the can. He shifted the pile then snatched up two hessian sacks just like the ones his own bindle was made from.

"How'd you know those would be there?" Vincent asked, impressed.

"Well, what comes in bags like these, Vinny?" Elmer quizzed him.

"Dry goods, potatoes, onions." He could have kept going but Elmer stopped him.

"Ok, so, what store's trash do you think we are rummaging around in?" Elmer said knowingly, but not in an arrogant fashion.

"Oh yeah, nice." Vincent didn't bother answering and felt stupid for asking.

"Now pick up the rest of that and put it back in the bin. We don't want to leave a mess and give our ilk a worse name than they've already got."

After Vincent cleaned up the mess he had made, he followed Elmer a little farther down the alley to another dumpster. This one he didn't need to tip over as the item he was looking for was sitting neatly on top.

"Here ya go, new canteen."

The used bleach bottle was tossed at Vincent who caught it easily. Its dark brown glass cast an orange light on his fingers as he looked at it carefully. It had a lid, no cracks, and at least he was sure it was sanitary being it had held bleach. It would obviously need a good rinse, but he liked it much better than the whisky bottle that had been his previous choice. No one who saw this would assume he was a drunk at least—maybe a crazy bum who was drinking bleach, but not a drunk.

Next, Elmer led him away from town. On the way, he looked like he was watching the trees carefully as they walked. This put the hairs on Vincent's neck up. He wondered what had the old man so on alert. Then without warning, he dashed off the road and into the trees. Instantly scared, Vincent followed him, not wanting to be left alone and to his own surprise, he found that Elmer felt safe to be around. Ahead of him, Elmer grabbed a low hanging branch on a tree and gave it a good twisting yank. Nothing happened.

"Elmer, what the hell are you doing?"

Elmer looked at him and seemed shocked to see the fear on his face.

"I didn't mean to scare ya. I was just focused on finding the perfect stick for your bindle. I should have given you some indication." He looked Vincent over. "Are you gonna be ok? What the hell's got you so shook up anyway? What happened to ya?" Elmer winced seeming to notice that maybe he was prying.

"Well. Nothing that makes sense. Maybe I'll tell you about it when you tell me what you know about the code you were talking about last night." Vincent answered intentionally cryptically.

"Fair enough." Elmer winked back.

Neither of them was comfortable enough to share, not yet. Elmer got a knife out of his bag and cut a groove along the base of the branch and snapped it off. Then they kept walking to Elmer's mystery destination. Vincent wished he was more forthcoming with information on what they were doing, but Elmer seemed to enjoy keeping him hanging on, so Vincent played along for now. Elmer explained why that stick was special as they walked. It was a naturally twisted grain from a hardwood. He could use it for just about anything but mostly as a club if he needed to.

"Swing as hard as you'd like," he said. "It won't break."

He handed the branch he'd been working on with his knife to Vincent now after explaining its functions. Vincent was impressed; it was knotted and twisted and perfect as a weapon. He already felt safer.

The destination ended up not being that huge of a mystery after all; it was just the river. They stopped and before rinsing and filling their bottles, they both filled themselves. The water was clear and sweet, Vincent wondered if it was the same river he had drunk from in the last town, whose name he couldn't even remember. Another lost thought. There needed to be less of that, he warned himself. Vincent started washing the bleach out of his bottle and when he was finished, he filled it and put it into his growing collection of things Elmer thought were essential. Elmer told him they had one more stop and they continued down the road a bit. Vincent's appetite had returned, and he was feeling at the end of his rope physically again. The older man bounded along with a pep in his step, making Vincent wonder if he really could take him in a fight or if he might catch a beating instead.

With Elmer's seemingly uncanny ability to read his mind, the next stop was a bait shop/ café on a bridge over the river. As they walked up, the smell of meat cooking on a grill with onions in the background washed over Vincent, making his mouth water. What kind of torture was Elmer putting him through? He had to know how hungry he was. There was a growing thought that maybe he was getting a rise out of him when suddenly Elmer dropped his pants halfway and reached into the fabric behind his leg.

"Hey what are you doing? You're gonna...."

Elmer yanked his hand out quickly and buttoned his pants back up. Then with a grin, he flashed a fist of dollar bills at him.

"You can't keep this in your regular pockets or you're gonna lose it quick enough living this life."

Vincent recalled the conductor tossing him around and turning his pockets out. Elmer was proving to be wilier than Vincent had given him credit for. He had assumed he was an old lonely crackpot, but with every step he was regretting his initial assessment. He was cunning and useful, Vincent was learning that he was lucky Elmer had found him.

The two of them went inside and the smell of the patty melts was overwhelming. He wondered if maybe he could ask the clerk to do a side job to get himself one. He thought about Elmer's fistful of dollars and stopped himself from asking the obvious. This guy was going out of his way to be helpful, and Vincent didn't want to abuse his good fortune.

He didn't have to.

"We would like four of them patty melts with the taters, too, but we got some shopping to do first, so just have them at the counter for us," Elmer ordered like he owned the place.

"You got money, fella?" the clerk shot back rudely.

"You just get the food and let me worry about that," Elmer shot right back, not taking any shit. Despite looking like he did, his pride was very much still intact.

"You got it, fella," the guy behind the counter said, disappearing to the grill.

Vincent didn't want to assume one of those patty melts was for him, but there was no way Elmer could eat it by himself. He tried to ignore it and leave it on Elmer's plate for now. He didn't want to beg but if Elmer began to eat all four and not offer him one, he might.

"What do you need to get? I could grab it for you," Vincent offered to do his shopping for him, hoping to build some good will quickly.

"Not what I need; it's what *you* need," Elmer told him.

"I don't need anything, really," he lied, thinking of the food, "plus I left all my money at home." Another lie but it felt better than saying he had none.

"Well, I know that but if you're gonna make it out here for a while, you're gonna need some things." Elmer said not questioning why Vincent would have left home without his money.

Elmer walked through the couple of aisles in the small store. He grabbed a spool of silk fishing thread, some barbed hooks, a can of linseed oil, and a pocketknife. Then he reached for the matches and Vincent finally felt not so foolish. He pulled Dad's Dunhill from his pocket and flashed it at Elmer.

"Beautiful but keep that safe in your hidden pocket. You're gonna want to keep that close." This seemed to remind Elmer and he grabbed the needle and thread kit. "For the pocket." He winked at Vincent.

Elmer continued shopping and grabbed a bar of soap, some socks and briefs (which made Vincent feel a bit awkward), and two new undershirts. This made Vincent look at his own, seeing the now brown nipple stains and scorch marks.

Uncanny Elmer tossed him one of the new undershirts and told him to go to the bathroom and wash his face and change his shirt. Vincent did it with no arguments; he wanted the shameful shirt off his body yesterday.

By the time he came out of the bathroom, Elmer was sat at the bar. There were two plates, two burgers and a load of fries on each. The bag full of essentials was on the stool next to Elmer. Vincent could feel his eyes welling with tears at the prospect of a meal like that and Elmer's kindness. The flow of tears was quickly broken by Elmer shooting him a gleeful smile while he emptied the salt and pepper shakers into a leather pouch he had produced from somewhere.

"It ain't stealing, they can't tell me how much salt and pepper to use," he whispered. Vincent's mind ran over the day's conversations, thinking of the salty peppered fish from the night before and the explanation of what a frugal tourist was. It was another lesson from Elmer and for the second time in a day, Vincent laughed.

After lunch, Vincent was ready for a nap. Elmer, however, had other plans. He seemed to have a bottomless well of energy and was putting him to shame. The two patty melts and fries he had eaten were still sitting heavy on his stomach, and he wished he could relax and let it settle. He didn't want to risk losing it like the fish. Just thinking of the fish again on a full belly made his throat tighten.

"Let's get that bindle finished up so you can have one on each shoulder." Elmer laughed but the hint was noted. It was the least Vincent could do to try to begin to pay him back for lunch and the supplies, so Vincent nodded eagerly.

They went down by the river, where Elmer first tossed his line in with a bit of soap on the hook. He explained that the catfish loved the smell of soap and couldn't hardly resist eating it if they caught its scent in the water. This seemed crazy to Vincent; his own mom had put soap in his mouth once for cursing during Christmas dinner, and the thought of something seeking it out to eat seemed implausible.

Elmer sat down in a dry patch of sand that was hot from the sun which was setting and starting to blend into the tree line. He motioned for Vincent to sit down as he tied his fishing line to his big toe in a loose loop.

"Grab that oil out of the bag there and hand it to me. I'll show you how to use it and you can finish it." Elmer instructed.

Vincent was confused but complied anyway. Elmer flicked his knife open and grabbed one of the hessian sacks, the smaller of the two. Then he cut out the stiches from the side so it lay open in a large rectangle on the sand.

"Ok, now take a bit of the oil and rub it into the cloth like this." He dumped some oil into one palm and rubbed his hands together, then massaged one corner. "You do this to the whole thing then you use this as the outside layer of the bindle to keep everything else nice and dry even in the rain...well mostly. It ain't perfect but it's better than dripping wet."

Vincent listened closely, not wanting to lose anything forever. He was thankful that the lesson was going to involve sitting in the sun and not a ton of physical activity. He hoped it would give him time to digest for a little while. Maybe he would intentionally take his time. The warm oil felt good rubbing into his hands as he started to work the cloth. While he did, Elmer sewed a secret pocket into his pants for him, again making the joke that if someone wanted his money bad enough to look through his ass, they could have it. Elmer then slid the rest of his dollar bills into Vinny's new secret pocket without a word.

"Everything else stays folded and neat in the bigger bag here that we wrap around everything. In a pinch, the oiled cloth can be put above you at a pitch to keep your head dry and the bigger one can be used to keep your ass warm." Elmer laughed at himself.

Vincent was beginning to think Elmer was the funniest guy Elmer knew. But he'd gotten him to laugh twice today, so he couldn't argue. He was funny even if Vincent didn't think it was always intentional.

Just like that, Elmer let out a howl.

"Damn!"

He was reaching for his foot in an overly excited fashion. Then he dove forward and snatched his fishing line, which had been rapidly retreating to the water.

"Almost lost it."

He started winding the line around his thumb and elbow, pulling the fish closer to shore. Then with another hoot from Elmer, he yanked the fish onto shore. It was a huge catfish and Vincent was on top of it in an instant. He had been fishing many times and knew what to do. There was a rock in his hand and then in the head of the fish in an instant.

"Nice work, Vinny. Quick as Hermes."

Vincent held the fish up, shocked that Elmer's fishing with soap method had worked so well so quickly. The thought of eating the fish right now disgusted him but this trick could potentially save his life in the future. This felt like an important step toward self-reliance.

"Now you gut the thing and bring me the liver so I can get the line back in the water. No sense wasting all the soap."

Elmer explained that he wanted to fill his bag back up since Vincent had eaten his supply of fish last night. They sat by the river for a while in silence. Vincent started to feel restless and wanted to try to prove himself useful in some way. He knew the vegetation in the area—it was all still similar to what used to surround the farm before everything started drying up. The river was a refuge for green and it was summer berry season.

"Hey, if you're gonna fish for a bit, I'm gonna walk up the river and look around."

"Sounds like a fine plan. I ain't gonna leave without ya. I'll be right here." Elmer put the corner of the hessian cloth over his eyes and leaned back with his liver and soap-primed hook now tied off to his toe.

Vincent walked up the bank of the river. The rocks were smoothed from the water, warm from the last remnants of the sun, and felt good on his bare sore feet. He found himself looking for pretty rocks. He knew agates were around here and he had always been a rockhound. Maybe if he found a really nice one, he could sell it to a jeweler or a gem collector. The task of finding berries fell to the wayside as he found himself on a treasure hunt looking for gemstones. Going slowly, he was hunched over and looking at every rock. He wandered slowly up the bank zigzagging so he could cover an optimal amount of the rocks as he went. The best part was tipping over any rock that showed any promise of the pretty lacy patterns he was looking for. He was excited and lost in the fun of it.

That was until he almost stepped into a wooden trough coming from the bank of the river. It broke his trance, and he stood up straight. The small of his back pinched in pain from being stooped over for so long. His hands rubbed it as his eyes traced the little wooden river leading into the woods. Curiosity was now in charge and led him into the trees. His eyes were still trained down following the trough through the grass and he resumed his rock-hunting posture reflexively.

After making it about 100 feet into the woods, a voice cut the silence.

"Who the fuck are you, then?" A tough looking guy with a bowler hat was standing next to a series of wooden barrels, tubes, fire and jars.

The first thing that came to mind was the mad scientists from the books he loved so much. Frankenstein in particular. Like the child he was, he found himself quickly scanning the area for a man made from stitched-together dead people.

"I asked you a question, boy." Vincent turned instinctively to bolt back to the river.

"Yeah, kid, he asked you a question." Two hands appeared from what seemed like nowhere and grabbed Vincent mid-flight.

Vincent was screaming now. His eyes turned to the two men's shoes, and he found himself slightly relieved despite the situation when he saw work boots. The shock wore off and his scream faded.

"I'm nobody. I was just looking for rocks…well, I was looking for berries and then started to…."

"Berries and rocks? What are you talking about, kid? Why are you at our still site, then? There ain't no berries or rocks around here." The bowler hat man was closing the gap now.

"I was just following the trough; I didn't know what it was," Vincent said.

He was sure a beating was imminent, if not them stabbing his guts out and putting him in the ground under their still.

"Vinny, what the hell are you doing over here?" Elmer yelled from close behind.

Vincent swung his head around to see the older guy holding his own knotted, twisted bindle's stick like a cane. Vincent noticed Elmer's knuckles were white from his grip on it.

The two moonshiners exchanged glances.

"We better get back. Your dad and uncles are gonna be looking for us here in a minute if we don't show our faces pretty soon." Elmer started weaving a lie.

Now, the guy holding Vincent let him go and pushed him toward Elmer.

"Listen here, you two and whoever else you brought with you down to our river better get out of here before dark. There are worse things than bad men making moonshine when the sun goes down. If we see you again or anything happens to compromise this site, we will find you…understood?"

"Yeah, no problem, mister. I never wanted any trouble. I'm real sorry." Vincent ran to Elmer's side.

"We won't say a damn thing. Not to worry, you won't see us again." Elmer grabbed Vincent by the shoulder and led him away.

Elmer kept himself between the tough guys and Vincent until they got to the river.

"Jesus, Elmer, I'm sorry. I had no idea," Vincent started his apology.

"No need. I know you wouldn't have wandered into that on purpose. Only now we gotta get the hell out of town. They won't stop holding a grudge and the moonshine runs this county. It's why the soup kitchen eats like a fancy restaurant." Vincent realized his intuition was right when he saw the mobster's name on the billboard when he arrived in town.

The ominous warning about worse things after dark stuck in both of their minds, definitely not lost forever, though neither of them spoke of it. It echoed on in their heads as they assembled their kits as fast as they could. Elmer tossed the beautiful catfish onto the rocks.

"The crows can have it; we don't got time for it now." Elmer said offhandedly.

This made Vincent feel guilty for the fish and for wasting Elmer's time.

"Now what?" Vinny asked impatiently as he watched the remnants of the sun disappearing amongst the branches.

"Now we get on the train and get the hell out of town. We have officially worn out our welcome." He grabbed his own bindle this time, and the two of them hurried up the hill to the now closed bait shop they had eaten lunch at.

Vincent was turning over his first attempt at a train ride and the beating he caught.

"Are we gonna buy tickets?" he asked nervously.

"Nah, it ain't that kind of train, Vinny." He laughed but in an exasperated fashion. "This one's cargo only. Cept the conductor don't mess around with bulls and don't mind if you catch a ride."

"Are you sure? What's a bull?" The two questions overlapped.

"Umm, yes, Vinny, I'm sure. I don't want to catch hell any more than you do, and a bull is an asshole train companies pay to make sure you pay for your ride." Vincent could sense the old man's irritation and tried to walk the rest of the way quietly.

"Oh." He couldn't help himself.

Vincent struggled to keep pace with Elmer at times. The old man seemed to float along with no effort at all. Meanwhile, Vincent was stomping along in his clumsy work shoes and with sore feet. He had never been on a train that was in motion and found himself a little excited at the prospect. Halfway through town, a train whistle broke the silence between them.

"We've gotta run now, Vin." They both started running. "Vinny, sorry." Elmer corrected himself.

"It's fine, let's go." Neither of them wanted to be left in this town another night after their encounter with the moonshiners. It was a long way across town to the barn they had spent the night in the day before, in the dark. They kept running past the safe haven all the way into the train yard. The yard was mostly empty, except for a couple of workers moving the loading ramps away from the now full cargo cars.

"ALL ABOARD," came a booming voice from somewhere up ahead.

Elmer started laughing as he boosted Vincent into the closest car. No time to be picky Vincent thought wishing it was a passenger car with a bar and a food cart.

"Least this conductor's got a sense of humor," Elmer chuckled.

The joke wasn't lost on Vincent as Elmer had explained that this was a cargo train and not a train for people so the 'all aboard' was intended for the stowaways. They both laughed, feeling relief being in the safety of the car. Vincent felt important and in the know with Elmer's information. He turned around and pulled the older man up into the car with him. Vincent was still panting for air after the run across town. The old guy, on the other hand, was barely winded.

There were a couple of other guys on the train who seemed pleasant enough. They had a bottle of moonshine and Elmer passed it back and forth with them a few times. Vincent refused and drank from his bleach bottle instead; it left a slight taste of bleach. The taste reminded him of the way Dakin's solution had smelled when he had used it on Dad's leg, he put the lid back on the bottle losing his desire for another drink. Elmer gave an approving nod at Vinny's sobriety, and took a swig of whisky for himself.

The train was rolling now, and the sensation of motion with the rocking of the train on the uneven tracks was like a mother rocking a child to sleep. Vincent was reclined on a bag of something loaded on the train, holding his slightly oily bindle on his lap and watching light spill in through the crack of the mostly closed door.

What came through was a zoetrope of rural America. Patches of farms, homes, lives, families, industry—all of it washed through the crack and into his mind's eye. It brought thoughts of home and his dad. He wondered how his brothers were doing and who they were bothering now. Sadness started to take over. Then he thought of the mongoloid saboteur and Mom. Anger balanced the sadness out and he started to push them both aside, instead listening to Elmer ramble on. He was busy talking to the other two guys on the train. They were mostly drunk by now, he figured by the way the babbling had taken over. Dad did that same thing; the booze choked out rational thoughts and replaced them with inane babble. He hated it most times but now it felt comforting and thought it may help him fall sleep like his parents arguing had done not so long ago.

He listened to Elmer warn the men of the code of the bottle and two X's. "Like this," he had told them. Vincent opened one eye to see Elmer draw it in the dirt on the floor of the train. It was the same one he'd seen in Kingston. The two passengers laughed at Elmer now to Vincent's surprise. He had come, in a short time, to respect the older man. The laughter from these more mature grown men made him question it. Maybe Elmer was just a crazy old guy who just happened to be useful. Did it matter? Vinny didn't think so, not yet. He enjoyed his company and so far, his advice had all been good. Both of Vincent's eyes closed again so he could resume focusing on just listening.

The now slightly offended Elmer didn't seem to mind. "Hey, Vinny boy, look here." He tapped his foot from where he was sitting. "You see this?" He drew a circle in the dirt with an X in the middle. "Know what that is?"

"I've got no idea, Elmer. What?" Vincent half-expected an off-colored joke.

"That's the symbol for, this is an easy place to beg a meal." His fingers swished the dirt around and refreshed his dirt canvas. "It's a part of the code you were asking about that night I met you passed out at the soup kitchen. It's a way of communicating that some of us frugal tourists and bums alike have developed by word of mouth. We try to use it to keep each other informed on what's on the trail ahead or what's fresh for the pickin' right where you're at." Elmer's gaze narrowed for a minute "But, I got the feeling something has figured out our code and is using it against us or with us. I'm not too sure about which but I've been around enough places and seen enough code to know that our little secret code ain't so secret anymore."

Now, Vincent was getting interested. Elmer's fingers scratched at the dirt again, the glint in his eyes returned with a smile. This time his rough dirt sketch was of a familiar cat.

"How 'bout this one?" Elmer pointed with the emptying bottle of moonshine.

Vincent recalled the drawing and the unkept yard with the cat lady who had the warm, inviting smile.

"Umm, a friendly old lady who will help you out." A look of shock smacked Elmer's face. Then was quickly replaced with the biggest smile he had seen from the old guy.

"I knew you were worth the work, Vinny boy. You are sharp." His hands flew back to the dirt, excitedly now.

Vinny smiled at his enthusiasm for teaching him, and his own intuition about the cat lady being right.

"Ok, smart guy, how about this one?" Elmer challenged pointing to what looked like a cross.

School was in session. Vinny didn't care he always liked school before his mom pulled him out. The thoughts of sleep were gone from him, replaced with excitement and the possibility of starting to unravel the mystery of this hobo's code. Maybe he would get some answers about the man with the smooth-soled shoes. Maybe he could ask Elmer about him. But not tonight, not in the dark.

"That part of the code means, Talk about God here and get a meal." Elmer never even gave him a chance to answer this one.

Vincent laughed and paid attention to everything Elmer said. Nothing was lost.

"Vinny." His foot was getting tugged on. "Vinny, wake up. We gotta go. We're here."

Vincent had been in a deep sleep, rocked gently by the train into a near coma. It took his brain a minute to realize where he was and adjust to his surroundings. His eyes caught up and gave him some feedback. The train was stopped now, and the other two guys or bums or whatever they were had already departed, it seemed. The bay door was still slid open just enough to allow their exit.

"Where's here," was the first thing Vincent wanted to know. He wondered if they were even in the same state. He wondered how long he had been asleep.

"Would it matter if it had a name? What does matter right now is the fact that the conductor of this train may have been friendly enough to make jokes and let us get a ride, but we don't know how the guys at the train yard are gonna feel with a bunch of frugal tourists and bums spilling into their yard." Elmer seemed exasperated at his questions rather than actions as he bulged his eyes and motioned his finger in quick circles in front of him; clearly, wheels spinning faster was what it meant.

Luckily, his bindle was still packed, and Vincent was able to jump to his feet and scoot out the bay door in a flash. Elmer tossed him his own kit and the rest of the bottle he had been sharing with the other two men. Part of Vincent wanted to toss it on the ground like the beast of a man who pulled him from the fire in the bramble had. Instead, he reached up and helped the older man down from the train.

The yard was relatively empty. The few guys who were working seemed desensitized to the flood of vagrants that washed off every train that stopped. They wormed their way around, staying out of the way and made it to the backside of the yard facing town. There was a set of benches, where Elmer sat down and adjusted his shoes. Vincent scanned the street back and forth nervously. He felt less welcome in each town he visited. Was it the towns or was it him? Was he becoming more bum-like by the day? Did he now exude an air of desperation that people who were barely hanging on themselves loathed? The questions made the ever-growing self-conscious part of him feel ashamed.

"Now what?" he asked Elmer, wanting to be off the main strip as soon as they could. Maybe the gentle urging would get him up and moving.

"Why? You got somewhere to be?" Elmer asked, his head now tilted back, soaking up some morning sun.

"Oh, no, guess not."

Vincent went back to scanning the streets. His eyes landed on a smudge on the bench Elmer was now reclined in. He looked closer now.

"Elmer, holy shit, look." He rarely cursed but he was shocked. It was the bottle with the two X's.

Elmer sat forward and looked at the code for himself.

"Well, that changes things," he said, looking at the bottle in his hand. Then his hand slapped his forehead. "I gotta be more careful; towns are changing, and you never know if it's gonna be the same one you stopped in last time." He rummaged through his bindle and grabbed his canteen while also tossing the bottle of booze into the trash. "I better flush the system, plus we don't need the law seeing us with some illegal hooch, do we?"

With that, he upended the moonshine bottle and finished it. He seemed genuinely scared but acted like he was ditching the bottle for the police, and not whatever he was really afraid of. Vincent, however, was relieved; he was glad to be rid of the bottle. He hated the way people looked at drunks and didn't want Elmer getting that kind of attention.

While he waited for the older man to warm his blood on the bench, Vincent noticed a newspaper under Elmer's discarded bottle in the bin. It was clean, so he pulled it out, sat down and started to read. Most of the front page was littered with stories of the mobsters they were calling mafia families. The idea was appealing to Vincent. A group of people you chose as friends who dressed in fancy clothes that drove all the ladies wild, flashy new cars, piles of money, and power, but most important of all, respect. No one liked to cross them—not even the law. When they did catch them, they used all their piles of money and connections to either serve soft terms behind bars, or no time at all.

Maybe Vincent could find some of those guys and try to impress them somehow. He wondered if maybe he missed an opportunity the other day with the moonshiners. Sure, they were jerks, but he had walked up onto their site. Vincent may have done exactly what they did in that situation if the roles were reversed. They didn't hurt him, after all, and when Elmer bluffed them, they had let them go easily enough with just a warning about the woods after dark.

He flipped the page of the newspaper and was reading about fertilizer prices and seed stores. It made him think of home. He felt himself feeling homesick. He wondered what everyone was doing. A ball of anger burned in his stomach at the thought of being tossed aside by his family, but another urge surpassed it. He grabbed the page of fertilizer and seed news and headed for the tree line.

"Be back in a minute. I gotta hit the head."

Elmer pointed to the trees he was already headed to without opening his eyes. "I won't leave without ya. Take your time."

After he was done cleaning up and burying his mess with a stick, he was wrestling with his pants and admiring Elmer's work on the secret pocket when he saw the bills poking out. Elmer must have put them there without saying anything. It was eight dollars. More money than Vincent had ever had at one time. Probably more than his Dad as well. This made him feel grown up but also guilty because he hadn't earned it. He wondered how to address it with Elmer. If he brought it up, he risked embarrassing him or offending him. The best course of action seemed to be to hold onto it and pay him back somehow. Either with money of his own or with some work of some kind. He wondered how Elmer had made so much money to begin with. Maybe he could show him? Vincent wondered how to bring it up as he walked back to the basking old man.

Elmer seemed ready to go now. Vincent was starving, and the money was already burning a hole in the secret pocket. He wanted to offer to buy them some breakfast, but that would let the cat out of the bag and he would be forced to address the money.

Uncanny Elmer chimed in.

"Well, 'bout time for a bite to eat, don't ya figure?" He was walking with intent now, clearly familiar with where he was going.

"Yeah, why? You know where to get something?" Vincent asked, already knowing the answer.

"Of course, I do, Vinny. Remember the cross code from last night?"

Vincent did remember but was shocked that Elmer did as well. He figured Elmer had been drunk and like Dad would have no recollection of his babblings the next day. Many promises had been broken in that fashion growing up.

"Follow my lead." Elmer grinned.

They rounded the corner of the main street and a huge white chapel stood tall in front of them. Vincent could smell sweetness in the air that only came from cooking corn. It had to be johnny cakes. They held a special place for Vincent and his mouth filled with saliva.

Elmer marched up the steps to the priest, who was out front greeting people.

"Hello, Father, good morning to ya."

"And good morning to you." The priest was looking down his nose, but he was friendly enough.

"Me and the boy were coming to have a blessing before we hit the road again and couldn't help but notice the smell of your johnny cakes." He paused but not long enough to leave room for input from anyone else. "You see, the boy's mother passed." Elmer crossed himself and closed his eyes, pointing his nose heaven-ward. Vincent took his cue and did the same. "We are trying to make it out West to live with my sister who runs a mission, so we can have a roof over our head in these trying times and serve the good Lord. But we haven't had a meal in days."

Another lie but it was a means to an end for a meal, still it felt ugly to watch. That was until Vincent looked at the priest's face, which had softened into pity.

"I was just wondering if you wouldn't be able to spare a couple for the boy. I will be ok to fend for myself; the Lord will provide, but I do worry for him." Elmer tousled Vincent's hair now, making him feel even more involved and guilty.

"Not another word, of course we will. The Lord would never turn one of his flock away and neither shall we. Now the both of you, make your way around back and get something to eat." He smiled and motioned them around the side with his robed arm.

Elmer shot Vincent an elbow to the ribs when they were around the corner. He felt bad but he was starving. The people around back all gave them sideways glances, but no one was rude. As they were in line waiting and suffering the shame of the stares, the priest came back and started whispering to groups of hens and the ladies serving the food. Suddenly, the entire crowd shifted. They were now tilting their heads to the side and giving soft, understanding smiles. The lie was moving at the speed of light.

They sat down with the stacks of cakes on their plates and dressed them with butter and syrup from the table. No one bothered them while they ate. The table was lonely except for them. While they ate, Vincent thought of Dad's johnny cakes he made every once in a great while as a treat. The cakes weren't necessarily the treat, but Dad's good, seemingly sober mood was. It was a rarity growing up, but those moments of clarity were some of his favorites to look back on.

Uncanny Elmer could sense his sadness.

"What's up, Vinny? Get your fill. Don't worry about these folks. They got plenty to spare." He smiled and chewed.

"It's not that…well, it's not all that. I hate lying to people, after all. It's just thinking of my dad. He used to make these sometimes. Well, before he got his leg smashed." Vincent was talking without inhibitions. Elmer felt safe and his guard was never up around him now.

"How's that?" Elmer asked in an open-ended way that left Vinny responsible for continuing the conversation. Vinny could tell he wanted more so offered what he felt comfortable with.

"Well, when I was eleven, Dad was chopping wood, and maybe drinking a little, and he had this big burl he was trying to hack through. Well, he must've let the ax go a little wild or hit that burl in a way that it bounced the ax right off and it buried itself in Dad's leg." Vincent took a bite and a breath and before swallowing continued. "I was in the field playing with rotten pumpkins when I heard the smacking sound. At first, I thought someone had smashed one of those pumpkins behind me, but it was followed with a yelling from Dad that scared the life right out of me." He took another bite. "Well, Mom had me run to the neighbors' and they came with their horse and buggy to take Dad to Kingston, I think. Then we got left with them, they took us to their house and cared for us for a while. I remember them talking about my sister, who has mongolism, and it hurt my feelings but other than that they were real nice. Then Dad got home. He was different, really. He stayed different, maybe even got worse when he started drinking even more than before. But at the beginning, Mom was so big she couldn't help with his leg, so I took care of it for him." The last bite stuck in his throat now, almost being replaced with a gag. He dropped his fork onto his plate.

"It's ok, Vinny, you don't gotta tell it," Elmer said.

"I felt like I was helping but I was terrified. Dad's leg was disgusting. I tried to keep it clean with Dakin's solution, but it didn't help much." He could smell the rot and the topical antiseptic over the johnny cakes. "Mom quit doing much of anything but eat, yell, and smoke. And my sister started to hate me, I think." Vincent swallowed hard. The words were falling out of his mouth with no control, and it felt good to get it off of his mind. "Even though I was doing all of Dad's chores and Mom's mothering work, they all seemed to resent me. Dad's leg finally stopped rotting a few months later, but the damage was done. He was never the same. He was still Dad and I love him. He just had a real hard life and Mom was always so overbearing." The excuses felt shallow, but he wanted to save some respect for his dad. "It wasn't like he could argue with her about what my sister said I did." Vinny suddenly blushed and felt ashamed, and he decided to omit the story Jamie Lynn told. "Mom paid for all the bills, and he wasn't much for working after his leg and the laudanum, but he was a good dad and he loved me. I think he was sad when I had to leave.... he gave me this." He pulled the Dunhill from his pocket and didn't realize he had started to cry, but just barely. He wasn't full but he also wasn't going to be able to eat any more.

"It's ok, Vinny. We are all broken out here. Ain't no one gonna judge you except the folks that you probably will never see again once you blow in the wind and find the next town." He tested Vincent. It worked and the boy smiled. "Plus, you know what? It was all to your advantage anyway. Look how damn strong and smart you turned out. You toss me out on the streets at your age and they would have definitely been scraping me off the street from the soup kitchen alley I found you in. Not you— you pulled it off and now you are on your own path. Just fill your life with experiences worth having." He paused slightly. "You know, seeing the country this way is gonna give you a lot of insight that lots of folks won't have. It's a blessing in itself." The irony of his last statement being made at a church made them both laugh.

"Thanks," Vincent said. He stayed quiet and let Elmer eat in peace.

When they were about to head out, a couple of ladies who seemed to represent the crowd at the church approached them.

"This is from all of us. We hope it helps you get to where you're going along with a guiding hand from the Lord." She handed Elmer a fresh fistful of cash. Was this where the pile in his secret pocket came from? Was it all ill-begotten cash? Did it matter?

"Oh, ladies, you're too kind and we both thank you. Now we better get on the road, but first we need to clear our souls with a prayer." He led Vincent into the church and they both knelt and prayed. Well, Vincent prayed. He wasn't sure what Elmer was doing; he wasn't sure if he was even religious.

On the way out of the church, Elmer took the fistful of dollars and pushed it into the donation box. Then he turned and winked at Vincent.

"I ain't a thief and I won't take more than I need." This redeemed the lies he'd told to get the cakes, and reaffirmed to Vincent that he was a genuinely good person. He felt lighter as he walked. Telling someone about home felt good. The pressure had been released and there was no judgment—just advice and encouragement.

The rest of the day was mostly uneventful. Elmer knew a fishing hole and made a makeshift smoker out of branches and old wood to cure what he caught. Vincent pitched in and used his new hooks and silk line to catch his share. The thought of fish was less repulsive as the days went on. Elmer let Vincent know that he knew a place where they could sleep and it would be safe and not in the dark, and before sunset they headed that way.

It was an abandoned mill of some sort. There were piles of sand around the building, obscuring most of it from view. As they approached, they could see a fire illuminating the hidden side of the building. Then the bellowing voice of a babbling drunken fool came through the night, cursing and full of hate.

"We'll just keep to ourselves and go around the other side," Elmer warned, hearing the same problems in the drunk's voice that Vincent did.

People like that were never the kind you wanted to spend any time around, or they would end up causing you trouble. Trouble neither of them had an appetite for. Elmer held the too-full pouch of fish close to his side to keep it from falling out as they hurried past.

They made their beds and Vincent had a sudden realization. This was a town that had the warning with the two X's bottle and that guy was definitely drunk. Just as he was about to tell Elmer he might make his way over to warn him, there was a smacking sound from the other side near the community fire. The smack was followed by the crying of a woman and a kid screaming.

"I told you to leave me the fuck alone. I'll get her something to eat when I can," the drunken asshole said as he took another swig from his jar of illegal booze.

He then proceeded to berate a few of the assumed weaker drunks around the fire. None of them said a word in return. So, the insults continued to flow.

Never mind, Vincent's thoughts of warning him evaporated. He's more trouble than he's worth and if Elmer's warnings carry any weight, he'll get what's coming to him. Vincent wondered if Elmer had considered warning him, but he was already out cold, so apparently, he wasn't overly concerned. With that, Vincent tucked into a makeshift hay pallet, pushed his oily bindle under his head and fell asleep. He spent most of the night tossing and turning thinking about home, wondering if they were thinking of him.

Sometime during the night, an urge to piss woke Vincent up from what little sleep he had managed to get. It was dark; the community fire had almost died completely, and its safe orange glow was almost gone. Better stay close, he thought, and walked to the open doorway to piss outside, not step outside. As he stood there draining himself, he heard a gurgling breathing noise followed by a rustling sound. Jeez, the drunk had some stamina if he was still up drinking. He sounded like he was trying to suck the last drops from his bottle as sloppy slurping noises echoed on the walls.

Vincent sneaked back to bed, not wanting to be the only person awake to draw the drunk's ire. He struggled to close his eyes with the sucking noises continuing on but eventually sleep lured him away again.

An hour later, the screaming from the drunk's wife and her child woke him up for good.

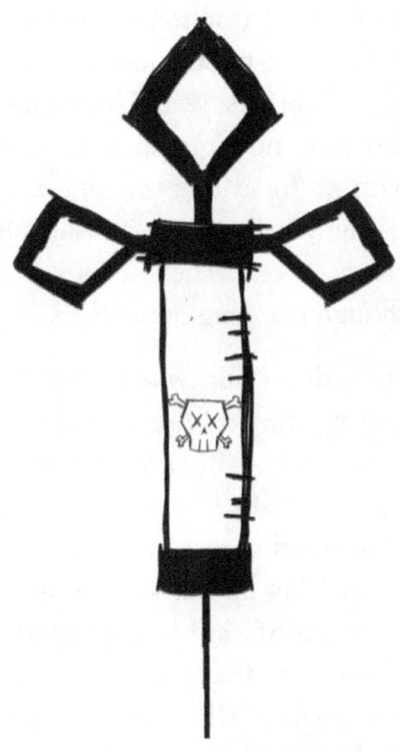

Without thinking, Vincent's hand shot into his pocket and held Dad's Dunhill in his palm. The weight of it was comforting. The bloodcurdling screaming continued to echo through the shell of the former mill. He looked at Elmer, who was more practically clutching his knobby bindle stick and sliding himself between Vincent and the screaming.

"What the hell is going on?" Elmer asked as he scooted past, still seated.

"I don't know. I'm the same as you. I woke up to it, too," Vincent said, wide-eyed in the grey pre-dawn glow.

The two of them exchanged glances and decided the best course of action certainly wasn't inaction. Elmer stood up and

Vincent followed his lead around the corner. As he was ready to peek around the bay door, he was looking down to make sure he wasn't stumbling on bricks when something caught his eye. Footprints in the dirt, nothing unusual there, but they were smooth-soled with no tread like the kind a fancy businessman would wear. The familiarity of the unusual shoes in an unusual place stood his hairs on end. Then he looked up to the source of the screams, although his imagination was now distracting him.

There was a dirty, thin woman holding her equally thin and dirty daughter by the neck, restraining her as she pawed at the dirt trying to make forward progress. Vincent's eyes followed her intended path. A barrel-chested man was curled into a semi fetal position in a corner near the burn pit. His eyes were wide open, and his mouth was twisted into an abnormal position. There was no life in his grey eyes; he was dead. One thing that stood out was that the man's belt was undone and hanging loosely to his side. His pants were up but low enough to see the top of his buttocks. The smooth-soled footprints trailed up to and surrounded the body.

The sound of sirens pierced Vincent's already ringing ears. The girl's screams must have alerted someone from the nearby neighborhood who in turn called the cops. Vincent's first instinct was to flee. He spun around and got ready to run back for his bindle, but Elmer grabbed him by the arm.

"That's not smart, Vinny. Just stand by. If we take off running like that lot…" He motioned to three bums hightailing it. "Just looks like you're guilty. We got nothing to hide so we got no reason to run." He paused. "But we don't want to be involved if we don't need to be, neither."

Elmer led Vincent back to where they were sleeping, and they got their kit together. The police were now getting the mother and daughter calmed down as the screaming was subsiding and being replaced with wailing. Vincent was shocked that she seemed so upset about someone who was slapping her out in public and drinking the family's dinner with a group of bums around a fire just the night before. He thought of his own defense of his dad when he told Elmer about his family at the church and felt stupid. She loved him, of course.

"We got a couple over here—father and son, looks like. They look to have been sleeping." The officer acknowledged them. "Hey, you two see or hear anything?"

"You mean besides the screaming?" Elmer asked and chuckled. The cop gave him a funny look. "Sorry, no, we were fast asleep over here."

"Well, you two stand by in case we have some questions," he ordered and went back to the crying girls.

Vincent paced around nervously for the half hour the cops stayed. Elmer reclined on the dry grasses. Vincent couldn't take his mind off the code and the smooth-soled footprints. He wasn't sure what it was but there seemed to be a connection between this guy and the burning bramble. The question begged for input from Elmer, but Vincent wasn't sure how to put it all together to ask him about it yet. It sounded crazy. The only thing more pressing than the footprints was the guilt. If he had warned the drunk about the XX code and that it was dangerous to drink here, he would still be alive. If he had only woken Elmer up and told him to do it…he seemed keen on warning people anyway. The words for this came easily enough.

"Elmer, I think this is my fault." The words seemed to shock the older man.

"Vinny, shut your mouth. Are you trying to get yourself arrested for a free meal or somethin'?" Elmer seemed angry.

"Well, what about the code we saw when we came into town? The bottle with the X's. You fell asleep right away, but I was up and thinking about it and I knew he was in danger, and I didn't say anything. It's my fault." Vincent's chest tightened and he felt panicky.

"You didn't do shit, Vinny, by the time we got here, he was already drunk. Ain't nothing on Earth woulda sobered him up before this morning." He waited, gauging Vinny's response. "We have more trouble than just one drunk, Vincent. Something is hunting us."

Vincent nearly screamed when he said this and confirmed his fears of the man with the smooth-soled shoes. Elmer must have seen the fear on Vincent's face and continued on trying to calm him.

"Well, not us necessarily Vinny, but us as in vagrants, tramps, hobos, derelicts or in our cases frugal tourists."

Vincent eased slightly but not much, as part of him was now convinced he was being hunted.

"I'm not sure about all of that, but I can feel it, too," Vincent said.

"Look how they treat us." Elmer said trying to prove his point.

Elmer pointed to the scene below them in front of the mill. The women were being led into the paddy wagon as the body of their father/husband was tossed casually into the back of the ambulance. The drunk's legs dangled out of the open door, limply swinging in the wind. He was still fresh and not stiff yet. Whoever had killed him was probably still very close. The cop who had tossed him in the ambulance now heartlessly jammed the legs into the back and swung the gate shut before they could tumble back out. Then he banged on the roof and the ambulance sped away, followed by the now encumbered paddy wagon. Seconds later, the cops loaded into their car and sped away leaving the scene empty except for Elmer and Vincent.

No one had even bothered to come and ask any questions or chase the hobos who had fled across the field. It was over. Just another dead bum and two new mouths to feed for a community that could probably ill afford it. Humanity was losing to the Depression.

"We are easy targets, Vinny. Best thing we can do is warn as many people as we can about the code, we gotta teach them the symbols. That and pray they have enough self-control to resist their vices in towns where the code says it's not safe, regardless of how readily available it is." Elmer gathered himself and started walking. "Time to move on from this town, Vinny."

Vincent didn't argue. Elmer's advice made sense and sounded good, but he still felt terrible. He was distracted by the guilt as they walked. There was an expectation of catching a train, but as they walked, Vincent realized they were headed away from the train yard.

"Where are we headed?" Vinny asked.

"Does it matter?" It was a running joke, but Vincent didn't laugh this time. "We are gonna head to the gas station and catch a ride to get closer to a train yard running north and south. I don't wanna be hitting the coast."

Catching a ride sounded ambiguous. It could have meant nearly anything by Elmer's logic. But Vincent resigned himself to following Elmer's lead. He was too distracted to question his methods. As they made their way down Main Street, Vincent avoided the gazes of the judgy nobodies; instead, he focused on their shoes. He scanned each pair he passed, thinking he might see Mr. Smooth Shoes among them and sound the alarm. Or run. There was nothing, just regular people with regular shoes.

Soon enough, they were parked on a bench at the gas station. Cars rolled in and out and Elmer sat on the bench biding his time. He said he was waiting for the perfect ride. Vincent wondered if it existed but waited patiently anyway. The cross code and the bottle code were scratched into the bench and kept him pacing. They were beginning to feel ominous, and he wanted to keep his distance from the symbols.

"You think we will get to a town without a warning code?" Vincent was wondering if life was going to stay this hectic on the road. "Or find a job in one?"

He wanted to pay Elmer back as soon as possible, and any income he made could be used to get the two of them some stability. Maybe a room somewhere they could both have a fresh start. In a town with no code.

"Well, Vinny, that's a big ask. You see, last time I was in this town, there were no warning codes, just codes telling you where to grub a meal or find a dry place to sleep. The situation is dynamic. However, if you are patient, the answer to your second question will come with the seasons."

Vincent couldn't be bothered to decipher Elmer's cryptic dialogue, so he let it rest. He would just keep pressure on Elmer and hope a job would come in time.

Then, without any warning, Elmer sprang to life. "Excuse me, sir, you mind if me and the boy catch a ride south with ya?"

"Nah, hop on. I got an empty load and it's the company's fuel. Just so long as you don't mind riding in the cargo hold." The truck driver was an older guy with ragged clothes, and work boots. Vincent was still distracted and lost in his own head.

"Sounds good to us, don't it?" He pushed the small of Vincent's back to get him walking.

Vincent ignored the prod for input but followed his lead by walking to the truck and hopping in the back.

Once they were on the road, Elmer tried to make small talk, but Vincent was unresponsive. They rode in silence most of the way, Vincent feeling guilty for getting the drunk killed and Elmer feeling bad for not making Vinny feel safer.

They bounced around for a week or two like that on trucks in little towns, headed south always. Sometimes they found the elusive perfect ride; others they had to walk a long time between towns to find. It was consistent: Elmer never failed to produce at least one meal a day, most of the hot meals provided by the good grace of others. Some meals involved nefariousness, like stealing from a local farm and eating their fill. Elmer had told Vincent that as long as they planted the seeds from whatever they ate, it would pay the farmer back tenfold in the future, so it wasn't really stealing. Again, Elmer's fuzzy logic seemed to make sense even though it felt wrong. Only twice did Vincent have to resort to eating the salty/peppery fish. His taste for it had improved as he could at least eat it and keep it down with a good dose of water to go with. That didn't mean he liked it any better. Maybe he was ruined for it for good. He told Elmer about his dislike for it the last time they ate it, but it seemed to hurt his feelings, so Vincent would try to keep his disdain for it quiet.

As they made their way south, they spread the code. To anyone who would listen, and even to those who wouldn't sometimes in Elmer's case. They scratched the warnings into the dirt whenever they could, saying, "Watch for the bottle with two X's." Most of the time, they were met with laughter. People would talk around the fire—after they left—about the crazy old man and his son who were spreading tall tales. Even if more than a few of them stopped drinking for the night, just in case. More than a few more would end up dead as well. Vincent and Elmer missed seeing more bodies, but the gossip was everywhere now. Dead young men here, old faded drunks missing there. No answers anywhere. The whole transient community was bubbling just under the surface now with a nervous energy. They were less likely to help each other, and community burn barrels were becoming a thing of the past.

Then one night while eating dinner at a community rodeo that was having a pig roast for all in attendance, they were approached by a young man who was a missionary traveling around to cities, trying to organize more events to feed the hungry so the mafia wasn't cornering the market on helping the needy. At first, he seemed nervous and made small talk, finding out that Elmer and Vincent weren't father and son but just friends. He eventually warmed up and got to the point. His fingers went to the dirt, and he started to draw. He etched the bottle with two X's into the dirt with his nail and then gave them a speech they were all too familiar with about a code warning people to avoid their vices. Vincent and Elmer exchanged glances and laughed. The young man, feeling insecure, erased the etching with his foot and excused himself.

Elmer stopped him and they proceeded to tell him they knew of the code and were laughing out of relief that someone was finally sounding the alarm beside them. They agreed that they got more laughs and jeers than anything but even if they could save just a few downtrodden men, it was a success. Before the conversation ended, the young man shocked them one more time. He told them of a new warning code; this one was a syringe with a skull inside. At first, he said he believed it was a warning that heroin was deadly, and so he thought it was a positive warning sign. That was until young men in towns with the code were dying and disappearing at rates faster than in towns adjacent to them. Many attributed this to overdoses, but the traveling missionary had seen a different story. Towns with the warning had little to no active heroin addicts, and towns with no warning code always had a fair number nodding off in dark alleys. Now with the alcohol warning as well, he was convinced it was something more dangerous than careless drug addicts killing themselves with overdoses.

Vincent and Elmer were shocked. They had seen the code once or twice but hadn't paid much attention to it. They were too preoccupied with the alcohol code to consider the skull syringe as a warning itself. Now armed with their newfound code, they said their goodbyes and promised to warn as many souls as they could.

As they walked out of town and away from the rodeo, Vincent kicked a rock in front of him, trying to digest his dinner as well as the information about the heroin warning code. The missionary was a nice guy whose voice would carry more weight than both Elmer and him combined. Vincent hoped the missionary kept moving and kept warning, as they were making little to no progress keeping people away from danger themselves.

Suddenly, Elmer jammed his elbow into Vinny's ribs.

"Well, hey, would ya look at that. It's some mafia fellers." Elmer pointed, then quickly realized his mistake and nodded in their direction instead. Vincent caught the act and wondered if it was respect or fear that changed Elmer's mind.

There was a group of them coming out of a fancy restaurant. "Italian Bistro" was printed on the sign, but it wasn't necessary; you could smell the egg noodles and pasta sauce a mile away. They came out laughing and smoking, women on their arms...both of them, not a care in the world. Vincent looked at his rags and compared them to the suits they were wearing, and he slowed his step and worked his way to the other side of Elmer. Maybe they would see the dirty old man first, feel sad for him and never even notice his younger shadow. This was unrealistic, he realized quickly. These men would never give Elmer a second glance, let alone make it past his visage to Vincent. They were miles above them.

As he stared and his jealousy grew, his gaze did its natural diversion and went to their shoes. Plain dress shoes, nothing unusual there. Then an older man with no women and a slightly different style pushed his way through the crowd of younger mobsters. Vincent expected them to give the man some shit and maybe even rough him up a bit. Instead, they gave him a wide berth and all of them avoided eye contact. One of the younger guys ran ahead to an all-black car that was pulled up out front. He opened the door then stood by, waiting as the stranger climbed in. Vincent caught a look at his shoe just before it disappeared into the darkness of the car. Fancy, shiny leather...smooth soles. Vincent's blood ran cold, and he grabbed Elmer by the hand.

Elmer had been staring at the ladies, mouth hanging open, but the sudden handful of trembling fingers distracted him.

"Vin, what the hell is wrong with you? You ok?"

Vincent's cold sweaty hand clung to Elmers despite the act making him feel like a child. Vinny still hadn't found the words to tell Elmer of the first night on his own with his pack and the footprints, the fire at the tree, and the smooth-shoed man. It was too crazy, but the pieces seemed to be falling into place. Soon he would be ready to spill his guts to Elmer, but not yet, not with the sun well past setting.

"NOTHING," Vincent almost yelled. Not because he was mad, but because all he could hear was his own breathing. His ears had plugged up from fear and the whooshing in and out of his own breathing had replaced almost all other sounds.

Elmer bristled at the sound of his voice.

"Vinny, I'm serious. What's going on? Do you need to go to the hospital?" He was worried the boy had been sick and hadn't said anything, wearing himself into exhaustion. He had been acting differently since leaving the town the drunk had died in, but Elmer had just chalked it up to him feeling guilty for not sounding the alarm about the code.

"No, I'm fine. Can we just find somewhere to sleep, somewhere with a light?" Vincent said in a more neutral tone.

Elmer could see his eyes were locked on the crowd across the street, scanning them so quickly that his eyes were vibrating in their sockets.

"I'll do ya one better, Vinny. Let's get the fuck out of town." The curse from Elmer shook Vinny out of his trance.

"Yeah, let's go."

After a small disagreement Elmer sat across the fire from Vincent, but too far away from it to enjoy its heat despite the unusual chill in the summer air. The older man seemed reluctant to start the fire to begin with. Though Vincent didn't need to press very hard to get him to agree to make it. When they had reached the outskirts of town where the streetlight faded to black, Vincent refused to go any farther. Elmer was inclined to agree, as the new moon was making it almost too dark to follow the glow of the concrete road. They ducked off the road blindly until Vincent found the Dunhill and sparked it to life; its now familiar shape felt good in his hand. Elmer seemed shocked and backed up. Then when Vincent started to light a pile of sticks, he stomped it out. He explained that the fire might draw people in, but Vincent explained to him that he wasn't sleeping out here in the dark. Seeing his fear or sensing his anger, Elmer gave in and sat away from the growing flames.

The fire didn't last much longer than the small row. The chill in the air must have been a premonition of rain, because the skies opened up. Elmer in a flash had his bindle in his hands and was unwrapping the oily hessian sack from the outer layer. Vincent followed his lead. The two of them combined their oily rags and layered them onto a couple of branches directly above their heads. The cold drops stopped landing directly on them and they both held their now exposed bindles close. They sat side by side, backs against the tree for the rest of the night. At some point, Vincent fell asleep, and when he woke up, Elmer was still wide-awake staring into the dawn. He had been using Elmer's shoulder as a pillow and gave him an awkward look when he opened his eyes.

"Bout time you woke up. You ready to get out of the woods?" Elmer seemed tired and crabby.

Feeling sheepish, Vincent didn't argue and took charge of shaking the oily sacks out and re-wrapping the bindles. He then swung both over his shoulder and gave Elmer a look that said he was ready to go. Now a little warmer either from the sun or Vincent's effort to make it right by carrying his pack, Elmer gave him a smile.

"Let's get to the next town and get something to eat. That sound good to you?" he asked redundantly.

On the walk, they saw another code scratched into a series of telephone poles. It was a simple triangle. Vincent would have walked by a million of them but Elmer, who was keen to find the code wherever he went, had a gift for locating it. Vincent was getting better at finding it, though. Nothing was being lost forever, he told himself, as Elmer's early advice echoed in his mind again. This simple triangle code pissed Elmer off. He explained that it meant the road was spoiled with bums and hobos, and few if any frugal tourists. There would be no help in their near future as the overwhelmed towns would likely chase them out or make them feel so unwelcome, they would leave on their own. Elmer wanted to spare them the shame and made a decision on the fly.

"We need to head south, Vinny. It's getting close to being time to head that way, anyways," Elmer said matter-of-factly.

Vincent, however, was confused; he hadn't realized they had a destination, let alone a deadline.

"Where we headed?" Vincent asked, already knowing the answer.

"Would it matter if you knew?" predictable Elmer asked.

"Nope, guess not," a now slightly annoyed Vincent retorted.

Elmer seemed like a parent excited about a Christmas present, because they could hold the mystery above their child's head as leverage. Vincent was like a kid wondering what he was going to get.

They ended up catching a ride on another truck later that day. Elmer had been hanging his thumb out in the lane for hours and finally, someone had stopped. Vincent hadn't bothered introducing himself as by the time he got close to the driver's side door, Elmer already had the ride secured.

"You and your son can ride in the back." The driver shot out his window as Vincent got close.

It struck Vincent that most of the people they had met and who had actually spoken to them had just assumed that they were father and son. It didn't bother Vincent so he wouldn't correct anyone unless Elmer did. It seemed to be part of Elmer's racket now, and Vincent didn't want to betray his confidence. He got the sense that Elmer enjoyed the assumption anyway.

"Hop on, Vinny. He's gonna take us as far south as he's going." The trucker referring to them as father and son had obviously made Elmer happy.

Vincent could tell by the look on his face that he wasn't about to correct the trucker. His intuition told him the older man enjoyed the mistake and maybe part of him felt like it might be true.

Oddly, there were already three men in the back of the truck. It had surprised Vincent when he jumped in. Elmer, however, just gave them a "howdy" and made himself comfortable. They all had on shoes that looked comparable to Elmer's holey nightmares. Vincent relaxed as well. They gave the men the warning about both of the danger codes, the XX's and the syringe with the skull. None of them cared and continued talking amongst themselves. It suited Elmer and Vincent just fine as they made small talk the rest of the trip, laughing and joking, just the two of them.

Their next stop was the biggest city yet. Elmer told Vincent to get his fill quickly because they wouldn't be in town long. Everything was electric—the atmosphere, the signs, the people. Despite the Depression, people here seemed lively. Vincent scanned the shop windows; the eight dollars in his secret pocket were eager to be spent. He hadn't yet acknowledged

Elmer giving it to him, so it wouldn't be right to spend it, but he sure wanted to.

There were pretty girls everywhere. None of them paid him any attention, but he sure paid it to them. One girl in particular had on the prettiest dress he'd ever seen. She was busty and leggy and beautiful. The man holding her hand almost disappeared in Vincent's fantasy; his eyes were busy working her body over, moving down the woman's exposed legs to her heeled shoes. Then in a flash, her boyfriend was in the fantasy with them. Striding next to his beauty, wearing his shiny smooth-soled leather shoes. The hairs on Vincent's arms went to attention.

The guy looked average enough, not that dissimilar to him, except clean and wearing nice clothes. Nothing for Vincent to be scared of. Not in the light of day, right? The guy then made eye contact with him and smiled. It was friendly, not a warning. Vincent felt relief—at least he hadn't looked at him with familiarity. That would have sent him running in fear.

Now, Vincent's eyes were darting from person to person, shoe to shoe. The lust for city life was gone. With so many shiny smooth-soled shoes, how would he ever be able to tell friend from foe? The only impetus he felt now was to get out of town...again.

"I'm already ready to go, I don't have any use for being here." Vincent said coldly.

They walked to the edge of town in agreement on being glad to be putting the hustle and bustle behind them.

The city blended into a dirty little suburb. The sun was setting and neither of them had slowed down to eat or drink all day. Elmer had pointed this out an hour ago, but Vincent hadn't slowed his pace. He needed some distance from the city and the smooth soles. Without warning, Elmer sat down on a bench. "I gotta get a drink and eat a bite o' fish." He offered the still bulging pouch of fish to Vincent.

"No, thanks, my stomach is in knots." It wasn't a lie but even if he was starving, he doubted he would want to eat more fish.

Vincent sat down and gauged their surroundings. Something stood out. It looked like a forward-leaning h.

"Elmer is that a code?" he almost shouted, excited to have beaten the old man to the punch.

Elmer ripped a chunk of dried fish from the bigger piece with his perfectly white teeth and casually looked over.

"Oh, shit." He spat the fish on the ground and was flying through the ropes on his bindle, resecuring it all.

"What?" Vincent asked, shocked at the response.

"Vin, that's the code for run. It means this town isn't safe for anyone—not addict, nor frugal tourists, nobody...you hear me? You see that symbol, you beat feet, got it?" Elmer almost seemed angry.

"Yeah, no problem. Let's go." He grabbed Elmer's bindle and hurried behind him. "Where can we go though?" Vincent asked, thinking they were stuck in this now terrifying suburb.

"Train yard up ahead." Elmer was winded and the black bags under his eyes were noticeable even in the dark.

It was the first time Vincent had seen the older guy even get winded, but he was past that. He seemed exhausted. Vinny wondered if he had stayed awake all night in the rain watching him...protecting him. The thought of a sick, tired Elmer scared him more than whatever empty threat this town could hold.

"Slow down, Elmer. You're gonna hurt yourself." There was a panic in Vincent's voice now.

"If we don't get out of here, we might both get hurt. Now get your ass moving, Vin."

Another ten minutes of running in the mostly darkened streets, and they could hear the hiss of the train yard and the many boilers. They made it. Vincent's neck was beginning to hurt from tossing his head over his shoulder to look behind them every couple of seconds. Thinking of his own discomfort felt bad as he looked at the sweating, puffing, ragged-looking old man leading him to safety.

Without missing a beat, Elmer dodged through the yard. He was mysteriously familiar with just about any town or train yard they came across, and Vincent had never been more thankful for his wisdom. Vincent tried to plant every footstep exactly where Elmer's had just been, mimicking him through the yard. They passed the loading area for passengers and Elmer ducked a bit while passing the windows of the ticket station. Vincent copied him. They picked a path to the cargo side of the yard and Elmer started testing doors. Nothing at first then finally near the end, when Vincent was losing hope and considering using the secret eight dollars to just buy tickets out of town, a bay door slid open. There was just enough of a gap in the door for the two of them to sneak in.

Once they were inside, it was pitch black. Visions of shiny shoed men appeared from Vincent's imagination. His hand scooted to his pocket and in a flash, the Dunhill was illuminating the car.

Elmer let out a shriek and slapped a hand over his own mouth, not wanting to betray their free ride.

"Sorry, Elmer. I had to check." He was beginning to realize that Elmer had an aversion to fire. He would do his best to accommodate the fear in the future; no sense in piling on. He put the lighter back into his pocket, but his hand held it tightly for a while.

"No problem. You just scared me is all. Guess I'm a little jittery...can you blame me?" They both laughed at this.

Then Elmer did something Vincent hadn't seen him do before. He grabbed a board from the cargo pallets and jammed it into a space behind the bay door, an action that would prevent it from sliding open. It would stop any other passengers but would also make a bull think the door was locked and secure. It was genius and Vincent would make sure it wouldn't be lost forever.

As soon as the board was in place, Elmer was nesting. He was moving a tarp from the cargo to make a mattress. Before the train even started moving, Elmer was snoring. It was Vincent's turn to guard him while he slept. He sat up, watching the crack in the door. His eyes were burning, and his mouth was dry. While he was fishing his bleach bottle out of his kit to quench his thirst, he hoped the smell of Dakin's solution had faded. The lid spun off and he sniffed the bottle. Just a hint of bleach left not so much like Dakins anymore but still not just sweet river water either.

Vinny gave it one more sniff to maybe conjure a memory of dad and home.

Then, like someone was mocking him, he heard a sniffing sound. Instinctively, Vincent looked in Elmer's direction, but the sound of his snoring couldn't be mistaken for the sound of sniffing. Then the door rattled next to him. It was subtle but Vincent knew he had heard it. Another sniff from the crack in the door put him into fight mode. He ripped the bindle off the gnarled club beneath and held it so tightly, his knuckles hurt. Another sniff from the door now but this time it was followed by a less discreet prying at the door.

Vincent heard Elmer's snoring pattern shift, and he hoped he was being alerted and waking up. Vincent was too scared to move or try to urge Elmer awake with his voice for fear of letting whatever was sniffing know he was hiding. Elmer snored even harder and the door shook a little more violently.

The urge to scream was barely stifled. The fear of alerting whatever was out there sniffing right beside him outside the door kept his mouth shut. The door rattled again creaking on its hinges. This time there was intent, like whatever was out there was now sure that whatever it wanted was behind this door.

Mercifully, the train hissed, and Vincent could feel the brake let loose as the train sprang to life and started to roll forward. Not giving up easily, the assailant tried again to force the door. This time, Vincent could hear a noise that scared him almost more than the sniffing. It was Elmer's door jamb splintering. Vinny kicked his foot forward, aiding the board in keeping the door shut. The train was picking up speed now and Vincent thought he could hear footsteps keeping pace. He imagined smooth soles slapping the gravel. Then in a fit of what could only be rage, there was a banging at the door as the footsteps receded and the prying on the door ceased.

"Everything ok, Vinny boy?" Elmer said in a sleepy fog.

Terrified but aware that the old man was barely hanging on physically Vincent swallowed the lump in his throat.

"Yeah, it's fine. Just reorganizing the space over here so I can stretch out, and a box fell off the stack." He needed Elmer to be at his best and if he was scared or up all night protecting him, he wouldn't be.

However, in the very near future, he knew he needed to spill his guts to Elmer about all of it: the fire, the shoes, the stalker. It sounded nuts but he had to tell him. Maybe they could compare notes and come up with some answers.

For now, he needed to protect Elmer, even if the train was moving faster than whatever was trying to get in could run. He imagined the smooth soles climbing onto the moving train, the stalker not wanting to let its prey escape so easily. Vincent pushed his foot harder against the closed door and Elmer's splintered door jam.

Twenty minutes later, Vincent was sleeping. The train had rocked him to sleep once again. It was irresistible and he was tired.

They moved south and then west, stopping only for meals and then right back onto a new train to continue to Elmer's mystery destination. There had been so much on Vincent's mind that he didn't care about not knowing the final destination. Vincent had been turning Elmer's constant refrain of 'would it matter' in his head all day and had come to a realization. Maybe only today mattered? One step at a time, he told himself. Maybe that was the key to Elmer's success, his ability to roll with the punches.

The farther west they got on their journey, the less warning code for booze they saw, but it had been replaced with the ominous syringe-skull combination. It seemed the vice of choice in this area was heroin or morphine. Vincent wasn't sure of the difference, but he knew it was the same poison that had finished pushing dad off the cliff of uselessness; so, he wouldn't have a hard time avoiding this vice any worse than the last. Vincent and Elmer warned who they could, but it seemed even less useful with the junkies than it had with the drunks. At least the drunks seemed interested in their warning of the code before laughing in their faces. Hell, a few had tossed their bottles to the side without questioning them. The junkies, however, were suspended in a state of nodding off and helplessness with the need for another shot. They had no interest in warnings or codes—just the next fix.

Vincent continued to harass Elmer about a job as they moved along. Learning the ropes of the hobo lifestyle was a good start and he was glad for the help. But this was not the life he wanted. Elmer could wander and be a frugal tourist and be happy with it, but Vincent still wanted to get a good job, work enough to get money, and go home for dad and his brothers. Mom and Jamie Lynn could stay and conspire by the cauldron full of smoky soup.

The thought of the smoky soup made his already upset stomach boil more vigorously.

"What's for dinner?" he asked Elmer, hoping his answer wasn't salty peppery fish.

"Well, this is an unusual situation for me. I can't seem to recall this place and I'm not sure if we are gonna find much of anything outside of my fish." Vincent groaned internally. "We can scoot around town a bit. Just keep yourself alert."

They were both still on edge from the series of towns they had been either chased out of or scared out of. Without having to emphasize it, they both would also have a keen eye for the code to help guide them through this unfamiliar town.

There was no soup kitchen, no fancy Italian restaurants, not much of anything, really. This town seemed to have succumbed to the Depression. But it was comfortingly quiet. It felt like it was outside of the mafia's influence, as the soup kitchens were a dead giveaway of their involvement in local affairs. There was little to no life on Main Street, aside from a couple coming out of the only shop that seemed to be open. It was a general store and as they passed, Vincent saw the same fancy candies he had brought home to share from Kingston for his siblings a lifetime ago. His brain growled, now hungry for a taste of that moment in time.

There was no luck in finding a meal, no code, no line of people with empty plates waiting to be filled at the trough of food goodwill had provided. Just the prospect of more of Elmer's fish. Vincent was glad to have the option, but it didn't mean he liked it.

At the edge of town, Vincent once again beat Elmer to the punch.

"Hey, HEY, what's that one?" Vincent almost yelled pointing at the unfamiliar symbol. He was excited about its mystery, hoping it was going to mean food, or a nice bed at least.

Elmer had to move a little closer to see.

"Only reason you beat me to it is cos my old eyes prolly need some glasses. I wonder how much shit I'm missing." The old guy seemed genuinely concerned.

"Well, that's why I'm here, I guess," Vincent said, beaming. It was the first time that he felt truly useful to Elmer instead of it always being a one-way street of kindness from him.

"Indeed, Vinny. Let's see what you found." He leaned closer to the fence post on the side of the road. The code was small, but it was there in the same black, thick lines as the rest of them. It looked like a dipper for a well, a simple, small rectangle making a cup, with a line coming off the side at a forty-five-degree angle making the handle. Elmer let out a hoot that scared Vincent, who was looking around like a scared bird. The laughter that followed eased him almost instantly, though the hairs on his arm took their time to go back prone.

"Jeez, Elmer, what's it mean?" He was a little annoyed but still excited to figure it out.

"Let me ask, Vinny, did we see a warning not to drink hooch in this town, any double X's?"

"Not that I can remember."

"Well, Vinny, this may be my lucky day. This sign here means whoever the owner of this fence is…" He motioned to the house at the corner of the lot that occupied the interior of the fenced area. "…will be selling moonshine."

Vincent's heart sank as he realized what was for dinner. He didn't drink so this code was useless to him. Still, nothing was lost forever as he logged the code for later.

"Oh," he said with zero gusto.

"Let's do another walk through town to make doubly sure it's safe." The old man said slightly sheepishly.

Elmer seemed acutely aware that he was not as adept at picking up codes as Vinny was getting. Vincent thought he needed his eyes to make sure the warning was absent from town. And that he probably needed a drink.

"You ok with that, Vinny?"

Vincent couldn't say no, of course. Plus, it was the first time Elmer had ever asked for his input on a plan. Vincent usually just tagged along.

"Yeah, that's fine with me, but how are you gonna pay for the shine?" The eight bucks were no longer burning a hole in his secret pocket; it just felt heavy.

"Oh, don't you worry about that, Vinny. If I don't find a warning, I won't have no problem getting a bottle...or two."

They were back on the road to town now. There was still plenty of daylight left, so they had plenty of time to scour the town for double X's.

An hour later, they had crisscrossed every street a number of times, probably looking insane. Thankfully, no one was around to see them. Or they were but they were sticking to themselves and not making a fuss about them like the other small towns had. Vinny liked it—it felt safe.

They also had spotted a perfect place to camp. It was a ramshackle hut near a small pond that was boiling with fish, Elmer said, noticing all the action on the surface and happy with the prospect of filling his satchel with dry fish again. Vincent, not so much. However, the abandoned single room building had a roof and a floor, most of the walls were still intact, and there was a single bed; the mattress was shot but still miles better than the floor. The chimney seemed in good shape as well. Elmer had Vincent use his Dunhill to spark some dry grass to test the flue. As Vincent put the flames to the grass, he had a flashback of the smooth shoes and the tree burning. He was glad they found a safe place where he could keep a fire going all night if he wanted to.

"Ok, Vinny, I'm gonna go round me up a bottle. You gonna be ok for a bit on your own?"

Vincent was fine with it. He would take a turn on the mattress, figuring there was no way he would ever let Elmer sleep on the floor. He was tired from walking all over town numerous times, and a nap in the safety daylight provided sounded great.

"No sense watching an old man stoop for a bottle anyway. Leave me with some dignity." Elmer laughed at himself and tossed his bindle in the corner.

The money in Vincent's pocket felt dirty now. He wished he could give it back, but that would hurt Elmer's feelings. Vincent needed a job. It was a desire that was starting to consume him.

"Well, while you ask around, see if you can't find us some work, too." He felt bad being so persistent, but he got the feeling Elmer would be content with never working again.

"Soon enough, Vinny."

With that Elmer spun on his heels and sped away, now clearly on a mission.

"I'll be back, Vinny. I won't leave ya so don't worry bout that either," he yelled, turning around and waving.

The reassurance wasn't needed but it felt good to hear anyway. Vincent waved back.

Vincent tried to sleep on the mattress, which ended up being very comfortable, but that may only be because he hadn't been on a bed since he was back at home. He started to think about home again, wondering what they were doing, wondering if they cared what he was doing. All of a sudden, it felt overwhelming, and he wanted to cry. He missed it all, even Mom and Jamie Lynn. Part of him thought if he went back now, they might even let him stay. If he told them of all the stuff he had been through: the beating he caught, the fire, the moonshiners, the mafia guys, the smooth-shoes man who was stalking him. Vincent looked around nervously at the thought of him. He wondered if they would welcome him back, if they even missed him at all. Maybe they were looking for him because they regretted their decision and chores were piling up. Would they let Elmer stay? If not, maybe he wouldn't, either.

Vincent's stomach let out a loud roar. He was starving and did not want to eat fish at all. Maybe now that it was closer to dinnertime, he would have a better chance at grubbing a meal from somewhere closer to the heart of town. He scratched a message for Elmer on the floor with some coals.

'Be back soon, I wouldn't leave you either, Vinny.'

He signed his name as Vinny for the first time. It made him smile a bit.

Town wasn't any more active at dinnertime. In fact, he couldn't even smell dinner in the air, which seemed odd to him. After making a full lap through town, he passed the general store with the fancy candies in the window. He couldn't stop himself. He went around back and lowered his singed pants enough to worm his hand into the secret pocket. The secret pocket that Elmer had made and filled with money for him. Thinking of it made him feel worse for what he was about to do.

The store was spilling over with possibilities. There were the fancy candies, of course, which he put on the counter. Then some chocolate caught his eye; his favorite was Abba Zabba, but a new one caught his eye. Mars bar. He grabbed it and a Baby Ruth. Also, some gummy candies and a glazed doughnut the man at the counter said was freshly made. He also asked to see some money, which Vincent gladly produced before continuing on his shopping spree. There was a stack of books, and he couldn't help himself. He immersed himself in their jackets before settling on a collection of sci-fi short stories. There were model cars that caught his eye too, but he had to be realistic. The last things he added to the pile were a soda, some dinner rolls (again fresh-made), a good-sized chunk of cheddar cheese, and some mustard. No fish tonight.

As the guy behind the counter was ringing him up, he looked at Vinny's pants.

"You sure you don't wanna spend a buck on some jeans? Got 'em right over there in the corner."

Vinny's face got hot with shame.

"Uh, yeah sure, thanks."

He was hoping no one had been noticing the burnt spots on the jeans, but apparently, they were more obvious than he had imagined. The low-pressure sales tactic had worked.

"What are you, about a thirty-two by thirty-four?"

"Umm, I'm not sure. I think so." He had no idea. It was something Mom had taken care of for him. He was hoping the guy knew his sizes well.

The clerk brought the pants over and spun Vinny around, then yanked at the back of his pants probably looking at the leather tag.

"Yep."

He let Vinny go and spun him back around to the counter, which he was returning to. The man started to punch numbers into the register and Vinny watched the total grow. He was starting to feel terrible. But the bag of goodies would help.

He left the store, now burdened with the heavy load and guilt. The place they were camping at was a bit of a walk and halfway there, Vinny got cold feet. He ducked into the woods and started eating. He started with the candy; after his jaw began to hurt from the gummy candies, he went in on the chocolate. When the candy was gone save the fancy ones he had shared with his siblings, he still wanted more. Despite his stomach being full, the sugar had left a desire for something savory. There was no way to cut the cheese for a sandwich, so he simply took a bite from the block, dabbed the roll into the mustard, and mixed it all in his mouth. It was amazing and the first thing he had gotten to pick out to eat on his own since leaving home. Now almost bursting at the seams, he eyed the doughnut, then inhaled it. He washed it all down with the soda.

All that was left of the food was some rolls, cheese and mustard as well as the fancy candies. The guilt was awful as he thought of Elmer eating salty peppery fish. He almost gagged thinking of the taste of it. Vinny thought about taking some leftovers back and letting Elmer finish it, but that would give away the fact he had spent the money on himself. Then there was the matter of the book and pants. The book was easy enough to tuck into his bindle. It wasn't as if Elmer would be carrying it.

The pants would be harder to explain. Unsure what to do, he pushed it aside for now. One thing at a time.

The rest of the walk back to the camp was awful. He was so full, it hurt to walk. He popped one of the fancy candies into his mouth and it brought the taste of home with it. That combined with the guilt for betraying Elmer made the tears start. Not long after, he had to duck behind a tree and watch all the treats come back up and mix with the dirt. Chunks of half-chewed cheese and gummy bears fought for space in the quickly disappearing puddle. It made him cry even harder.

He finished sobbing and stashed the rest of his shame in the woods near the camp. He didn't feel like coming up with any lies to cover his tracks tonight. He just wanted to get some sleep. The fire was going inside, letting him know Elmer was back. When he walked through the door, Elmer leaped off the bed, clearly drunk. His mission was a success. Vinny wondered how he ended up getting enough money for a bottle. Maybe there was work and he could replenish the eight bucks and pay Elmer back.

"Vinny, whatta ya know?" Elmer said.

Vinny wasn't sure if it was a question or a statement, so he faked a smile for a reply.

"Well, I found the nicest guy, got a nice little family, coupla cute little kids that helps him. Real nice people, Vinny. He lemme get this bottle here on credit so we gotta stick around till I can settle up. Seems like a nice town, though, Vin. Safe." He took another chug from the bottle. "Well, safe for *this* anyway." He shook the bottle in Vinny's face.

Vinny didn't like this side of Elmer. But he was glad he was too inebriated to ask many questions. Regular Elmer, uncanny Elmer, would have instantly known something was up. There were still tears drying on Vinny's lashes.

Elmer started back in talking about the family he spent the evening with, and how they offered him something to eat but he refused because he couldn't eat without his son. Vinny was crying now, facing the fire as Elmer rambled on behind him. He felt like throwing up again to get rid of the last of the shame. Instead, he listened to Elmer and pretended nothing was wrong.

The rambling was familiar and comforting, like Dad's, and it washed the guilt he felt away slowly. Vinny let his mind wander with Elmer's babbling. Elmer blended with memories of Dad and before he knew it, he was up in his own bed at home, comfortable and safe. Sleeping.

The next few days were exactly what the two of them needed. It remained quiet in the safe little town, and they rested. It felt good to put the string of bad towns out of their minds and relax for a bit. Elmer drank every night, babbling about something or other. Vinny was growing to resent the fact he had pointed out the code for moonshine. He didn't like drunk Elmer; too many parts of him reminded him of the drunk, awful parts of dad. The guilt from the binge in the woods was wearing off, and he had even put the new jeans on without a word from Elmer. The older man had noticed and flashed him an approving smile, but Vinny's shame kept his eyes on his own shoes for a change.

He kept his space from the drinking and babbling by wandering the sleepy streets of town, picking through collection bins for newspapers or anything interesting. Really, only returning to the safety of their little abandoned cabin in the woods when the daylight started to fade. Despite the docile nature of the community, the smooth-soled stalker was never far from his mind, and it kept the fear alive in him. The last couple of days he spent finding bottles that were returnable. The new, non-returnable kind were everywhere but with a little digging through other people's filth, deposit bottles were still to be found and money to be made. There was no way he was going to replenish all of what he had spent on his spree, but it was a start.

In contrast to busy Vinny, Elmer kept himself busy with a fishing line tied to his toe, a bottle on his lips, and his fish smoker bellowing behind him. It was simple but Vinny was realizing it was probably enough for him.

There was a curiosity about how Elmer had scraped up enough cash to buy the moonshine, but he had hinted at keeping it to himself so Vinny didn't press. Then out of nowhere Elmer revealed his method of obtaining his shine casually over some bacon and bread he had somehow gotten ahold of. Vinny's own stash of ill-gotten cheese and bread was long gone; he had munched it away while biding his time away from the drinking.

"Vinny, we got us a little job. We already been paid for part of it but the last of what we're owed is all yours if you help me get it finished." Elmer shot him a sheepish drunken smile.

The couple of empty bottles lined up at attention in Elmer's corner suddenly made sense. Vinny now wondered what Elmer had roped him into, but he wasn't angry as he didn't mind helping him. Elmer had always helped him after all. Even if his help was nontraditional at times, it wasn't going unappreciated, plus Elmer had said he the last of the payment for the job was his, and Elmer wouldn't risk offending him by lying about giving him the rest of the pay.

"Well, what do you have set up for us?" Vinny said, smiling.

Relief washed over Elmer's red face, and he continued.

"Well, the guy that makes the hooch in town wants us to help him finish a dugout for his moonshine still out on his back five." That didn't sound so bad to Vinny. "And then help him move his still into it." Still not too bad, Vinny thought.

"That it?"

"Yep, that's it." Elmer laughed.

"Well, when do we get started?"

"Now, we actually gotta get a move on, Vinny." For the first time in a week, Elmer spun the cap closed on his bottle and tossed it on the bed. "Don't bother grabbing nothing. They'll make us lunch and feed us dinner if we are there too late." Elmer was already halfway out the door.

Surprisingly, he wasn't stumbling or slurring anymore. Somehow, he had sobered himself up in the few minutes it took to explain the job to him.

The farm was a short walk from town, and they made quick work of it. When they got there, some young boys were wrestling a wheelbarrow down a hill that disappeared behind the house. Vinny figured that was the still location, and he was correct as Elmer almost ran to catch the boys.

"Sorry we're late, fellas. Vinny likes to sleep in." Elmer laughed and looked over his shoulder at Vinny, who was shaking his head and keeping pace.

The boys laughed and Vinny took over the wheelbarrow for them. Their dad was friendly enough when they showed up late. The atmosphere was relaxed as he explained the layout for the dugout. It was ambitious and clever. Vinny was impressed. The boys were obviously copies of their dad and followed him around like two little shadows. It was nice to see him include them and make the boys feel like an asset while they were trying to help, though they were mostly getting in the way. He never lost his temper with them once. Vinny was jealous, but a bigger part of him felt good for the boys because he had seen how hard it was for everyone in the towns he had passed through. At least they were still happy and oblivious to the Depression consuming everyone else.

Their mother was even nicer than their father. She was sweet and pretty and non-judgmental. Just a never-ending supply of lemonade and smiles while the men worked. Her daughter was always close by her side with cute little dresses and yes sirs and no ma'ams. It was a far sight from Jamie Lynn. Vinny wondered how Mom would have been if Jamie Lynn hadn't been born with mongolism. Was Mom always predestined to be fat and unhappy with life? Or was Jamie Lynn the precursor to a life of misery? Somewhere in Vinny's mind, he recalled a thin, happy version of his mother in similar pretty dresses, but those memories were tied to so many others of contention that they almost had disappeared.

The dugout went smoothly. Elmer worked like a pack mule, hauling the dirt away and moving it farther downhill while

Vinny and the father worked the shovels. The vision the man had was clear enough that within three days, they were nearing the end of the excavation portion of the job. There was the matter of moving the heavy still, but he was still forming a hood for it, so it wasn't ready yet.

During lunch on the last day of digging, Vinny had mentioned his complaints about the non-returnable bottles and the father's ears had perked up. He apparently was always on the lookout for more bottles and as long as they were not cracked, he could fill them with shine and cork them. He would pay Vinny for a couple of loads if he was interested. He would even loan Vinny a wagon to make it easy on him.

Vinny was most definitely interested. He had already located every bottle in town, so the work of digging through rubbish was mitigated. With a solid afternoon of work, he could probably fill half of Elmer's and his cabin with bottles.

After lunch, that's just what he did. He went back to town with wagon in tow and got to work. There were a few sideways looks with all the noise and digging in bins, but Vinny never left a mess and always met them with smiles and a wave. It was hard to be mad at someone smiling and working. So, they left him alone...most of them.

'It's going to be getting dark soon,' the length of his shadow told him. The green and blues of the glass were being projected onto the grass beside his twenty-foot shadow. It looked like stained glass from a church window as it mixed with the oranges of the sunset. Vinny was distracted thinking about church on Easter and why that was the one day a year his family decided to be religious. Vincent wandered into an alley near the end of the row of businesses but before the residential area started. A no-man's land of detritus and puddles. As he neared the bins at the end of the alley, he heard a click behind him.

Vinny spun around ready to scream but was met with a flash of red and the taste of blood filling his mouth. His jaw popped hard in its socket and the fading red was replaced with tears from pain. Then without warning, he was spun around by his belt loops. His first thought was of the general store owner who had spun him much the same way when buying these same new pants.

"Wait..." Vinny started to plead. Then his throat was pinched shut by a stunningly strong fist.

"Shut the fuck up, boy." Another blinding flash of pain from the back of his head now. "Just shut the fuck up. Nod if you understand. If not, you're a dead man." A cold hard object replaced the fist on his throat. Vinny understood it to be a knife instantly and nodded.

No sooner had he nodded than the blade was removed from his throat. It went to the back of his pants and Vinny heard a tearing and felt a gust of cool afternoon air hit his now exposed butt. His new jeans slid down to his knees without resistance.

"I'm warning you, one fucking sound...." The man hocked some phlegm in the back of his throat and Vinny could hear him spitting into his hand.

Suddenly Vincent was aware of what was happening. His head was swimming from the blows, and his heart was beating so hard, it was all he could hear outside of the whooshing of his breath in and out of his lungs. A hundred thoughts went through his mind about fighting back, trying to run, screaming, but every option outside of submission ended with death. He was frozen in fear, pushed over a garbage bin, his butt in the air, his humiliation on full display. Then the coolness of the night air on his butt was replaced with something warm and slippery trying to find its way into him. Reflexively, he squirmed away, only to be met with another blow.

The fight was over.

Vinny gritted his teeth and looked between his legs at the ground. He saw a horny big toe pushing through the top of a destroyed boot. Its nail was like a rusty blade that had wormed its way through the leather, just like its owner was about to do to him. Instead of focusing on what was about to happen, Vinny tried to put his mind elsewhere, but only came up with visions of the smooth-soled stalker. Maybe the threats were more numerous than he had previously imagined as now the man with the hole in his shoe was a much more real threat than the smooth-soled stalker.

The slimy creature returned to his buttocks and tried again to force its way in painfully.

CRACK.

Splinters of wood shot past Vinny's head onto the brick wall in front of him. A knobby piece of wood landed on the top of the pile of trash he was bent over. Vinny recognized it instantly. It was the top of Elmer's walking stick. Vinny had been carrying it for so long now, it was practically a shared possession.

There was an immense weight pressing on him. The slimy creature was no more. Now it was the weight of this assailant threatening him, suffocating him against the trash bin.

More cracks thudded behind him. He could feel the blows landing through the man's body. Then the weight slid off Vinny and onto his side on the ground. The blows continued. Vinny finally had a good look at the man. He was bearded, filthy, toothless and huge. He was every bad thing you thought of when you imagined a problem in a dark alleyway.

The blows continued.

The man's eyes were wide open, but he was clearly unconscious...or dead, Vinny thought. This snapped his brain back to reality. He grabbed Elmer, who seemed to be in a trance beating the possibly dead man to death.

"Elmer, we gotta go."

There were tears flowing down the old man's face.

"You ok, Vin?"

"Yeah, Elmer, I'm good but we gotta get the hell out of here." Vinny pulled up his pants and went to button them, only to realize they were buttoned but loose because the man had slit them to the crotch. He held the slit together with one hand and grabbed the wagon with the other.

"Go ahead, Vin, I'll meet you there." the intentions were all over his face.

Vinny couldn't let him do it, so he left the wagon and pulled Elmer instead. He needed the older man still, if only for comfort. Elmer going to jail for this was not going to benefit anyone. He dragged him all the way back to the cabin with little resistance, but Elmer was miles away mentally.

Without any words between them, Elmer went inside and grabbed the bottle from the bed. He emptied it. Vinny couldn't care less. He had just prevented him from having his first sexual encounter—non consensually with a disgusting bum. He could feel the slimy protrusion on his butt again.

Vinny took off the destroyed jeans and grabbed his burnt ones from his pack, along with some fresh clothes and soap. The pond was warm, and Vinny stayed in, scrubbing vigorously until the sun was completely gone. Only then did the darkness chase him inside.

He wondered if Elmer had killed the guy. He hoped so.

Elmer was wrecked with booze by the time he got back inside. Nothing was said. Vinny felt shame about the fact that he had to be saved again, and saying thank you would only add more shame. Maybe it would disappear in the morning.

Vinny tossed and turned for an hour or two. Elmer fed the fire in silence and every once in a while, a gurgling from a bottle would break the silence. Vinny wished Elmer was babbling now. He didn't think sleep would come but the comfort it offered would be welcome. He didn't get babbling in the end, but he did get something.

"Sorry I wasn't there, Vinny. Won't happen again. I would do anything to keep you from that part of the world. You're a good kid. I love you." Elmer was crying again but not the same way he had earlier.

"I love you too, Elmer." He waited a minute, wondering if the time was right. "Thank you for saving my ass back there."

Elmer laughed so hard it hurt Vinny's ears, but he joined him in it. Elmer motioned the bottle at him in the semi-dark of the room. Vinny just shook his head and smiled. Ten minutes later, he was sleeping.

The little moonshine farm was an oasis from the misery that surrounded it in the rest of the country. The safety of the town seemed magical almost. But it had been shattered in an instant last night. Upon waking this morning, the first thought in both of their heads was that it was time to move on. Elmer was busy fussing with his gear and trying to fit every bit of dried fish into his satchel, as there was an overabundance now. Reluctantly, Vinny looked for his burnt pants but couldn't find them.

"Hey, Elmer, you see my pants?" he asked without looking back.

Smack.

"There, try those. I tossed them burnt ones in the fire this morning. They weren't fit for a bum, much less you."

"But...." Vinny was looking over the pants, which last night had been split to the crotch and were un-wearable. The split was gone.

"Got bored listening to you fart in your sleep so I sewed 'em up for ya to kill some time."

"Thanks."

Vinny felt terrible for not telling Elmer about how he got them in the first place. He needed to come clean. But only after he had the eight bucks to pay him back. Vinny suddenly wondered about the wagon and the bottles they were to take to the moonshine farm on their way out of town, after collecting their pay. There was the familiar weight in his front pocket from the Dunhill. Vinny suddenly thought of Elmer burning the old pants and realized the secret pocket had the rest of Elmer's money in it. Without him thinking, his hand went to the back of the new pants, only to find a new secret pocket. There was what felt like bills inside and a couple of coins.

He looked at Elmer sheepishly. Elmer said nothing, but only smiled and winked. Vinny felt shitty but the wink eased his guilt. Paying Elmer back was now even more of a priority.

Elmer opened the front door, and blue and green light flooded in. Vinny looked up to see the wagon still full of bottles outside the door now.

"What the hell?" he wondered aloud.

"Well, I also needed to go for a walk to clear my mind a bit, and I figured I may as well fetch the wagon." Elmer was beaming, clearly pleased with himself.

"Damn, Elmer, how'd you manage that without waking me up?" Suddenly he was worried for him. "Please don't go out alone at night anymore, though."

"I won't, Vinny. Just had some loose ends."

Vinny thought of the rapey bum with his bulging wide-open eyes. Had he seen him breathing after Elmer's assault? It didn't matter, he told himself again. If Elmer said he tied up a loose end, it was good enough for Vinny. Aside from the shame of almost being raped, that was the last thought Vinny gave to it.

"Ready to go, Vinny? Say goodbye to the cabin cos we ain't coming back." Elmer was already moving along, clearly attached to nothing except Vinny.

It was harder for Vinny. Part of him wished they could stay here forever. However, it wasn't in the cards, and he caught up to Elmer with a slight lump in his throat.

The walk was quiet as they made their way through town. Vinny was wondering how much they were gonna make from all the hard work and the bottles. He hoped it was enough to cover Elmer's eight bucks plus a little extra, maybe they could stop at the store before leaving and grab a few candies. Also, he wanted to buy something for Elmer, maybe a bottle for the road, even if Vinny did hate booze himself.

Elmer seemed slightly more on edge. He was watching carefully for signs that people suspected them for yesterday's trouble. No one did and by the time they reached the edge of town, they both doubted anyone ever would. He was a monster of a human that likely had no one that gave a shit about him. Not like Elmer, not anymore, cos Vinny had told him he loved him, and it was sincere.

They were nearing the moonshine farm when shots rang out.

The outside world had caught up with the safe little town and the safe little oasis that brewed specialty moonshine. Apple-pie bourbon was Elmer's favorite, he had told Vinny earlier that week.

There would be no more of that.

It sounded like two or three hundred rounds had been fired in less than half a minute. Because of the proximity and the unsure nature of their intent, Vinny and Elmer hit the ditch on their bellies. Elmer put his arm over Vinny in a protective gesture.

They stayed face-down in the ditch until the gunfire stopped. Then without returning to their feet, they started to assess the situation. No sooner had they poked their heads up than they heard the rumble of vehicles approaching them, matched with a cacophony of whooping and yelling.

Two cars sped toward them now from the direction of the moonshine farm. The cars were overburdened with young men. Young men in suits, all armed, all excited. As the cars rolled closer, Elmer tucked his head back down. Vinny, however, was affixed to their shoes. Fancy, all of them. He got a good look at three pairs as three mobsters were hanging off the side of the cars on the siderails, guns still in hand.

Vinny looked up at the last one in the series and they made eye contact. It was brief but it left an impression. The mobster was living a carefree life as an apex predator, not a care in the world. Vinny was a scared animal hiding in a ditch, prey. As if to accentuate this point, the kid, who looked not much older than he did, leveled his pistol at him and fired a round. The car never slowed, and the kid turned around to rejoin their celebratory cruise, never again thinking of the bum in the ditch whom he shot at.

The bullet struck the dirt a few feet in front of Vinny, splashing him with a blast of dirt. Luckily, it wasn't more but Vinny's hands flew around his body to make sure. Elmer was doing the same.

"Where'd it hit, Vinny?" he said, panicking.

"I think it just hit the ground. I'm fine. What the fuck was that?" Vinny didn't like to swear but it was the only thing that came to mind.

"Not sure, Vinny, but it was coming from their place." He was pointing at the moonshiner's house now, obviously concerned more for them now that Vinny was safe.

"Let's go."

Without another word, they sprinted the rest of the way to the farmhouse, not knowing what to expect.

They were met with a sight they were not prepared for. The father was lying face-down in the front yard. His hand was clenching a pistol, and his body was riddled with holes, his back full of exit wounds and his chest and belly wrecked with entry wounds. He had stood his ground to the end and never fled despite the odds, it seemed.

Elmer was working on his body to try to find a sign of life. It was useless.

"Vinny, you gotta find the kids."

Vinny was already running toward the house and hollered back in agreement.

"I know!"

He hadn't made it very far when his heart sank in his chest. The mother was lying there in a sad heap. There was a bullet hole in her throat, which was sad, but the worse part was she was lying there half naked. Her breasts were exposed, and the blood was running in a stream down between them. She was dead and it looked like as if she had tumbled and her dress had ripped, or one of the mobsters decided to have a look. It didn't matter which. Her daughter was just behind her, lying face-down.

Vinny prayed she was ok and just hiding her pretty little face from the horrors that surrounded her. As he rolled her over, he screamed.

Her face was completely gone. Everything forward of her hairline and ears was missing. It was as if someone had scooped out her brain through her face. Vinny screamed again and his stomach turned. Elmer came behind him and whimpered as he shoved Vinny's face into his chest to protect him from the gruesome sight. He ripped his overshirt off his withered body and covered the girl's mangled head.

"Where's the boys, Vinny?" he asked, trying to stay composed for Vinny's benefit.

"Jesus, Elmer, why'd they do that to her?"

"Vinny, we gotta find those boys." He slapped Vinny hard.

It worked to get his body moving, but the hole in the girl's head was consuming him. Blindly, he tagged behind Elmer. Elmer was up the porch of the house now, yelling for the boys. He darted inside and went room to room in the small house. It didn't take long to realize where they must be.

Both of them shot out the back door down the hill that disappeared behind the house. To the dugout they had made.

The boys were there.

They were just as riddled with holes as their father. Their arms were wrapped around each other, and they were tucked into the far corner of the dugout. Both of their faces were still intact, but not much else. There was no hope of finding life in either of them, it was obvious. Vinny saw his brothers in his mind from the shock he was in.

On top of killing the entire family, the mobsters made sure to send a nice clear message about why this happened. The new still the father had been working on was more holes than copper. They had absolutely shredded it like the bodies of the boys.

Through his tears, Elmer managed.

"We gotta go, Vinny. Ain't nothing more to be done here by us cept to get ourselves landed in jail."

He was right, but Vinny didn't know if he had the strength to leave them behind like this. What was next? Just another town full of fear and misery? It felt pointless to keep pressing forward.

"We can't, Elmer. We can't just leave them like this."

Sirens broke the tension that was developing between them as Elmer's pleading look turned to panic.

"We aren't leaving them for the crows. The cops will be here and if we are standing around, they will pin it on us just to have it be done with."

He was right and Vinny reluctantly agreed.

They left the danger of town behind them and walked south. There was no paycheck for all their hard work. Just a family destroyed and a wagon full of bottles left behind. Vinny couldn't help but notice that it was essentially the booze that caused all of this, along with desperation because of the Depression. It gave him yet another reason not to drink.

Vinny also realized there was a criminal enterprise preying on the desperate and addicted. It wasn't just a group of guys running from cops selling illegal hooch to other guys who wanted to relax with a drink in the evenings. It was destroying lives behind the scenes, and no one was going to stop it.

On the way down the road, the police siren was screaming more loudly now, but Elmer stopped long enough to pull out his pocketknife and walk over to the fence. He located the post with the code for booze and peeled it off. He then took a minute to scrape the double X's and a bottle.

They walked most of the day in silence. As the shadows grew on the road in front of them, so did their unease. Every car that passed was a potential threat now. It could be full of mobsters looking to get rid of witnesses. That wasn't the only thing concerning Vinny, though. The girl's missing face was haunting him. Out of everything that day, it was the only thing that stuck aside from the impression that his little brothers had been shot. He knew that hadn't happened, but it was already in his mind, and it was hard to convince himself otherwise.

Vinny didn't want to walk in the dark. Uncanny Elmer returned and stuck his hand up at the next passing truck. By chance, it was a friendly guy who stopped. He offered to let them ride in the cab, but Elmer politely declined, just saying they were exhausted and wouldn't mind lying in the back for a bit to catch some sleep. The truck driver obliged, and they climbed in back.

It was a quiet ride to the next town, mostly. They both fell asleep eventually. Both dreamed of faceless little girls and bodies strewn about the yard. Vinny woke them up with a scream a couple of hours later.

"You ok, Vinny?"

Vinny waited a second. "I guess so. Maybe not right now, but I will be."

"Well, that's good." Elmer took a deep breath. "I'm sorry you had to see that."

"Me too."

"Well, if there is a bit of good news, Vinny, it's that we are now on the way to a real job."

Vinny wasn't sure what he meant. "How's that?" he asked.

"It's seasonal work, it's always available as long as you don't mind breaking your back for a month or so." Elmer could see Vinny's spirits rise a bit and continued. "It ain't glamorous but it pays good."

"So, what is it?" Vinny said, not thinking of the girl's face for the first time today.

"Hoeing spuds."

Vinny was familiar with the work of mounding dirt around the green tops of growing potatoes to increase yield. He had never done it but wasn't afraid of learning.

"What's it pay?"

"A couple of seasons ago, it was twenty-five bucks per acre. You could hoe an acre a month and if you broke your back you could do maybe three acres in that month or however long the work lasts."

Vinny was shocked. "So, we could make over a hundred dollars."

"I guess we could, but I ain't much for breaking my back anymore, Vinny. I'll prolly sit this one out."

Suddenly, Vinny was terrified. Had Elmer had enough of taking care of him? Was he going to drop him off at the job and wave goodbye like Dad?

"Don't worry, Vinny. I'll hang around and keep myself busy. I got plenty of things to occupy me during the day. Not least of which is replacing my walking stick. Might take a month to find something suitable," Elmer joked. "I'd never leave ya," he then reassured.

The truck bumped to a stop sometime later in some new town full of threats. Elmer and he wandered around town looking for codes, looking for warnings. There wasn't much except a cross carved into a tree outside a church, which looked empty. No one home to sweet-talk with words from the Bible however. They walked a bit more and Elmer found a bench to rest on. Vinny waited and killed some time reading a paper he found. It was a local rag, not as interesting as a national paper but still good enough to kill an hour or so.

He read about the local sports teams, local politics fighting over water rights, and other items not worth remembering. Then he saw a face he thought he recognized. He read the story a bit further for some insight.

"Missionary found murdered, suspect still at large."

That was all it took, and Vinny remembered the man at the rodeo who had told them of the heroin warning code. Fellow shepherd of hobos, trying to lead them to the light and away from danger. The hairs on Vinny's arms stood up as he read. The man had been found with his throat slit. There had been a symbol carved into his chest that was unidentifiable. The warning codes flashed in Vinny's mind, and he wondered what the unidentifiable symbol had been. He finished the article, which was mostly about the missionary's life and surviving family.

Vinny pushed the paper to Elmer, who generally couldn't care less for reading. At first, he scoffed at him then when he looked at the paper, his eyes got wide, and he grabbed it from

Vinny. He looked like he read the entire article and had the same thoughts as Vinny.

Was he killed because he was warning people about the code? Was this a message like the one the mafia had sent by killing an entire family? Was it just a coincidence? Vinny felt the latter was least likely. Something was going on and they were getting too close to it.

"Time to go, Vinny."

Luckily, the train yard was quiet. Not a lot of bums looking to catch a ride and not a bull in sight. They picked a car after they saw them do a final cargo check. They sneaked into the car full of cabinets and made themselves comfortable, careful not to damage anything. The first thing Elmer did was jam the remnants of his bindle's handle into the door as a wedge, like he had done in the dangerous town with the code, the forward leaning h, that told to run away from some unknown danger.

"Don't need any company," Elmer said.

Vinny thought about telling him about the night he fell asleep on the train, and something tried to pry the door open…but he changed his mind. There was already an overwhelming amount stuff to worry about without dragging that into it as well. If Elmer hadn't been drunk the last week or two, he probably would've told him then, but the drunken babble was always in the way. Soon, he would tell him his working theory and they could collaborate on it. There would be time at the new job.

This got Vinny thinking about the job. About the money he could make. At first, he imagined his spending spree at the end and all the goodies he would buy, all the books he could read. Then the guilt of the last spending spree came back.

No, this time he was gonna spend it on something to help Elmer and himself get out of this lifestyle for good. If he worked really hard, he bet he could do four acres. If Elmer's recollection of the pay was correct, that was a hundred bucks. Surely, he could secure a room for a hundred bucks. Something to call home even if it were temporary. Plus, he could give Elmer his eight bucks back and have a clear conscience.

It seemed Elmer knew his train routes well, or he had gotten lucky as this particular train stopped at the town Elmer wanted to end up in. There was no more hopping trucks or begging rides. Just a couple of miles' walk out of town. By the time the farmhouse and the bungalow came into view, they were already choking on the dust from a few dozen men in the fields hard at work hoeing.

Vinny felt a sense of urgency and wanted to sprint to the main house to ask if they still had any openings. Elmer, on the other hand, had seemed to slow down as they were getting closer.

"Well, Vinny, this is it. Now you have the world in your hands, and you won't have a use for an old curmudgeon like me." He laughed to cover his discomfort.

"No way in hell. This is gonna get us both on our feet. Just like you'd never leave me, I'd never leave you, either" he tried to reassure him but could tell it hadn't worked.

"Well, if you don't see me for a few days, I'll just be down the road a spell by the lake."

"What do you mean?"

"Well, work starts early so you sleep there in the bungalow, but that's for field hands only. They ain't gonna let me sleep and eat for nothin'."

"Oh. Well, I could just walk here in the mornings." Already, it seemed like a bad idea. He had no desire to walk in the dark or miss one second of work if he wanted to hit his goal of four acres.

"Nope, you just work hard and be a good kid and I'll be waiting when it's all done." He smiled. "Just don't forget I'm down the road if ya need anything. Now run up to the house and get a job before they are all gone." He laughed.

"Ok, well, I'll see you tonight or tomorrow. Either way, I'll let you know how it goes, and I'll bring you something to eat if I can."

"Don't worry about me. I been at this a long time. Hurry up, get going."

He thought Elmer sounded like he might start crying. He couldn't wait for that, or he might as well.

Vinny sprinted up the road to the house, excited to get to work. To be a man. He got to the front door and felt small and unsure of himself. He looked down the road, expecting to see the back of Elmer walking down the road. Instead, he was still standing exactly where they had parted, waving and smiling. Now urging him with hand motions to knock. He never turned his back on me, Vinny thought as he thought of Dad limping inside the night he left home.

He knocked on the front door with confidence.

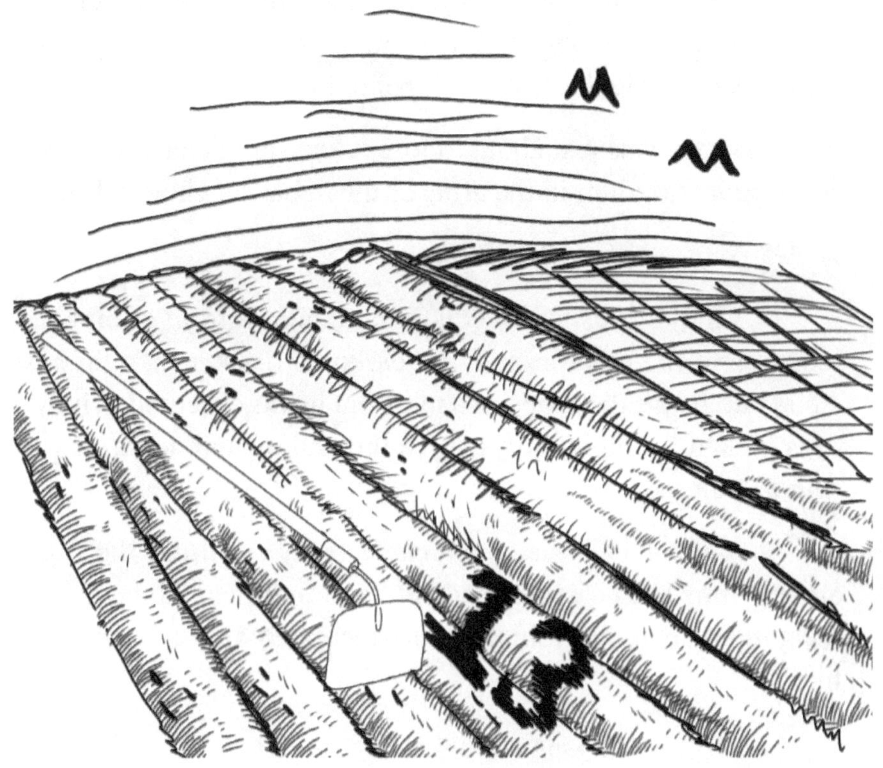

The alley was darker than last time, almost pitch-black. Why did he think another trip through town was a good idea? The green and blues of the non-returnables glinted in the moonlight. He would just be fast and get it over with. Before he got to the bottles, two huge hands grabbed him from behind and forced him over the bins. He was naked somehow, he realized as his hands, feeling almost too heavy to move, searched for the protection his denim might offer. Then there was a sliding slimy feeling on him again. Vinny looked down at the horny toe poking through the front of a destroyed boot.

Not this time, Vinny thought and wheeled. He expected the bulging eyes of the disgusting bum again, but instead found the man had been replaced by the moonshiner's daughter, her face scooped out along with her brains. A gurgling came from somewhere inside the cavity left behind.

Vinny was just about to lose it and start screaming when something froze him in the arms of the hobo-daughter hybrid.

Sniff, Sniffff...SNIFFFF

Vinny's eyes left the disfigured hulk in front of him and looked into the moonlit alley. A darkness blacker than the rest stood out. It was the shape of a man, but it was obscured. Vinny's eyes looked for an identifying feature and looked down. It was smooth soles.

A great belly laughter came from it, filling the night around him. The beast that had held him tightly let him go. Now the gurgling coming from its cavity increased. It was laughing at him.

Now Vinny's screaming started.

Thump

"Shut up, kid. You do this shit almost every day. I need some damn sleep," a voice from somewhere not in the alleyway said.

He was confused. And still screaming.

Thump

He opened his eyes and moonlight filled the bungalow. He instantly knew where he was and what was happening as another thump hit his chest and his screaming stopped.

"Damn, kid, I thought I was gonna have to use my fist instead of a pillow." It was Vinny's bunk mate.

He was only a couple of year older than Vinny but had the build of a man and the experience to back it up. Vinny thought he was cool.

"Sorry, Mac." Vinny wasn't sure what name Mac was short for or if it was a nickname. "I don't know what the hell is going on," he lied and was thankful for the darkness in the bungalow.

He could feel his face burning red hot with shame. The more time that passed from the bum's attempt at his virginity, the more shame he felt from it. He should have fought back or something, but he had relied on Elmer to save him again.

"It's fine, kid. Get some sleep. How's your hands?" Mac asked, sounding concerned.

"I'll be fine," Vinny lied.

He could feel his pulse in every inch of his palms. His hands hadn't been hardened enough for this work, and the constant plunging of the hoe into the dry compact soil was taking its toll.

"You two, shut the fuck up," a pissed-off voice in the darkness sounded off.

Vinny lay back down. He thought of the unsure look on both the owner of the farm and his foreman when he asked for a job...begged for a job. The man was kind enough to give him a shot but had warned him if he couldn't keep up, he was gonna give his hoe to another, stronger man. Vinny had assured him it wouldn't be an issue. The foreman had showed him the tool shed and provided him with his new torture device. He also assigned him a bunk and showed him where meals would be served. Then he led Vinny to his first plot, maybe his only if the foreman was right. Vinny hoped not, as he still planned on his goal of four acres and a hundred bucks.

The first time he smashed the hoe into the ground, it rebounded and made the foreman laugh. This drew the attention of a few guys working the plots next to him. Ok, now with a crowd, he had to perform. He swung as hard as he could, and the hoe only buried itself halfway into the hardpacked earth between the rows of vegetative growth. He pulled the soil toward the plant and the crowd roared with laughter.

It was going to be a long day.

By the end of his first shift, he was getting the hang of it, but his hands were starting to hurt. By the end of the second shift, the shaft of his hoe was covered in brick-red stains. By the end of the third day, Vinny wanted to quit.

The only thing that kept him going now was the thought of the paycheck and the foreman's daughter. She was in charge of wheeling down the meals from the kitchen and making sure the water barrel was full. Vinny saw her and fell in love instantly like any other boy his age would have. She was stunningly pretty and friendly.

Vinny thought he caught her giving him a double-take at lunch, but he was sure he was wrong until Mac gave him shit about it at dinner. He had ribbed him in front of the group of younger guys Vinny was desperately trying to fit in with. They had all agreed that for whatever reason, the foreman's daughter had her eyes on Vinny. There was no small amount of jealousy in all of them, as any of them would have killed to have the girl's attention. It had solidified him a spot in the group (even if it was at the bottom) out of slight admiration, something Vinny had never felt from peers. He loved it.

The lids of his eyes were heavy now, and Vinny fell asleep thinking of the foreman's daughter and not smooth soles or the faceless bum rapist or the murdered moonshiner family. It was the best sleep he had had since arriving.

When he woke up the next morning, his hands were stuck to his sheet, and he had to peel them off. This started the blood flowing. The foreman was shaking people awake and took notice.

"Vinny, you're done. You can't work like that."

His heart sank. He was being fired. It wasn't a surprise, but it hurt. He was starting to feel like he fit in and was making friends his own age. Plus, he thought he was in love with the foreman's daughter. But it fit with Vinny's track record of bad luck. Stupid hands. He looked at the peeling, bleeding nightmares and felt his throat get tight. He didn't want to cry in front of his new friends, who were looking at him now.

"Ok" was all Vinny could get out without giving away the lump in his throat.

The foreman gave the pathetic boy another onceover and looked to ponder the effort he had put in the past week.

"I ain't firing you, just uh, well give yourself a few days and when that heals up and stops bleedin' so bad, you can come back to work as long as there is still a hoe for you," he said, knowing he would make sure there was a hoe for him if the kid decided to come back.

"Yes, sir," Vinny said, relief washing over him.

The rest of the men went out to the fields now, leaving Vinny bored and alone in the bungalow. He thought about getting breakfast but wasn't sure if they were going to feed him if he wasn't working. The best thing to do was feed himself and save himself from some embarrassment. Instead, he decided to check in on Elmer. He hadn't seen him in a few days and the last time, he thought he hurt Elmer's feelings.

Elmer had shown up after dinner one night a couple of days ago. Vinny was joking and laughing with the guys around the fire by the bungalow when Vinny heard his familiar voice from behind him. It was Elmer just checking in, but it was dark. Vinny's nightmares were keeping the fear fresh in his mind, and he didn't like the fact Elmer was walking around in the dark. He had scolded him for it and could see Elmer getting hurt. Vinny tried to make small talk for a few minutes, but Elmer was deflated and hurt, so there wasn't much in the way of conversation. He left shortly after, leaving Vinny feeling bad for barking at him. His new friends had questioned him about the old man and asked if it was his dad. Vinny told them he was just a friend and they laughed at him for his odd choice of friends.

Now he walked with his burning hands toward the lake down the road. He was sure he would be able to spot Elmer by his fish smoker puffing away. A couple of days had passed, and he hadn't seen Elmer, which felt odd but refreshing. Vinny came to realize that his reliance on Elmer was keeping him from being a man himself. If Elmer was always there to save him or keep him from figuring things out on his own, he would always be reliant on him. The thoughts brought guilt, too. He really did care for the older man, but his independence was beginning to feel like more of a priority. Anyway, Elmer would be fine, he thought. He had been at this a long time by himself just fine.

Elmer was exactly where he said he would be, and like Vinny expected, his nose led him right to him.

"Vinny, what a surprise. What are you doing here?" Concern was in the last part of his question.

Vinny held his hands up and they explained everything.

"So, you got canned, huh?" Elmer asked, sounding mildly happy. "That's ok, Vinny. We can move along and find us something else to do, if you're still set on making some money. I can find us some...."

Vinny cut him off. "No, they are letting me come back to work. I just gotta let 'em heal up a bit."

Elmer looked deflated again. "Oh, well, let's see what we're working with." He took Vinny's hands in his own and looked at them intently. "First we gotta dry them out, then we gotta lube them up and keep them covered."

Vinny wasn't very sure what he had in mind but trusted his lead once again. Elmer practically dragged him to the sandy beach by the lake.

"Find a nice patch of hot, dry sand and bury your hands in it. Every few minutes, rub them around and rebury 'em. Keep that up till they are dry and cracking, then we move on to the next step." Elmer seemed pleased to be helping. Vinny did as he asked and pushed his hands into the dry sand. It hurt at first then the warmth felt good on the rawness.

They made small talk for an hour or so, Vinny going on at length about his new friends and the prettiest girl he'd ever seen, who actually liked him. Elmer was excited for him outwardly, but his eyes showed he could feel himself losing Vinny to the new exciting lifestyle. Vinny was too excited to notice the hurt and kept talking. Elmer nodded and smiled at all the right spots.

After Vinny's hands were dried out by the sand, they already looked better. Elmer then helped him peel the edges of the blisters off, so they weren't making pockets for infection.

"Now we gotta clean it out," Elmer said, leading Vinny back to his makeshift camp.

He pulled a bottle from his bedding. Vinny was shocked Elmer had another bottle. Besides wondering where he'd gotten it, he was mad he was drinking.

"Elmer, are you sure it's safe for that here?" He motioned to the bottle.

"Well, if not, I'm mighty lucky cos I been stinking drunk every night and most every day." He laughed then looked at Vinny and stopped. "Yes, I'm sure, Vin. I looked over the town and back down the road for a warning code and there weren't any." Then he added, "Would've been nice to have your young eyes to help look for them, but yes, I'm sure." There was a touch of resentment in his voice.

"Oh, sorry." Vinny felt bad for him and buried any thoughts of telling him off.

Elmer grabbed his hands and abruptly dumped a couple of shots worth of booze on them. It burned like fire. Elmer giggled a bit and told him to toughen up. After the booze, Elmer went to his smoker and came back with a leaf full of oil drippings from the fish.

"Elmer, what the hell are you doing?"

Before he could argue, Elmer was already smearing the oil into his palms.

"This will keep them from cracking and keep any infection out. You keep putting that on every coupla hours and you'll be back to work in two or three days, I bet."

Vinny questioned his method but knew Elmer wouldn't hurt him on purpose.

"Ok, thanks, Elmer."

The smell from his hands made him want to throw up. It reminded him of the day he met Elmer in the town full of the fishy smell and the salt dream. It was going to be a long couple of days.

"No problem, Vinny." He tipped the still open bottle back and took a big drink.

They had a quiet couple of days. Fishing and oiling hands and drinking. It made Vinny miss the farm and made Elmer miss Vinny.

Vinny woke up screaming the first night. Elmer woke him up and knew what he was dreaming by the look on his face. He didn't ask any questions, thankfully, because Vinny didn't think he could ever speak of the events that took place in the "safe" town again. Especially with Elmer, who had saved the scared little boy version of him from being raped.

The fish oil was working wonders and by the third day, Vinny was ready to get back to work. He left Elmer by the lake and promised to visit again soon. Then he sprinted the couple of miles back to the bungalow. Just like he hoped, they hadn't started to work yet, and Vinny had time to run inside and reclaim his bunk. He was putting the things from his bindle into the drawers they provided the workers when he grabbed something he didn't immediately recognize. His hands recoiled and he looked into the bindle's opening. Whatever it was, it was tan and smooth to the touch. He reached back in and pulled it out.

It was a brand-new pair of buckskin gloves. What the hell? Vinny wondered for a split second, then knew. Elmer. When did he have time to pull this miracle off? The old man sure had a knack for sneaking around. Vinny pulled the soft leather over his hands and felt guilty for the thoughts of abandoning Elmer.

"Oh, you're back," came a soft, feminine voice from behind him.

Vinny spun around and almost fell. It was the foreman's daughter. The sun was shining through her white flowery dress, highlighting her legs through the fabric. She was smiling and holding a plate of food.

"Here, I made it just for you," she said, still smiling. "I thought you'd be back yesterday, so I had to give the last ones to Mac."

A tinge of jealousy flared in him.

"If I knew you were cooking breakfast just for me, I wouldn't have missed it for anything," he said clumsily. "Sure, as hell wouldn't have let Mac eat it."

She laughed at the jealousy and pushed the plate at him.

"Well, you enjoy. I've got work to do." Her face was red.

Vinny loved it.

"Thank you," he hollered after her, smiling from ear to ear.

After she was gone, Vinny took the plate of fritters to the table, where the rest of the men were eating oatmeal, eyeing his plate and his new gloves. Mac took a noticeably longer look at the plate then at Vinny. Vinny could almost feel the jealousy as he chewed the fritter.

That day, Vinny out worked the men adjacent to him by a long shot. The gloves and the attention from the foreman's daughter had him floating all day long.

There was gossip at lunch about one of the workers who had gone missing two days ago while Vinny was camping with Elmer. Most guys assumed he got drunk and wandered to a new town with lesser expectations for work. A few guys who knew him better said he liked to drink but also loved to work and were shocked that he would leave his things behind. Vinny paid little to no attention to the gossip as he was busy staring at the foreman's daughter whose name, he learned, was Sarah. The name had echoed and bounced around his head all day, distracting him from the work while the gloves buffered the pain in his hands. The thought of her in the doorway with her almost transparent dress was driving him mad with lust. The first thing he was going to do with his paycheck at the end of this was to take her on a date...then he would pay Elmer back.

Sarah waved at Vinny across the benches and smiled.

Elmer who?

The next couple of weeks went along much more smoothly. With the gloves and his muscles adapting themselves to the work, it was getting easier by the day. Unfortunately, that meant he was now working himself out of a job, along with the rest of the men. Vinny was growing closer to Mac's group of friends. At the same time, Mac seemed to be growing more jealous and less friendly toward him. It was directly related to the amount of attention Vinny got from Sarah. No matter how many times Mac took his shirt off in the field or acted like a tough guy at meals, he just couldn't catch her eye. Vinny, on the other hand, was bumbling and awkward around girls but regardless, Sarah's eyes were fixed on him.

Vinny had only seen Elmer once since he had helped him with the blisters on his hands. The foreman needed some baling wire from town, and offered a bonus to Vinny if he could run to town and be back before lunch. It was an easy enough task. Until he bumped into a drunk Elmer on the road back. Part of Vinny wanted to avoid the stumbling drunk coming down the road, even after he recognized who it was. Elmer, on the other hand, saw Vinny and nearly tripped on his own feet running up to him.

Without slowing his pace, Vinny greeted him and made small talk when he could, but Elmer was relentless. He was talking about everything and nothing at the same time like every confused drunk before him. As they neared the farm, Vinny tried to excuse himself, but Elmer wouldn't stop talking. Vinny could see Sarah making her way down the hill with her cart full of lunch. He stopped Elmer mid-sentence and told him he would see him in a week or so, and without waiting for a response, sprinted up the hill with his wire under his arm. He never looked back. Elmer stood and watched for a minute until he disappeared into the crowd gathering around the tables. Vinny saw him walking back toward the lake a few minutes later and tried to wave but Elmer was already well on his way.

Vinny was now three acres into his goal and halfway done with his fourth. By his estimation, there wouldn't be enough acres left for him to secure another one on his own. So, at lunch, he proposed to Mac that he and his three friends should snatch up one of the last acres and split it five ways. Mac agreed and a couple of days later, as the boys finished their own plots, they trickled in and started hilling the spuds in what would be their last acre.

As they worked, Vinny caught wind of a plan the other boys had of all getting in Mac's jalopy and pooling their resources to get to the next job, where they would split work again. They could live like that for the foreseeable future, they all agreed. Vinny was still insecure about his position in the group and didn't want to seem desperate, but he couldn't help himself.

"You guys think you'd want to take me with?" he asked after dinner while the boys discussed their future in front of him.

Vinny was hoping they would just say, "Sure, we thought you were coming anyway."

"Dang, wish I could, Vin," Mac said with a sneer that Vinny didn't really understand.

He thought he and Mac were friends at this point, being bunkmates and all. The jealousy had been boiling in Mac for a couple of weeks now, but Vinny was oblivious to it. He had assumed Mac, like the rest of the guys, was happy for him and just giving him shit when he noticed the attention Vinny got from Sarah.

"With all of our gear and the number of seats in my jalopy, we wouldn't have any room to breathe if we packed you in, too." Mac explained.

Vinny wanted to argue his case but could tell it was a dead issue and he would only look pathetic. He thought of returning to the life of a frugal tourist with Elmer and although he missed him, he shuddered. There was so much fear and shame tied up with that life that going back to it felt like a step backwards in his pursuit of independence. He needed another plan. The first thing that came to mind was running away with Sarah, getting a job in the city, and starting a family. They were lofty goals, but he settled on taking her out on a date first, if she would go with him.

Vinny waited for the perfect opportunity to ask her, but it was taking its time revealing itself. Any time he built up the nerve, someone or something interrupted. The acre he was working with his friends was shrinking by the hour. It was now or never.

Vinny stood in line for lunch shaking and sweating. Knowing what was coming made his stomach churn. He sidestepped down the line, now standing in front of Sarah, his face on fire.

"So, umm, Sarah…" he started like the village idiot. "When we, uhh finish working, are you going to be around at all after that?"

"Yes, Vinny, for a few days, anyway," she said sweetly. She added a smile that put Vinny's nerves at ease a bit.

The sound of his name on her lips made him vibrate even harder.

"Well, if you would want to, I don't know, maybe go to town and get something to eat or we could go see a talkie, or both."

Sarah smiled even harder. There was a look of shock on her face from the fact that he had actually managed to ask her.

"Of course, I will. I think all this will be done by Friday is what my dad says. If you want, we could just meet after dinner then." She took control of the conversation, needing it to speed up so she could finish serving the now impatient-looking working men.

Mac and his buddies were listening in and suddenly all, except mac, erupted with ooohs and aaahs, making Vinny's ears ring with giddiness. They were giving him shit, but it was in good fun. They were actually happy for him...most of them.

They all went back to work that afternoon, but Vinny was the only one floating. The other guys all agreed to go out drinking at a speakeasy someone had found during the season and were bugging Vinny to go with them. Mac egged him on, saying that now that he had a date, he was a man and the only way to celebrate was with a drink. There would be little to no work tomorrow, as they were nearing the last of their spuds and they would only have to wait for the other men to finish theirs before the owner paid them all off for the season.

Vinny hated booze but the peer pressure was irresistible. He just wanted to be one of the guys and if it took going out and drinking with them to make it happen, he would do it. After he got off work, he washed himself at the back of the bungalow and changed into a clean shirt and put his overshirt back on, wishing it was nicer.

The first thing he was going to do with his paycheck was go into town and buy himself some clothes for his date. Then a tinge of guilt struck him—and pay Elmer back, he reminded himself. It was almost an afterthought, but he still needed to do it. He also needed to say goodbye. For now, what was left of Elmer's money was going to buy drinks for him and his new friends, as most of them were strapped for cash and he wanted to show them a good time for taking him with and accepting him as a part of their group. He still held some hope for a spot in Mac's car to take him to the next job with them.

The ride into town in Mac's jalopy was exciting. Not only because he had only been in a car a few times, but because he was surrounded by a group of peers who accepted him. It was the first time he had felt really happy since leaving home. The car bounced into a parking spot full of potholes and cigarette butts, to which his buddies added their own. He was covered in the smell of smoke now, something he hadn't missed from Mom chain-smoking in her corner stinking up their house. It was a small price to pay for inclusion, he thought as they made their way to the bar.

Vinny bought the first shots and was offering to pay for the next as well when Mac told him to put his money away.

"This one's on me, bud." Mac got doubles for them all this time.

Three drinks in and Vinny was already regretting this decision. The looser his friends got and the more fog that collected in his brain, the less relaxed he felt. He found himself scanning the shoes of the patrons and newcomers to the bar. The feeling of being unable to handle an emergency outweighed any joy he was feeling from being drunk. At least he was surrounded by people he trusted; he thought as another round was pushed in front of him.

"Let's go, Vinny. You're falling behind," Mac started. The rest of the guys joined in ribbing.

Vinny poured it down his throat despite his better judgment. It was too late; the booze was calling the shots now. He vaguely remembered shoving another couple of drinks down his throat and then the night started to fragment.

There were bits of him singing along to some song he only knew because he was drunk. Mistakenly taking a piss in the ladies' room to the roaring laughter of his friends. There was a vague recollection of an altercation that he didn't even know if he was involved with. Then there was the worst part of all. Vinny started babbling. Just like Dad. Just like Elmer. He could feel himself spilling his guts about his family giving him the boot and crying like a baby, his now uncomfortable friends consoling him against their wishes in the closeness of the car. Vinny segued into the filthy bum trying to rape him and Elmer fighting him off. His friends were not laughing anymore.

Somehow, Vinny made it back to his bed that night. He woke up to puke shortly after and spent the rest of the night curled up on the back porch like an old dog. The night air felt good. He hardly noticed the rest of the men get up for work and eat breakfast around him. He never saw the look of disgust on Sarah's face as she tried to serve breakfast. In fact, it was nearly lunch before he was shaken awake.

"Vinny, you seen Carl?" it was Mac. Sober and clear-eyed looking slightly frazzled.

Vinny still felt drunk as he tried to stand up.

"Um, no. I've been, uhh, sleeping, I guess. Where is everyone?" He was thirstier than he could ever remember being.

"Shit," Mac said, looking around. "Well, we left him at the bar last night to bring you back and ain't no one seen him yet this morning. I guess we gotta run to town and look for him. You gonna ride with us?"

"Sure." Vinny blinked hard against the sun.

Vinny stood up and dusted himself off. He stopped at the water barrel on his way to the car and drank as much as he could. Now he really was drunk again. The water sloshed around in his belly stirring up the booze. He saw Sarah up the hill and gave her a wave. She turned and walked back to the house without returning it. Vinny figured she just hadn't seen him, and he hurried to jump into Mac's car, which was now pulling away. He tripped on his own feet and almost ended up underneath the tire, barely catching himself on the frame and pulling himself in.

The drive to town was quiet. Mac was racing like a madman and Vinny was regretting the little tidbits of last night that were resurfacing, and hoping the rest of the guys were drunk enough to forget about it. They pulled into the bar parking lot and Vinny saw a familiar sight. Around the side, police were gathered. Through the crowd, Vinny could see Carl. He was in a semi-fetal position with his pants halfway to his knees. He was dead. Vinny thought back to the wife-beating drunk he and Elmer had woken up to, what seemed like years ago.

"It's time to go," Vinny said.

Mac looked at his white face and without waiting for the police to notice them or someone in the crowd to connect the dots, they left.

The drive back was almost as quiet as the drive to town. It just took twice as long. They were both terrified but for very different reasons. Mac didn't want to go to jail. Vinny didn't want to be next.

"Guess that means there's room for you if you still want to go with us," Mac said coldly, shocking Vinny with his callousness.

"I mean, I didn't want it like this."

"Do you want to go or not?"

"Yeah," Vinny said, not wanting to be left behind. It felt gross.

"We're leaving tomorrow morning, assuming we get paid tonight."

"Ok."

They stayed quiet the rest of the drive back. Vinny was frantically considering his date tonight with Sarah. He wished he had a car so he could just drive her himself. As it was, they were looking at a walk back, in the dark. Vinny had felt safe here but after seeing his friend dead, he wasn't so sure it was safe anymore. Maybe it was just a bar fight gone wrong, he tried to convince himself. He knew better. It felt too familiar. The danger was close again.

Vinny waited around, hoping the paychecks would come soon. He needed to say goodbye to Elmer and wanted to pay him back. But the sun was threatening the horizon again and he was out of time. Elmer would understand him not paying him back, but he wouldn't understand not saying goodbye. He owed him that much at least. Vinny jumped out of the still moving car and started sprinting.

By the time he reached Elmer's camp, he was out of breath. He had sprinted the whole way, knowing he was racing the sun. Elmer was there; he seemed on edge, but he was sober. The fish smoker had been disassembled and the camp looked to be getting taken down. This was perfect—it looked like Elmer was getting tired of waiting and was going to leave anyway.

"How's it going, Vinny?" Elmer said.

"It's ok. How has it been down here?"

"Fine, just fine, and how's the spud business?" Elmer asked already knowing the job was done.

There was a shift in the older man's demeanor that told Vinny he knew more than he was letting on and the question was meant to feel out his intentions for the future.

Suddenly, Vinny felt guilty. He couldn't explain it. He knew he needed his space to grow, but saying goodbye to Elmer was feeling impossible. It would hurt his own feelings, but it might destroy Elmer's.

"Good. We are almost done. Maybe a couple more days," he lied, now unable to face Elmer. His eyes were locked on his own work boots for a change.

"Oh, really? Well, that's good I guess, close to time to move on, huh?" he asked Vinny, and Vinny knew the question was more bait used for feeling him out indirectly.

Vinny hesitated and the two exchanged awkward glances that said it all.

"Don't worry about Elmer. I can wait a while longer and whenever you're ready to go, I'll be here." The tone in his voice was saying goodbye even if neither of them could.

Vinny felt the tears stick his eyelashes together.

"Ok, well, I gotta get back, Elmer. It's gonna be getting dark. I just wanted to check in on you. I'll be back in a coupla days...thanks for everything."

Out of nowhere, Elmer took a step forward and surprised him a little. He put his arms around the younger man and hugged him. They both were crying but neither of them wanted the other to see.

"You better hurry back before it's dark on ya. Take care, Vinny." He let him go and turned back to his busy work with his bindle and satchel full of smoky fish.

"You too, Elmer, and watch out for the warning codes. I don't think it's safe here anymore." Vinny turned and ran away.

He wished he had more time to tell him of the stalker and Carl in town and the smooth-soled man. He wished there were time for a lot of things, but it was time to go. The darkness was growing all around him.

***

Elmer watched him disappear through the trees, remaining until Vinny was out of sight. Then, unceremoniously and with a tear in his eye, the old and abandoned man packed up his meager belongings and started to clean up his camp. He did his best, trying to leave the area looking like he had never been there at all.

***

On Vinny's sprint back to the farm, his heart was pierced a second time. A car was approaching and rather than cower in fear like a scared little boy, he tipped them a wave like a man. Only to realize he was waving to some little rich prick in fancy clothes driving with Sarah seated next to him. As they passed him, the rich kid flashed him a smile and a wave, oblivious to the fact he was driving Vinny's date around. Sarah, on the other hand, sneered at him. The look on her face told him everything he needed to know. They would never be going on a date.

Vinny was confused and dejected. He wanted to stop and find a hole to crawl into and die. But his paycheck and ride out of here were waiting. So, he cried and ran, checking over his shoulder every few seconds as the shades of black darkened around him. By the time he got to the farm, he was angry. He couldn't wait to get his money and get to the next town with his friends. Leave Sarah and Elmer behind and start fresh, no more shame or humiliation.

He was thinking of all the nasty things he would like to say to the little rich prick and Sarah. He wanted to make her feel as small as he felt, maybe call her a whore or a tease. Venom was coursing through his veins now.

His blood cooled when he saw Mac's car was gone from beside the bungalow. He was probably back in town answering questions about Carl, he hoped. Vinny walked into the back of the bungalow to see his bindle was the only bit of luggage left inside. Now confused, he started seeking out his friends. He asked around among the few people who were left, with not much help at all. Then he saw the foreman and ran up to him.

He looked pissed.

"Hey, Vin, I thought you were taking my daughter out, then she comes inside crying about you getting drunk and blowing her off. You really hurt her feelings, you know." The respect the man had grown to have for Vinny's hard work had disappeared.

"What, I'm not sure...." Vinny thought back to the night before and waking up on the porch. "Can I just get my pay?"

Now, Vinny felt bad for cursing Sarah in his mind. He was the one who messed up. She probably only went with the rich prick to piss him off. For the second time in his life, Vinny swore off alcohol. This time he meant it.

"Yeah, here it is." He pushed an envelope he'd taken from his pocket into Vinny's chest.

Unable to help himself, Vinny tore it open. After all that had happened, he was still excited to see the fruits of his labor.

It was short.

"Hey, I'm sorry about Sarah. I was a real jerk but...."

"I don't think she's gonna care, Vin," he said, cutting Vinny off.

"Oh, ok, but why is my pay short?"

"It ain't short, four acres at twenty-five per acre is one hundred bucks. That not what's in there?"

"Well, yeah, but I did that last acre with Mac and the guys. We were gonna split it," Vinny said.

"Uh, sorry to say, Vinny. I didn't know that. Mac took his pay on that last acre and he and the guys left about an hour ago. Said they were going to chase farm work farther north."

Vinny's heart sank. Not only had they cheated him, but they left him behind.

"Oh."

"Also, gotta clear out the bungalow tonight or you'll get chased out. They are cleaning it and getting it ready for the migrants who'll be up picking weeds starting tomorrow. Already got a whole crew from last season on their way up on a bus.

Gonna be here bright and early." He finished and turned his back on Vinny without another word or a thanks for the hard work.

The season was over, and Vinny was worse off. Sure, he had a pocket full of money but now he was on his own again. And it was getting dark.

Vinny only had one answer, inspired by Elmer. Catch a train and start over. Luckily for him, the train yard was close and if he ran fast enough, he might beat the dark.

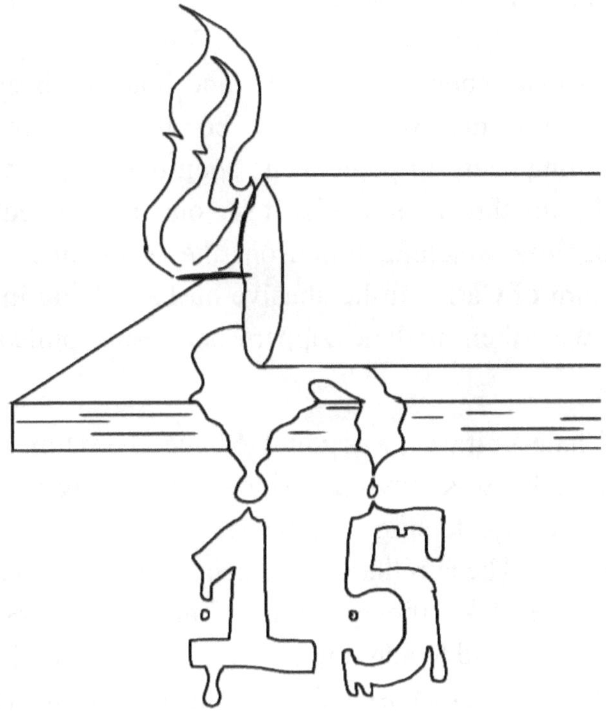

The dark was winning the race, and Vinny couldn't help himself as he turned off the main road that led to the train yard. Elmer's camp was on the way to the yard and if he was lucky, he would have his fire nice and bright. He wanted to leave town as an independent man, but with his unfortunate afternoon and his hangover, this was the path of least resistance.

The smell of fish had been haunting him since almost the start of his life on his own, but tonight he wanted nothing more than the safety the smell would offer in the dark. As he neared Elmer's camp, his stomach sank. There was no fire, no smoker, no fishy smell, no Elmer. He was gone.

More of Vinny's anger boiled inside now. For the third time today, he had been abandoned. Vinny let out a yell of frustration that echoed off the lake and bounced back at him, reminding him that he may not be alone. There was an overwhelming sense of panic as he spun in circles a few times looking for the threat. He couldn't see one, but he could feel it; something was watching him from the wood line. Thoughts came to him of Carl and the abusive husband lying in the fetal position with their undone zippers and pants pulled slightly down.

Whatever it was, was going to have a hard time removing his pants if he was running. Vinny sprinted away from the abandoned camp, feeling like he was leaving a part of him behind as well. The part that trusted people. The stupid old drunk had abandoned him after grifting off him for weeks now, or months. Vinny tried to add it up, but his anger clouded his brain. It didn't matter. He had used Vinny as his son for free meals and rides and places to sleep. Sure, Vinny was benefiting but that wasn't the point. Vinny was seething now. Fuck Sarah and her fancy lad with a car and suit, Vinny thought as his feet pounded the gravel even harder. Fuck Mac and the 'friends' who had bailed on him after teasing him with an invitation they knew he wanted more than anything. His ears were ringing now, and the field of view his eyes were providing had narrowed to slits focused on the light rapidly approaching from the yard.

Fuck them all.

The train yard was mostly quiet. There was some action at the other end a half-mile away, but nothing to concern himself with. Vinny half-assed his way through Elmer's routine, scanning the yard and looking for potential cars that looked easy to sneak into. His attention was solely focused on the bastards who had left him behind. There was a car ahead whose door was left halfway open by some careless bull. Vinny counted his blessings as he stood up to make a dash for the door. Just as his feet were ready to push off, he was snatched from behind.

He tried to let out a scream, but a muscular hand was against his lips stopping him. His mind rolled backward to the faceless bum monster trying to rape him. Then instinctually, he looked between his flailing legs, expecting to see the big horny toe of the bum. Instead, it was a pair of shoes he was all too familiar with. He relaxed against the fight and gave in.

Elmer let him go.

"Jesus, Vinny, you trying to get yourself killed?" He was whispering and motioning to the top of the train.

Vinny's burning hungover eyes were still filled with anger, but he strained in the blackness to see what Elmer was pointing at.

It was a bull, a beast of a man with a shotgun in his crossed arms. He was perched on top of the car with the open door, trying to minimize his silhouette but not being very successful. The open door was bait and Vinny had almost swallowed it hook, line and sinker. Once again, Elmer had saved him. He was thankful to have been spared a round of birdshot, but his anger was still right at the surface.

Elmer was out of breath, which was unusual, and Vinny got the impression that he was the person he had felt following him.

"We're gonna have to wait till he gets off that catwalk on top there and catch a car at the back." Elmer said hesitantly.

Vinny could see Elmer trying to measure his anger in the darkness, but it was radiating off him and there was no hiding it.

"I can hop one on the next set if you want, Vinny."

Vinny still had a soft spot for Elmer and the tone of his voice made him feel guilty. He wasn't really mad at Elmer; he hadn't left him even when he should have. It was everything else. However, articulating that while hungover and seething wasn't an option.

"No, it's not you, Elmer, it's just this life."

"I get it."

The train was hissing now, signaling that it was about to lurch into motion. The bull was headed forward, still on top of the cars, hopping from catwalk to catwalk toward the engine and giving them the opportunity to check the cars at the back.

"We better get a move on unless we want to sleep in the yard."

Vinny agreed with his feet. They both ran to the cars towards the back of the set. No luck, the doors were all buttoned up. Their only option was the bait car—the bull had never shut the door. They sprinted to the car, which was rolling away almost faster than Vinny could run. Elmer was putting him to shame. Vinny's thick, dry blood was pounding in his veins and his head was starting to spin. He wished he had drunk more water. Elmer had warned him about that after the salt dream, Vinny remembered. He was glad he found it as it was almost lost forever.

Elmer made it to the car and grabbed the frame of the open door. He flung his hand back to Vinny, who wanted to make it on his own and refused the hand at first, pumping his legs as hard as he could. It wasn't working.

"Come on, Vin," Elmer almost screamed in a panic.

Vinny could see the old man struggling against the speed as his feet started to tangle and drag gravel. His hand still outstretched, not wanting to leave him behind. Vinny had a vision of Elmer tripping and ending up under the wheels cut to bits for his attempt to get Vinny on the train.

Reluctantly, Vinny offered his hand. Elmer gripped his hand like an eagle on a salmon. Vinny could feel the small bones in his hand start to crack. Then with a strength that shocked him, Elmer tossed him forward into the door. The older man's feet lost traction with the gravel, and he was holding onto the doorframe, his feet were dragging and kicking up dust. Just as he was getting ready to let go of Vinny and the train, the younger man grabbed him and hoisted him up.

"Thanks, Vinny," he said with a thud. He seemed shocked that Vinny had dragged him along.

"Sure," Vinny said. "Thanks yourself."

There was an awkward feeling in the air between them. Vinny was ashamed that he had been caught in the act of abandoning Elmer without saying goodbye. Elmer was ashamed that he felt he pushed Vinny away by being too clingy.

In reality, Vinny was bursting with things he wanted to say. He wanted to thank him and apologize. Tell him thanks for the loan and pay back the eight bucks…with interest. Tell him about Mac and the other jerks that had bailed on him. And finally talk about the smooth-soled stalker and the code and what it all meant. Vinny knew they were related now and had to know what Elmer really thought, what he really knew about the code.

Elmer stymied those thoughts with a twist of the lid on his fresh bottle of whisky. Tomorrow then, Vinny thought, not wanting the opinion of a drunken Elmer.

The sound of air filling the cavity Elmer created in the emptying bottle echoed around the car. It was how Elmer coped. They didn't know where they were going to end up in this mystery car, or if it would be safe to drink once they got there, so Elmer had better get his fill now. He quietly drank half the bottle while Vinny boiled in silence. He pulled out some dry fish to munch on as he drank. The smell hit Vinny and his red puffy eyes responded by closing. It was a comforting smell and the familiar rocking of the train put him over the edge as he fell asleep.

The anger helped germinate the fears in his mind and he dreamt of faceless girls, rapey bums, and chortling sniffing smooth-soled stalkers. He was just about to scream himself awake when in his nightmares he heard a sobbing and babbling, familiar but miles away. He focused his thoughts and woke himself up gently.

It was Elmer sobbing in the darkness of the cargo bay muttering under his breath to persons unknown.

"It's my own damned fault. I knew the boys liked to play with 'em." He sobbed and pulled at his bottle. "Fuckin' Elmer, always putting chores off, getting by with the minimum," he cursed himself, "and the boys, oh my boys, burnt to crisps, along with you…" Another loud swig. "…Laura, I'm sorry I wasn't home and I'm sorry I left the candles burning on the table. I'm sorry I didn't run into the blaze myself... I was only gone for a minute, all for A GODDAMN BOTTLE." There was the unmistakable sound of breaking glass. "And I'm sorry for pushing Vinny away. He's a good boy just like ours and I fucked that up, too."

Vinny was at a loss. Elmer's aversion to open flames made sense now. He really did have a home and a family. A pit of guilt started burning in his stomach. For all his own selfish reasons, he had been pushing Elmer away. Elmer, the one person on Earth who cared if he lived or died and had saved him from more than one bleak ending. Vinny wanted to say something to Elmer. Tell him he loved him, and he wasn't going to leave him after all, something, anything to comfort him and stop the crying. But nothing came. Instead, he sat in silence like a coward until eventually, the snores of Elmer let him know it was ok to wait to talk to him about it in the morning.

He sat awake for a bit longer, hungover, eyes burning, but eventually, the repetition of the snoring and rocking of the train lulled him back to sleep. Another sleep filled with monsters in the dark.

Not long after Vinny was awakened by a screaming that was not his own for a change. His eyes flew open, and he looked in Elmer's direction, thinking the old man may be dreaming of his life going up in flames, reliving the nightmare of listening to his family burn to death. However, his snoring was still there, under the screaming.

Something was wrong with the screaming; it was mechanical sounding. Vinny thought of the sci-fi robot monsters from his books and shivered. The train lurched forward, and Vinny could feel its momentum bleed into the brakes. They were slowing rapidly.

"Elmer, wake up, we got trouble." Vinny crawled with his hands outstretched, feeling his way to Elmer. "Elmer, get up."

"WHAT?" Elmer yelled, clearly not impressed.

"Something's wrong with the train."

They were crawling now toward the door. They both pushed on it and moonlight flooded the bay. The train wasn't going much faster than they were on their hands and knees. As if to make a point, it ground to a halt. The mechanical screaming reached a fever pitch but stopped in tandem.

Both men rolled off the train half-asleep, mostly drunk or hungover, and confused. They could hear the engineer yelling, doling out verbal abuse to everyone and anything in his path. From what they could gather, this train wasn't going anywhere anytime soon.

Luckily, they were on the outskirts of some town and not in the middle of the prairie, miles from anywhere. Elmer tried to stumble along with Vinny as he walked ahead to the lights in the streets. Neither of them wanted to be out in the dark in an unknown town with unknown threats. After they reached town, it was clear Elmer was going to need help. Vinny let him hold his shoulder and steadied him by his waist as they looked for a place to tuck in.

Vinny scanned every tree, post, or anything that could be used as a makeshift canvas. Finally, after dragging Elmer through most of the small town, he found what he was looking for. It was a bed with an arrow pointing forward with ½ beside it.

"Ok, Elmer, half a mile and we got us a bed, it looks like."

"Sounds right as rain, Vinny." He was now in the giddy stage of drunk, it seemed.

They stumbled along for a few blocks then out of nowhere, Elmer's talon-like fingers dug into his shoulder, causing Vinny to shake him off. The old man fell to his ass.

"Jesus, Elmer, what the fuck are you doing?" Vinny was rubbing his shoulder.

Then he caught a look at Elmer's face, which was twisted with fear. He was pointing at something, and his finger was shaking in the streetlight.

"Shit." Vinny said.

The tree ahead of them had a bald spot on its trunk, a makeshift canvas. Something was carved in its center. A bottle with two X's.

"Oh my God, Vinny. What have I done?" Elmer's face was white with fear. He still hadn't stood up.

"Nothing, Elmer, we just gotta get off the street to the safe place to sleep. It's gotta be close now."

Vinny wrestled with the drunken old man and got him to his feet. Managing as fast of a pace as they possibly could, they reached what had to be the safe spot to sleep. It was an open-bay barn. It wasn't lit but it was safer than the streets. They hurried inside. He could feel Elmer shaking as he helped him to a corner.

"I'm sorry, Vinny. I should have been more careful." He seemed like he was slurring less. Maybe his uncanny ability to sober up in emergencies would come in handy again, Vinny thought, and relaxed a little bit into the soft dry hay beside Elmer.

"It's fine. I'm gonna stand guard for a bit, but we might have to take turns." Vinny was exuding way more confidence than he felt.

Maybe it was his turn to take care of Elmer and prove he really was a man now. He could do it; his hand clutched the Dunhill in his pocket, and it steeled his nerves.

"Well, we can both sit up for a while. I don't feel much like sleeping anyway, to be honest." His voice was not confident but drunk, shaky...scared.

"Ok." Vinny tried to think of something to talk about, but nothing came. It was easier to listen. Nothing came from Elmer, either. So, they sat in silence, both intent on the possibly imagined threat in the night.

***

After sitting in silence for a while, waiting for Vinny to give him an opening, Elmer said quietly, "Thanks for pulling me onto the train, Vinny. You didn't have to."

Vinny had no response. He was already asleep. That was ok, Elmer thought. He didn't mind, he would stay awake and

184

protect him despite the booze still making the barn spin. He loved him and the boy needed his sleep.

...sniff...sniff...SNIFFFFF

***

The hay was soft and warm, and it mixed with the sunlight spilling through the bay doors. Vinny's bones felt hot, so he turned his body to the cool side to let it warm up as well. As he rolled over, he saw that Elmer had sat up all night pulling guard duty. In fact, he was still sitting upright in the same position Vinny had placed him in last night. Then he blinked the sleep out of his eyes and looked again.

"AAAAAAHHHHHHH!"

The screaming started just after the blinking stopped. Elmer was still sitting up, his eyes wide and bulging, his hands reaching toward Vinny, his lips screaming in silence. He wasn't blinking...or breathing. The thick fabric that he called pants was down around his ankles, exposing his flaccid cock, but Vinny's eyes landed on the gaping wound on his inner thigh. Elmer's blood painted the hay between his legs like the blood on the grass the night of the fire under the bramble and his encounter with smooth-soles. Still screaming, Vinny moved his eyes up to Elmer's no longer rising chest. His shirt had been torn away, revealing a fresh canvas. In the center of the pale white background was an intricate carving torn into Elmer's flesh. The symbol was of a pair of lips being shushed by a fist and one extended finger. Even in his panic, Vinny recalled the mysterious symbol the paper had mentioned in the death of the missionary; nothing was lost. The pieces were falling into place amid his panic.

A new warning code had revealed itself in the carving on Elmer's chest, and the message was clear. Vinny had better shut his mouth.

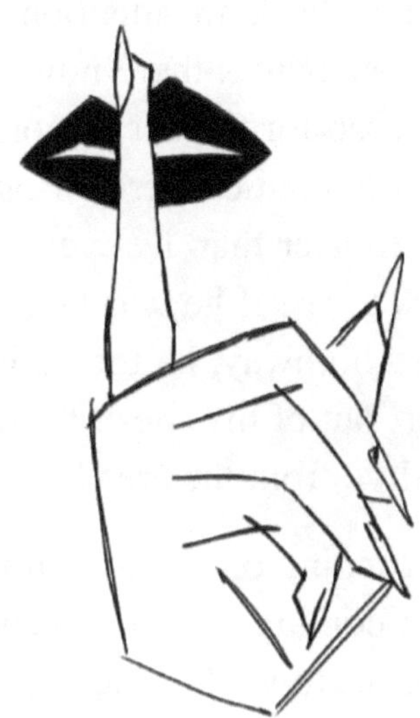

There was no time to process anything. By the time Vinny's screams faded, he could hear another that had been masked by his own. Vinny turned his head and saw a young boy standing in the bay pointing at him. The boy's screams quickly changed into pleads for his father. Who, by the sounds of the running on gravel, wasn't far behind.

It was time to go.

On instinct, Vinny grabbed his bindle and Elmer's as well. He had been carrying it for so long for him that it was only natural to swing them both over his shoulder. He was still trying to figure out if this was a dream. It had to be, but the air burning his lungs told him it was real. He was breathing so hard that when he sprang to his feet, the blood went right to his head, and he swooned.

"He's dead! That guy killed him and took his stuff," the kid yelled accusingly.

Vinny snapped back to attention and shook the sleep from his eyes. The father was there now, looking at the scene, and at Vinny. Vinny ran for the back door; certain the man was right on his heels. Both bindles were swinging like flags behind him, and he sprinted faster than he ever had before. There was no time to look back to see if he was being chased. By the time he reached the paved highway, he forced himself to slow, so he didn't blow his heart out of his chest. As he slowed to a jog, he heard sirens come alive from the area he had just ran from.

Vinny kept running on the road for a bit, but before too long he heard sirens coming from up ahead of him, now in the opposite direction of the town. For the first time, he looked back. There was no one following him and no cars coming down the road from that way. He was shocked they were making such a fuss over Elmer—not that he didn't deserve it, but he thought of the abusive father and Carl, who both seemed to be forgotten as soon as they were loaded on the paddy wagon. He felt bad for hoping they would just forget about Elmer, but his own safety surpassed his emotional connection to him.

The sirens were racing toward him, so he decided to return to old behaviors and hide in the ditch until they passed. As the car got closer, he recognized it as a state trooper, not a local sheriff's deputy. All the warnings people were hearing, and the number of dead homeless people must be raising the attention of higher powers. The realization hit him that he would be a nice, tidy way to explain at least some of the deaths. Running from Elmer and taking the bindle was a mistake, but there was no way to explain it away now. He was at the bottom of society and justice didn't favor that.

As the staties passed him, he could have sworn the man in the passenger seat turned his head and made eye contact with him. All his guilt welled up and chased him into the tree line. He ran for what felt like hours into the woods. Vinny's legs were turning rubbery, so he slowed to a shuffle. The new warning code was still burned into his mind's eye and every time he blinked, he saw Elmer's screaming face and the carving of the lips being shushed. Eventually, Vinny was forced to stop walking, he had no idea what time it was, but he was deep in the woods. The spit in his mouth was thick and foamy—he had been hoping for a river to stop at but hadn't been that fortunate.

Vinny pulled his bleach bottle out and took a drink. The smell reminded him of both Dad and Elmer now. Tears threatened him for the first time that day, but he managed to put them aside in favor of fear. The darkness was growing quickly now. There was no going back the way he had come, even if he wanted to; he realized as he scanned his surroundings, he knew he was well and truly lost. The thought of being so lost was almost comforting. If he didn't know where he was, whatever had killed Elmer couldn't possibly know either, or the staties for that matter. Vinny's hand reached into his pocket for the comfort the Dunhill still offered.

Holding the cool silver in his hand made him want to go home. If he told Mom and Dad what had happened in the past few months, they would have to let him come home…maybe. He wondered if he would even be able to find his way home from wherever this was. He knew the city and state, but there was no way without Elmer he could find his way back on the random trains and lucky rides. If he could find his way back, it would take months maybe, and he would just be bounding from town to town facing the dangers they all held alone. There was no going back the way he had come. That part of his life was over. He had to move forward on his own. The tears started now.

He wasn't sleeping in the dark.

Quickly, he gathered as much wood as he could, then used Dad's Dunhill to get it going. He didn't have to worry about scaring Elmer with an open flame, so he let it roar. At first, he was worried that it would alert the staties to his location, but the growing darkness convinced him to toss another log on the fire. He was still thirsty but only had a little water left, so he let his throat burn.

The fire offered some security, and he let his mind wander to his exploits with Elmer. He always hated his drinking, and it pissed him off now thinking back. Elmer knew better but chose the bottle over him just, like Dad always had. Vinny's growing anger was starting to send ripples out in all directions, changing his past memories and altering future ones. The ripples were slowly eroding the good memories of home so that all that remained was the bad. Maybe that was the way it was for everything, Vinny thought as he stewed by the fire for the rest of the night. He remembered hateful memories of his fat mom and his cowardly dad, knowing he was the furthest thing from their minds tonight as Mom ate and smoked in her corner and Dad drank and got high in his. Elmer's made some appearances during the night as well, but most of them were regretful and not hateful, not yet, the ripples hadn't finished eroding away the good bits.

After the day full of fear and hate and regret, he drifted off to sleep so close to the fire his forehead would hurt like a sunburn for days. It was a restless sleep that didn't last long. He dreamed of the rapey bum with the faceless head of the girl. The laughing, smooth-soled shoe man was there too, stalking and laughing at him though this time he was accompanied by an all-too-familiar sniffing sound. There was someone else there tonight, though—it was Elmer. Walking toward him in the dark alley, his shirt ripped open and his pants missing completely. Blood was trickling down the carving in his chest to join the flow of blood from his inner thigh. Vinny looked harder in the moonlight and Elmer's screaming face was being shooshed by a pale finger he was holding up.

Vinny was tired of waking up screaming.

He threw two more logs onto his still roaring fire and swept his head around, scanning the blackness around him. There was a touch of grey to what must be the east. It wasn't nearly bright enough to give him comfort yet and wouldn't be for at least an hour. The night was hot, but he still huddled close to the flames, sweating out what little liquid was left in his body. The rest of the night Vinny spent listening for footsteps and sniffing, or Elmer making that shooshing noise.

That day was lost in sleeping and dreaming and crying. Hating was a part of it as well, not at one person in particular now that he was cooling off, but at life in general. He understood life wasn't fair, but this life seemed particularly cruel and unfair. Pity was a part of it now too, and it was growing.

The night was lost to fear and pity and hate and more nightmares, real or imagined. It was hard to tell anymore. Vinny stood guard when he could but like usual, fell asleep. He couldn't take waking himself up screaming again, so, he just stayed awake again, through the night.

He finally snapped out of his downward spiral on the third day...or was it the fourth? It didn't matter. What did matter was that Vinny was dying of thirst. He remembered Elmer digging gypsy wells a few times next to stagnant water to let the ground filter it a bit and make it more palatable. The ground around him was damp, and not completely from tears, so he thought there was hope in digging a shallow well and having it slowly fill up from the surrounding soil. He dug until there was a two-foot-deep hole and plenty of bloody knuckles. He knew it would take time to fill up if it was going to, but he wasn't sure if he could wait.

Elmer's bindle was staring at him from next to the fire. He still hadn't opened it, but he knew there was a bottle of water in there and the temptation was too much. As respectfully as he could, he untied the bindle from the now well-worn walking stick, the one Elmer had to replace after saving him from being raped. He started to cry and stopped himself, it never helped, it only made him dehydrate faster. He looked into the now open bindle and fished out the familiar water bottle. As he did, he peeked inside and saw a picture of a family. He strained his eyes and was shocked. It was clean-shaven Elmer with two boys on his knees and an absolute knockout sitting next to him. Elmer was smiling and young, but even more surprising was his clean-shaven face and nice suit. The family looked happier than Vinny's own had ever even pretended to be. It made Vinny's heart hurt for the misery Elmer must have felt every time he looked at the photo.

He snapped the bindle closed and thought for a second. It was all he had left of Elmer, and who knew what the old man had squirreled away in the bottom of the pack? But without a second thought he tossed the bindle into the fire, followed by

Elmer's walking stick. In some way it felt good like he was sending Elmer to the flames to be with his family, who had sadly met the same end. It wasn't perfect but it was all the closure he figured he would ever get. He wondered if Elmer was cremated or buried in a potter's field. It didn't matter—nothing would be lost. Not by Vinny.

He drank from Elmer's bottle, which had the faint taste of whisky left behind from backwash. It turned his stomach. But he couldn't waste the liquids, so he held it down. It seemed his body hated booze as much as he did. Good, he thought. He was never going to drink again for any reason.

By the end of that day, he was starving. Elmer's satchel of fish had survived the cremation next to him on the rock. He dug through and picked out a nice, dry piece. Part of him expected to hate it but he didn't. It actually tasted good, and he would remember to replenish the satchel with salt and pepper and fish in the future if he needed to. While he was eating, he remembered the salt dream with the sour stomach and made sure to finish off Elmer's bottle of water to ward it off. Nothing was lost.

His gypsy well never filled but that didn't seem to matter today as the skies opened up and rained on him. He was able to catch some drips in his bottles and quench his thirst, but not nearly enough to rehydrate him. It did, however, put out his fire right as the sun was setting.

He screamed at it to no avail. He tried adding more wet wood, which didn't help. He tried blowing on it, which just stirred the mud. It was gone. Now he was wet and plunged into blackness. Panic was setting in just as he remembered the oily cover for his bindle. He unwrapped it and put it over his head like an umbrella. Also, he put his dry pack in his lap to try to keep it that way. It reminded him of the night spent like this with Elmer and despite everything, he laughed to himself. There wasn't much he could do but be miserable and wet. Being afraid never seemed to help any more than crying did.

Then Vinny looked into the blackness of the night and saw hope.

Somehow, that night of fear and darkness steeled Vinny's nerves, and when it cleared the next morning, so did his head. He couldn't live being scared anymore. If something was going to happen, he couldn't stop it. All he could do was try to move on and protect himself. To always be prepared like Elmer was when he was sober. The warning on Elmer's chest flashed in his mind. Move on, and keep his mouth shut about the codes, he reminded himself.

The hundred bucks suddenly felt hot in his pocket. The hope he saw in the darkness came to the forefront of his mind, and he looked at the arrows he had made out of sticks in the darkness. They pointed to a glow that had revealed itself in the pitch black of the storm. If his fire hadn't gone out, he never would have seen it and may have stayed lost and thirsty in the woods. It was the unmistakable glow of a town bouncing off the rain clouds on the horizon. Now in the brightness of a new day the sticks now pointed the way. Sometimes, maybe there was more hope in darkness than Vinny thought possible. He finished off the last of Elmer's fish and put the empty satchel in his bindle. He would refill it when he got the chance.

He also took the time to get his pocketknife out of his bindle to keep in his pocket from now on. He didn't care what Elmer had said about police not liking finding a knife in your pocket. There was no way he would walk into a strange town unarmed ever again, and the police would likely not care about a knife when bringing in a mass murderer. He also unbuttoned his pants and stashed his money and Dunhill in his secret pocket. It didn't matter where he ended up; it seemed that threats were endless and everywhere. Losing Dad's lighter might feel like losing an anchor in a storm. He still needed it. Somehow, it still felt like home and comfort.

With one last look at Elmer's final resting place in the fire, he said goodbye and followed the stick arrow to the glow on the horizon. He knew he needed answers that no one else was going to find, but first he needed to protect himself.

Vinny hoped the town on the horizon had a gun store.

The walk out of the woods took much longer than he had anticipated. The glow had felt so close last night. Vinny started to worry that he might have to spend another night alone in the dark trying to get to it. There was a bit of relief when he came across a stream. It was muddy from the rain stirring everything up, but it tasted great. He filled his bottle and put it back, noting how much lighter his load felt without Elmer's bindle. He missed him, but not the extra weight.

Finally, an hour or so later, he could hear the sounds of a town up ahead. His anxiety spiked and he started to worry that there would be cops patrolling around looking for him, or that word had spread about him to regular folks. He needed to keep a low profile and stick to the back roads. Elmer would have known where to go and if they had a train or if they had to catch a truck. He always knew. Suddenly, the loss of the extra weight didn't feel as important. There was a decided advantage to being alone, though. No matter what he chose to do right or wrong, it would be his choice. There was a sense of freedom that came with that.

He chose to sneak around like a rat and avoid people at all costs. His desire for a pistol was outweighed by his sense of self-preservation. Before anything else, he needed to put some distance between him and the barn where Elmer died. He scanned anything that seemed like it could be used as a canvas on his way through the back alleys. Nothing. He wormed his way through town, trying to cover as much ground as possible while staying hidden.

The sun was past setting and only a faint grey was hovering on the horizon. There were streetlights, thankfully, and not many people that he could see from his dark corners. A group of young people had come out of a bar laughing and happy. For a minute, Vinny thought it was Mac and the guys from the fields, it wasn't. But that started him wondering where he would be if they had waited for him that day. It pissed him off thinking about them working the fields during the day in some new town, drinking at night, chasing girls at dance halls, everything guys their age should be doing. Not worrying if they were being hunted by the police and whatever got Elmer. He wondered if Elmer would still be alive if he had just left without him, if he hadn't pulled him on the train that night. The better question was what if Elmer could have just stayed sober. Vinny's anger was manifesting more and more. Involving itself in memories it had no business in. But Vinny knew at least part of the anger was right. Elmer had only been getting worse with the bottle.

There was no more time for feeling sorry for himself or Elmer. He could hear the familiar sounds of a hissing train yard. He nearly broke his cover and sprinted down the main street to the awaiting cars. But he stopped himself and scurried back to the alleys, taking the long way around. By the time he got to the yard, he could hear the brakes let loose and the wheels start to gain momentum. He had time. He pumped his legs and briefly thought about turning to see if Elmer was gaining on him, but he stopped himself and refocused. He was nearly to the train when a blinding light from ahead caught him.

It was someone, probably the bull (likely armed), shining a light from the engine. It was either a warning or someone lighting up their target for a better shot. Vinny didn't stick around to find out, but instead skidded to a stop behind a stack of railroad ties. He waited for shouting or gunshots but neither came.

There would be other trains and other cars. Vinny just had to be patient like Elmer. Luckily, the yard was well-lit. Unluckily, it seemed busy with bums. He hadn't taken the time to take stock of his surroundings while trying to catch the train, but now he was noticing them all coming out of the darkness. He scanned every pair of shoes he could. So far, just tattered leather remnants of shoes. His guard was up but there seemed to be safety in numbers, so he followed the slowly growing crowd. They knew something, it was obvious, but he didn't feel like talking so he waited and watched.

It didn't take long for their plan to reveal itself as a cargo train pulled in. There were three cars at the back that had the bays open on both sides. It was rare to see cars so empty, but the crowd of bums didn't seem surprised as they piled on, trying to balance their numbers as they did. Vinny quickly picked a car at random and pulled himself up. The first thing he saw was a bottle of booze and his heart sank. He might be in for a long ride. Part of him wanted to jump off and move to the next car, but it was probably the same story, so he tried to make himself comfortable in a corner.

Before the train even started moving, the babbling and arguing started. A few of the guys had given Vinny the once over, so he gripped his knife in his pocket and pretended to sleep. He was terrified. Any one of them could have been a twin brother to the guy who tried to have his way with him, whom Elmer had saved him from. Vinny's face got hot in the dark. The shame made him feel even more vulnerable. He had told himself that he would have started fighting back at any second if Elmer hadn't shown up and if it ever happened again, he would definitely fight back. Now, though, he wondered if he could. He wished the knife were a pistol. Once he got his hands on one, he wouldn't have to feel like this again.

Old Vinny would have been warning these drunks about the codes and telling them not to drink. But even if Elmer wasn't shushing him every time he closed his eyes he wouldn't have warned these people. They were everything people said was wrong with bums, and why Elmer and he were frugal tourists. In the future, he would never get on a train with so much filth. The knife in his hands started carving the side of the train. If he couldn't say anything to warn people, maybe he could show them.

He finished his masterpiece just as the train was rolling into its next stop. He dusted away the finer bits of wood that clung to the edges of the symbols, and he blew on it. It was a collection of all the codes he had learned—good, bad, and terrifying. He included a brief description with each symbol, making it clear enough even for a toddler. Nothing had been lost.

There were twenty of them now. There were likely many more, but he would add to it as he learned them and display them wherever he could. It would be his way of making sure Elmer wasn't forgotten.

He got off the train with the rest of the crowd but didn't follow them. He had no interest in what they were doing. He was looking for a gun store or hitting the road to somewhere that had one.

***

Had Vinny lingered much longer in the car, he might have seen the bull from the train make his rounds to the empty cars to ensure the bums hadn't left anything behind. Making sure the night crew would be able to load the very precious cargo. This train was kept empty on this run specifically for that reason, at a great expense to the owner. An expense the community would pay without their knowledge. The bull stopped at Vinny's corner of the cargo car and noticed the freshly carved symbols. He knelt to get a good look at it. If Vinny had stayed, he would have seen the smile on his face as he read the code. If Vinny had stayed, he would have seen his shoes, much too fancy for a trainyard bull's.

***

Vinny hadn't lingered, but instead had made his way to town. The sun was about to come up and he figured he would be just in time for businesses to be opening. He was right. The smell of pancakes and bacon greeted him on Main Street, and he couldn't resist. He dug around in his pants behind a shop and got out two twenty-dollar bills. It should be plenty for breakfast and a gun. Maybe some candy.

200

He ate alone. There were plenty of looks from the people eating and behind the counter, but after Vinny flashed his money, it was fine, and they brought him what he wanted. It was a pile of food: eggs, bacon, toast, pancakes, coffee, soda and a slice of apple pie. The taste was unmatched. He couldn't remember food ever tasting so good. By the time his plates were shining white, he was full, but barely. He asked the waitress about a gun store, and she told him not here, but he might have some luck down the road. He could feel the town telling him to move on, so he did.

There was another train leaving the yard he had left less than two hours ago, and he caught it. The car was completely empty, and the bull was missing from the yard which struck Vinny as odd but he welcomed the solitude and the easy ride. He regretted it a couple of hours later when the train made its next stop. It seemed an unusually short haul, maybe a half-hour or less.

This yard was covered in a fog that felt like it should have burned off by now, but the overcast sky was hanging around for too long. Vinny could hear movement. It sounded like two or three guys arguing and getting on the train, which immediately let the brakes loose and started chugging forward. There was no cargo loaded, and nobody got out of any of the passenger cars— just Vinny sneaking off the back. Now he was alone in the foggy train yard with a growing sense of unease.

He walked to where he hoped the main street was, hoping to find it bustling.

It wasn't.

There were no lights on in any of the shop windows despite the dreary morning, which should require it. There was no commotion of life going about as usual. Just an empty hollow feeling in the air with the mist. He scanned around, looking for anything moving, and his eyes landed on some graffiti. It looked freshly painted on a pristine white fence in barn red paint. Nothing like the secretive code he was accustomed to.

"BEWARE THE MOON KING"

It sent chills through Vinny's blood and his hair stood on end. Who was the Moon King? It was much less cryptic than the code the bums had been using, but much more effective. Now his eyes darted around, looking for the Moon King. What was he looking for? His imagination wandered as his fear grew. Then it was broken by a sound in the fog up ahead. A motor was running. This eased his nerves for a moment. At least there was someone else in this town. His pace quickened. Then he saw something that scared him so badly, he fell on his ass.

He finally found a bit of the hobo code. But it was the one that was the scariest to him, the one he understood the least but drew the most visceral reaction. It was the forward-leaning h... run was what it meant. And run was what Vinny did.

He ran down the road to the sound of life in the car motor. Only to find the car parked sideways in the street with no occupant. As Vinny made his way closer to the car, he wished he knew how to drive, because he would take it right now, consequences be damned. He thought he might be able to figure it out and got even closer. The passenger window was covered in blood and the beige seats were painted in it. Vinny backpedaled in terror and almost lost his footing.

He gathered himself and ran at full speed down the middle of the road. No one stopped him, No one was left. His eyes spun nervously in their sockets, seeking whatever threat may present itself. The marquee in front of the theater had seemingly joined in to warn the rest of the town as it read:

"BEWARE: THE MOON KING IS REAL"

Vinny was flying now. He had no interest in solving this mystery. He didn't want answers. He just needed to get the hell out of this town. The muscles in his right hand were cramping from gripping his knife so hard. For a moment, Vinny thought he heard a sniffing. It was subtle, and he was moving too fast to get a better listen. He wanted to look back but lacked the nerve.

By the time he reached the outskirts of the Moon King's kingdom, his lungs were burning. He felt like if he kept running, he would pass out and be even more vulnerable. So, he slowed his pace to a jog but kept it up until he hit a junction in the highway. There he had a bit of luck. A truck was coming from the direction he had just run from. At first, he was scared when the truck slowed next to him. The man asked if he needed a ride. Vinny only stared at him, wondering if he was a threat. The trucker told him he had just driven through a town that didn't feel quite right, and it was probably not a good idea to be walking alone.

Vinny hesitated and stuffed his hand back into his pocket with his knife. Then he got a look at the driver's shoes, just regular work boots. He wasn't sure it was a true test of whether someone was a threat, but at least the boots weren't out of place. He climbed in and said thanks but stayed silent the rest of the ride. The driver didn't seem to mind as he sang along with some country tunes on the radio.

Eventually, they pulled into a busy little town. The hum of life felt like a relief. He thanked the driver and offered him two bucks for the ride. He declined and told Vinny to take care of himself.

Vinny was going to take care of himself right now. He marched downtown with a purpose. Surely this town would have the ability to fill his desire. He wasn't disappointed. The neon glow of the pistol-shaped sign led the way.

Once he was inside, he felt slightly overwhelmed. The man behind the counter was rattling off numbers and digits and Vinny had no idea what they meant. He had shot Dad's varmint gun a few times, but bullets were expensive, and he had other things to spend his money on, like laudanum. The man asked about his experience level, about which Vinny lied. He asked what he was looking for and Vinny said something to protect himself with. When the man asked him from what, Vinny surprised himself.

"The Moon King." He felt stupid and quickly added, "Or just guys trying to hurt me."

The gun store owner suddenly got serious.

"You got someone trying to hurt you, boy, just go to the police. Killin' him ain't gonna do nothing but get you in even worse trouble than you might be in. You need me to call 'em for you?" he asked, seemingly genuinely concerned.

"No, mister. I just need a gun." Vinny was starting to get mad. He pulled the money from his pocket and slammed it on the counter. "What can I get for this?"

"Ok, ok, calm down. Let's see here." He thumbed through the bills eagerly. "Well, anything from here, really." And he motioned to the counter full of pistols. "If you're lookin' to stop somebody from hurting you and you don't want him to get up, I suggest this." He pulled up the pistol that probably came the closest to the amount of cash he laid on the counter.

Vinny didn't care how much it cost. Just looking at it felt safe.

The owner could sense his fondness for it.

"Pick her up and get a feel for it." He was grinning and pushed the gun into Vinny's hands. "You buy that, and I'll even throw in a coupla boxes of ammunition."

The cold steel felt cool in his hands. The size of the bore made him feel dangerous, like a man, not a victim. He never wanted to let it go.

"What you got there is a 1911 Colt model ACP .45 caliber. Guarantee you if you put a round or two from that into someone tryin' to hurt you, hurting you will be their last thoughts." He giggled at himself. "Now, I'm not advising you...."

"I'll take it," Vinny cut him off. He pushed the pile of money across the counter, not bothering to count it (the gun store owner didn't, either).

Vinny walked away from the gun store back to being as heavy as he was with Elmer's bindle. The extra weight he carried now was his own version of courage. Maybe it would offer the same safety Elmer did.

This town felt less dangerous already. The fear of the police recognizing him from a description that a farm boy gave them was fading. He scanned for codes and saw there was booze available to buy somewhere, soup kitchens that served anyone, places to sleep, and even part-time work. No warning codes, however. Maybe he would settle here for a bit. The town seemed friendly enough to frugal tourists. Vinny was tired of running scared and the vitality of the town was comforting.

Something Elmer had told him was if you had some money to spread around in a town you were going to stay awhile in, do it. Nothing was lost. Elmer said the money bought goodwill as well as whatever it was paying for. So, Vinny got a bite to eat at a diner and stopped and got some sweets, which he ate in one sitting under a tree at the park. While he worked on the jawbreakers, his idle hands worked a fresh piece of canvas, recreating the collection of codes he had learned. He hesitated when he got to the hushed lips, feeling like it might be a bad idea. Elmer flashed in his memory, shushing him as well. Vinny finished the series anyway, feeling bold with the cold steel now pressed against his hip.

***

The fresh symbols carved into the trunk of the tree didn't go unnoticed.

206

The local soup kitchens were well-funded and with the number of symbols telling people illegal hooch was available, it was obvious the moonshiners and their mobsters had organized the crime in this area. Aside from the number of drunken bums stumbling and babbling around town, it was to Vinny's benefit. It almost seemed like the community was catering to the homeless people. The free food was plentiful as well as delicious, places to sleep were numerous if not overcrowded, and the law seemed to turn a blind eye to the goings-on.

The added weight of the pistol and ammunition gave him a confidence he hadn't felt while wandering on his own before. He remembered the lie he had told about his experience with guns. It would behoove him to get some practice, he thought, looking back on the conversation with the gun store owner. So, after a quick bite to eat at the same café (with the same cute older waitress), he wanted to head into the woods and shoot some cans.

After breakfast and what he thought was some light flirting from the waitress (Vinny was glad he had used the last of his soap the day before), Vinny wanted to grab some supplies and something for lunch just in case he was out in the woods later than lunch. While in a general store gathering the supplies to refill his bindle, he noticed a locally made pemmican with berries. It stored well like the fish, but it tasted so much better, and he bought a whole block.

There was an aisle dedicated to shoes also. Vinny walked past the fancy shoes with smooth soles, giving them a wide berth. The feeling they gave him inspired his next purchase. He grabbed the fastest-looking pair of shoes, black canvas Keds with rubber soles and white laces. They were made for running and something told him he wasn't done with that yet.

Now resupplied and armed with running shoes and a pistol, Vinny made his way out to the woods for some target practice, feeling tough. He passed a bottle dump and grabbed a few cans to be used as pretend stalkers. He had a limited knowledge of guns but he was intuitive and he quickly figured out the workings of the well-designed pistol. Getting the magazine out was the most difficult part. He didn't realize for a few minutes that there was a release button. After, he filled it with as many bullets as his scrawny fingers could manage to stuff into it (he realized it probably held more than five bullets, but that was plenty if the gun shop owner was right about its power).

He pulled the slide back and chambered a round. It was loaded, the hammer was already cocked, and Vinny understood that meant danger. With more than a little hesitation, he held it up and aimed at the stalker can down in front of the hill. He lined up the sights and pulled the trigger.

BAM

The pistol snapped out of his hands, leaving his wrist screaming in pain. It hit the dirt and so did Vinny, thinking it might go off again. He got back to his feet and looked around the woods, praying for privacy. No one was there. His hands dusted the dirt off his clothes, then grabbed the pistol from the dirt tentatively. It was still cocked, he noticed, and he pointed it away from his feet.

The can downrange was missing so Vinny went to get a better look. The can was destroyed. There was a finger-sized hole in the front and the back half of the can was all but missing. He was a good shot. This reinforced the notion that he needed to get more confidence. So, he spent the rest of the day burning up a box and a half of ammunition. There was always more at the shop, and he still had a fair amount of money. By the time he decided to be done for the day, his confidence with the pistol had grown. His fingers were blistered from reloading, but he felt good about it. He had also learned how to de-cock the hammer so he could keep it loaded while he carried it without fearing it would blow off his manhood.

He took a late lunch before leaving the woods, snacking on the pemmican, which was so much better than the fish, he vowed to never eat it again. It made him think of Elmer, who Vinny thought would be proud of him for learning to protect himself. The pemmican swallowed harder after that. A few pieces of candy later, and Vinny was back in good spirits. The Dunhill in his pocket needed some love from the months of use now. The store sold a lighter rebuild kit, which Vinny had bought. Now he took his time and removed all the lighter's guts, replacing the wick and the batting, along with adding a new flint and some fuel from the can that came with it. He struck the lighter and the flame rose brighter than it had in some time. It reminded him simultaneously of Dad and Elmer. It felt good. He tucked it back into his secret pocket with his money and made his way back to town. The sun was starting to set.

By the time he made it back, it was dusk. The town was well-lit and still busy. Before Main Street, Vinny saw a younger guy stopping the people ahead of him. As he approached, Vinny realized he was next.

"Hey, guy, what do you know?" the strange but friendly man asked.

Vinny was about to reply when he continued.

"You need a bottle? Two bucks, your choice of flavors."

"Nah, no thanks," Vinny said as politely as he could through his disgust for the booze.

"You sure...well, I've got other things as well, if you know what I mean." He held out his forearm and slapped his wrist. It was obviously him indicating he had heroin.

"No, really, I don't need anything," Vinny said. Now feeling slightly pestered.

"Ok, good for you, kid." The guy looked maybe two years older than him.

He flashed him a genuine smile and waved before hurrying to the next potential customer. He must be doing well,

Vinny thought, noticing his fancy shoes as he walked away, for the first time in recent memory not feeling terrified of the shining leather.

Vinny thought he could use another bite to eat, despite not feeling terribly hungry, the cute waitress not being the smallest reason for his visit. He sat at the counter and to his shock, she seemed to make him a priority. They made small talk about the pies and the menu, but Vinny thought he could feel her interest in him. He questioned why briefly but her smile melted away his worries. He didn't care as long as she was paying attention to him.

By the end of the meal, which Vinny forced himself to eat every bite of, he thought she might say yes to him if he asked her to go on a date. Just as he had worked up enough nerve, she grabbed the ticket from in front of him and said...

"It's on me."

Vinny hated how the attempt at kindness felt. It felt like pity. Was that all this was? Her taking pity on a little street urchin? Even if it was her way of flirting, it had deflated Vinny's ego enough to where he wasn't going to be able to ask her out tonight. When he left and said goodnight, he thought he could feel a bit of disappointment in her, which made him feel better. Maybe she was just flirting.

He continued the argument with himself as he made his way back to the edge of town, where he had been sleeping under the trellis of a bridge. Was she flirting? Was she feeling sorry for him? Did he even care if he could get her into a bed? All of this swirled around his hormone-riddled mind. It distracted him so much that he almost stumbled into the middle of a conversation between two guys that they looked like they were trying very hard to keep private.

They were huddled near the edge of the park at which he had spent the afternoon carving the warning code into a tree. One of the men was whispering to the other one. Vinny saw him pass a bottle from his hand to the other man's, who took a huge drink and almost as soon as his lips left the bottle, they returned for even more.

Vinny was curious now and the thoughts of the waitress fled. He tucked himself into the shadows (disappearing was something he was getting better at daily, it seemed) and watched some more.

The man drinking the bottle with such greed at one point offered the other guy the bottle back. He only waved it away and tugged at the man's hand, trying to get him to follow him. When they turned and walked under the streetlight, Vinny recognized the shine on the shoes. It was the bootlegger that had stopped him earlier on his way back into town. Vinny saw that he had finally found a customer, and maybe more. Vinny wondered where he was leading the man and suddenly thought of Elmer, the abusive drunk, and Carl.

Was this a part of the warning code mystery? Vinny's hairs stood on end, and he found himself grabbing his pistol. He was going to find out.

He followed them, trying his best to keep to the shadows. The park was absolutely crowded with trees but devoid of anyone except the three of them. They made their way to the picnic area with gazebos and benches when Vinny saw the bootlegger started to scan the area. Vinny was barely able to duck into a bush before being seen. In the process, he lost sight of them. It was only for a second, but they just seemed to vanish.

Vinny hurried down the worn path being less quiet and careful, hoping to catch up with them and find out what they were up to. He moved along at a good clip for five or ten minutes and never caught sight of them. Feeling deflated, he wormed his way back to the main entrance, hoping if he was quiet, he would hear them off in the distance and resume the chase. As he got closer to the picnic area, he thought he could hear something ahead of him. Something very close. He listened harder, frozen in fear.

It was a wet, sucking sound peppered with gagging, swallowing sounds. It sounded alien and terrifying in the dark. Vinny pointed his gun in the direction of the noise and crept forward in the dark. The noise was coming from inside the gazebo. Carefully, Vinny leaned around the corner and looked in, his pistol leading the way.

In the moonlight he could see the shine of the bootlegger's shoes behind him as he knelt between the legs of the drunk. The drunk's pants were off, and the bootlegger was bobbing his head between his legs, sucking and slurping and gagging. The drunk was laid back on the bench, head turned toward the sky in ecstasy, arms up on the bench, hands clenching the rails. It was quickly obvious to Vinny what was going on, and the drunk was not in trouble. He seemed to be enjoying the attention the bootlegger was giving his cock.

Vinny could feel his face burning. He had heard of men having sex with each other and giving each other blowjobs. Hell, he had almost been raped himself. But seeing two men be as bold as that with each other in the park shocked him. Suddenly, he felt ashamed of himself for watching and hustled away with much less care about being quiet.

***

It didn't go unnoticed. The bootlegger lost in ecstasy and now drunk himself saw Vinny hurry away. The look he flashed him in the dimly lit gazebo said he would deal with him later.

***

Vinny hurried back to his camp and tried to shake the thoughts from his mind. Not only of the sex in the park but the stalker. And in the full moon, another thought came to him. The Moon King. He gripped his pistol even more tightly. Tomorrow he would buy a proper holster before breakfast. With that, the hormones took over and he fell asleep dreaming of the waitress. He spent the whole night holding his pistol and woke up the next morning holding himself.

After cleaning himself up, he made his way back to town regretting the fact he had to pass through the park. He needed a new place to sleep. He wondered to himself what the waitress's sleeping arrangements were. The park seemed busy this morning. There was a throng of people up ahead, and it looked like a crowd was forming around the same gazebo he was spying on the drunk couple at last night.

The images of the blowjob flashed in his mind, and he started to feel anxious. As he approached, his heart sank in his chest as he saw it was the same gazebo from the night before. The drunk was still on the bench, frozen in what Vinny had thought was pleasure but was now obviously a death pose. His hands were still clenching the bench, his head was still tilted back, but his pants were now pulled up. Although, Vinny could see a red stain on the demin on the inside of his thigh. The same place Elmer had been torn open.

The cops were arriving and moving the crowd back from the scene. They were asking everyone if they knew his name. No one did. Someone said he had only been in town a couple of days, that he came in with the last wave of bums. Vinny felt ashamed to be lumped in and looked around to see who noticed him. He also looked for the bootlegger, although something told him he wouldn't find him during the day. Nothing was out of place in the crowd of confused faces.

One of the cops made a remark under his breath that stood out: "Why do they always pick our town to kill themselves in?"

Vinny wasn't sure what happened or what he saw, but he was sure it wasn't suicide. He realized that this murder was going to go unsolved just like Elmer and the others. Something inside told him he had to warn the vagrants despite Elmer shushing him every time he closed his eyes.

By the time the cops finished loading the body into the ambulance, the crowd had mostly dispersed until Vinny was the only one left. This drew the attention of one of the officers and Vinny knew it was time to finally say something.

"Excuse me, sir, umm, well, I think I might know what happened to him."

"Oh, yeah, kid? Enlighten me," he said with a smirk.

"Well, there was this guy selling booze who was kinda nice earlier but later when I was walking, he was giving drinks to the dead guy from his bottle. I followed them and found them in the gazebo giving a blowjob, but that's not what happened. I think he killed him." Vinny spilled it out in one breath.

The officer's attitude went from contempt to anger suddenly.

"Where did you say you were walking to, kid? And what's your name?" He seemed to ignore all the pertinent information Vinny had just given him and focused on him instead.

Vinny suddenly imagined wanted posters with his face on them. Did the cop think he had done this to the drunk? That Vinny was a predator going from town to town killing bums like Elmer?

"Nothing. I was just going, umm, home, my name's...Elmer." It was the first thing that came to mind. He didn't want to use his own name in case it was in the papers.

Vinny spun and started to walk away.

"Hey, wait a minute. Elmer who?" Vinny looked back and the officer was tucking his writing pad into his shirt. He looked like he was going to give chase.

Vinny wasn't going to stick around and with his new running shoes, he sprinted off. Behind him, the officer was less than interested in chasing a lightning bolt who was telling tall tales, and he shrugged it off. Going back to forgetting they had just scraped a bum off a bench.

By the time he got back to his camp to retrieve his bindle, the only thing left on his mind was getting out of town. Again. He was sick of running but he doubted he would like the electric chair any better. At least he was armed this time. There was a tinge of sadness thinking of the diner and the cute waitress he should have asked out last night rather than trying to solve a mystery he was terrified of solving. He bypassed town and the diner and any prying eyes that might now be on the lookout for him, and he made his way to the train yard.

For some reason, there was no traffic on the rails that day. Not a single train came in or out or even passed through. By the time Vinny realized he would be stuck in this town for another night, it was already getting dark. He should have started walking hours ago but had gotten caught up drawing another series of the codes he had learned into a bench in the yard. He was getting better at it.

There was no desire in him to go back to town, but he needed somewhere to tuck in for the night. He was walking around the yard looking for a place where he had a stroke of luck. There was a fresh carving on a post near the front of the yard. Wood chips from the carving still hung around the bottom of the post, and fresh charcoal had been rubbed into its grooves, making it stand out. Vinny figured since it was so fresh and there was no train traffic, the sleeping arrangements would likely be unoccupied or at least not crowded.

The post's symbol indicated it was a quarter of a mile in the direction away from town. That was perfect as it would keep him away from everyone's prying eyes and the bootlegger. It started to drizzle as Vinny walked, and he was doubly thankful that he had located a roof for the night.

Very soon, he would come to regret that "stroke of luck" for the rest of his life.

The moon wasn't quite full, but it was close. The brightness of the night made for easy walking. Some of the trees had started to lose their leaves that he kicked as he went along. The leaves had always reminded Vinny of a Midwest version of seashells. Each was unique in color, size and shape, some whole, most in pieces. He collected a few with his eyes as he went. The crunching under his feet stopped as he thought he heard an engine approaching. He listened but it was either now too far away or no longer running. Either way, it was no longer a threat. The wind picked up and like a wave at the beach, washed in a new batch of Midwest seashells onto the road to distract him. The raindrops were getting bigger but not any more intense. Vinny hoped the sleeping arrangements included a roof, or it would be an oily night under the bindle rags.

He thought of Elmer and him huddled in the dark. It was a good memory now, but it didn't last. Another ripple was ruining his memories. The next image that flashed was dead, screaming, naked...helpless Elmer. When he tried to blink it away, it only revealed nightmare Elmer shushing him.

The near-full moon poked through the trees and Vinny could see it was still a deep orange from the harvesting in the air. His dad had always called it a blood moon. The thought instantly conjured visions of the Moon King. Was it a monster of some sort with slimy skin? A wendigo type monster that changed like the wind?

Almost on cue, another batch of shells washed across the road.

Vinny was scared now and the orange glow from the blood moon offered no comfort. The rain increased in volume as well as size now. The post in the yard had read it was only a quarter of a mile, but this was starting to feel like many more miles than that. Maybe he took a wrong turn? He spun his head around, feeling his anxiety build. His clothes were starting to soak through with rain.

Finally, there was a building coming up on his right. The road split and he followed it up the tight driveway to what looked like an abandoned house. The windows were missing replaced with particle board, and the front door was boarded up with 2x4's. Vinny had slept in more than one boarded-up abandoned house with Elmer, so he knew you had to get creative sometimes to gain access.

SNIFF

Vinny's feet ground to a halt in the muddy driveway. He knew what he thought he heard, but now all that was coming was the wind and the rain hitting dry leaves. He thought of the dead drunk and the bootlegger performing some act Vinny's thought was sexual but ended up being lethal. The drunk's pants were down just like Elmer's. Carl's belt was undone. The drunk was also unbuttoned, he thought, trying to remember for sure. Then he remembered the first time he heard the sniffing. It was the night of the tree fire. And before, on the train going out of the first town that had the forward-leaning h symbol telling them to run. Was it all connected from the beginning?

Smooth-soled shoes ran through his mind.

Vinny held his cocked pistol in one hand and his lighter in the other. There was too much to consider in the now obscured blood moonlight. His mind could wander for days on all the fear he experienced since being kicked out of his home. The rain was increasing, and the cloud cover was about to ruin his chances of being able to see enough to find a way in. He needed a roof tonight, and walls.

Everything was closed up tight. The smaller windows were shattered, the larger ones boarded over. By the time he made his way around back, he was worried he was going to end up sleeping on the porch. He paused every few seconds to whip his head around and listen. The back door was missing a patina of rough lumber hammered into its frame keeping it sealed shut.

Vinny made his way up the steps and tried the knob. To his disbelief, it turned, and the door swung open.

"HELLO!" Vinny yelled.

His hair stood up again feeling tired of the act. Vinny could sense of something closing in on him. Without waiting for a response from inside, he jumped through the door—the feeling of being closed in on by some unseen predator had chased him. He slammed the door behind him and pushed against it. His fingers scrambled for the lock and couldn't find it. He looked up to the window to try to see his attacker, and lightning flashed.

Vinny screamed.

The flash from the lightning revealed nothing but his cowardice. He found himself holding his lighter while the gun was jammed into his waistband again, finding the comfort it provided more necessary. The thunder shook the house to its footings. Producing another scream from Vinny.

He was too on edge. He needed light. The bottom floor of the home had a small fireplace and after some searching, Vinny found enough scraps for a fire from broken chairs and barnwood, which hadn't been suitable for making barricades so had been abandoned to rot on the floor of the once nice home. The Dunhill came in useful for its intended purpose of starting fires and before long, Vinny had a little fire going in the fireplace. Nothing that would draw attention from the outside but enough to keep Vinny feeling safe.

The thunder and lightning continued but thankfully, his screaming had not. He felt mildly safer in the house with a fire going and a nice bite or two of the pemmican. He wished it was a burger from the diner with the cute waitress. The resentment he felt for having nowhere that he felt like he belonged was growing. He didn't need people anymore. Any time he got close or even felt interested, something came along that he couldn't prevent. Jamie Lynn's and Mom's lies, the fire he started to protect himself in the bramble, getting chased from town to town by cops and misfortune and the mobsters, Sarah and that fancy lad, getting left by Mac and the fellas, the bootlegger and the drunk in the gazebo, and even Elmer being a drunk.

He was done with the outside world. From now on, he was going to stick to himself. These thoughts of solitude and being left alone by everyone were the ones that were with Vinny tonight. He got comfortable on his bindle by the fire and tried to relax. Before long he was out, dreaming of the faceless girl, shushing Elmer, and the smooth-soled man.

This time, it was different. Instead of laughing, he was sniffing, and the moonlight was bright red, not the usual pale blue. He sniffed more loudly now in his corner of the alley. Elmer was shushing silently, and the faceless girl-bum amalgam was gurgling away.

SNIFF SNI... the world shifted and blended in his mind.

...FF SNIFFFF "Yeah, he's in here." There were footsteps now, more than one set. Except Vinny could feel them on the floor. He could also feel the heat from his dying fire in the small fireplace.

Vinny wasn't dreaming, he was awake.

The footsteps made short work of the space between the back door and the living room, where Vinny was. A flash of white interrupted the orange glow now, washing in through the open back door.

BOOM

The thunder cracked and shook the house.

Vinny was surrounded. His back was to the corner of the room and four men crowded the space between him and any escape.

BOOM BOOM BOOM

Vinny fired three rounds. His hands had done it just hours before and it felt familiar still. He even knew what he was doing. In the heat of the moment, he at least had the sense to aim for the man shaped like a barrel.

None of them flinched.

The barrel-shaped man laughed in the darkness.

"This one's full of fight. He's gonna like him." He took a step toward Vinny, who pulled the trigger two more times but only hit the floorboards. He leveled the pistol at the man's face.

CLICK

Vinny's heart sank. He wished he was strong enough to put more bullets in the gun. He dropped the gun and had his knife in his hand before the big man took a swing. The blade intercepted the man's swing and buried itself to the hilt in his forearm. The beast of a man only twisted his arm counter to Vinny, wrestling the blade from his grip with little effort. Then came a punch so hard, it knocked the sense out of Vinny. His legs buckled and his vision swam. He held his hands up in front of him to shield from another possible blow.

"WAIT!" Vinny shrieked. "Don't hur...." Vinny stopped talking.

His vision had cleared enough to make shadow from light, and he saw their shoes for the first time.

They were all nice shiny leather. Way too nice to be in an abandoned house at night fighting some homeless kid. This wasn't them stumbling across him—they had been hunting him and he was caught.

Vinny went limp and his survival instincts failed completely. There was no fight or flight left in him. All he could do was stare at their shoes.

One of the pairs of shoes approached him. Vinny was vaguely aware of something like a bee sting on his neck.

His last conscious thought was of Elmer, eyes bulging, pants around his ankles, and shushing like a madman. The codes Vinny had been carving into any available canvas flashed in his vision one by one, finishing with the shushed lips, and everything faded to grey...then blackness.

The familiar rocking of the train was comforting. Vinny was still so tired he almost felt drunk, so he decided to keep his eyes closed and steal a few more minutes of sleep. His mind drifted into the halfway world between being awake and sleeping where the two mixed into madman dreams that had just enough of a touch of reality to scare you.

Mom was in the corner, and he could smell her cigarettes. His mind was filling in gaps and the rocking of the train became the sensation of walking down the steps into the main room of the house. Reliably, Mom was there in the corner. The glow of her cigarette lit her face up in the darkness. Vinny went to open the curtains but was cut short.

"Stop, Vinny."

Her voice was different; it was masculine and brutish, not the overly soft girly voice she affected to hide her lack of femininity. Had so much changed since he had left that now her voice was different?

He looked at her again in the corner, now hulking in her chair. She was so white she was almost glowing in the darkness. Another detail shook Vinny: Her skin was shiny, and he could see way too much of it. She was naked.

"What are you looking at, Vinny?" She took pull off her cigarette again and this time it lit up a face Vinny didn't know. Fat, white and human but just barely. There was a hollow look that the smiling monster in Mom's chair had, like a smile from a statue. It was there but it meant nothing. It was only trying to keep up appearances and look human…but the closer Vinny looked, the less it was convincing him. He could smell Mom's soup now and with the fear he was feeling, his stomach churned.

"You saw the marquee Vinny. The Moon King is real," the Mom monster said under its breath.

Vinny lost it and started to scream but was cut short by his last meal.

He woke up gagging silently, feeling like he was suffocating. The next retch brought up the remnants of dinner that were stopping his breathing. His arms weren't responding, and his body felt impossibly heavy.

"I know I saw some writing on a fence about the Moon King too, but I wasn't worried about him. I'm more worried about pissin' off the guys at the top if we don't take care of him soon. He's drawin' too much attention." Someone Vinny couldn't identify was talking behind him.

He went to push his body up and finally realized his hands were tied behind him. Panic started to gain momentum and his breathing increased. Flashes of the fight in the abandoned house were coming back to him now. His hands flailed around, trying to reach into his pocket for his lighter.

"Oh, shit, he's waking up. Give him another one. It oughta be enough to keep him sleepin' til we get there or at least until they get the chains on him." An unseen voice advised behind Vinny.

Chains? The sound of that word escalated his panic into terror. He wriggled around and pulled at the restraints as hard as he could. A stupid part of him wished Elmer would jump out and save him.

There was no one coming to the rescue this time.

He was screaming now, and his doped body was slowly gaining strength from the adrenaline now coursing in his blood. He flopped hard and managed to face his attackers.

"Oh, perfect, you see that? He saved me some work; I was gonna have to flip him over, but he really wants another one bad." He started laughing at himself and was joined by two others Vinny couldn't see.

The man grabbed him by the hair, and every follicle screamed in pain. He hadn't grabbed enough to distribute the weight and it felt like a patch of his scalp was about to give way. Then another bee sting in his neck. Vinny saw a needle and syringe in the gloved hand of the man who had ahold of him.

"So, it's not a bee?" was all Vinny's drug-addled brain could manage.

It drew a roar of laughter from the assailants. Then, more blackness for Vinny.

***

The train floor was now cold and motionless. Vinny felt the surface and was surprised at its smoothness. His eyes were blinking out the sleep and slowly, a dimly lit white room was coming into focus. There was a desk in one corner with the lamp that was providing the yellow light. There was a radiator next to it and a shelf that held what looked like neatly folded sheets. He turned and as the rest of the room came into focus, Vinny realized he must still be in that halfway world of wake and sleep where things got scary.

There were three men either sitting on or standing next to concrete blocks protruding from the walls next to them. The blocks had a white cushion on top of them and each man had a bucket near his feet. They each also had chains. The chains were connected to the walls with heavy bolts secured into the white concrete that matched the floor. The other side of the chains were connected to the men by way of a ring that had been inserted into their necks and around their collarbones.

The men all looked lifeless. Like someone had propped corpses up into almost lifelike positions. They were all thin and sickly looking. The only reason Vinny could tell there was any life in them at all was the sound of their chains clanking against the concrete as their visually imperceptible motions were captured with the sounds. The one farthest from him seemed to be fighting sleep more than anything else. His head was bobbing, his chin bouncing off his chest, and his eyes fluttering, trying to remain open. The man in the middle was nervously rocking on his feet, just slowly enough to keep the scraping of the chains quiet. The other man closest to Vinny was sitting, back against the wall and was using one hand to hold the chains up, obviously

228

trying to keep the weight off the rings, which were caked in blood from the fresh-looking wounds around his collarbone. The man's free hand produced a bottle, and he took a drink. Even from here, Vinny could smell the rotgut.

As the man lowered the bottle, he looked at Vinny and they made eye contact. Vinny could see the man was or recently had been crying.

"What is goin..." Vinny started and was cut short.

The man shook his head and shushed Vinny like Elmer had. A scream threatened to show up and Vinny tried to snap himself awake.

"If we talk now, we are gonna catch a beating," the man whispered, snatching Vinny back into the moment.

He was as awake as he was going to get.

Vinny still felt drunk from the "bee sting." His heavy hands pulled themselves forward and Vinny realized he too was connected to the chains and bolts in the wall. Only, he was connected via some very old-looking handcuffs that were cutting into his wrists. He pulled against them, producing some rattling noises of his own for the first time. This drew the attention of the nervous man.

"He's awake. Oh, he's awake. Now it's gonna start for him, too. He isn't ready, this one's just a boy, he's gonna break too fast. I was just a boy, too, but I been tossed around the world a bit before this, and now they got me locked up here. Prolly gonna die here, too. I wonder what they are gonna make him take. They got us all on something all the time. I hear them talking sometimes and I think that pretty soon, I'm going to get a new dose cos mine just ain't enough anymore." The flurry of words came so fast, Vinny couldn't make any sense of any of it. "I swear I heard someone talking in the hallway yesterday but I ca..."

"Shut the fuck up," the drinking man next to Vinny hissed. "You're gonna get us all whipped again if you can't shut your damn mouth... if I could reach you, I'd choke the life out of you." He took another drink of the booze he had.

Now it was the sleepy guy's turn as he jolted awake.

"I didn't miss him, did I? I went through my doses already, and I need more or I'm gonna get sick again."

"Nope, he's coming back anytime now for the new one. He won't leave him like that for long. He'll be back and you can get your fix and he can get his whisky, and I'll get more of that FUCKING POISON." The shouts from the nervous man echoed off the walls and down the hallway.

Their fighting continued as Vinny finished his survey of the room. It was a sterile white concrete room. There were two drains in the floor that broke the white background like two unblinking eyes. It looked like there were four occupied concrete beds including his and two blocks that were unused except for the empty chains that hung there.

SQUEAK SQUEAK SQUEAK

The repetitive high-pitched metal on metal sound came down the hallway that the echoes had disappeared into. The noise had silenced the fighting and the men returned to their fearful, lifeless states. The nervous one was now chewing on his fingers. The drinking one was putting the lid back on his bottle.

SQUEAK SQUEAK SQUEAK

It was closer now, but the hallway must be impossibly long. Vinny thought he could hear crying in a layer underneath the squeaking, but the sound of his own breathing and his heartbeat were drowning it out. As he waited for the noise to enter the room, Vinny realized he was barefoot. His new shoes were gone, just like the life he had been living yesterday.

A stainless-steel bed made its way into the room, followed by a thin older man. He looked around the room and shot each of them a nasty look. Vinny, the last object of his ire, was lingered on and a small grin formed on his lips before he went to the desk in the corner and started retrieving objects from its drawers.

Vinny wanted to ask what was going on, but his intuition and the look the man had given him left no room for questions. He watched him place some matching stainless-steel tools on the metal bed. Then he took a bundle from his pocket and unrolled it on the table.

It was a spoon and needle with a little brown jar. The man went to the hall and returned with a pitcher and four glasses. Vinny suddenly realized how thirsty he was and swallowed hard.

"Are you ready?" the man pushing the cart asked to the thin air. "Are you going to be able to give it to yourself or do you need my assistance?"

Vinny was confused, then the nodding man chimed in, "No, I got it. I just hope you brought more this time. It's just not enough."

"It's plenty."

The thin man walked the supplies, a glass of water, and a candle over to the nodding man, who in turn started to cook a dose. Vinny wasn't dumb; he knew what this was. The man was fixing a shot of heroin that the man with the cart had provided him. Vinny's confusion was growing.

"And you?" The man was looking at the drinking man next to Vinny.

"I've still got plenty." He shook his bottle of whisky at the man, proving it.

"I suggest you don't get too dried out, lest you might infuriate the boss." The man smirked.

The drinking man took the hint and took a big swig from the bottle.

"You're right. Actually, can I get another one just in case?" And he shook his bottle, now emptier than a second ago, to prove his need.

The man laughed.

"I thought so." He went to the hallway and came back with a new bottle.

Vinny wondered what kind of dungeon this was. It was nothing like his books except for the chains. There was no dripping dirty water. There was no filth. In fact, the room smelled of chemicals from cleaning and was dry as a bone. And the prisoners were being given drugs and alcohol? None of it made sense.

"And you?" The man was pointing to the nervous man with a needle he had retrieved from his bundle.

"Jesus, please, no. I can't take any more of that shit. Give me something else, please," the nervous man begged.

"Oh, I'm sorry but this can't be helped." The man giggled. "We have someone who has a desire for this so as long as the need is out there, you will be subject to it."

He took three steps forward and grabbed the nervous man by the hair, exposing his neck, and jammed the needle home with no regard for the other man's pain.

"I haven't slept in days," the nervous man said in a now deeper voice that sounded on the verge of tears or panic.

"I'm quite sure you haven't as *I've* been in charge of your doses, not the boss." He laughed again and went back to the table to roll his bundle up.

Vinny's heart was racing. He was hoping to be ignored completely.

"And you?" The man was now staring at him.

"I'm not sure what you want," Vinny choked out, completely terrified.

The man burst into a belly laugh. "Oh, it's not what I want. It's what *they* want."

"What do they want?" Vinny asked.

"For you to be cleaned. Strip your clothes off," the man barked, losing interest.

"Strip my clothes...."

BAM

The man hit Vinny so hard, one of his back chewing teeth bounced off the roof of his mouth. Vinny could hear it hit the floor as blood filled its void.

"Don't make me repeat myself."

Vinny could see him winding up, and to avoid the hit, he started stripping. Satisfied that he was underway, the man went back to work at the table. Vinny pulled his shirt off and up over the cuffs, so it was on the chains. Then he started to take his pants off. By chance, he felt the weight of Dad's Dunhill in Elmer's secret pocket. It sent ripples of comfort into him. He had to hide it. Vinny looked back at the man, who was still busy at the table. Then he scanned the other prisoners. All busy with their own problems. Like a flash, Vinny pulled the lighter and his leftover cash out and tucked it under his mattress. Then after making sure, he hadn't been caught pigeonholing them away, he took his pants off completely.

"Drawers too," the man ordered, now focused on Vinny.

Vinny almost protested but thought better of it and took his underwear off. The man approached him with a pair of scissors and cut the shirt from the chains. He handed Vinny a bar of soap then disappeared into the hallway, returning moments later with a hose.

"Scrub" was all he said then let loose with a blast of cold water.

Vinny did as he was told and scrubbed. He was used to cold water showers and baths, so that didn't bother him as much as scrubbing in front of people. He tried to be modest but there was no use. The pressure of the water hit his testicles and knocked them together, dropping him to his knees.

"Keep scrubbing!" the man yelled over the blast of the water. He was obviously enjoying this, based on the smile plastered on his face. "The boss doesn't like a dirty cup."

This statement confused Vinny, but he kept scrubbing anyway, spitting the blood out of his mouth and at the same time trying to get a drink from the splashing hose water. He watched the red swirl around the white concrete down into the drain. It looked like a peppermint wheel candy.

He got a good look at the man's shoes while he was on his knees scrubbing. They were athletic running shoes, much like the ones Vinny used to own. The question of what would make him want to run answered itself as Vinny heard footsteps coming down the hall.

The glee washed itself off the thin man's face like the filth had been washed off Vinny's body. The smile was gone and replaced with a no-nonsense stern look. He cut the water off and stuck his hand out for the soap. He went to the rack next to the desk and tossed a dry, clean towel to Vinny.

"Dry off." He took the hose out to the hallway, leaving Vinny to dry off and hide himself with the towel by wrapping it around his waist.

Hiding his privates made him feel slightly safer. But the anticipation of what was next was making his chest hurt.

"Is he ready?" came a man's voice. It had a European sound to it, but Vinny couldn't pin down any particular region.

"Yes, cleaned and stripped, the table is ready. Do you want me to get him strapped down?"

"No, I want to get a look at him first."

Vinny saw his shoes first. It was what he expected for a change. They were shiny, fancy, leather shoes—the kind with smooth soles. Then a man in an expensive suit followed them in. At least he looked like a man. He had the same hollow look that the Mom monster had in his dream. His eyes were bloodshot to the point they were almost completely red. When he entered the room, it felt like all the air had been sucked out. It was heavy and hard to breathe now, and there was a smell of lit matches underpinning every other scent. The thing stood in front of Vinny, who didn't have the strength to get to his feet. His hair was still dripping wet. He was shaking so badly; the drips were flying in all directions.

"This is the one they said was full of spirit?" the thing said.

"Yes, sir. They said he put up a hell of a fight. He shot Bobby three times and stuck a knife through his forearm." The thin man was acting like a scared puppy now that this thing was in the room. "Said he was hard to track down, too."

"Well, I guess the truth of it will be exposed in the very near future. We will see how full of life he really is." The thing in a man suit paused and shook its head, looking disappointed. "Get him on the table."

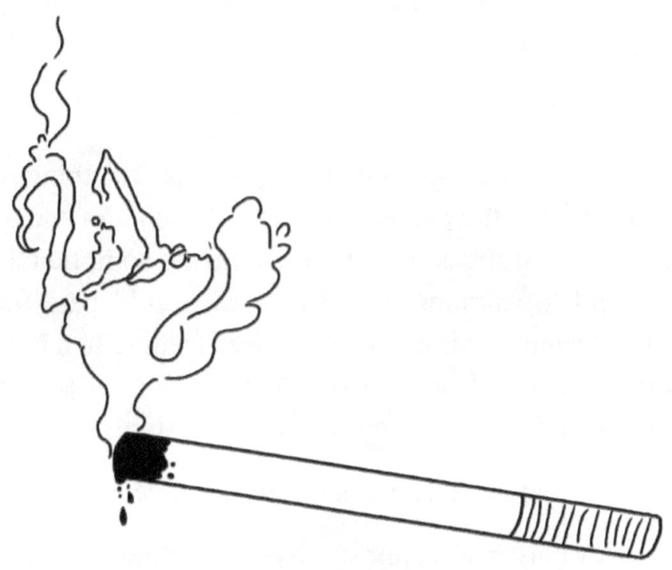

The subservient yet aggressive puppy man did as he was told. Vinny's mouth was still full of blood and the inside of his cheek was starting to swell. He wanted to fight and try to talk his way out of what was coming on the table, but there was no use. Puppy man undid his shackles with a key from his pocket, giving Vinny a look in the process that dared him to resist. He did not. The shaking had increased in intensity but not from the cold, though he was freezing.

The thing was at the table with the lamp, looking at a book. Vinny's stupid side wondered what book it was. His thirst for books knew no limits, apparently. The thing in a man suit flipped the cover closed and it gave the heavy sound of a leather-bound hardcover, indicating it was not a cheap dime store book. Then there was the mechanical sound of a switch being flipped, followed by the sound of classical music.

Vinny, now horrified, looked at the puppy man, who in return looked almost giddy.

"Lie down or I'll lay you down myself."

There was no room for arguments. The thing was just feet from him, and the puppy man was between him and the door. He just wasn't strong enough to resist. So, he complied. He took just a second to examine the table. It was cold bare metal with a channel running around its perimeter leading to a hole. The only other definable feature was the straps. Vinny pictured himself lying there in the next few seconds and started to cry.

"That ain't gonna help, get up there," puppy man said.

Vinny could almost sense a pleading in his eyes that told him if he didn't get on the table now, the thing at the desk was going to get involved.

Vinny climbed onto the metal, tears rolling down his cheeks. Shaking harder than ever as the coldness of the metal sapped what was left of his body heat.

A cackling came from across the dungeon, and Vinny raised his head far enough to look at who it was. It was the nervous man, who now looked absolutely insane. His eyes were bulging and red, his skin was red, and sweat was dripping from every appendage. He was screaming with laughter.

"Shut him up," the thing said without turning around, then went back to work on whatever he had in front of him.

The puppy man had only tightened one side of the straps on Vinny's right arm. He gave Vinny another warning look, daring him to misbehave. Then he went to the shelf and grabbed something. He proceeded to walk over to the crazy man in the middle and stuffed the object—which now looked like a washcloth—into his mouth, then wrapped it with a bit of rope and secured it with a knot. The crazy man laughed the entire time, only stopping when the rag hit the back of his throat, forcing a gag. Followed by muffled laughter.

Pleased with the results, he returned smiling ready to finish Vinny's restraints, which took little to no time as Vinny wasn't resisting.

"Well done, William. Now don't forget the bottle. His blood is going to be very hot, and I don't want to waste a drop."

Puppy man who was William complied. There was a row of empty jars next to the glasses he had used for water for the other prisoners. William took one and placed it beneath the hole that was at the end of the channel on the table's perimeter. Its function became clear.

"Please don't do this," Vinny pleaded to the room.

He didn't care who helped him; he just wanted off this table. Why had he let himself be restrained without a fight? There was no way out now. If he had taken his chances, he might have escaped. They were too busy, and he missed his opportunity to try to flee. Now he was begging fate for a second chance.

Who was he kidding? He never even would have made it out of the room. The tears flowed freely now. He didn't plead any further as William returned with a bit of rope and a rag, asking him with his eyes if it was necessary. It wasn't. Vinny closed his eyes and waited for the inevitable.

Vinny could hear the thing approach him minutes later and then it leaned over him. Its breath was putrid and sulfurous.

He was breathing deeply like he was inhaling Vinny's essence. Vinny turned his head to avoid the smell, only to feel like his face was placed into a vise. He opened his eyes and was face to face with this thing pretending to be a man, its hands pressing the sides of his head.

"You are the one who was so full of fight, yet you can't look me in the eyes. I can't say I'm not disappointed. I was hoping to feel you wriggle like a fish under my knife." The thing was staring into his now open eyes.

Vinny met his stare for a second and lost. He started screaming. No sooner had it started than William was behind and above him stuffing the rag into his mouth.

"That will do," the thing said.

Fumbling around with the instruments that were laid out on the desk, he made a choice and came back to hover over Vinny, who was fighting the gagging feeling in his already dry throat.

"Are we ready?" he said coldly.

Vinny fought and squirmed on the table, pulling at the restraints so hard the bones in his wrists popped. He thrashed his head, only to be met with a thick leather strap tightening on his forehead. He kept fighting the impossible fight until the thing spoke.

"Now, that is more like it."

The pleasure in the thing's voice was unmistakable. Vinny wasn't going to give him any more satisfaction from this than he was already going to get. He stopped struggling and lay perfectly still. Even when the knife flashed before his eyes, he resisted fighting or crying. He closed his eyes again and tried to prepare himself.

With no ceremony or hesitation, the thing pushed the blade into the flesh between his collarbone and his neck. The blade slid through the skin easily enough. It stung but it must have been sharp, because all he could feel at first was the warmth of the blood running down and warming the flesh on his shoulders. He was so cold it almost felt nice.

The creepy music from the radio was underpinning everything like a bad joke.

Then the blade started on the sinewy tissue and the pain started. Vinny could almost hear them break like piano wires strung too tightly as the blade pressed into them. He screamed against the rag in his mouth and pinched his eyes closed even harder. The sound of air being pressed out of the thing's nostrils in a muffled laugh was barely audible over the screaming in his head. He tried to stay motionless to deny him the pleasure, but it was getting harder by the second.

The blade moved to the underside of the collarbone, now digging a tunnel to meet the hole he had started on the other side. Vinny reflexively pulled his arm away, only to be met with a cold hand that felt inhumanly strong. It pressed his body down so hard against the table, movement was no longer possible. He continued excavating the channel under his collarbone with knowledgeable precision. Obviously, he had performed this operation more than once.

Finally, the cutting stopped. The warmth in the fresh hole was replaced with cold steel. Vinny couldn't help himself and opened his eyes. He saw the thing pushing a C-shaped piece of shiny metal into the hole he had cut through him. There were no more screams left in Vinny, but the tears were streaming down his face. The last time he had seen this much of the inside of a human was changing the bandages on Dad's mangled leg. He could feel his stomach churn. The flesh in his head started to feel like pins and needles starting with his lips and tongue.

The thing finished pushing the C through the hole, bringing a chunk of Vinny with it as it made it through. The thing pulled the flesh off and sucked on it, then tossed it onto the table. Then without pausing, it took the quarter-inch steel shaped like a C and pinched it, effortlessly making an O out of the C.

"One down, one to go," the thing said, and laughed maniacally.

Vinny looked into its blood red eyes, his own bulging in fear. The thing then popped his fingers into his mouth and sucked on them until they were clean. He used his thumb like a squeegee to push the blood on the table into the channel, which led to the bottle that was slowly filling up. He licked his thumb clean and the redness in the whites of his eyes softened into a burnt orange color. The color reminded Vinny of the full blood moon on the night he was captured; it had painted everything in that same eerie orange.

"Sorry, I had to stop for a treat. I'm so famished." The thing's laughing continued more intensely as the radio orchestra reached a crescendo.

Vinny's fear climaxed now and the tingling in his lips went to his brain. The world around him turned a now familiar shade of grey and then black. To his benefit he remained asleep for the rest of the procedure. By the time William was unstrapping him and bolting the chains to the newly installed rings, Vinny was only just coming back to life. Then a familiar smell took him back into a half-conscious state. It was Dakin's solution. He was vaguely aware of the feeling of cool water on the burning wounds and someone cleaning the area gently with a rag. However, all rational thoughts were being reserved for the dream world, so little attention was paid to the cleaning of the wounds.

Vinny was much more focused on Dad's leg that needed attending to. The Dakin's label had reminded him to do it before the infection set in. He moved his hands in the real world and in his imagined one. Now that Dad's leg was undressed, he could smell it. It was the smell of decay and infection. He looked closer at the wound; was there movement? Little white beads were moving in the blackened parts of his dad's leg. He pulled at one and produced a maggot.

"It's ok, Vincent. It's eating the bad parts." That's what Dad had told him. His name felt weird on his lips as he repeated it. It was lost until a second ago.

He needed to wash the leg but while he was filling his bottle, he realized it was his bleach bottle/canteen. The one that smelled like Dakin's. Is that what brought him here?

"Hopefully, the next thing I remember was the last thing I forgot. Otherwise, I fear something's been lost forever." Elmer laughed beside him.

Vinny looked at him and was shocked to find him bare-chested, the lips freshly carved and bleeding on his chest. Only this time, Elmer had no face, like the little girl and was holding a finger in front of the gaping hole, making hissing noises from the tube that used to lead to his mouth.

On some level, Vinny realized reality had to be better than this nightmare, and he fought himself awake.

The thing was gone, and the room was silent again except for the sounds of William cleaning up the mess, clanking away at the metal table. The smell of Dakin's was strong. His fresh wounds were screaming in pain and the weight from the chains pulling on them made it worse any time he breathed. The prisoner he had seen holding the chains up made sense as he coiled his own on his chest to relieve the pulling sensation. He was lying on the concrete slab with the thin mattress and could feel the bulk of the Dunhill just below him—it was still there. Relief washed over him; he could feel the comfort Dad's lighter still offered even through the mattress. Dad might be out there looking for him right now.

Vinny heard a slurping noise and looked to see William licking the table clean. When he sat up, a coil let loose from his chest and clanked to the floor, producing a whine from Vinny from the fresh pain it caused by yanking on the wound. William heard the movement and looked at Vinny from across the room, blood dripping from his chin.

He put one finger up to his lips and gave Vinny a shush.

Vinny fainted again, but this time was given mercy by not dreaming at all for the rest of the night...or week.

***

Vinny had no idea how long he had been lying there. Just brief moments of clarity when he was given water by William, who seemed to have softened a bit now that there was no hope left. He had used the bathroom a few times in the bucket provided by leaning on his side and putting the bucket up to his naked body. Every time it was used, William emptied it without question, always bringing a fresh clean bucket back.

Everything hurt when he moved and there was heat radiating from his shackles. He hoped he wasn't going to rot like Dad's leg. William had been religiously taking care of the wounds and even though it had likely only been a few days, the pain was starting to recede, or Vinny was adjusting to it.

The other prisoners were uselessly inebriated constantly. Their babbling and fighting never seemed to end so Vinny just ignored it for now. Vinny had a vague recollection of some other men coming into the room and talking and joking around while the drunk next to him was whimpering, but it was an unfocused memory that was quickly lost in the confusion surrounding him.

The fog lifted within a few days and then there was clarity when he was slapped awake one morning.

"It's time," William said and tossed Vinny a pair of white clothes like the other prisoners were wearing.

Without arguing, Vinny spat the blood from his lip into his bucket and swished some water from his cup around in his mouth before swallowing. He put the drawers on first. That made him instantly feel like he rejoined the human race. The pants followed and by the time he got to the button-up shirt, he was already warming up. He was very careful pulling the chains up to the front of the button-up, trying his best not to jostle the wounds. Despite his care, a fresh trickle of blood appeared on the shirt.

"Shit," William said under his breath. "Take it off."

Vinny did as he was told while William retrieved some bandages and a fresh shirt. His hunger pangs were controlling his thoughts now. He hadn't eaten since before he was captured. Was his last meal pemmican or a meal at the diner? He couldn't remember but his stomach didn't care either way as it rumbled.

"So, you're hungry, huh? Well, the sooner you do what he wants, the sooner you get food."

"What does he want?" Vinny asked.

"Don't you ever fucking speak to me unless I ask you to," William said and slapped him again, this time keeping his fist open and sparing Vinny's teeth. "He wants what he wants, and you better be ready to make him happy or your short, miserable life is going to get even shorter."

William was gently bandaging him now, cleaning the wound with some fresh Dakin's before dressing it with cotton and tape. When he was done, Vinny put the shirt on even more carefully and sat on his bed rubbing his cheek.

Footsteps started down the hall and puppy man William tucked his tail and stood in the corner waiting, wringing his hands like he was nervous. If he was nervous, Vinny should be terrified...he was.

After an eternity of listening to the footsteps (the hallway must be miles long), they finally reached the door. It was the thing that had installed the shackles. It was clear that he was in charge, and nothing went on without his permission.

He had a small bag in his hands and a box of matches. The contents of the bag were dumped out on the desk and William ran over to put them away. It was cartons of cigarettes. William was stacking them on the shelf with the cups and bedding.

The thing plucked a pack from the carton and was busy smacking it against his palm, packing them. The noise brought back memories of Mom doing the same in her dark corner. Vinny had a flash of the naked Mom monster pulling on her cigarette, lighting up her hollow face.

"These are for you." The thing pretending to be a man tossed the pack at Vinny, who reflexively tried to catch it.

Vinny only managed to knock his coiled chains to the ground, making his shackles pull on his raw flesh. The pack of smokes bounced onto his bed.

Vinny picked them up and looked at the logo on the front. It was Mom's brand.

Without thinking, Vinny said, "I don't smoke." He instantly regretted it.

There was a look of fury on the thing's face, and he took a step forward toward Vinny and raised his hands. His red eyes flashed with anger and then eased just as suddenly as he lowered his arms. Vinny was a beaten creature and he realized he had only spoken out of reflex.

"You do now, and if you ever speak to me again, I will have William take you out with the next day's shit buckets." He smiled at Vinny. "Got it?"

Vinny only nodded in agreement.

The thing tossed the box of matches now and Vinny actually caught it.

"Now, smoke that fucking cigarette," it said, still smiling but biting at its own lip anxiously.

Vinny opened the pack and produced a single cigarette. He put it between his lips and there was a sense of disgust or guilt that washed over him. He looked at the thing, who looked even less patient than he had a moment ago. Vinny struck the match and lit the cigarette, gently pulling on it with his mouth. A bit of the smoke made its way into his throat, and he started coughing wildly.

The nervous prisoner in the middle started laughing at this. He had been given a fresh dose of "poison" with the others despite his objections to William, but while the heroin junkie nodded off and the drinker cried in his bed, the man in the middle spun out of control. Finally losing it at the sight of Vinny coughing.

The thing nodded at William, who understood instantly and grabbed the rag/rope combination from the shelf. He made his way to the nervous man, who was begging him to stop.

Vinny pulled on the cigarette again. The taste reminded him of Mom and her smoky soup, and he gagged and coughed some more. The thing was watching intently. This time, Vinny took a drag but left it in his mouth, then quickly blew it out before he had to breathe in. The thing looked unimpressed, but Vinny tried again. He pulled on the cigarette and just as he was about to blow it out, the thing punched him in the stomach, forcing him to inhale. Vinny blew the smoke back out, coughing and puking into the bucket, spraying it all over the place.

The thing took a step back to avoid the puke and looked at Vinny, undeterred. "AGAIN!" he shouted.

Vinny smoked the rest of the cigarette without trying to fake it. His head was swimming and he felt drunk. The taste was awful, but his stomach was already so empty, there was nothing left to retch up. He tossed the still glowing butt into the bucket as he finished.

"AGAIN." The thing was growing impatient, obviously. Vinny didn't know what to do except comply. Had he smoked it wrongly?

He tried again. This time coughing less as he learned to pull small amounts of smoke into his throat at a time as he inhaled instead of all at once. His stomach was aching now, and his lips felt cold. He reached for his water to rinse the taste out of his mouth and was stopped short.

"Not yet, finish it," the thing said.

Vinny was close to being done, so he took two more drags and tossed the butt into the bucket with the rest. As he was watching the ember fade in the bucket, the thing suddenly grabbed him by the hair and forced his head back, revealing his neck. He produced an empty syringe and with an excited look from his blood-red eyes, he plunged the needle into Vinny's neck. He released his grip on Vinny's hair and pulled the plunger back on the syringe. As Vinny's blood filled the empty container, the thing's breath was choking him. He wanted to turn his head but with the needle buried deep in an artery, he stayed still.

As soon as the syringe was full, the thing pushed Vinny away, removing the needle at the same time. The thing held it up to the light for a moment, admiring his prize, then took it and squirted its contents into his mouth. He tilted his head back as he swallowed and stayed that way for half a minute or so before Vinny could see relief wash over him. When he opened his eyes, they had faded from a blood-red into a pale yellow. He almost looked human now.

"God damn, that's good; it's been too long since I've had the pleasure of a cigarette." He turned and looked at Vinny, now obviously pleased with himself. "You will smoke one of those once every fifteen minutes." He pointed at the clock on the desk. "If you miss one cigarette, you will be killed like any of them that miss a dose." He motioned to the other prisoners. "As long as you serve a need for me, you will stay here in relative safety. As soon as you stop serving a purpose, you're dead."

Vinny nodded in confused agreement, feeling as scared as he looked.

"Now feed him. The blood is thin, no body, like a bad wine." The thing spun around and stumbled, then shook his head and walked away as he said, "That went right to my head." Then he laughed his way down the endless hallway.

William followed shortly after.

Vinny's stomach growled and reminded him how hungry he was. He wondered what these monsters' idea of food was.

While he waited for food, he took the pack of smokes and the matches in his hands. He looked at the clock, noting the time so he didn't miss his deadline. He suddenly felt very sorry for himself. Why did Elmer have to get drunk that night? Why did his parents have to kick him out? It was their fault he was here. His anger towards all of them was growing.

He blinked and shushing Elmer reminded him it was his own fault.

"Fuck you," he thought at the apparition, and the bulging-eyed Elmer disappeared.

He had been replaced by a cart full of food William produced from the hallway.

It was time to eat.

By the time he was done eating, Vinny felt like he could pop. When William first wheeled the food cart in, Vinny could hardly believe his eyes. It was full of food he was normally lucky to get once a year, if that. Kidney pies, liver and onions, eggs done in any way you could imagine, beans with ham, chili, dark greens raw and cooked in bacon fat, nuts Vinny had never seen (and some he had), prunes and plums, and best of all desserts. The cake caught Vinny's eye first. He was wary of the food as William pushed the laden cart toward him and scooted back. It had to be poisoned or full of drugs, Vinny thought.

"You eat or you die. It's that simple." William paused. "And he won't wait for you to starve to death." He smiled and nodded at the food.

Vinny was starving and before he knew it, he was pulling plates off the cart, stacking them on the mattress next to him. The tiny space filled up quickly. When he was done making his choices, William pushed the cart to the drunk next to him. There was a bit of guilt as Vinny hadn't considered that the cart was for everyone. He looked at the pile of food next to him and looked at the other prisoners. They didn't seem to care, about anything really. The drunk took a meat pie and a cup of pudding. The nervous man took what was left of the desserts. The junkie was nodding off and not responding so William made a selection for him and set it on the edge of his bed.

Then William pushed the cart to the other side of the room and brought them all glasses of water. He sat at the desk and clicked on the radio.

"Hurry up. I don't want to be down here all night."

Vinny looked at the food. His stomach was growling again, then he looked at the others. Half of the dessert was gone from the nervous man, and the drunk was tucking into the pie. He saw Vinny eyeing the food.

"It's safe. It's the only bright spot in this miserable shit hole, so you might as well enjoy it," he slurred and took a swig from his bottle.

"Shut up or I'll gag you all until tomorrow morning," William warned.

Vinny looked at William and he tapped his wrist.

"Shit," Vinny said inaudibly as he looked at the clock. He needed to smoke to keep on the pace set by the thing. He grabbed the pack of cigarettes and a match and pulled lightly to get it going. The coughing came next. When the smoke cleared, Vinny made good use of the next fifteen minutes and gorged himself. The only bad part was that when he chewed, it rattled his chains, which in turn pulled on the still very sore holes. He cleared almost all the food from the plates he had taken, and even managed to get down half of the piece of cake before he needed to smoke again.

As he finished up and tossed the butt into his bucket, William started back around with the cart, and collected the dirty dishes. He stopped and gave the nodding man a slap; he didn't even flinch. William put his full plate with the tub of plates and pushed the cart out of the room. Vinny thought that was the end of it for the night. He felt tired and was going to try to get some sleep. Then he had a panicky feeling. How was he going to keep to his schedule if he was sleeping?

Luckily, William popped back into the room. This time the leather bundle of drugs was in his hand, along with a bottle of scotch. He lit a candle and started preparing doses. Vinny weighed his options and figured losing another tooth was better than losing his life, as miserable as it was.

"How can I smoke while I sleep?" It was a timid, pathetic sound that came from him.

William seemed startled by the sudden burst of noise, as sad as it was. This made the nervous man start laughing uncontrollably.

"You shut the fuck up. I've got your poison right here and in minutes you'll be miles away." He pointed the needle at the now quiet nervous man. "And you, I told you not to speak to me and if we didn't have customers on the way, I'd blacken the other half of your face. As for smoking in your sleep, you better just stay on your toes and be ready whenever he is."

Vinny nodded in agreement but was more confused than he was a minute ago. Customers? Be ready when he is? None of it made sense to Vinny. Yet.

The sound of shoes slapping concrete interrupted Vinny's train of thought. It was more than one person and there was laughing and talking mixed in. Puppy man William got nervous and raced around the room wiping faces with a wet rag, and cleaning up crumbs that had spilled from the sloppy bums eating their dinner. He rushed to the desk for the prepared doses and jabbed them both into their respective targets. The nervous man looked like he was going to argue but the sound of the rapidly approaching people kept him quiet as he looked toward the doorway. Lastly, William raced to the radio and switched it off.

Just in time. Three men entered the room. At least at first, Vinny thought they were men. He realized the one in back was the thing that had installed the collar shackles. He had his hands on the shoulders of the other two like he was leading them into his den for after-dinner drinks. Vinny was more right than he knew. He looked at the drunk, who was shockingly already halfway done with his fresh bottle of scotch. He looked at Vinny and mimed smoking a cigarette. It was a warning and the drunk seemed familiar with this routine. Elmer and his good advice came to mind, so Vinny lit a fresh cigarette. The thing noticed and gave Vinny a smile that made him want to get rid of the food he just ate.

Then the thing turned on the radio and furrowed his brow when he was met with a jaunty tune rather than the classical music, which he quickly found with the turn of the dial. He looked at William, who in turn looked at the ground, standing with his tail tucked in the corner by the radiator. There was a look that was well understood by everyone in the room. William would be taught a lesson later.

"Gentlemen let's get you what you came for. You've both paid. William, we need one heroin and two scotches," the thing said.

No sooner had he stopped talking than William was speeding to the drawers at the desk. He pulled out a handful of glass syringes and screwed needles onto them at lightning speed.

It wasn't fast enough.

"Sorry for the wait, gentlemen."

The thing was now obviously pissed at William, who was already exposing the neck of the junkie and filling one syringe. He put it in the pocket on the front of his leather apron and sidestepped to the drunk. The drunk made it easy for him and craned his neck upwards. He grimaced as the syringes plunged into his neck, but he held still for both. William sped to the desk and put the full syringes on a tray. The classical music was picking up with the anticipation Vinny was feeling. He could see the guests licking their lips and their red eyes were almost glowing in the light from the desk. They were just as hollow as the other thing. They were missing something crucial that Vinny couldn't place, something human.

"Would you like to go to the sitting room?" the thing asked. Vinny looked at him grinning at his guests and it suddenly made sense.

He was the bartender, and they were his customers.

"No, we might want seconds," one of the customers joked. All three of them laughed heartily.

"Well, that's fine, too. Just so long as we don't take more than four vials from any one prisoner in a day, they should live long enough to return my investment. And if you are still hungry after, we can fill that need as well."

The two customers looked at each other and nodded in approval.

William held the vials on the tray up to the men. The bartender grabbed them and handed two out, keeping one for himself.

"Enjoy."

With that, all three of them held the syringes up and squirted them into their mouths. Almost immediately, one of the customers spat out the contents.

"This one is nearly spoiled!" the pissed-off thing yelled at the bartender.

The bartender grabbed the syringe and wiped his finger on the end, then popped it into his mouth, quickly spitting on the now polka dotted floor. He spun and went to the nodding man, grabbing him by the chains and lifting him while sniffing his body deeply. The sniffing sounds brought even more fear to Vinny. They were too familiar. The thing spun and stood up stiffly.

"I'm sorry, gentlemen. My pathetic assistant should have caught the warning signs. We will get rid of him and have a fresh source in the morning." He looked pleadingly at the customers, who were now standing, arms folded in front of their mobster-style suits. For a second, Vinny thought they were going to pull out pistols and shoot. He thought they might set him free in the process.

"Well, he ain't spoiled yet. You care if I finish him off?" The words killed the hopes Vinny had that these men would cause problems for the bartender and possibly save him.

"By all means." The bartender motioned to the sleeping man. "Just do be careful as he was freshly dosed, so his blood will be potent."

Without hesitating, one guest took off his jacket and took three giant steps to the sleeping man. He grabbed him by the hair and pulled it back, exposing his neck.

"I don't gotta drink from the groin, do I?"

"Not in here, my friend. Anything goes in here, no need for secrets like on the street," the bartender said.

The thing proceeded to chew a hole into the side of the now dying man's neck. Vinny watched him grab a significant chunk with his teeth and rip it free. The vein he ripped into snapped loudly enough for Vinny to hear across the room. His stomach responded and he gagged. Now there was a slurping and corresponding gagging sound from the patron as well. It was the same sounds Vinny had heard from the bootlegger at the gazebo in the park. This made him think of the torn chunk of flesh from Elmer's inner thigh, his groin. The pieces were falling into place, but it was far too late to matter now. These things had hunted Elmer and him into extinction. But it was these things, these hollow-looking men, that were killing the unfortunate and addicted. In all the small towns with all the warnings Elmer and he had spread, the warnings were meant for these things. The pants were always down on the dead men and Elmer so they could feed from the blood that ran the heaviest there. No one much cared if an addict bum died, especially not enough to go searching around his groin for a cause of death. It was the same reason Elmer had put his secret pocket in inside of the pants by his butt, nobody wanted to search a homeless man's ass.

"Well, while your friend finishes up, would you like another drink, on the house?" the bartender asked the other patron, who was standing there looking envious.

"Sure would."

William snapped into action from his corner and prepared two more syringes quickly. The drunk, now looking terrified, had his neck ready before William was even close to him. He filled them quickly and handed the needleless syringes to the bartender.

The bartender thing took the syringes and returned a backhand that echoed off the walls.

"You ever embarrass me like that again and it will be the end of you." He looked at the patron without missing a beat and handed him a syringe. "Sorry you had to see that." The patron only smiled and held up his syringe.

"Cheers," he said as they both emptied them into their mouths.

The gagging sounds had ceased from across the room and William was rushing over a clean washcloth. The patron snatched it from him and cleaned his blood-soaked face as he rejoined the others near the desk. He stumbled as he neared them and steadied himself on the desk.

"You weren't kidding. Despite it being slightly sour, that blood was loaded, and now, so am I." The patron was slurring and clearly high as his eyelids fluttered against the drugs.

"And this one must have straight booze for blood cos I'm finely tuned off of two drinks." They both sounded like Dad after too much laudanum and booze.

Vinny was beginning to think he would escape being tortured for the night.

"Well, the conversion isn't like having a regular drink, but I will dial it in as I experiment with dosages." He paused and gave Vinny a look. "Would you gentlemen like to have a cigarette before we finish? It's my personal stash but I'm willing to share."

William was already preparing a fresh syringe. Vinny knew what was coming, and if he could manage to avoid a beating, he would. He looked at the clock and realized it was time to smoke again already, so he lit up.

While he smoked, the three of the things gathered in front of him and watched him finish. The cigarette was burning too quickly. Vinny was hoping it would last long enough to avoid the inevitable. It didn't. As soon as he was done and the butt was still glowing in the bucket, the bartender took a step forward, syringe in hand. Vinny was still choking on the smoke and trying to stifle a cough but didn't want to resist. So, he produced his neck like the drunk had done. The coughing was forcing his head to bounce on his shoulders despite his efforts to remain still. The thick, cold needle pressed into his skin; the bee sting feeling was now familiar to him. The coughing was forcing the needle in and out and he could feel it puncturing his esophagus.

"Shit, William, hold his head still." William's vise-like hands came from nowhere and Vinny was locked into place. The needle found its home quickly this time and Vinny grimaced as he watched the glass tube fill with his blood.

The patrons were laughing at the scene, clearly amused but also intrigued.

The bartender thing pulled the now full syringe out and turned back to the others. They passed it around, each draining roughly a third of Vinny's nicotine-laden blood into their mouths.

The patrons looked at each other nonplussed at first, then within a few seconds their faces changed.

"Holy shit, it actually works." William was smiling from ear to ear at this response from the customers.

"Yes, yes, of course it does. I told you it was good. Now this one is for personal use, but there are more coming for public consumption, as well as many other vices you may miss from your previous lives."

They chatted for a while longer before Vinny could tell the booze and drugs were winning out. The bartender seemed to pick up on the waning conversation and started to guide them out of the dungeon.

"Well, gentlemen, I do hope you enjoyed yourselves. I apologize for any hiccups, but they will be ironed out before you return." The bartender turned back into the room and looked at William. "Clean them up and straighten this place up, then I want you upstairs so we can...speak." He turned back to his guests. "I hope if you were happy, you will tell your friends. I have a feeling business is about to be booming."

The last statement put the hairs on Vinny's arms at attention. He wasn't sure if he was more upset about being a product or being a product for the bartender's personal use. It was clear no matter what that there was little to no hope of him ever getting out of here alive.

While William did the busy work around the dungeon, scrubbing it back to its former sterile state, he was cussing under his breath. Vinny watched him work and tried to make out what he was muttering, but there was no use. The nervous man was back to babbling nonsense about living in a park and eating at soup kitchens. None of it made sense. Every once in a while, William would stop to tell him to shut up, but it was no use; his mind seemed to be gone.

There was a pool of "spoiled" blood gathering around the feet of the junkie. The shade of red was the only thing distinguishing him being dead from being alive. He had been a nodding sleeping motionless thing without hope since Vinny had arrived. Now, he just had a fresh coat of paint. Vinny felt pity for him but doubted the man himself cared he was dead; he was probably just happy to be out of the dungeon.

William unbolted him and the rings on his collarbone swung freely now, no more nervous clanking. Vinny watched the soles of his feet disappear out the door as William dragged him away. There was the sound of a heavy metal door and a few minutes later, the smell of burning hair. William returned shortly after, humming now, not cussing. His mood seemed better.

William had pulled a hose into the room with him and the drains made sense as he washed the shit/piss/blood combination down the two eye-like drains. The polka dots of blood followed. Three cigarettes later, it was all clean, waste buckets empty, fresh bedding for all, full glasses of water, and a fresh pack of smokes for Vinny.

The last thing William did was warn Vinny.

"Stay on your toes, keep smoking. You never know when he's gonna want another." The warning caught Vinny off guard. It almost seemed friendly. Hope rekindled in a matter of seconds in his mind. Maybe he could appeal to his humanity. William didn't seem to be hollow like the other things. His eyes still looked human...white. But Vinny knew it was too soon. He would have to bide his time, maybe befriend William and get the fuck out of here.

William disappeared into the hallway and his footsteps echoed away. Vinny's hand disappeared under his cushion and retrieved the Dunhill, Elmer's eight bucks, and the rest of his money from hoeing. He snatched them and shoved them into his pocket again. His fingers massaged the Dunhill. Relief washed over him, and memories of Dad and Elmer calmed him down. At first. Then the ripples of drinking and babbling and abandonment washed the good memories until they were faded and angry. He was gripping the lighter so hard it hurt his hand.

He popped a cigarette into his mouth. He was a little early, but he doubted the thing would care if he smoked more often than directed. The Dunhill came out of his pocket and sparked to life as he pulled on the cigarette. He looked around to see if the drunk or the nervous man noticed his contraband. If they did, they didn't care.

After the smoke, Vinny fell asleep angry, and his dreams reflected it. They were full of faceless monsters and hollow, laughing men with red eyes. He woke up screaming sometime later and was promptly cussed out by the nervous man and the drunk. The Dunhill lit another cigarette as he looked at the clock. It was either 3 a.m. or 3 p.m., it didn't matter either way.

Footsteps interrupted his train of thought, and he was glad for the screams that woke him up to smoke. He would hate to disappoint the bartender and catch a beating, or worse. Though it was William not the bartender who appeared. His face was bruised, and his lip was split almost all the way to his chin. Vinny avoided eye contact and finished his smoke. Now was not the time to try to make friends. He watched William out of curiosity, maintaining his discretion.

William pulled something from his pocket. It was a bit of rope with a handle on either end, a garrote. He jumped forward toward the nervous man, who was now shrieking. He also knew what the item from William's pocket was, and he was scared of what was coming. The rope twisted around his neck and William pulled on the handles in opposite directions, tightening it, then he backed up until he was playing tug of war with the nervous man's neck and the chains holding him to the wall.

"There is no more fucking NEED FOR YOU!" William screamed at the top of his lungs. The nervous man was choking and clawing at his neck.

It was over suddenly, and the fighting stopped. William stood shaking and pulling on the garrote until there was a pop and one of the nervous man's shackles broke free, pulling the bone through the skin and clanking to the floor. Only then did William drop the now limp body to the ground as well. He stood there panting for a minute then calmly stepped onto the dead man's chest and ripped the other chain free with another sickening cracking sound. Then unceremoniously he dragged the man's body out of the room. Vinny watched the white soles of his feet disappear around the corner.

There were four empty spots now. As well as a drunk and a terrified Vinny, who lit another cigarette with his Dunhill and cursed his family and Elmer for letting this happen.

The empty spots on the concrete slabs had been filled in a matter of hours. Some well-dressed mobsters had brought four new bums and chained them to the walls, all of the bums asking questions at first then after the beatings started, they were silent. They stayed silent until the first of the collarings started. That was when the screaming started. Vinny couldn't stand it. He lit a cigarette with a match, not wanting to betray his Dunhill, and hid his face between his knees, which were pulled up to his face. The Cigarette dangled from his lips between his legs and his hands muffled the screaming. He only unplugged his ears for a moment to toss the butt into the bucket. The crying and screaming and laughing mixture were terrifying enough, but the orchestra playing behind it all made his pulse quicken. By the time it had finished, the beds were all full and the smell of Dakin's was overwhelming.

William was scurrying about, cleaning up the mess, changing bedding, dripping Dakin's on the wounds, placing gauze around the fresh shackles, and getting clothes for the naked half-conscious men. He seemed to get better with every changing. Their system was improving and with the seemingly endless supply of bums, they would only get better.

The bartender, now finished with the installations, was sitting at the desk marking something down in a logbook or something similar from what Vinny could tell. He was always taking notes when he visited. Vinny remembered him talking about dialing in dosages and figured it had to do with that.

Now that Vinny's initial shock was wearing off, he looked more closely at the thing. He was tall and muscular but not bearish. He always wore a suit, sometimes with a jacket, sometimes with a rubber apron. The smell of sulfur seemed to follow him and the patron things as well. If you saw him on the street, you'd expect women on his arms and flunkies following him around. Men probably wouldn't like him, but they would more than likely respect him.

As if he could feel Vinny taking stock of him, the bartender turned his head over his shoulder and gave him a grin.

"Time for a smoke." He opened the drawer in front of him and pulled out an empty syringe. "William, you better make sure these don't run out. They are getting low."

"Yes, sir," William sniveled back and disappeared into the hallway.

The bartender walked across the small gap between them. Vinny tossed his butt into the can and produced his neck. There was no sense resisting. The needle poked around and relatively quickly was removed with just a partial vial being produced. While still staring into Vinny's eyes, the bartender emptied the blood into his mouth. He took a few deep breaths, still staring, looking like he wanted to finish Vinny off and leave a dry corpse. Then his blood-red eyes softened to the creepy orange, and he spun on his heels, not saying a word. He shut the logbook on the desk and left the room, leaving Vinny with the new prisoners and a crying drunk.

Business seemed to pick up just as the bartender had predicted. The new prisoners adjusted as did Vinny. There was a sort of routine they could expect. They only had so much blood so there were only so many pokes in a day. Sometimes, prisoners would complain of being cold and the bartender would make notes. One was always dosed with cocaine, which they forced him to inhale from a tray. This one was an asshole. Another was always injected with heroin. This one nodded to sleep. The nervous one was given something called amphetamines. He was itchy and paranoid. Then there was the drunk, who was emotional. Another one seemed to be a catch-all gap filler who was sometimes fed bottles of booze to handle overflow. Sometimes dosed with another drug to handle a sudden rush. Always high on something, he was always sick.

Nothing changed for days, maybe weeks. It didn't matter anymore. Vinny could feel the heavy meals taking their toll on his body. His once well-defined chest was becoming soft and fleshy. For the first time in his life, he was getting a belly, which just slightly hung over his waistband now. The syphon sites for blood were beginning to leave deep sores that oozed pus regularly. Vinny could almost see concern on the bartender's face one evening when he squeezed one of the swollen sites until the pus ran onto his fingers. He rubbed it between his fingers and sniffed it, then wrinkled his nose.

"William, make sure you are cleaning these sites with Dakin's, as well as the rings," he ordered and went to make some notes in his book.

Vinny lit a cigarette and hoped for an infection.

There was no coughing when he smoked anymore. The taste had grown on him, too, and the cigarettes were a momentary escape from the dungeon at times. The food cart squeaked in the hallway and the nervous man lit up with insanity. It seemed Vinny wasn't the only one who looked forward to the food. It was the only other escape outside of cigarettes. Talking wasn't allowed. This didn't discourage whispering occasionally between Vinny and the asshole, sometimes the drunk, though Vinny found he couldn't stand the drunken babbling so usually just stayed silent. The nodding man slept. The man being force-fed cocktails of booze and drugs was puking in his bucket or sleeping, no good for talking. The fighting between the asshole and the nervous man could be entertaining until William or the bartender heard them, and the entire room was whipped with a thick leather strap that left gouges in the welts. This left Vinny with lots of time on his hands while he watched the clock. The hands marching forward his hatred of all the things that had led him into this dungeon.

Then one day, some excitement finally.

There was a different feeling in the air as the first guests for the day made their way in. For one, they were all dressed in costumes. Some wore masks, some were painted, some were in sheets, some in highly elaborate getups resembling skeletons. All scary. Knowing the faces behind the masks were those of the hollow things made them worse. The other surprise for the day was that some of the costumed men were accompanied by women. It was Halloween and all the spooks were out...with their dates.

A man dressed like a cowboy from a book walked in with a Southern debutante with the accent and all under his arm. She was talking like a proper Southern lady and making all the hollow things laugh. She was beautiful and Vinny couldn't help but stare in excitement and wonder why she was with this thing.

"Drinks, anyone?" the bartender offered, knowing the answer already as William was rushing from the desk to the drunk.

The perpetual drunk put his bottle down and looked to the sky until the syringes were full.

"Ladies first," one of the patrons said as William pulled the first one off the tray and offered it up.

To Vinny's horror, he saw the woman snatch it greedily and spray it into her mouth. He hadn't noticed the redness in her eyes before, as her body had distracted him. But now the makeup and the costume weren't nearly enough to hide the hollow monster underneath. Naively, Vinny had assumed all the monsters were men. He was wrong.

The rest of them toasted with the full vials and followed the woman thing's lead, slurping and gagging down the alcohol-laden blood. The bartender was giddy from their pleasure. He was in a good mood for a monster. The holiday had seemed to soften him and bring out a glimmer of what was left of the human he had replaced. He was smiling and laughing right along with the patrons. William was tucked into the corner by the radiator, waiting to be needed.

Vinny lit a cigarette, figuring he was next. However, shortly after they did another round, this time from the man who filled a need—who had been fed booze all day in anticipation—they all filtered out including William, leaving Vinny and the other men to digest the woman who had entered the room.

"I don't care what she is. If I wasn't chained up, I'd fuck her," the asshole on cocaine said.

"I bet you would, you degenerate," the nervous man started in on him.

Vinny thought it was vulgar and couldn't disagree more. She terrified him more than the other things because he hadn't seen her for what she was instantly, like the men monsters. He could be lulled into comfort by a monster like that. His pants rose in agreement, and he cursed himself. He pulled his knees up to his chest to hide the fact it excited him, too.

The argument between the two prisoners lasted four cigarettes' worth of entertainment. Vinny clicked the Dunhill in his hand and listened to pass the time. The drunk was babbling something about getting caught at a soup kitchen, which caught Vinny's ear. He was the third or fourth person he had heard talk about that since he had been in the dungeon.

"Did you say you were at the soup kitchen?" Vinny whispered, thinking it was safe enough if the others were doing it, too.

Through his sobbing, the drunk finally responded, "Yeah...why?"

"Well, I've heard a few guys in here now talk about them and was just wondering if they had something to do with this place."

The drunk was suddenly angry. His mood shifted by the drink.

"Are you fucking kidding me? Is that what they do, then? Get us while we are eating?" He was yelling.

He was about to start yelling some more when there was a soft padding down the hallway. Someone was coming, and they were alone. This usually meant it was William making his rounds feeding, cleaning, or watering them. However, miles of footsteps later, the bartender came in alone with a ceramic tea pot steaming away on a tray with some other things.

"And who was yelling, and what about?" The thing usually never spoke to them, so they all stared in shocked silence. "I said, who was yelling, and about what?" There was no mistaking his irritation about asking twice.

Everyone looked in unison at the drunk, who saw the stares and started fuming.

"It was me. This kid told me that you all catch us by waiting for us at the soup kitchens." He motioned at Vinny, whose stomach sank. "That's pretty messed up even for something like you."

"Shut up," the bartender said to the drunk, but his eyes were locked on Vinny.

He took a cup from the shelves by the desk and poured a dark liquid into it. Then he made his way to Vinny and handed it to his shaking hands, smiling the whole time. Vinny could smell it now. It was coffee.

"Drink," the bartender ordered.

Vinny did and poured the boiling hot liquid into his mouth, scorching his tongue in the process. He finished in one drink. The bartender smiled and grabbed the kettle to Vinny's dismay. He approached and refilled the cup.

"Drink it, take your time." He paused and his smile faded. "Explain to me what you told him."

Vinny felt like he was being baited into making a mistake, but he couldn't see how lying would help at this point.

"Well, I've heard a few guys in here now that have all mentioned a soup kitchen, so I was just asking him if he was at one too." It was the most he had spoken in a long time. It felt nice.

"To what end?" the bartender asked.

"Just tying up some loose ends in my mind. I guess I still had questions," Vinny said without hesitating, suddenly hopeful for some reason.

The grin returned to the thing's face.

"Well, well, seems you've figured out a secret of ours. Yes, we do use the soup kitchens to our benefit. We own and operate almost all of them, in fact. It's like a buffet of the indignant and addicted, easy pickin's really." He smiled smugly now. "In fact, we make the booze they drink in those communities as well. The soup kitchens keep us in the locals' good graces and in the meantime, we can pick and choose the ones who won't be missed."

Vinny thought back to the nice little moonshine family who had been mowed down by gangsters, the little girl with no face, and he hated the monster just a little more than he had a minute ago.

"It's just one of our avenues of income, including this little venture that you have become a part of, as an unwilling participant though you may be."

The thing was preparing himself a drink from the emotional man next to him. The coffee was starting to make Vinny even more jittery and shaky than normal; his chains were clanking against the wall.

Then there was a commotion in the hallway, interrupting the bartender's drink. He placed it on the desk and went to investigate. Moments later, he returned with three patrons from earlier who were looking for another drink.

"Like I told you, he is at his limit for today. Any more would kill him, and that, my friends, will cost a premium," the bartender said, protecting his investment.

"Whatever. I don't give a fuck. We want a smoke, too," the patron in charge ordered.

The bartender shot Vinny a look and Vinny lit a Cigarette.

"I usually reserve this one for myself, but if you are paying what I ask, we can reach an arrangement. From now on, you order ahead of time. Understood?"

"I said whatever. Are we good?" the man said, getting pissed.

"Indulge," the bartender rattled.

In a flash, the three men were on the emotional man next to Vinny. He was squealing for a brief moment, until one of them sank their teeth into his throat, replacing the squeals with gurgles. They drank and joked until they were satisfied. Leaving a dripping husk of a drunk on the bed next to Vinny.

William would clean it.

Vinny found it harder and harder to feel anything about it.

The drunk things were now joking about their costumes while Vinny craned his neck skyward, hoping the thing would avoid jabbing him in the same spot as last time. It was still sore, possibly infected, judging by the bartender's reaction earlier.

One of them looked at Vinny and laughed, pointing him out to the others.

"And what are you for Halloween this year little boy...a pack of smokes?" They all roared with laughter at the joke.

"Actually, he's a pack of smokes and a cup of coffee tonight," the bartender added and laughed himself. "Let me know what you think."

They all took a shot of Vinny, and within moments were all in agreement that the bartender was onto something special with that one.

The party cleared out shortly after. Leaving Vinny with the burning remarks. Maybe he was just a pack of cigarettes and a cup of coffee now, after all. It echoed in his mind until the bartender returned.

He looked at the dead drunk.

"Pity, that one could hold his liquor." He shrugged looking at the drunk's body. "He did have a big mouth, however."

Then he grabbed Vinny by the hair unexpectedly and jammed a needle in with no regard for his discomfort. He took the full vial to his desk and drank both Vinny and the dead drunk's blood from the vials he had prepared. He sat listening to the radio for a while, which Vinny enjoyed since it was regular music for a change instead of opera. The thing almost looked pitiable sitting there trying to pretend to be human. Trying to cling to the things that once made him human. The holiday must have rustled some memories along with the drunks blood.

"You know we have men everywhere." The booze was in his voice. "The only reason this was possible…" He motioned to the dungeon with his arms flailing. "…was Mr. Ehrlich's research with the blood brain barrier. It gave me this idea, use your blood to get our vices to our brains since we lack the fluid of life ourselves."

Vinny wasn't sure what he was talking about, but he could tell he was bragging.

"We also control some of your newest distractions. The talking pictures, movies, what have you. We've made some of our own, in fact. The quite famous *Nosferatu* picture was modeled after its director. What better way to mislead the masses than to make a picture to blame their fears on? We no longer exist except in the imaginations of the mentally feeble and children afraid of the dark," the drunk bartender continued.

Vinny did understand this reference, and for the first time realized monsters were in fact real. These weren't hollow men things. They were vampires.

The bartender vampire finished bragging shortly after and left without another word, seeming embarrassed at himself for talking drunkenly to a prisoner. The vampire left the radio on, either in an act of humanity that he was trying to hold onto or by accident. Either way, Vinny didn't care. He listened to the songs, which turned to local and national news. By the sounds of it, the other monsters in suits hadn't been doing a great job getting Wall Street back up and running. Also the men in overalls hadn't done a great job farming as the soil was blowing all over hell and back. Late to the party were the locusts, but they were quickly bringing up the rear.

Maybe the vampire's dungeon wasn't as bad as it could be. Vinny wondered how the family farm was holding up. He caressed the Dunhill and lit a cigarette, thinking about Mom and Dad specifically. He hoped they were buried in dust and locusts.

The addition of the coffee made sleep almost impossible, so Vinny smoked and ruminated on his hatred rather than sleeping the days away waiting for the vampire to need a smoke. The ripples of hate were becoming waves and slowly eroding the better memories he had. All he could seem to remember about home was how much he hated it when he was there. How much he hated Mom and Jamie Lynn and even his cowardly father. There was still a soft spot for the boys, but even that was disappearing to the waves of hate. What was left of Elmer was regret and anger. If he only could have controlled himself around the booze. If only Vinny had heeded his warnings to shush, imagined or not. No hate was lost.

Vinny's small belly was now swelling, and he could feel himself gaining weight in other areas as well. There wasn't much that could be done about it at this point. The shackles were preventing any kind of exercise. His shoulders were still raw, as the constant pulling from the chains seemed to be slowing the healing. Plus, the food was amazing, and Vinny couldn't seem to get enough. He looked forward to the food cart most of all. So many nights were spent worrying about dinner and bouncing from town to town. Now when given the opportunity to eat, he couldn't help but gorge himself.

The growing belly reminded him of fat, smoking Mom in the corner eating her smoky soup. In some ways she was just as much trapped in a dungeon as Vinny was, only hers was created by her fat body and her fear of being judged for it. She hadn't left the house in so long, hell, she hardly even left her corner. Maybe that had changed? Maybe right now she was out with Dad looking for him. Vinny caressed Dad's lighter and he had the fleeting feeling of hope. He looked at the clock and flicked the lighter to a fresh cigarette. His sense for predicting the bartender's need for a cigarette was getting better and most of the time, he was close. He looked at the half-finished cup of coffee and drank it as well. It was cold, but he knew if it wasn't empty when William came in to prepare the bartender's syringe, it would not go over well.

Just as Vinny was finishing the smoke, a set of footsteps started echoing down the impossibly long hallway. Right again, Vinny thought, and waited the eternity it took them to get to the room. The visit was typical at first. William made his rounds and dosed the prisoners. Then he started the cleanup, buckets, wounds, new bedding. While this went on, the bartender gathered a syringe and eyed Vinny.

"Smoke another cigarette quickly," he ordered.

Vinny groaned internally but complied. He pulled the cigarette down within four drags while the bartender watched. Vinny's stomach churned from too much nicotine and his head was spinning from it. As soon as the butt hit the bucket, the needle was in his throat. Then it just stayed there motionless. Vinny looked over his upturned chin at the vampire's forehead, and then to his blood-red eyes. There was concern in them.

He finally pulled the needle from Vinny's neck and squirted just a few drops into his mouth, followed by a smacking of his tongue.

"You're souring." He squirted the rest of the vial into his mouth and wrinkled his nose as his eyes faded to a mild yellow. "That won't do at all, will it?"

He looked at Vinny now then squeezed some sores on his neck, inspecting the fluid with his nose. Then he dug a finger into the holes the shackles were forming.

Vinny grimaced but stayed motionless and silent. The bartender retrieved his now pinkish finger and tasted the fluid. His nose wrinkled again.

Vinny started vibrating, the overdose of nicotine not helping his nervousness. He had seen what happened to people with sour blood in the dungeon. His eyes darted around the room to find William. He expected to see him running at him with the garrote in his hands, ready to choke the life out of him.

"Something will have to be done." And without another word, he left Vinny to wonder and worry with William slinking around the room.

William simply finished his chores and then went to retrieve the food cart. He only briefly stopped at Vinny's bed while delivering the plates of food. Vinny was nervous but he couldn't resist. In fact, he grabbed more food than he usually would have. It may be his last meal after all, and it would probably make him feel better. Only when William echoed his way down the hall did Vinny let his guard down and dig into his personal buffet.

The junkie was making gagging sounds out of his meal or his own phlegm. Vinny couldn't tell which. It sounded like the gurgling some of them made when they died. He tuned it out and ate. The only thing he liked less than being stuck in the dungeon was being stuck in it with the dregs of humanity. There was rarely a good conversation to be had. All they wanted to talk about was their own misery. After the first dozen or so new prisoners who had come and gone, Vinny was numb to it. He had heard all of their sob stories before.

As soon as the meal was finished, Vinny felt like he would be sick. William returned later for the dishes, but Vinny was already asleep in a food coma. He woke up hours later screaming in his sleep. He couldn't remember the dream this time, but the jeers from the asshole and the nervous man were enough to stop the screaming.

Vinny felt hot, his muscles were tight in his legs, and a sheen of sweat was covering his body. The sweat was soaking through his clothes, and it started him shivering. He pulled his knees to his chest and smoked a cigarette.

A solitary set of footsteps started down the hallway. Vinny was sure it was William, ready to choke the life out of him. Maybe it was for the best. He was growing accustomed to this place, and less and less he felt like himself. How long before there was nothing left of Vinny? Just a pack of smokes and a cup of coffee for vampires. That wasn't the life he had in mind when he was forced from home.

The footsteps were closer now, just about there. Vinny steadied himself. He was ready. He wouldn't put up a fight and make William rip him from the wall by his bones.

The bartender entered the room and shocked Vinny, who gasped at the sight of him.

"Still scared of me, boy?" He laughed to himself. "Well, after this morning, maybe you will be singing a different tune...or not." He laughed again.

Vinny had no idea what he was talking about but held his breath in anticipation as the bartender approached him.

"This one goes *in*." He produced a syringe that was already full of a dark red liquid that resembled blood, and he jammed it into Vinny's shoulder, depressing the plunger as he went in.

Vinny could feel the cold fluid enter his bloodstream. He was even more confused than he was a minute ago. Had he been injected with blood?

The uncanny vampire was in his head.

"You think that was blood, do you? Well, I'm sorry to disappoint but that is only reserved for my kind. In fact, you have been given a test injection of an antibacterial drug called

Prontosil. It was developed by some men we have inside a company called Bayer. It's in the old world, but they have some new exciting possibilities for us." He chuckled again. "You see, we may feed on you like cattle, but we need you nice and healthy to do so, so we benefit the greater portion of mankind by only eating those that don't benefit the greater good, and develop medicines for those that do. It's mutually beneficial in this way." He was obviously pleased with himself. Vinny was offended that the bartender thought he didn't matter to the greater good, but he was right. He was just a bum when he was captured and would probably have stayed that way for the rest of his short, miserable life. Vinny thought of Mom and Dad again. This was their fault.

The bartender, now finished with his gloating, left without a smoke. Vinny sat shaking and sweating and hating.

Within a few days, the stink and sweat had left Vinny. Every day, twice a day, the bartender came in and administered the Prontosil. He would examine the sores on his body, nod and take notes. On the fourth day, the results must have been promising as the bartender started administering it via William to the other prisoners as well. From that point forward, the shackles started to heal and within two weeks, he was back to being a pack of smokes. He was healed now, and the shackles no longer hurt. The abscesses in his neck had abated as well. On some level, Vinny felt cared for. Not like at home, where he did all the caring for everyone and nursing Dad back to health after he shattered his leg or caring for his mongoloid sister. Here he was being looked after, and all he had to do was smoke cigarettes and drink coffee on schedule.

Speaking of, Vinny looked at the clock and produced his Dunhill to light a cigarette. Close enough. Halfway through his smoke, Vinny heard an unfamiliar gait coming down the hall. It was a clumsy, shuffling sound, not the firm slapping footsteps of the vampire or the soft padding of puppy man's feet. Vinny looked around at the rest of the hopeless. None of them cared enough to even notice. They would shortly, however.

The shuffling approached the door and a slim, dirty figure leaned in with a lunatic smile plastered on his face. His blood-red eyes and hollow look gave him away as a vampire instantly. But there was something off about him. He was wearing average-looking clothes for one, not a suit like the rest of them. There was also the manner in which he moved. He was darting his red eyes around nervously, and his tongue kept running across his lips. The fingers on both hands were rapidly curling and uncurling. It reminded Vinny of a rabid dog that had trapped him and his brothers on the roof of the barn until Dad sobered up enough to wake up and shoot it with the varmint gun.

"Hello," the thing whispered. "Are we all alone?" He looked into the corners of the room and down the hallway. "Looks like it, now don't be scared, boys, I'll be gentle."

He started at the far side of the room with the junkie Vinny thought had aspirated on his own vomit last night. Apparently not, as the junkie stiffened up and tried to start a scream before the vampire clapped a hand over his mouth then his teeth around his throat, ripping out a lethal chunk. The gurgling started as he let his hand fall away from the junkie's mouth. The now free hand started peeling strips of flesh from the dying man's face as he drank and gagged away. As soon as the life was gone from the junkie, the thing stood up and made his way to the man who filled a need for overflow. The man pleaded with him to stop but it was no use. He ripped his throat out in the same fashion. Only this time, he spat out the blood.

"Nothing in this one. What a waste." Vinny realized the man must have been sober, waiting for a need to be filled.

He moved on to the nervous man on amphetamines, who was busy looking for invisible bugs in his skin and hardly seemed aware there were people dying right beside him. He would soon enough. The ripping sound of flesh was followed by the gagging and sucking sounds the things made when they ate. The nervous man seemed to have a moment of clarity as his eyes darted around the room, seeking a savior but only seeing dead men and bums tied to the wall. The life in his eyes left him quickly thereafter.

Vinny suddenly realized this thing was going to eat everyone in the room. The thing's eyes had faded to a burnt orange but his lust for killing them and getting higher only seemed to increase as he rushed to the asshole on cocaine. The asshole put up a fight and got a couple of good shots in on the thing, but they didn't even faze it. He walked through the punches like they were from a toddler and pinned the asshole against the wall. Then he proceeded to chew through his throat sloppily. The kills were getting less clean the higher the thing got. The asshole was able to talk while the thing took its time and drained him slowly. Obviously, he liked the cocaine.

The panic was full blown now. Vinny could see it on the drunk's face as well. Not having any other option, they looked at each other and both started screaming for help. The drunk yelled ambiguously to the ether for help while Vinny was much more targeted.

"WILLIAM, HELP!" Vinny put the screams on maximum volume and repeat. So did the drunk.

The screaming only seemed to excite the junkie vampire.

"I told you boys it's going to be fine." And he laughed as he wiped the blood from his chin. "I'm feeling better already." The twitching and sickly look he had upon entering the room had faded and he was looking fresh and dangerous now. "Except now, I need a drink." He looked at the drunk.

Sniff sniff.

"That must be you, then."

The drunk was crying now, still pleading for help at the top of his lungs. There was none. The vampire dug his teeth in and spat out a chunk of flesh, then the sucking, gagging sounds started. The drunk was hitching like a child who was all cried out.

Vinny was losing his voice but continued to scream for William. He knew the sucking sounds were not going to last long and then it would be his turn. He was right. The vampire stumbled backward from the drunk. He bent forward and a torrent of blood was puked onto the floor in front of Vinny.

"Too much yet never enough." He looked at Vinny. "Well, we can't leave you here by yourself now, can we?" He took a step forward and grabbed Vinny by his shackles.

CRACK

The sound came from behind the vampire, who let out a shriek in surprise or pain. Then he spun and Vinny got a look at

William, who was armed with a baseball bat with shiny spikes driven through it.

CRACK

William smacked the thing in the face, this time driving the spikes into one of its eyes. There was a hissing, bubbling noise coming from the wound and an acrid smoke was rising from the base of the spikes. William removed the bat and swung again.

CRACK

CRACK

CRACK....

The smacking went on until there was nothing left of the vampire's head but a puddle of mush that blended with the pool of blood it had puked up.

William stood there panting for a minute and surveyed the room. The carnage was unbelievable. Vinny was numb to it. His blood felt cold. Something about the way William came in reminded him of Elmer saving him from the rapey bum, and he forgot himself for a second.

"Thanks for saving me," he said to William.

"I told you to never speak to ME!" William screamed as he looked at Vinny.

He slung the bat over his shoulder and looked like he was going to bury it in Vinny's head. Vinny just leaned forward to meet it. He had no fight left in him.

For some reason, this made William laugh and he softened.

"Sorry, boy. Guess my blood was a little hot."

Vinny looked at the bat regretfully and nodded to William.

"Fucking withdrawals make them crazy." He nodded at the vampire's corpse. "I better get the boss."

A few hours later, the bartender came to inspect. He looked tired. Vinny looked at the clock, which read 5 o'clock, a.m. or p.m., he wasn't sure. The bartender inspected the room and shook his head. He got ahold of Vinny and scoured him for marks.

"Did he bite you or scratch you anywhere?" the bartender thing asked, its sulfur smell mixed with the iron smell of blood in the room, creating a toxic-tasting air.

Vinny shook his head no.

"Well, at least there is that. Them I can replace." He motioned to the dead bums surrounding them. "You, I've put too much work into at this point."

Vinny wondered if it was meant to make him feel better. It didn't.

"Well, I guess it's time to tighten security," the bartender said now. It made Vinny shudder. If the dungeon wasn't safe, what was?

That night after William had cleaned up the mess and Vinny sat alone in the room for the first time, the quietness provided an opportunity. With all the background noise from the bums gone, Vinny could hear conversation coming from somewhere down the hall. It was tough to make out but if he strained, he could make out most of it.

First, there was talk of an empty train that had already been filled, so there was nothing to worry about as far as filling the dungeon back up with prisoners. It reminded Vinny of the creepy empty train that had pulled into the last town he left. He wondered if they were using it to move bums around from soup kitchens to dungeons. Had he ridden on it to get here?

Next, they discussed security and the need for more daylight hour guards. There seemed to be a disagreement about how to get said guards, but in the end, someone said they had a plethora of willing and unwilling slaves. This drew laughter from the entire room, and they moved on to the next topic.

The Moon King.

They were apparently familiar with him as well. Vinny could hear someone say.

"He drained the entire town. All that was left was warnings and blood. At this rate he's drawing too much attention and he's gonna get us all caught." There was a chorus of agreement.

Someone suggested they put two trackers on him and figure out where he moved on to. When they found his new whereabouts, they would put a hunting party together and put the glutton down. More agreement from the crowd.

Then it was time for smokes. Vinny could hear William race across the hallway, his soft padding footsteps making quick work of it.

"Smoke another cigarette, boy," he instructed Vinny, who was already preparing one. He almost slipped up and sparked the Dunhill, forgetting it was contraband, but caught himself just in time and used a match instead. Vinny raced the cigarette down and arched his neck for William. He ended up taking four full syringes and Vinny was left lightheaded and sore. The repetitive poking was taking its toll on him mentally as well.

They finished their meeting with Vinny's blood and by the next morning, five new bums were marched in. It was going to be a busy day of collaring. Vinny hid his face and smoked most of the day, trying to avoid the screams for help the best he could. He thought about the night he was forced to leave home and how he had thought it felt like a dungeon being stuck in the house with his family. He was so wrong. This was much, much worse. He rubbed the Dunhill now hidden in his pocket, hoping it would bring relief.

It didn't.

The days were lost to monotony and terror. Vinny tried to keep track of the days but eventually found it useless. It was easier to track the passage of time with the growth of his now prominent belly. The bartender had recently added cigars to his list of needs, so at almost all times, Vinny was now either smoking cigarettes or lovely-tasting hand-rolled cigars. There was no more nicotine overdosing—just the smooth, relaxing pleasure smoking offered by way of a distraction from the monotony of his days. The cigars just added to the distractions, and he loved the taste.

Today, the monotony was broken by an announcement from William.

"It's Thanksgiving and believe me, these fellas got an appetite, so get yourself smoking."

William was addressing Vinny, only, not talking to him but at him. Like you would a dog you didn't much care for but couldn't get rid of. Vinny was still rubbing the sleep from his eyes, but his fingers were mindlessly striking a match in agreement with William. He coughed up a ball of thick phlegm and spat it into the bucket. His lungs were starting to feel the wear of constant smoking.

Any time he felt like he was adjusting to the routine, the patrons would rip out another throat. Or peel a man's face off while he screamed for hours. There was no adjusting to that aspect of the dungeon. The fear was constant. Maybe another junkie vampire would sneak in and start on his side of the room first. Maybe a patron just wouldn't follow the rules and would do what he wanted. Maybe he would stop being useful and William would show up with his garrote.

If Halloween was any indication, today would be busy. Business had only increased since then, and Vinny was sure so had dungeon capacity down the hall, as he could hear the screams of pain and anguish every so often. Vinny felt bad for the other prisoners, knowing they were surely in for more syringes than he was as he was mostly private stock for the owner. The new drunk was actually not as miserable of an emotional babbler as the rest had been. He was friendly and could hold a worthwhile conversation every so often.

"Get yourself ready. Today's gonna be a long day," Vinny whispered to Paul the drunk and made a face of pity. He had offered his name openly one night when he was drunk. Vinny hadn't reciprocated.

"I'll be fine as long as no one pays to eat me." He faked a chuckle.

The padding steps of William returned to the door, and they stopped talking. He prepared the doses for everyone and a cup of coffee for Vinny, along with a fresh cigar and a pack of smokes. He busied himself around the room and cleaned the bartender's desk. Then they waited.

William wasn't lying—it was busy. There was a constant stream of vampires, mostly looking for booze, some just wanting to gorge themselves. The constant stream of screams coming down the hall was more than a good indication of that. Some came into the bar covered in blood, apparently looking for an after-dinner drink. William was flying up and down the hallway like a confused puppy learning to fetch. The bartender looked pleased and divided himself between the rooms, making small talk all the while.

The vampires all had different personalities, just like people. Some of the patrons were assholes and treated the bums in chains like dinner that deserved to die. Others were pleasant enough and just wanted their fix; it was nothing personal. One happened to run a library, where he bragged to his boss that he was "skimming billionaire philanthropists' money off the top with a shovel." Aside from his shady library management skills, he was friendly, and once when he had gotten drunk on Paul's blood he talked about books with Vinny. He seemed to find it very interesting that a chubby bum like him would have such an extensive knowledge of books and had read so many. He promised to negotiate with the bartender to get him some reading material, but Vinny didn't expect him to follow through. It was just more drunken babble like Dad and Elmer and every other drunk he ever met.

The crowd today was more of the same, a mixed bag. Some came in and eyed them like sides of beef or bottles of fine wine, some looked at the floor until their syringes were full. Then a customer came in and the air in the room changed. It seemed everyone could feel it, even William as he tucked himself into the corner by the radiator while the intimidating patron browsed the wares. He made his way around the room, looking at the bums and lightly sniffing the air around them. His muffled footsteps made their way to Vinny eventually.

At first, he sniffed lightly. Then his blood-red eyes darkened into an almost black. Then.

Sniff...sniff....SNIFFFF

It was a cadence that was burned into Vinny's memories, real and imagined. It had haunted him from underneath a burning tree all the way to his nightmares. Vinny's eyes flew to the vampire's feet in a panic.

Leather, Fancy, Smooth soles.

They were as unmistakable as his sniffing. Vinny swallowed hard as the thing stared into his eyes.

"That one's off limits. It's boss's personal use only," William chimed in, saving Vinny for a second time unknowingly.

"Curious," the tall, thin, older man-thing-vampire in an expensive looking suit said. He was even more hollow-looking than the others. "You think if I requested him, that your boss would dare deny ME?" The thing growled the last words.

Vinny's guts clenched inside him.

"No, sir, just telling you the rules. You'd have to take that up with him." William was almost a part of the walls now, joining them in the corner.

Sniff...sniff....SNIFFFF

"No bother. I wasn't in the mood for what's in his blood. I need heroin and a drink." William sprang to life, rushing to accommodate the request and hopefully get this patron to move along sooner rather than later. "There is just something about this one that is familiar. I never forget. I'll remember eventually... nothing is lost."

Vinny swallowed hard and hoped the liquor and heroin would muddle his mind. He wasn't sure what kind of power this vampire wielded over the bartender, but he didn't seem to mind stepping on his toes. As if to accentuate this point, smooth soles pulled the chair away from the desk and sat down. No one had ever sat in the bartender's spot before, and the nervous man chuckled at the sight. William ran across the room and turned his face red with the back of his hand.

Smooth soles sat there staring at Vinny. He emptied the first syringe in a single, gagging gulp. The second he took his time with. His eyes never leaving Vinny. Thankfully, William never left the room like he had the rest of the day. He must have sensed the danger to Vinny as well.

"Anything else?" William offered as the second the syringe was emptied.

"No, no, that's fine for now You and your boss are running a pretty interesting operation here. I like what I'm seeing." He seemed looser and at least more friendly to William.

"You should tell him that. He will be pleased to hear it," William responded, suddenly lit up with excitement.

"Oh, I will." He got up and pushed the chair in.

Vinny relaxed. Just before the thing was about to turn for the door, he spun and took two quick steps toward Vinny. He grabbed him by the face and pushed his sulfur-smelling mouth up to his ear.

"I remember you; you know. I was there in the beginning, and I will be there in the end. No fire on Earth can save you from me." He leaned back and grinned at Vinny then left the room.

This left Vinny and the rest of the dungeon shocked. They were all sure they were witnessing the end of Vinny, but he had restrained himself, something none of the other vampires seemed to be able to do.

The rest of the room had been left cautiously optimistic. Vinny was left terrified. Now he had the constant threat of smooth soles coming back to finish him off at any time. Luckily for the rest of the bums, there was no killing of anyone today, no throats ripped open, no polka dots of blood on the white floor. Also, the Prontosil was a miracle drug—there hadn't been a single spoiled blood loss in weeks.

The last event for the day was dinner. None of them expected what came through the door. It was a full Thanksgiving spread. Everything Vinny could think of that was associated with the holiday was crammed onto two carts that William wheeled in with a smile. The bums gasped and laughed openly. William didn't shush them. He only started his rounds, letting them all make their choices.

Vinny's nervous stomach disappeared at the sight of it. He had told himself to eat less unless he wanted to look like Mom before too long, but today wasn't the day to start a diet. By the end of his fourth plate of everything and his sixth cigarette, the appearance of smooth soles was almost completely out of mind. He lit an after-dinner cigar after the dishes had been collected, and he drank his cup of coffee. Surely, the bartender would be showing up for his need soon enough.

He was almost right.

The bartender did show up, but it wasn't business as usual. He was carrying a bottle of booze with a label printed in a language Vinny couldn't place. He set the bottle down on the desk and pinched the cork out with his thumb and forefinger. He held it up to his nose and breathed deeply.

"Aaaah, my boy, you are in for a treat, and soon enough so am I." He poured the bottle into a cup meant for water, not booze. "Now don't stand on ceremony and appreciate this too much. Get it down your gullet so I can have my turn." He handed the cup to Vinny, who looked at it with hatred. "Oh, not a drinker huh? Well, you are now." The bartender laughed.

Vinny didn't argue or plead his case. He simply upended the cup, drinking it all in one fiery gulp. It was smooth and smoky tasting—something about it reminded him of Mom's smoky soup. He gagged despite himself.

The vampire nodded in approval and laughed at the gag.

"You do have spirit." The bartenders attempted a smile.

The thing's eyes were less red and more yellow, which Vinny had come to realize meant he was satiated to some degree. He wasn't sure if it was that he was full or that it was another holiday stirring the humanity still left in him, but something made this hollow thing feel more human tonight. Vinny could already feel the foreign liquors effects in his nose and lips. It was spreading outward from his guts.

"I hear you had an interesting visitor today." The bartender still smiled at Vinny, who was getting drunker by the second.

Vinny's eyes widened in fear as he thought this might have been his last drink, like from the cowboy books he had read.

"Not to worry, you are safe for now," he said, seeming to peer into Vinny's mind again.

Despite the fact that they were coming from a monster, the words were comforting.

The bartender opened his logbook and made some notes while he waited for the booze to saturate Vinny. Before too long, he sniffed the air deeply and two syringes then approached Vinny, who was in the ready position. With a gentler hand than usual, he retrieved Vinny's alcohol-laden blood and returned to his seat.

The bartender squirted most of the first vial into his mouth then paused and tilted his head back, relishing it.

"It's so goddamn good I can almost taste it through the metal in your blood."

He held the bottle of foreign liquor to his nose and squirted the rest of the first vial into his mouth. Vinny was impressed, as it seemed like a smart way to subvert his senses.

"Close," the vampire said, smiling.

By the time the second vial was gone, the thing's lips loosened, and the bragging began.

"You know, the original idea to only occupy the top of the social ladder isn't specific to us. It's been used for millennia to keep certain groups out of the reach of the laws of man. We just perfected it. You see, justice isn't fair and balanced like the blindfolded lady likes to say. If one has enough resources, one can buy his way out of almost anything, or disappear. You see, the long arm of the law has a hard time reaching the top rungs of the ladder." He looked pleased with himself.

Vinny nodded in polite agreement, feeling drunk and stupid.

The thing continued, "In combination with our code, it is almost a surefire way to maintain a status of invisibility to the common man. It is our greatest power as a group, the ability to blend in at the top, if one can simply manage to follow the rules: Only feed from the useless, only bleed them from the groin out in the wild, don't encroach on another's turf, and don't turn anyone without permission from above....And above is what you met today, boy. Getting permission from him is nearly impossible. Yet we still get rogues that don't follow the rules and try to live normal lives according to their feelings, those are the ones that need to be hunted. And then, every once in a while, there is a glutton. Someone who can't control their appetite once they've turned. They will eat an entire town for breakfast and before long they become something else…something even more different than this." The bartender paused and motioned his hands over himself. "They must be dealt with, or they will alert everyone to our presence. But this one is different, though, maybe it wouldn't be so if I hadn't known him in the past."

His brow furrowed at this like he was deeply concerned. Vinny conjured mental images of the Moon King, sure that that was what the bartender was talking about when combined with the conversation he had overheard across the hallway the other night. Vinny was scared of him, too.

"Why just drunks and junkies?" Vinny slurred, shocking himself and the bartender as well.

The bartender's brow shot up in anger. Then his face relaxed when he looked at the drunk boy.

"Why just eat when you can satisfy your vices and feast at the same time?" the thing answered simply.

It enraged Vinny but it was logical.

It seemed to enrage the asshole on cocaine as well, as he let loose with a string of obscenities, his confidence seemingly bolstered by Vinny's question and the soft response from the monster. It was a mistake that the rest of the dungeon would suffer the consequences of.

The bartender jumped across the room in one motion and punched the man in the face so hard, the bone around his eye collapsed and his head bounced off the concrete behind him. Blood sprayed outward, painting the wall in an artistic spray.

"Shit, too hard. I don't need more losses." He looked at the still breathing but unconscious man and swayed on his feet, obviously drunk. He left the room in a huff, the bottle still uncorked on his desk, the used vials lying beside it.

Shortly after, William came in and cleaned the mess. He inspected the wounds on the still snoring asshole and shrugged.

"He's gonna regret this in the morning, and so will the rest of you."

After William left with his ominous warning, the booze was still in Vinny's head, and he didn't feel like sleep. Instead, he found himself babbling to Paul, who only nodded to the boy whose story he listened to completely. Vinny was recounting his adventures with Elmer at first. Stopping to cry at the part where he died. Then he swapped the tears for anger at him for not being able to control his drinking. Then he swapped Elmer for his parents and his anger with them for tossing him out. Vinny cursed them all while he lit a smoke with the Dunhill that was supposed to make him remember the family that loved him, and yet he only felt pain. Vinny could feel the spiral the drunken babble was getting him into, but he couldn't stop himself. He had never felt more like his dad.

Thankfully, his tolerance was low enough that passing out came shortly after the babbling started, saving him the embarrassment of further ranting.

He woke up the next morning to the sound of the squeaky table making its way down the hallway. The bartender wasn't bluffing, and neither was William. Today was going to be a long day.

The asshole was awake and looked to be holding his face together with his left hand. As soon as the bartender entered the room with the table, the apologies and the pleading started. He knew he had made a mistake last night, and there was no talking his way out of it. The bartender gave him a look that finally shut him up. Then he went to his desk and opened a book. He took a scalpel from the tray on the table and mimed some motions in the air while he read.

Then it started. Asshole first.

William undid the chains from the wall with his key and led the crying man to the table. Vinny lit a cigarette and watched. They laid him down and strapped him in.

"Are there any last words?" The vampire almost giggled in his face, leaning forward.

"I'm sorry," the asshole said.

"I'm not," the vampire laughed.

Then he dug the blade into the asshole's throat. At first, Vinny thought he was killing him. But he was being too meticulous, taking too much time to just be cutting his throat.

The screams which were being muffled by William's hand rattled then went silent. However, the asshole was still squirming around, so he wasn't dead. Vinny craned his neck to try to look over William's shoulder to see what they were doing. All he could see was blood and pink meat on the inside of his throat.

By the time they bandaged him up and walked him back to his bed crying silently, it was obvious what had been done to him. They had cut his vocal cords.

To the horror of everyone else in the room, the vampire yelled, "NEXT" at the top of his lungs, obviously enjoying his work.

William retrieved the nodding man, who put up no fight at all. He hardly seemed to notice. Then the next, the gap-filler. This all felt too familiar, like a more controlled version of the vampire in withdrawals that had gone around the room tearing out throats.

Vinny looked at Paul, whose eyes were wide with fear. He couldn't meet his gaze and looked away. Instead, he lit a cigarette and buried his head into his belly and knees.

By the end of the day, the only one spared was Vinny. Vinny wasn't sure why he was spared but he didn't question it. Everyone was in silent agony around him. The guilt would prevent eye contact for the near future. But Vinny would be lying if he said he thought it was a bad day. He was relieved to never have to listen to the asshole or the ravings of the nervous man again. He would miss the small conversations with Paul, but there were more ways than words to communicate if he had to.

From then on, when any new prisoners were brought into the dungeons for replacements, like the junkie who died shortly after his voice box removal, they were fixed with collar shackles and their vocal cords were also cut.

The dungeon was much quieter now, except for labored breathing. It suited Vinny at first. Then the lack of infighting and drunken babble was missed. The monotony returned. Only this time, he found himself looking forward to the next time someone would speak to him. Anyone or anything.

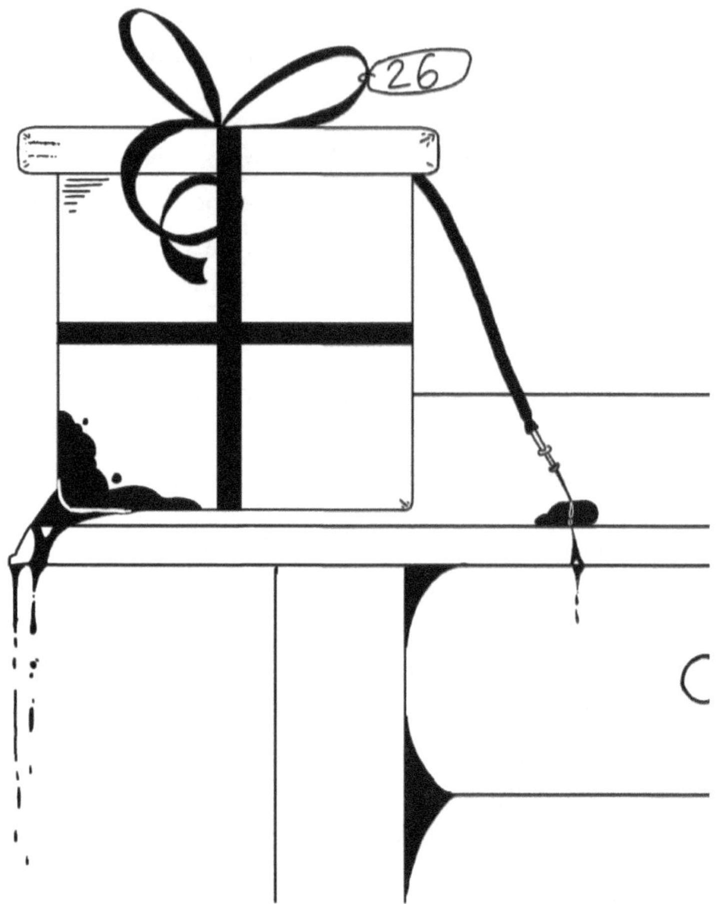

The silence hurt. The rarity of the chances to speak made them precious but they were too infrequent to count on for his sanity. There was the occasional drunken babble from the bartender, who was forcing more "good stuff" down his throat more often. The silencing of the bums was still fresh in Vinny's mind, so giving any feedback to the drunken bartender aside from nods of agreement terrified him. The newness and terror were waning, but the boredom grew by the minute.

December turned out to be a busy month. Vinny could tell it was December, because of the relentless stream of Christmas-themed music blaring from the radio, which had been left on more regularly, as if the bartender could sense Vinny's need for audible interaction. It helped. In some ways, hearing about the locusts and the dust storms and starvation made Vinny feel safe and secure in his dungeon. Every once in a while, smooth soles would show up in his nightmares, but Vinny always pushed it away with a smoke, a good meal, and a drink if he was lucky. His belly was still growing, along with the size of his arms and legs, but he cared less and less. What did it matter?

Vinny woke one morning to a new horror that spiced up his life. As he lit his morning smoke, he could hear a new sound mixing with the Christmas music. He couldn't define it but as William padded in, Vinny noticed he had a mysterious limp that he was favoring heavily. William could sense Vinny eyeing the injury.

"Don't get any ideas, tough guy." He looked at Vinny, almost looking pathetic. "I'm fine."

He started his chores but before he did, he cussed at the never-ending stream of Christmas tunes and flipped off the radio. Suddenly, the room was full of heavy, desperate breathing and the muted sounds of screaming children. Collectively, the dungeon bristled, and the bums eyed each other, some looking angry, others looking terrified. William seemed unfazed as he was more than used to the sounds of pain. Vinny could feel his blood boiling. It was the first time in a while that he remembered it was monsters that held him prisoner. He was so accustomed to his surroundings; he was forgetting to feel afraid.

Vinny tried to skip the meal being offered and stuffed his face into his knees and belly. He didn't even feel like smoking while the children's cries echoed in the hallway. Two plates clanked together as William left food anyway. Vinny tried to resist but after a few minutes of blocking out the screaming with his hands, one of them retrieved the slice of meat pie and he ate. No sense in going hungry. Plus, it smelled so good. He finished with a cigar.

Thankfully, the screaming stopped later that afternoon. Instantly, Vinny remembered the silencing of the bums and hoped the same fate hadn't befallen the children. Later that night, he gleaned that the children's end was even more bitter than he could have imagined.

Two patrons came in, accompanied by William and the bartender. They were regulars that were the "nothing personal" kind. They almost felt human when they feasted. Today, they were visibly upset as they entered the room, and immediately it was clear why.

"You're gonna let that fucking pervert Travis do that to kids in your place of business?" He spat on the floor. "We all know he's a fuckup but that feels too far away from what we used to be. There have been a lot of changes, but I can't agree to look the other way when kids are involved...whether they are our source of food or not."

"I'm with him. If you keep serving him kids, there are going to be problems," the other thing chimed in. His eyes were dark red and angry.

"Gentlemen, here, have a drink." The bartender handed them both syringes, which were slurped down and tossed onto the floor, where they shattered. "Listen, I am here to serve all manner of vices," the bartender said, getting pissed off now. "What should I do—turn him away, send him into the wild to feed at his leisure which could turn into *hundreds* of children? Only for him to get sloppy and then get caught and force us to step in." He paused. "Turn him away and have him go rogue like the glutton Moon King, who is a bigger problem than we already can't seem to handle? He's already draining entire towns." The men seemed to be seeing the logic in his thinking. "The cloak our lifestyle provides us can only shield us from so much. If we intervene and provide the degenerates among us their desires in a controlled environment, we are in control in the end, and that is all that is important."

Vinny thought back to the day he was kicked out of his home, and the fears he had the first night of all the stories of increased child abductions and missing children. His fears of being abducted didn't feel so unwarranted now. The missing children also made much more sense. They were filling those desires by any means apparently.

"Maybe you're right, but after we deal with the Moon King, things are gonna change around here, whether you like it or not," one of the men said as they left the dungeon. They continued talking as they made their way down the hall, but Vinny was lost in thoughts of kids being eaten by one of these things and the Moon King slurping down entire towns.

Vinny woke himself up screaming hours later after a group of kids with their faces scooped out chased him around begging for help in his dreams. Despite his efforts, he couldn't get back to sleep, so he sat and smoked. He had managed to achieve basic conversations with Paul using hand motions and spelling with fingers. It was limited and there was a shame involved because it was so easy for Vinny to communicate with his intact vocal cords. It still felt hard to make eye contact. Vinny almost felt like the vampire's pet while the rest were just below him on the hierarchy somewhere between food and rubbish. He didn't ask for it, but it was a fact and made him feel guilty.

They used their primitive language to vaguely talk about the kids. Both were disgusted and horrified. Paul managed to convey he missed his own kids at one point, and Vinny was shocked. He had assumed only single, desperate men were prisoners. They continued talking until a familiar squeak was heard coming down the hallway.

It was the metal table with the drains. It was never good news. Vinny lit a cigarette and waited for the table to be wheeled in. Surprisingly, it was the bartender, and he was alone. He surveyed the room and saw the fear on everyone's faces.

"No need to fear; this is only for the boy." The bartender warned the room looking at Vinny.

Vinny suddenly was sure he had heard him talking and was about to silence him as well. He powered through the cigarette and lit another.

The bartender flipped on the radio and instantly started whistling the tune without missing a beat, as if he knew what was playing before it came on. Then he took out his logbook and made some cursory notes.

"Ok, my boy," he said as he straightened up and turned. "I have an early Christmas present for you. Brought to you by the advances in modern medicine. I believe it will make you much more comfortable. Although you might not appreciate it to begin with, you will come to love it, I'm sure."

Despite his fear, this didn't sound like a silencing and Vinny found himself curious. Maybe it was something good, the stupid part of him thought.

"Finally, technology has caught up with the dreams of one of ours from many years ago. An intravenous port has been developed and should limit your bodies exposure to pain and infection while giving me reliable access. Are you excited?" He was positively giddy and blowing sulfurous breath into Vinny's nostrils, he was so close to him.

Vinny wasn't sure what he was going on about, but he nodded in appreciation, forcing a thin smile.

"Good, good, good. I'm happy for you as well. Now let's get it started. I promise just one last poke, the poke to end all pokes." He pushed the table closer. There was a scattering of tools and tubes. "First, we will lace this needle right here into this vein in your arm." Vinny was more interested than scared now and listened intently. His brain was still thirsty for knowledge. "Then we will secure it to your arm with surgical tape and attach the tube and the valve. And voila, we are done."

Without hesitating, he followed his own steps. It was painless, mostly. Vinny was fascinated as he watched the needle slip into his vein. A squirt of blood started out of the other side of the hollow needle. Quickly, the bartender captured the flow into the tube, which led to the valve and stopped the squirting. He paused to lick the blood off the back of his hand, and secured the tube to his arm and taped the needle down.

"There, that was easy enough. Maybe if it goes well, it will be common practice from now on." He eyed the other prisoners. "Well, let's give it a test run, shall we? Smoke, boy." Vinny did as he was told, and the bartender retrieved a crystal shot glass from the shelf. As soon as the cigarette was hissing in the bucket of piss, the vampire was opening the valve on the tube in his arm and filling his cup.

It worked and Vinny was pleased about not having to be poked in the neck. The drawback was that now he felt like a tapped keg. Some of the last glimmers of hope were dying inside him. He was truly owned. In his self-pity, he eyed the valve on the rubber tubing. If nothing else, it could offer an easy way out if he were just to open it and close his eyes.

In the long run, Vinny came to love his gift.

***

The Christmas music was still playing on the radio days later. It had to be getting closer now. The newly installed IV was itchy but was cleaned regularly and seemed to be fine. The screaming kids had continued to trickle in. But there was another, more interesting development for Vinny.

Women.

A group of three of them had become regulars. They were Vinny's age and gorgeous. Sure, they were hollow things like the others, but his prick didn't care. Any time they came in, it was a treat to Vinny's senses. They smelled good, they looked good, they sounded good. Every part of Vinny wanted a part of them. He was suddenly self-conscious about his newly cultivated girth.

It wasn't like they had any interest...or did they? Vinny could swear that the one he had his eye on the most sometimes gave him a look of interest. He wasn't sure what interest she would have in a fat bum pack of smokes, but he didn't care very much. Part of him was jealous when they drank from the other men.

When they left in the evenings, the other men had obviously had the same feelings as Vinny, as the noises of self-abuse were surrounding him, along with satisfied panting. Vinny tried to imagine he was better than them but, in the end, he abused himself after they fell asleep as well.

He found himself looking forward to the women's next visit more than the food cart. It also motivated him, along with Paul's advice on exercises to do (which he demonstrated silently from his bed), to try to get his belly under control. The exercises were hard at first but Vinny had nothing but time to get better.

Christmas day finally came. Vinny found out it was the day of because the librarian finally followed through with his promise of a book. He was the first customer of the day and he practically bounced into the room.

"Hello, boy, look what I have brought for you. I spoke to your owner, and he agreed that I can bring you in a novel every so often. And not to worry; you will have all the time you like. Consider this book a donation from Carnegie." He chuckled. It was an obvious reference to his embezzlement scheme.

Vinny didn't care about the moralities of it. He was practically giddy with excitement, and he forgot himself.

"I don't even know how to say thank you for this," Vinny offered.

Only to be shushed by the librarian. The act sent chills down Vinny's spine as he thought of Elmer for the first time in a while.

"Don't thank me—just read and enjoy, and for God's sake, don't get caught talking."

Shortly after, William appeared and prepared his syringe of heroin. The nodding man didn't argue. He didn't care. Then a glazed-over librarian left, giving a squinty-eyed look of approval to Vinny. No sooner had they disappeared than Vinny was buried in the book. He didn't stop until he finished. Then he ate dinner and read it again as the bartender enjoyed his evening smoke listening to the news on the radio.

Then there was a crash down the hall, followed by an unearthly howling.

"BOSS, WE NEED YOU!" It was William.

More howling from the hallway. The bartender stood up so quickly that the chair shattered against the wall behind him. Before he was upright, he already had a pistol in his hand. It surprised Vinny that he was armed. What did he need a gun for? What scared him? What was that howling down the hall? Was the Moon King here?

The bartender raced into the hallway to greet them.

"Jesus, I'm glad you're here," William said in a frantic voice. "They found him, but he surprised them and got the drop on 'em."

The howls had faded into a sobbing, growling sound now.

"Who, who got the drop on them?" the bartender asked.

"The Moon King," William said, his voice cracking.

Then the sobbing thing appeared. He was covered in a black, shiny fluid and his arms were missing, leaving behind pink, meaty stubs saturated with the same black fluid. Upon seeing the bartender, the armless thing starting panicking.

"Holy shit, Arvid, he is so fucking big. We found him in a cave outside town. He was holed up and we thought we had him cornered, but he tore through the others like paper...FUUUCK." The bartender shot Vinny a look at the sound of his own name. He knew by the look Vinny gave back that the secret was out.

The armless thing hitched and sobbed.

"I'm the only one that got away. That fucking thing stood on me and pulled my arms off like wings off a goddamn fly." He looked around the room. "I really need some heroin and a drink."

William was already dosing the nodding man.

"Yes, of course, take him and have your fill." As soon as William pulled the needle from the nodding man's neck, Arvid took him by what was left of his shoulder and led him to the junkie.

Arvid lifted the junkie by his head and pressed his neck into the face of the armless vampire. There was no hesitation. A lump of flesh was spat onto the floor and the gagging slurping ensued. Arvid let him drink much more than his fill and by the time he stopped drinking, the armless vampire was well-lit.

"I'm sorry, Arvid. We tried but there was no way. We are gonna need a fucking army," he slurred.

"Don't you worry about him. If it's an army we need, an army we shall have. I'm gonna send word up the ladder to the men at the top. The Moon King will be no more." Arvid sighed, maybe in regret. "You have no more need for stress or worry. Have your drink."

William handed a newly filled syringe to Arvid, who sprayed it into the armless vampire's mouth.

Paul watched nervously his chains clanking on the wall. His eyes told Vinny he was hoping it was enough and he wasn't next to be held up for his throat to be ripped out.

"Would you like a smoke?" Arvid asked.

"Hell yes," the armless monster barely got out. He was wobbling on his feet now.

Arvid snapped his fingers and William was retrieving a glass for Vinny's blood. He held it up to the armless thing's lips, but he wasn't responding so he dumped it into his mouth. The armless thing choked on it and spat blood into William's face. William didn't even blink, only licked his lips.

"Enough," Arvid said and pushed William away. "It's time."

He led the man out of the room, who was barely walking now. He was being pushed along by Arvid out into the hallway.

"Arvid, I can still be useful for something. You don't gotta do this," the thing pleaded.

"I said your worries are over. Now, just relax," Arvid calmed his nerves.

There was giggling down the hall, followed by some gasps.

"Ladies, I'm sorry. We have had a situation. Can you maybe return at a more opportune time?" Arvid said, echoing in the hallway.

"Oh, lord, what is that?"

It was the girls.

Despite the recent events, Vinny perked up. He had lost some weight, he thought, and wanted to see if he caught her eye even more now.

"Well, all we want is a drink. Can we still get one?" another girl said, seeming not to mind the dying thing in front of her.

"William, get them their drinks and join me quickly," Arvid ordered, obviously irritated with the girl's persistence.

By the time they got to the room, Paul had his neck craned and William was already halfway done. He made short work of the other half and handed the syringes to the girls.

"Here, enjoy." And with that, William went to join Arvid.

The girls giggled and drank. The cute one with the dark hair was wearing a dress that showed off her body and Vinny's own responded to it. He tried to hide it by pulling his knees up.

"Did you guys see that guy's arms? What do you think happened?" one of the two blondes said.

"I don't know but it was gross," the other blonde offered.

"Who even cares? Did you guys see the new guys at the theatre? I think they are a part of that new crew that's been working in the area," the dark-haired girl said. "Where were they going after the film? After this, we should try to find them."

Vinny imagined the sexy vampire girls rolling in the hay with the men they were talking about, and he felt even more jealous than when they drank from the others.

"I want another drink first," one of the blondes said. "Should we go find that guy?"

"No, I don't even care. I'll just pay for it myself. Let's just finish him, he'll forgive me." She smiled and batted her eyelashes.

Paul, who had relaxed, thinking his evening was over, was shocked and had a look of disbelief on his face as the two blondes approached him with want on their faces. They drank and gagged and slurped.

Vinny never bothered to learn any more names or start any more friendships. It hurt too much.

Meanwhile, the dark-haired girl had a different appetite. She stood in front of Vinny and leaned forward exposing the majority of her breasts in the process. Vinny couldn't help himself and glanced down her shirt.

"You like what you see, huh?" She stood back a step and her wonderful sulfur smell faded. "My turn then. Stand up."

Vinny's heart raced with excitement and fear as Paul was sucked dry next to him. He did as he was told but tried to lean forward a bit to hide his excitement. It was no use. It poked wildly away from his body, pulling the fabric with it.

"What do we have here?" She flicked the tip of his prick through his tight pants. "Pretty nice for a fat little boy like you." She leaned forward and took his bulge in her hand and massaged it slightly. Vinny nearly climaxed with the brief touch. "It's never going to do anyone any good."

With that, she clapped a hand over Vinny's mouth. The other hand still held his testes and she started to squeeze. She didn't stop squeezing, even when Vinny cried out in muffled pain. She didn't stop when there was a sickening pop, and Vinny's knees went weak. She only stopped when her friends behind her started to puke.

She spun, surprised, and Vinny fell to his knees, gasping against the pain radiating through his groin up into his belly and onward.

"Gross, are you guys finished?" She looked at the spinning blondes. "Jesus, let's go."

And with that, she left Vinny crumpled on the floor and Paul slumped forward against his chains dripping the last of his blood onto the floor from two gaping wounds in his neck.

The pain in his groin grew until the valve on the IV looked more tempting than it ever had. A fine sheen of sweat had become a river that was flowing to one of the drains. Vinny was building the nerve to flip the valve when William made an appearance.

There was a screaming howling from down the hallway and the sound of a heavy door being slammed.

"BOSS!" William called for help the second time that night.

Arvid came in looking distraught and tired. The smell of burning hair and steaks followed him.

"What the hell is going on tonight?" he asked as he surveyed the room. "It was those fucking girls, wasn't it?"

"I think so. He's dead and something's wrong with the boy," William explained.

"Stand up." The order from Arvid fell on deaf ears as Vinny was incapable of complying. "Boy, what did she do to you?"

"Ughh," was all Vinny got out at first. "She squeezed me, and I think it burst," he managed, holding his crotch with both hands, making it obvious what he was talking about.

"William, get the table...RUN," Arvid ordered and what seemed like seconds later, the squeaking table made its way into the room, followed by William.

Arvid spent the few moments it took William to get the table poring over a book he pulled from the desk. Then William unbolted Vinny. Even with his current misery, the missing weight of the chains felt good. He knew to get on the table, but it wasn't possible. Arvid and William each grabbed a leg and an arm and gingerly lifted him to the table.

"William, get him something for the pain." William disappeared. "Luckily for you, my boy, I can make you feel better than you ever have in your life and remove the damaged tissue. You should be fine in a week or so, I imagine…if everything goes well." He looked at Vinny, who had remained stoic the entire time, not shedding a single tear. "Now that you've learned my name, what should I call you?" Arvid said almost like a doctor with a good bedside manner.

Vinny was in disbelief. Maybe it was the holiday stirring his humanity again or maybe it was sympathy. But the human part of this monster seemed to care about him.

"Vincent...Vinny," Vinny said, forcing a smile through his pain.

"Well, Vin, not to worry. You'll be back to normal in no time."

The sound of his name grated on his nerves. He hated the sound of Vin—it was what Mom called him, and getting back to normal was no release from anything. He hoped he would never wake up. If he did, there was always the valve on his arm.

William returned with the pain medicine and Vinny slept until it was over. He woke up later, half the man he used to be but twice as mad at the world.

By the time he was healed from the forced castration, Vinny was forgetting to remember, and things were being lost. The better parts of him were going first, followed closely by any fond memories of home. All that remained of both were empty black holes that only had room for hate. The "good stuff" flowed freely now, along with the coffee, cigars and cigarettes. He was drunk most nights but thankfully, there was no babble. There was no one to babble to. The other prisoners hated him for how he was treated so specially by Arvid. Vinny stopped caring long ago and kept himself busy with his newfound vices, and his books, which the librarian had continued providing. Vinny had accumulated a nice collection beside his bed. They were the anchor for his sanity in the long, monotonous days...weeks...months? It didn't matter anymore, maybe it never did.

Arvid was sitting at the desk listening to a gloomy opera and nursing a drink, and William was busying himself with cleaning. Business had slowed and Arvid's drinking had increased. There were rarely any long diatribes of the vampire's superiority, but Vinny craved them and enjoyed them when they came. He still wasn't allowed to speak freely or much at all, really, but the interactions were some of the only things to look forward to.

William's limp had healed slowly, and the padding of his feet was returning to its usual cadence. Vinny could hear him padding back down the hallway now, hopefully with more cigars.

When William entered the room, Vinny saw he was right and the tightening in his chest from his craving eased a bit. Before he even went to the cabinet to put the rest of the supplies away, he stopped at Vinny and peeled a cigar from the box and handed it to him.

Vinny pulled the Dunhill from his pocket and shook it, trying to force the little if any fuel oil that was left to the wick. It had smelled more and more of burning wick, and Vinny feared it would spark its last cigarette or cigar any day now. It hurt to think about, even though it had become a reminder of how much he hated home. The thought of dad handing it to him still made him feel like he wanted to cry. It was something other than hatred and he still needed it.

He struck it once...twice...three times and on the fourth it produced a weak flame, which he sucked up into the cigar, quickly puffing to get it going. He snapped the flame off and inhaled deeply, then looked around the room, already feeling relieved.

Arvid was staring at Vinny in disbelief, with his mouth hanging open and his hand frozen halfway between his lips and the desk, still holding his glass of Vinny's blood. William in turn was staring at Arvid, gauging his reaction to the illicit lighter. Vinny realized too late that he had gotten sloppy. Everyone in the dungeon had their eyes on the lighter. Vinny clapped his fist closed around it and shoved it into his pocket.

"Vin, where the hell did you get that?" He stood up and walked over to Vinny while he shot William a look. He stood in front of a fat, scared Vinny, towering over him. "Well?" he asked with a tone that needed a reply.

"I uh, well, I had it when I came. It was in a secret pocket in my pants. You must have missed it. I'm sorry," Vinny said.

Arvid grabbed the arm that was still jammed into his pocket, and he pulled the clenched fist out.

"Let's have it." He held an open hand out.

Vinny hesitated but released the lighter and dropped it into his palm. It instantly hissed and sizzled like spit on a hot stove. Arvid winced and looked like he was going to drop it. But he steadied his hand at the last second. His other hand grabbed his handkerchief and used it to pick up the lighter. Vinny could see a red imprint from where the lighter had touched his pale skin.

Arvid rolled the lighter around, admiring it, and even sniffed at it like a dog.

"I'm astounded that a bum like you would have such a beautiful lighter. Who did you steal it from?" He laughed, not really wanting a response to the question/insult. He tossed the lighter to William. "Replace the innards and fill it for him. No sense in taking it away now." He looked at Vinny with curiosity. "What else do you have on you? Do I need to search or are you going to give it to me freely?" He eyed Vinny carefully, trying to measure him.

"No, you don't gotta search. Just this." Vinny pulled his wad of cash from his pocket and dropped it into Arvid's waiting hand. He flinched, maybe expecting it to burn as well. "It's not mine, well, not all of it anyway. Eight of it belongs to someone else. I just never got a chance to pay him back." Vinny's throat tightened and he felt like he might cry.

Arvid saw his eyes glisten and laughed so loudly, it woke up the nodding man, whose chains shook in fear.

"Oh, well, we can't have that. You better hang onto it then, in case you bump into him sometime." His laughing continued and he spilled the bills onto the floor.

Vinny picked them up and felt stupid. He looked at the valve on his arm and thought maybe he would bump into Elmer sooner rather than later. By the time he finished picking up the bills, he was winded and wheezing for air. He sat back on his bed, sweating and missing the weight of the Dunhill in his pocket.

William came back later that evening with the Dunhill. It was polished and shining now. Brand new guts and wick, and the smell of fuel was thick around it. Vinny was so happy, he forgot himself again.

"Thanks, William." His brain tried to pump the brakes, but it was too late. Vinny braced for impact.

"You're welcome, Vinny." And he padded down the hallway, disappearing forever.

***

By lunch the next day, everyone in the dungeon was getting antsy. Chains were clanking in discontent and stomachs were growling. By dinner, it was a full-on riot as the bums started banging their chains on the concrete and making throaty, choking sounds in protest. Vinny was getting worried, too. He was nearly finished with his cigar, and he could sure use a drink of the "good stuff". Something was wrong; they could all sense it. There was never this long of a gap between visits from someone—Arvid, William, patrons or junkie vampires looking to eat everyone.

Vinny tried to keep his spirits high, but by day two he, too, was starting to panic. They were all going to die of thirst in this place. Vinny had started rationing his water and cold cup of coffee early, knowing from life on the streets that it was better to conserve resources. The buckets had filled to overflowing and some of the bums had regressed to just pissing and shitting on the floor, not even trying to aim for a drain. The smell was overwhelming, almost forcing a gag with every breath. Vinny resorted to mouth breathing. The cigar was long gone, and he was down to four smokes. The craving was constant but again he saw the need to ration them.

That evening, there was a familiar choking sputtering sound from the nodding man. He was dying. As if to punctuate Vinny's realization, the man's bowels let loose loudly as he defecated. Now he was dead. Vinny surveyed the other bums. They were sweating and shaking mostly. They all looked manic. None of them even seemed to notice the dead junkie. All they could think about was the doses they were missing. Vinny couldn't judge very much as he lit one of his last smokes. He justified it because he needed to settle his nerves. His coffee was long gone, and his water was at the bitter end as well.

The fear of dying of thirst must have been too much for the drunk, who had been shaking uncontrollably, because when Vinny woke the third day and surveyed the room, he had wrapped the chain around his neck and knelt forward with his weight. His face was blue, and foam was coming from the corners of his mouth. He was dead, too. Vinny eyed the valve on his arm then his pack of smokes with only two left. He grabbed it and burned one down.

The dungeon now resembled the ones from his books. Filthy, wet, full of broken dead men and a distinct lack of hope. It was just as bad as it had always felt in his imagination while he put himself there when reading. Maybe worse.

Questions of what was going on were less important than the fact that Vinny had smoked his last cigarette hours ago and was now sweating like the remaining bums. He looked at his almost empty glass of water and shrugged before drinking it. Why delay the inevitable? Vinny believed the asshole on cocaine died in his sleep as he hadn't moved all morning. The remaining two just sat silently, no more energy for banging chains.

Vinny sat without hope, feeling the desire for a smoke overwhelm him. The valve had never looked better. Could he do it, though? His fingers played with it, letting the stream grow, then cutting it off, again and again. The puddle of maroon grew at his feet. His head swooned when he looked at it and he cut the valve off for the last time. Something inside him still wanted life, even if it was this life. He thought about yelling for help, but it had been too long for something like yelling for help to do any good.

Vinny fell asleep or passed out a bit later that day and didn't wake up until he heard footsteps echoing down the hall sometime later.

There was hope after all.

Vinny forgot the rules and started yelling for help, not wanting to pass up an opportunity to be saved.

"Shut up," came a response from down the hall. "I'll be there in a minute." It was Arvid but he sounded different. He sounded angry and something else…scared.

There was a clanking of chains minutes later and Arvid appeared with some gaunt, tired-looking women who had been silenced and collared as well.

"Get this place cleaned up." He reached into the hall and pulled in William's cleaning cart.

The girls immediately got to work. Vinny avoided eye contact out of shame as they scrubbed up his and the others' mess. His bucket was overflowing with feces and butts. There was a squeaking Vinny recognized as the table making its way to the room now. Arvid pushed it into the room, and unceremoniously plucked the dead men from their chains and stacked them three high. He gave each of the others a slap to check for life and was satisfied with the results. The bodies were wheeled out and a smell of hair and steak returned minutes later.

Vinny's stomach growled and his throat clenched for a want of water. Surpassing both was the need for a smoke. He looked at the women now pleadingly.

"Can you get us some water, and a pack of those smokes." He nodded toward the cabinet with the pitcher and cartons of cigarettes.

The woman looked shocked to hear his voice. She probably assumed they had all been silenced as well. She only shook her head, wide-eyed in fear.

"Please," Vinny pleaded.

"Oh, get him some fucking water and a smoke. I need one anyway!" Arvid yelled from down the hall. "In fact, get them all water before I incur more losses I can't afford."

Vinny blushed, not realizing he was being listened to. But he also needed that smoke. He motioned to the same scared woman to hurry now that she had Arvid's permission. She complied and no sooner had the fresh pack hit his hands than he was tearing into it for relief. The dryness of his throat combined with the smoke only produced a choking feeling.

"Water, please," he asked the woman, who looked dazed and confused. She vibrated from her toes to her hair.

Vinny felt bad but needed that drink.

"GO!" he yelled at her.

She snapped to attention and went to retrieve a pitcher then into the hallway, where he could hear the tap turn on.

Arvid returned just behind the woman with the water.

"Smoke another and another." Vinny complied as Arvid grabbed a bottle of "the good stuff" and poured an almost full glass.

Vinny eyed the foreign booze greedily while he rehydrated and smoked.

Arvid brought him the nearly full glass.

"Don't fuck around. Drink up."

Vinny complied eagerly. There were more than a few memories he would like to fade away from the last few days, and the booze would help.

While Vinny did his best to drink the booze quickly, Arvid prepared a dose of heroin on a spoon, something Vinny had never seen, as it was William's chore. As soon as it was prepared, he took the syringe along with an empty one over to the man who filled in gaps, and he jammed the needle into his neck. When the man's eyes looked heavy, Arvid jammed the empty syringe into his neck and produced a full vial. He looked at Vinny.

"Are you about finished?"

Vinny poured the last bits down his throat and tipped the cup over to show it was done.

Arvid refilled the cup then sat down at his desk. He put his hands to his face and held it as he braced its weight on the desk. He took two nervous-sounding deep breaths like he was steeling his nerves. Then he grabbed the heroin-laden syringe and emptied it into his mouth and gagged it down. Shortly after, his posture eased, and Vinny could sense him relaxing. His eyes told the full story when he looked at Vinny. They were less red than they were when he entered, but they now carried the weight of heroin and fluttered against it, just like the nodding bums.

Vinny came to realize—maybe too late in life to matter—that his habit of judging people by their shoes was reckless. He had been fucked over from smooth soles, hiking boots, shoes full of holes, work boots, running shoes. It seemed everyone from every walk of life was out to get him. He was now realizing it was all in the eyes. If they were wet, they belonged to a drinker. If they were wide and crazy, someone on amphetamines. Heavy lids, probably on heroin. Blood-red, they probably wanted to eat you. Vinny wished he had paid more attention to the eyes in his past.

Arvid filled his cup from Vinny's valve and sat back at his desk, nodding a few times before taking a drink. Vinny's head was spinning, and he felt like he could puke. He was starving and the booze went straight to his head. The cleaning women were making quick work of the room and already, the smell was fading back to its usual sterile taste as the bleach beat the funk back.

"I suppose you are looking for answers, right?" He looked at Vinny, who shook his head in disagreement. Arvid wasn't interested in communicating. He was just talking. "Someone," he continued, slurring his speech, "has gone too far but there is nothing I can do about it. That goddamn piano player Kroc got into someone's ear up top and decided my business practices weren't good enough for them, so they sent a message...." He paused and sniffed. "They killed William." He finished Vinny's blood. "They can't attack me. I'm protected, so they went after the next best thing."

Vinny was listening but his hunger was outweighing his interest.

Uncanny Arvid could tell.

"Get them some food from down the hall. It won't be your usual luxuries, but it will do."

The woman disappeared and reappeared quickly with a cart full of dried goods. Vinny wasn't picky—he was ravenous as he tore into the fruits and nuts. He sandwiched some jerky between some hardtack and broke it down with his teeth the best he could. Dunking it in his water helped. As his belly filled, his attention fell back to Arvid, who had been babbling away almost incoherently now.

"William was loyal to his own detriment. He could have left whenever he wanted, but he loved his family and knew if he did they would die. Hell, we all loved our families at one time. But he was different. He suffered a lifetime for them, only to be mowed down in a hail of gunfire. The least I can do is release his wife and kids as a remembrance of his service, willing or not. His death paid for their freedom. I suppose he would have liked that." Arvid hesitated. "I suppose he would have preferred to be one of us, but he died a human. I always had a feeling he was waiting for me to turn him. Though he knew that was unrealistic after the top rejected his appeal, he was just too useful in the sunlight."

Arvid seemed hot now and took off his suit jacket and undid the top two buttons. Vinny thought of William's unwavering loyalty to his family and realized that not all dungeons have chains. Maybe it was his love for his family that kept him at Arvids beck and call. The realization that William died a human struck Vinny as odd as he remembered the times William would sneak drinks of blood. Maybe he was emulating his master? Maybe he was trying to become him?

Arvid approached Vinny to refill his cup one more time. The smell of Vinny's blood was thick on his sulfur-laden breath. As Arvid teetered forward, the front of his shirt hung open and Vinny could see familiar-looking scar tissue. It was healed over but it was unmistakable. Arvid had been collared at some point.

Vinny's imagination swam with possibilities and his drunken mind almost blurted out the question on the tip of his tongue. He bit it back and let Arvid fill his cup in peace. The question weighed heavy on Vinny while Arvid nursed the drink. Eventually, Arvid left without another word, dragging the cleaning women with him.

Vinny never got around to asking his question, but it always stayed fresh in his mind. The dungeon was refilled with bums within a couple of days. The cleaning women took the place for William, while Arvid took the place of dosing bums and serving the few patrons who bothered to show up. Every night ended with booze and heroin for Arvid now. More often than not, he would fall asleep at the desk, nodding off into a drug-induced slumber. Vinny would wake up and Arvid would be gone each morning. The dungeon never returned to its previous machine-like precision after William was killed.

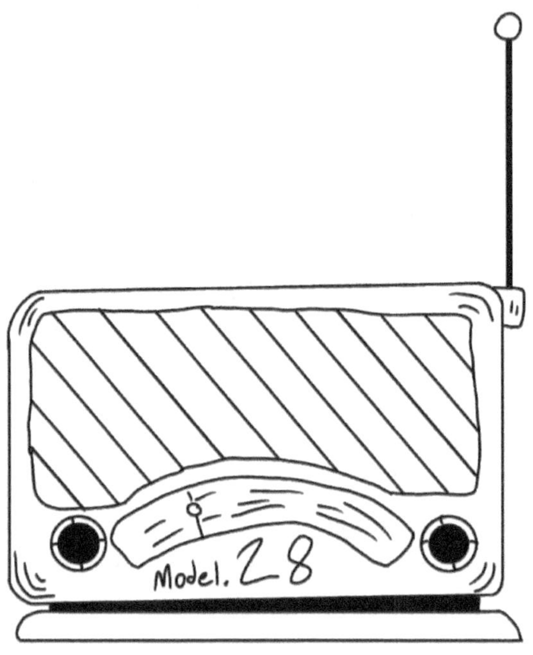

Many times, Vinny reflected on Elmer's thoughts on memories. He always hoped the next thing he remembered was the last thing he forgot or surely something would be lost forever. By now every good memory had been washed out by the ripples, leaving behind nothing but regrets and anger. He saw Dad wave goodbye and turn his back a million times, he heard Mom call him a pervert a million times, and he listened to what was left of Elmer's advice a million times. There had been too many cigarettes and cigars to imagine. So many, in fact, that his lungs hurt all the time now. Nothing was left of the old Vinny except a shred of hope that one day he would find a way out living or dead.

It was going on three or four (Vinny couldn't quite put his finger on it) Halloweens since the girls had taken his manhood. Out of the blue, they showed up again for the first time since the castration. They couldn't possibly have recognized him. He had grown so much in size; he was unrecognizable as the same boy the girls had left sweating on the floor. The girls didn't seem to be impervious to the ravages of time, either. When they showed up, they looked the part of monsters this time. They weren't the pretty girls who looked like they were out for a night on the town. The hollow part of them had taken over. The blondes looked as washed out as Vinny's memories felt. Their skin was gray and hung loosely from their cheeks. There were sores on their skin and the hair on their heads was thin and greasy.

The dark-haired girl that had crushed his manhood was as unrecognizable as Vinny was. Her beauty had faded completely. No more full breasts; they now hung deflated against her chest. Her eyes would never again be mistaken as human's; they were red and desperate. She had a distinct twitch that reminded Vinny of the junkie vampire that had eaten the entire room so long ago. Her clothes were still nice, but it looked like she had stolen them from the person they fit. Only once did she even look at Vinny, but it was only as a passing interest while she got a dose of amphetamines and heroin. They left without incident and Vinny returned to the monotony inside his own head.

William was never been replaced. Arvid simply used the slave girls to clean when it was needed. He had explained that the Kroc fellow was now working at the top of the ladder and had always had an eye for his bar. Upper management was always infighting, and Arvid just had to wait for the wheel to turn to see who he needed to listen to. Until then, he kept his head low and ran his bar, which never seemed to be as busy as it was before he started serving the pervert vampire who liked kids, Travis, Vinny remembered. It was Arvid's one regret, he often said while drinking Vinny's alcohol-laced blood and getting high on the nodding man's that that pervert was the death of him.

Suddenly, Vinny's reflection on the past was broken by the sound of footsteps slapping their way down the hallway. There was a panic in the sound that made quick work of the endless hallway. Arvid burst through the door and without looking around, raced to the radio and flipped it on. His fingers spun the dial, searching for something in particular. As soon as the spinning of the knob stopped, a broadcast started.

A man was describing a landing craft in a field somewhere in New Jersey. The landing craft seemed to be occupied by aliens. No one knew where they came from, but they were here.

Arvid looked at Vinny. His eyes were huge and red and full of terror, something Vinny had never seen. It scared him, too.

Now the alien seemed to be exiting the spacecraft, the voice was telling them. The army was standing guard, and a welcoming committee was standing by to greet it. Then, a tentacled monster wriggled its way free of the ship and without warning, pointed a gun at the welcoming party and melted them with it.

Now Arvid was truly scared.

"Vin, I need your help," he said.

Despite the aliens, Vinny felt flattered. It was the first time Arvid had asked him for anything, let alone help. Hope didn't wait for an invitation and rekindled in his belly.

"Sure, anything," Vinny said eagerly.

The radio was blaring but he could only focus on pleasing Arvid.

He stepped over to Vinny and took the chains in his hands. With no effort, he bypassed the lock and snapped the metal free from his collar rings. The links exploded, sending metal shrapnel bouncing around the concrete room.

"Hurry now, come with me," Arvid pleaded.

Vinny didn't hesitate. He followed Arvid out of the room and as soon as he was free of the door, his mind started absorbing everything he could see. There were heavy metal doors every thirty feet or so. Most of them were closed. The hallway stretched just a little farther past his room to the left, but to the right it went farther than he could see in the dimly lit corridor. He was racing to keep up with Arvid's pace. Very quickly, he realized his stamina was completely gone. He was huffing and puffing already. His belly bounced and his breasts shook with every step. It was his body, but he hadn't used it since it had gotten so big, so he felt clumsy in it.

Thankfully, the hallway eventually did end at a stairway that spiraled up and out. Vinny's heart was pounding more from excitement than his being out of shape as he made his way up. The stairs came up in a huge room covered in paintings and felt curtains. It looked to be a fancy smoking room.

"This isn't a museum tour, Vin. I've got to get the fuck out of here."

He pulled Vinny away from his amazement and scurried to another room. This time, Arvid loaded Vinny with some expensive-looking antique watches and some other goods he had stuffed into a crate that he handed Vinny.

The radio was blaring in every room up here, Vinny noticed. The army was attacking the alien ship now.

Arvid stopped loading the crate he was working on to hear how the assault was going.

Not well.

Just as the army opened fire, the ship produced a tripod-like weapon that fired on them, setting the woods ablaze. The broadcast shifted and suddenly a panic was in the voice of the man providing the news. He was aware of many craft now as reports were coming in. They were deploying weapons that were tearing up buildings and roads. It was an invading army.

Arvid snapped to life once again, grabbing Vinny by the shirt and leading him through this amazing mansion. He stopped in a beautiful entryway and slid into the shadows of a room near the huge doors to the outside. There was a pale gray light spilling in through the cracks.

"The sun is still too high for me, Vin, so I need you to take that crate and put it in the back seat of the car parked out front while I get the rest of what I'm going to need." He paused and eyed Vinny.

"Understood?" There was a warning in that statement that Vinny could understand all too well.

Through his puffing, Vinny managed a reply.

"Yeah, sure, I can do that." Part of him was giddy with the prospect of going outside. Part of him was giddy with the prospect of Arvid setting him loose. Aliens be damned.

Vinny checked that Arvid was tucked into the shadows and carefully opened the front door. The sun, as low as it was on the horizon, still burned his eyes. He stood on the front porch and took a huge, deep breath of fresh air while his eyes finished adjusting. The wood of the porch was warm and felt good on his bare feet. As he blinked the pain from his eyes, he looked skyward for any approaching alien craft. Nothing.

"Hurry the fuck up, Vin!" Arvid yelled from the house as Vinny made his way to the car in the driveway. "Vin...VIN!"

Vinny put the box in the back seat of the car and surveyed his surroundings. He had no idea where he was just by looking. Did it matter? He looked all around. There were no guards, no one watching him. He stood there puffing, out of breath, debating with himself. Should he run? He wanted to, but there was no use. He was fat and out of shape, had no idea where he was, and these monsters would catch him like they did before.

"VIIIINNNNN!" Arvid was practically screaming now from the house.

Vinny ran back up the steps to the house, not answering because it felt good to make Arvid wait for a change. He couldn't run away but maybe if he helped, he would be set free as Arvid fled from the alien invasion.

A look of relief washed over Arvid's face as Vinny appeared in the doorway. He was backed into the shadows but holding another crate in front of him, this one full of ancient-looking leather-bound books.

The radio was now talking about the various craft and their attacks across the Eastern Seaboard. New York was under attack now—there were "five great machines wading through the Hudson like men wading through a brook." Something about the phrase was familiar and it stuck in Vinny's mind, echoing around as he took the second load outside. He looked at the books in the crate and thought of his own collection. Then his stomach sank. He knew the story on the radio. He had read it a million times.

He put the books in the car and stood stupefied for a minute. The sun was almost gone from the horizon. He wouldn't get far if he ran, as night was upon him. Vinny thought of just letting the story play out, letting Arvid panic and leave, but part of him thought Arvid would kill everyone before setting anyone free. Then he had a stroke of genius. Maybe he could be the new William. Maybe he could assuage Arvid's fears and talk some sense into him, gain his trust.

Nervous about his plan, Vinny ran up the steps, pausing for a moment to enjoy freedom for one more second. He looked at the orange and pink glow from behind the trees and promised himself it wouldn't be the last.

Arvid was gone from the shadows in the entryway and the radio was still going on about the invasion. Only now, it was almost funny to Vinny, who couldn't wipe the smile off his face.

"ARVID." It was the first time Vinny had spoken the name out loud.

Out of the shadows, Arvid appeared with another box full of his favorite treasures.

"What." There was no cross look or mention of the use of his name. The fear in him was real.

"Arvid, I'm pretty sure it's all fake," Vinny said, still smiling.

"What's fake?" Arvid snapped, pushing the crate into Vinny's arms.

"All of it. The whole thing. The alien invasion isn't real. It's just a story. I used to own the book and I've read it a hundred times. Its H.G. Wells' *War of the Worlds*." Vinny was delighted with himself for remembering. Nothing was lost.

Arvid stood there digesting the words Vinny had just told him. Then he snatched the crate of goods back and set it on a table.

"You're sure?" he asked, still sounding uncertain.

"Yes. Listen, next, they are gonna talk about the smoke and cylinders landing all across the country," Vinny said, trying to convince him.

The radio instead chimed a commercial tone followed by, "You are listening to a CBS presentation of Orson Wells and the Mercury Theatre on the air, in an original dramatization of *The War of the Worlds* by H. G. Wells...." It continued but the point had been made.

A smile crept across Arvid's face as relief washed over him.

He snatched Vinny by his collar rings and pulled him close to his face.

"So, you think you're so fucking smart, huh? Like I wouldn't have noticed that myself. You could've said something sooner, but you like me to look fucking stupid, don't you?" He pulled on the rings so hard, Vinny could feel his bones creak.

"No, NO, that's not how it was. I told you as soo...."

Smack

"Shut your mouth, don't you ever argue with me." He was pulling the rings leading Vinny back to the smoking room. Where the steps descended back into the dungeons. Vinny's pulse quickened. He didn't want to go back. He'd rather be dead.

"Please, no, don't put me back in there. I can help, I can clean and prepare the syringes. I won't run or argue. PLEASE don't put me back in." Vinny was crying now, something he hadn't cared enough to do in years.

The dragging continued and they were in the endless hallway now.

"Please... I could have run while I was outside, and I didn't. I promise, Arvid...."

Another smack shut his mouth as it erupted with blood.

"Oh, so you think now that you are so smart that I owe you something." Arvid laughed. "Honestly, if you had run, I wouldn't have even bothered to come looking. I was so caught up; I would have been long gone and so would you have." He laughed even harder at this. "I guess not so smart to take an opportunity when it comes knocking, huh, Vin?"

Vinny was done pleading. It was useless. He was also done crying. It had never helped. The last shreds of his hopes burned out as Arvid bent new chain links around his collar rings and he sat on his all-too-familiar bed completely defeated.

"Smoke," came the order from Arvid, and Vinny snapped the Dunhill in response.

He was never going to get out of the dungeon alive.

Vinny gave up on hope during the failed alien invasion, but it didn't take much longer for hope to give up on him as well.

Business had been shifting for a while and finally, the wheel had turned just as Arvid had anticipated. He had fed Vinny an extra-large drink of "the good stuff" to celebrate. A few months ago, Vinny would have welcomed the opportunity to talk or be talked to. However, it was a lost cause, and he only had enough phoniness left to nod in agreement while he got the drink down as quickly as possible. Every so often, Arvid would ask a question that required an answer more involved than a nod, and Vinny would give him what he wanted but nothing more. The monster seemed to have a sense of pity for the beaten boy, but it didn't matter anymore. Vinny was gone.

Arvid bragged and explained that since he had been patient and hadn't ruffled any feathers, Mr. Kroc had put him in charge of many new operations in various cities. The boss's dream was to have one of Arvid's bars in every metropolis to cater to the needs of their community. Arvid had sloppily complained that he was losing the close feeling he had with the customers and running a small business offered. But the tradeoff was so much bigger, it was "a turning point" for the entire vampire community, Arvid had boasted, obviously proud his bar had become the blueprint for success.

He had looked at Vinny for approval after the bragging session and found none. He was staring at the floor, smoking a cigarette.

Arvid's visits happened less and less after that. Every so often, he would stop by and drink or get a shot of heroin, which he seemed to prefer over booze more and more. Vinny felt phased out. Maybe it was for the better. His books sat unread now. There was nothing left of reading except a sore spot H. G. Wells had left. The Dunhill was the only thing that stirred any emotion in him anymore. Each time he sparked the flame, he saw his dad turning his back again. Each puff of smoke was followed by Mom's laughter for being so clever to get him out of the house. Vinny hardly thought of Elmer anymore. When he did, it was when he was drunk and tuning out the babble from a stoned Arvid.

There was a new slave. Vinny never learned his name. William was always an asshole, but this new one was pure evil. He took pleasure in shorting the constantly rotating cast of bums' meals and water. When they stepped out of line, it wasn't a punch to the side of the head but a raining of blows until the culprit was unconscious, or dead. Every so often, after he was done with his chores cleaning the dungeon, he would leave and

Vinny could hear one of the large metal doors open, followed by muffled whimpering and crying. He was nothing like William.

Then the coughing started. It was short bursts at first. Vinny's lungs had hurt for a while now, but the tickle grew and grew until he was coughing all the time. He was glad the rest of the bums had been silenced, as he could see the look of frustration on their faces when Vinny's coughing fits started while they were sleeping. The looks of frustration and hate were enough. He was glad to be spared the words of hate that would have accompanied them.

The new slave was cleaning, and Vinny was coughing the first time the blood showed itself. It was a particularly nasty coughing fit and after Vinny spat on the floor, it was clear to anyone in the room that he wasn't long for the dungeon now. The slave took a particular interest in the bloody phlegm and examined it closely. He looked at Vinny knowingly and gave him a look they both understood.

Vinny took one finger and extended it and held it up to his blood-stained lips.

SHUSH

The act stirred memories in Vinny that brought with them a flood of emotions that manifested themselves as laughter. He wasn't sure why he was laughing but he couldn't stop himself. The slave got a look of shock on his face at the sight of the fat, bloody shushing man laughing at him.

The slave didn't finish his chores that day. He scurried from the room, keeping an eye over his shoulder and on Vinny as he did.

Vinny lit a cigarette and smiled. He looked at the valve on his arm and was glad he wasn't going to have to use it after all. The way out had presented itself and now all he had to do was wait.

It didn't take long.

That night, Arvid made a rare appearance. He brought a bottle of "good stuff" that was from the old country. It was one Vinny was really going to enjoy, he had told him. Vinny didn't care. He drank with the same gusto that he always did, and the booze was gone in a flash.

"Take your time, Vin. Better to savor and enjoy that one," Arvid mused.

Arvid was in an exceptionally good mood tonight and it couldn't help but rub off on Vinny. Vinny smiled despite himself. Maybe it was the booze.

Before long, they were chatting like old friends.

Vinny forgot himself and found himself answering personal questions that Arvid had never asked before. Where he was from, what he had done before this, if he had a girlfriend before he was captured, if he drove a car. Just casual conversation, but it felt so good. Vinny had almost forgotten how it felt to have someone take an interest.

"So, after the potato fields, then what? Where did you and Elmer end up after that? Did you catch up with Mac or Sarah?" Arvid slurred, genuinely interested in the story Vinny was weaving.

"No, after that is when one of you bastards got Elmer." Vinny laughed drunkenly. "I never saw anyone I knew again. I spent my time running and trying to protect myself, but a lot of good that did me. I should've tried to go home but I was so far away and thought I could take care of myself once I got a gun." They both started laughing at this.

Vinny's laugh suddenly turned into a coughing fit. He retched and coughed and tried to stifle it, but it was no use. The blood sprayed from his lips and onto the floor, making the all-too-familiar polka dot pattern.

Arvid's laughter stopped. This was why he was here. He was confirming that his merchandise was spoiling after the reports from the new slave. It should have been easy to deal with—hundreds of bums had met their end in the dungeon. They looked at each other, now both understanding what was coming.

"Well, Vin, it's been a long night. Why don't you get some sleep, and I will see if I can bring you something for that cough in the morning." He was lying and they both knew it.

Vinny nodded and smiled, he was glad the end was near.

"How about another drink?" he asked, feeling lonely all of a sudden.

"Of course," Arvid agreed.

They sat and drank late into the night. Vinny finished his story and Arvid hung on every word. It was the first and only time Vinny ever enjoyed being drunk. He fell asleep before Arvid left the room and stayed that way until the next morning.

***

The squeaking started before Vinny had a chance to open his eyes. He sat up and straightened out his clothes. His belly was straining against the buttons. If he had lasted any longer, he would have needed a bigger size. Vinny was nervous and lit a cigarette. Would it be his last? If so, he wanted to enjoy it. He held the Dunhill up to his heart, hoping it would give him one last burst of happiness...it didn't. All he felt was anger for his family for abandoning him to the evils of this world. He wasn't ready to be on his own, but then again, maybe no one ever was. He shook the thoughts of his family from his head and focused on his smoke.

The squeaking got closer, and Vinny realized as it entered the room that it wasn't the metal table with the drain. It was a huge antique wooden mirror. It was being pulled by Arvid, who entered the room first. He was followed by someone Vinny couldn't place at first but found familiar. It only took one look at his shoes to remember. Vinny wondered why smooth soles was here. Then Vinny remembered what he whispered to him the first time they met. Vinny remembered him saying he would be there at the end. It didn't matter.

"Would you like a drink, Vin?" Arvid asked.

"Yeah, please." His nerves were screaming in his head, but he remained calm. It was almost over.

Arvid poured him a shot and brought it over. Vinny lit another cigarette with a shaking fist and poured the drink down.

"Fix him up, too," smooth soles said.

"Give him a minute," Arvid argued, buying Vinny some time to finish his smoke.

"No, it's ok. Let's get it over with." Vinny was ready. He tossed the cigarette into the bucket with one final hiss.

Arvid nodded and fixed a dose of heroin above the candle on his desk. When it was ready, he walked over to Vinny, who had never had heroin but knew the routine. His neck was stretched out toward the ceiling.

"Sorry, Vin." And Arvid sank the shot into his neck.

The warmth spread instantly. Relief washed through every vein in his body and for the first time since leaving home, Vinny relaxed. It felt amazing and he was glad for the shot. He only regretted he wouldn't get a second one.

Smooth soles, looking pleased with himself, pushed the mirror in front of Vinny now. Vinny could see his own heavy eyelids starting to play the nodding game. As smooth soles walked in front of him, the reflection wasn't broken. Vinny couldn't see him in the mirror, despite him standing next to him.

The warmth had spread to Vinny's guts, giving the illusion of being full. It felt nice.

Arvid came up beside Vinny now. His sulfurous breath pelting the side of Vinny's face was comforting.

"Are you ready, Vin?"

A million thoughts raced in Vinny's mind, so many questions left unanswered. How long had smooth soles been following him, why not kill him when they killed Elmer, who or what was the Moon King...and did their army kill him? But there was only one question he had to know and had time to ask.

"Yeah...Just one last thing." Smooth soles sighed beside them; Vinny didn't care. "Were you a prisoner too?"

The question had been burning in Vinny's mind since seeing the scars on Arvid's neck. He saw the surprise on Arvids face turn into an approving smile and he leaned forward with his comforting sulphureous breath and whispered.

"I am, was, and always will be."

With that, both vampires sank their teeth into Vinny's neck, ripping free the necessary flesh to gain access to his flow of blood. It was curious there was no pain—the heroin saw to that. The men were invisible in the reflection, and it looked to Vinny like two lumps of flesh simply leaped from his neck. The blood flowed outward and disappeared into the voids the two monsters occupied.

Vinny watched his reflection as his vision started to fade. He tried to hold onto any good memories he could find, but there were none. Elmer shushing. The faceless girl and her murdered family. His dad turning his back. Mom and the mongoloid laughing at their success. Nothing to cling to but hate. His hand clenched the Dunhill with the last bits of his strength. The world was turning gray now. The gagging and the slurping were all he could make out except for himself in the mirror. Then his reflection started to fade as well. The last thing Vinny forgot to remember was himself as he watched his reflection disappear and the world faded to black, everything was lost.

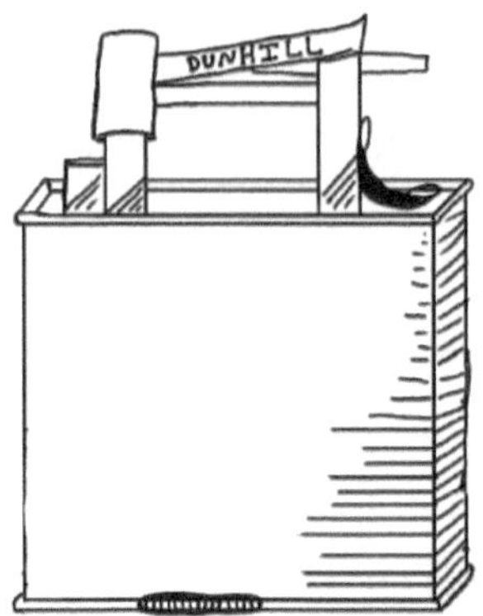

The familiar rocking of the train slowly woke Vin from a sleep he couldn't remember falling into. His senses were electrified, and he could feel himself in motion. How? He could clearly remember the dungeon and the mirror. How did he get here?

The light flooding in through the crack of the door was from a full blood moon. The familiar orange glow brought back memories of a night so long ago it felt like a dream. Then Vin focused on his sharp-feeling senses. The zoetrope of Middle America had changed. No longer was the broken light reminding Vin of families at dinner tables and kids playing games. The zoetrope had become a buffet. There were smells mixing with other smells that he never knew existed, but he wanted them all. He could smell booze mixing with blood in an old man. He could almost taste cigarette smoke and a group of young men smoking outside a bar. An appetite Vin never knew was growing inside him now as his stomach growled.

Searching for a clue of how he got here, his hands patted his body. That was when he realized the rings in his collarbone were gone. His fingers played with the holes they had left. The holes seemed to be closing up already, healing over like it had never happened. Vin also realized he was dressed in a fancy-looking suit. Complete with jacket and smooth-soled leather shoes. Vin laughed out loud. His hands searched the pockets of his new clothes. First, he discovered a piece of paper on the top of his pocket.

He unfolded it and was surprised that he could see the writing, despite the darkness in the car.

"Find your own town, don't feed in someone else's area...USE THE CODE."

The last part, written in capital letters and bold writing, caught his eye the most. Use the code? He thought back to the warning signs Elmer and he had spread wherever they went. They were never meant for them. It was never a warning for bums. It was a warning for other vampires, so they stayed out of each other's feeding grounds. The symbols were used to let other vampires know what they were feeding on and to move on if they were looking for the same. Vin shook his head in the darkness and laughed again.

Then his hand returned to his pocket, where he could feel the familiar weight of the Dunhill still pressed against his thigh. As his fingers pulled it from his pocket, he quickly realized it was burning him. The hissing was producing a thick smoke. He tossed the lighter across the train car, and it bounced into the opposite corner. He no longer had a use for it. The memories it represented were burned into his soul. The fact that his family had abandoned him was the only feeling he wanted to hold onto. Holding onto the silver lighter any longer wasn't only emotionally painful, now it was physically painful.

The burning of the lighter woke an anger deep inside him and visions of his family danced in his mind. The anger was accompanied by an ever-growing appetite and a growling belly. Vin was hungry—there was no denying that, but he sure could use a drink and a smoke. The lighter served its final purpose Vin knew where to go to quench this thirst...nothing was lost after all.

This book was for Sarah,

Who loves me

...and vampires

ACKNOWLEDGMENT

I extend my gratitude to Norbert Yates for his outstanding work on the cover art. His professionalism and dedication to traditional artistry, without the use of AI, are truly commendable. For those interested in contacting Norbert, his information is provided below.

I also want to thank my daughter for her incredible contributions to the table of contents and chapter art. Your creativity is my favorite part about you.

To my family, thank you for your patience and encouragement as I navigated the challenges of teaching myself how to write a novel. Thank you especially to my wife who worked two jobs without complaining so I could chase this dream.

True to my author bio, I invite readers to reach out to me with any mistakes they find. If you notify me, at the email address below, of an error and it is corrected, your name will be listed on this page as a contributing editor. Feel free to send hate mail or just say hi as well.

Stay Scared

KR

kristofferbooksfeedback@gmail.com

www.norbertyates.com

Contributing Editors:

Sylar Roland

Be on the lookout for my other upcoming releases:

A Midwest Horror

Cubiculum

A short story collection to resolve The Moon King

www.ingramcontent.com/pod-product-compliance
Lightning Source LLC
Chambersburg PA
CBHW030920300726
48970CB00001B/250